VALERIUS MAXIMUS

II

LCL 493

VALERIUS MAXIMUS

MEMORABLE DOINGS AND SAYINGS

EDITED AND TRANSLATED BY

D. R. SHACKLETON BAILEY

HARVARD UNIVERSITY PRESS
CAMBRIDGE, MASSACHUSETTS
LONDON, ENGLAND
2000

Library of Congress catalog card number 99-089336
CIP data available from the Library of Congress

ISBN 0-674-99541-4 (vol. I)
ISBN 0-674-99542-2 (vol. II)

CONTENTS

MEMORABLE DOINGS AND SAYINGS

    BOOK VI   2

    BOOK VII   102

    BOOK VIII   188

    BOOK IX   292

GLOSSARY   399

INDEX   407

MEMORABLE DOINGS
AND SAYINGS

LIBER SEXTUS

1. DE PUDICITIA

praef.   Unde te virorum pariter ac feminarum praecipuum firmamentum, Pudicitia, invocem? tu enim prisca religione consecratos Vestae focos incolis, tu Capitolinae Iunonis pulvinaribus incubas, tu Palatii columen Augustos penates sanctissimumque Iuliae genialem torum adsidua statione celebras, tuo praesidio puerilis aetatis insignia munita sunt, tui numinis respectu sincerus iuventae flos permanet, te custode matronalis stola censetur: ades igitur et ⟨re⟩cognosce quae fieri ipsa voluisti.

1   Dux Romanae pudicitiae Lucretia, cuius virilis animus maligno errore Fortunae muliebre corpus sortitus est, a ⟨Sex.⟩[1] Tarquinio, regis Superbi filio, per vim stuprum pati coacta, cum gravissimis verbis iniuriam suam in concilio necessariorum deplorasset, ferro se, quod veste tectum attulerat, interemit, causamque tam animoso interitu imperium consulare pro regio permutandi populo Romano praebuit.

2   Atque haec illatam iniuriam non tulit: Verginius, plebeii generis, sed patricii vir spiritus, ne probro contamina-

[1] *add.* P

2

BOOK VI

1. OF CHASTITY

Whence should I invoke you, Chastity, chief buttress of men and women alike? You dwell in the hearth consecrated to Vesta by ancient religion, you watch over the sacred couch of Capitoline Juno, you never leave your post on the pinnacle of the Palatine, the august habitation, and the most holy marriage bed of Julia. By your protection the emblems of boyhood are defended, by reverence for your divinity the flower of youth remains intact, under your guardianship the matron's robe is appraised. Come therefore, and hear of things that yourself ordained.

Lucretia, model of Roman chastity, whose manly spirit by Fortune's malignant error was allotted a woman's body, was forcibly raped by Sex. Tarquinius, son of king Superbus. In a family council, after bitterly bemoaning her injury, she killed herself with a sword she had brought concealed in her clothing and by so courageous a death gave the Roman people reason to change the authority of kings for that of Consuls.[1]

Lucretia did not brook the injury done to her. Verginius, a man of plebian family but patrician spirit, in order to

[1] 509: Livy 1.57.6–59.3 etc.

3

retur domus sua, proprio sanguini non pepercit: nam cum Ap. Claudius decemvir filiae eius virginis stuprum, potestatis viribus fretus, pertinacius expeteret, deductam in forum puellam occidit, pudicaeque interemptor quam corruptae pater esse maluit.

3   Nec alio robore animi praeditus fuit Pontius Aufidianus eques Romanus. qui, postquam comperit filiae suae virginitatem a paedagogo proditam Fannio[2] Saturnino, non contentus sceleratum servum adfecisse supplicio, etiam ipsam puellam necavit. ita ne turpes eius nuptias celebraret, acerbas exsequias duxit.

4   Quid? P. Maenius quam severum pudicitiae custodem egit! in libertum namque gratum admodum sibi animadvertit, quia eum nubilis iam aetatis filiae suae osculum dedisse cognoverat, cum praesertim non libidine sed errore lapsus videri posset. ceterum amaritudine poenae teneris adhuc puellae sensibus castitatis disciplinam ingenerari magni aestimavit, eique tam tristi exemplo praecepit ut non solum virginitatem illibatam sed etiam oscula ad virum sincera perferret.

5   Q. vero Fabius Maximus Servilianus, honoribus, quos splendidissime gesserat, censurae gravitate consummatis, exegit poenas a filio dubiae castitatis, et punito pependit voluntario secessu conspectum patriae vitando.

---

[2] *anne* Annio (*cf. SB Onomasticon to Cicero's Letters, p. 15*)?

---

[2] 449: Livy 3.44–48.5 etc.   [3] First century (mid?). The story is not found elsewhere.

[4] Not found elsewhere.   [5] *Ca.* 104: Ps.-Quint. *Decl. mai.* 3.17, Oros. 5.16.8; cf. Cic. *Balb.* 28. This Fabius is probably Q. Fabius Maximus Eburnus, Censor in 108 (cf. Broughton I.550

keep from his house the stain of outrage, did not spare his own flesh and blood. For when the Decemvir Ap. Claudius, relying on the power of his office, persistently sought to ravish his daughter, he brought the girl to the Forum and killed her, preferring to be the slayer of a chaste daughter than the father of a defiled one.[2]

No less strong-minded was Pontius Aufidianus, a Roman knight. Learning that his daughter's virginity had been betrayed to Fannius Saturninus by her tutor, he was not content to punish the rascally slave, he also killed the girl herself. Rather than celebrate a disgraceful marriage, he gave her an untimely funeral.[3]

Again, how stern a guardian of chastity did P. Maenius prove! He put to death a freedman, a great favourite of his, on learning that he had given a kiss to his daughter, a girl of marriageable age, even though he could seem to have done it in error, not lust. But Maenius thought it important that the discipline of chastity be implanted in the girl's still tender feelings by the harshness of the punishment; and by so terrible an example he taught her that she must bring to her husband not only unsullied virginity but pure kisses.[4]

Q. Fabius Maximus Servilianus, who consummated offices which he had filled with the utmost distinction by the grave function of Censor, exacted punishment from a son of dubious chastity and paid penalty to him he punished, shunning the sight of his country in voluntary retirement.[5]

n.3), whose father, Q. Fabius Maximus Servilianus, never held that office. Valerius has them confused, unless he wrote *Serviliani f.;* cf. Münzer, *RE* VI.1797. Orosius says that the father ("Q. Fabius Maximus") was prosecuted and condemned, which is confirmed against Valerius by Cicero, *Balb.* 28.

6   Dicerem censorium virum nimis atrocem exstitisse, nisi P. Atilium Philiscum, in pueritia corpore quaestum a domino facere coactum, tam severum postea patrem cernerem: filiam enim suam, quia[3] stupri se crimine coinquinaverat, interemit. quam sanctam igitur in civitate nostra pudicitiam fuisse existimare debemus, in qua etiam institores libidinis tam severos eius vindices evasisse animadvertimus?

7   Sequitur excellentis nominis ac memorabilis facti exemplum. M. Claudius Marcellus aedilis curulis C. Scantinio Capitolino tribuno plebis diem ad populum dixit quod filium suum de stupro appellasset, eoque adseverante se cogi non posse ut adesset quia sacrosanctam potestatem haberet, et ob id tribunicium auxilium implorante, totum collegium tribunorum negavit se intercedere quo minus pudicitiae quaestio perageretur. citatus itaque Scantinius reus uno teste qui temptatus erat damnatus est. constat iuvenem productum in rostra defixo in terram vultu perseveranter tacuisse, verecundoque silentio plurimum in ultionem suam valuisse.

8   Metellus quoque Celer stuprosae mentis acer poenitor exstitit, Cn. Sergio Silo promissorum matri familiae nummorum gratia diem ad populum dicendo eumque hoc uno crimine damnando: non enim factum tunc sed animus in

---

[3] quia *Gertz*: quod ita* AG: quo dita L

---

[6] Not found elsewhere.

[7] 226 (?): Plut. *Marc.* 2, who makes Scantinius a colleague of Marcellus. He may have been Plebeian Aedile (Broughton I.230 n.1).

I would say the ex-Censor showed himself too harsh if I did not see what a severe parent P. Atilius Philiscus was in later life, who as a boy had been forced by his master to earn money by prostitution. For he put his daughter to death because she had defiled herself with the guilt of illicit intercourse.[6] How sacred then should we think chastity was in our community, in which we see even the hucksters of lust becoming such severe chastisers of it!

There follows an example excellent in name and memorable in deed. Curule Aedile M. Claudius Marcellus summoned Tribune of the Plebs C. Scantinius Capitolinus to trial before the people on a charge of having tried to seduce his son. Scantinius asserted that as a holder of a sacrosanct power he could not be forced to attend and on that account asked the Tribunes for aid. But the entire board of Tribunes refused to intervene to prevent an inquiry concerning chastity from taking its course. Scantinius therefore was cited as defendant and convicted on the sole evidence of the person who had been solicited. We are told that when the young man was brought to the rostra he fixed his eyes on the ground and persistently kept mute, by which modest silence he contributed powerfully to his own avenging.[7]

Metellus Celer too showed himself a stern chastiser of lascivious intent by summoning C. Sergius Silus to trial before the people on account of money promised to a housewife and convicting him on this sole charge.[8] It was not an act but a state of mind that was then brought to the

---

[8] Probably as Aedile, perhaps in 88; or if Valerius means his adopted son, Consul in 60, perhaps in 67 (Broughton II.45 n.5 and 144).

quaestionem deductus est, plusque voluisse peccare
nocuit quam non peccasse profuit.

9   Contionis haec, illa curiae gravitas. T. Veturius, filius
eius Veturii qui in consulatu suo Samnitibus ob turpiter
ictum foedus deditus fuerat, cum propter domesticam
ruinam et grave aes alienum P.[4] Plotio nexum se dare adu-
lescentulus admodum coactus esset, servilibus ab eo verberibus, quia stuprum pati noluerat, adfectus, querellam
ad consules detulit. a quibus hac de re certior factus senatus Plotium in carcerem duci iussit: in qualicumque enim
statu positam Romano sanguini pudicitiam tutam esse
voluit.

10   Et quid mirum si hoc universi patres conscripti censue-
runt? C. Fescenninus[5] triumvir capitalis C. Cornelium,
fortissimae militiae stipendia emeritum virtutisque nomine quater honore primi pili ab imperatoribus donatum,
quod cum ingenuo adulescentulo stupri commercium habuisset, publicis vinculis oneravit. a quo appellati tribuni,
cum de stupro nihil negaret, sed sponsionem se facere pa-
ratum diceret quod adulescens ille palam atque aperte
corpore quaestum factitasset, intercessionem suam inter-
ponere noluerunt. itaque Cornelius in carcere mori coactus est: non putarunt enim tribuni plebis rem publicam
nostram cum fortibus viris pacisci oportere ut externis

---

[4] P. AP: C. LG
[5] Fescenninus A: Fescennius A *corr.*, LP: Pesc- *Pighius, edd.*

---

[9] In 321 (Caudine Forks). But Livy (8.28) calls the abuser L.
Papirius and the victim C. Publilius, whereas Dionysius (16.5),
not naming the former, makes the latter son of Ποπλίλιος, "one of

enquiry, and the wish to do wrong hurt more than the absence of wrongdoing helped.

That was severity in the popular assembly, this in the senate house. T. Veturius, son of the Veturius who in his Consulship had been surrendered to the Samnites because of a treaty dishonourably concluded,[9] as a very young man was forced by domestic ruin and a load of debt to give himself as bondman to P. Plotius. Plotius flogged him like a slave because he refused to submit to sexual advances and he made complaint to the Consuls. Informed of the matter by them, the senate ordered Plotius to be put in gaol. For it wished that chastity be secure to Roman blood in whatever condition that might be placed.

Is it surprising that the Conscript Fathers as a body thus decreed? C. Fescenninus,[10] Triumvir Capitalis, put public chains on C. Cornelius for having sexual intercourse with a freeborn youth, though Cornelius had served as a soldier with great bravery and had four times received from his commanders the honour of the First Spear[11] for his valour. He appealed to the Tribunes, not denying the act but declaring his readiness to wager that the young man in question had openly and without concealment practised prostitution. The Tribunes refused their intervention and Cornelius had to die in prison. For the Tribunes of the Plebs thought it wrong that our commonwealth should strike bargains with brave men for them to

the Military Tribunes who surendered the army to the Samnites." Cicero (*Rep.* 2.59) alludes to the story but gives no names.

[10] The conjecture Pescennius is usually read.

[11] He was promoted Chief Centurion. Apparently the rank might lapse after a campaign. He is noticed only here.

periculis domesticas delicias emerent.

11   Libidinosi centurionis supplicium M. Laetorii Mergi tribuni militaris aeque [similis][6] foedus exitus sequitur. cui Cominius tribunus plebis diem ad populum dixit quod cornicularium suum stupri causa appellasset. nec sustinuit eius rei ‹con›scientiam[7] Laetorius sed se ipse ante iudicii tempus fuga prius, deinde etiam ‹morte punivit›.[8] poenae[9] modum expleverat, fato tamen functus universae plebis sententia crimine impudicitiae damnatus est. signa illum militaria, sacratae aquilae, et certissima Romani imperii custos, severa castrorum disciplina, ad inferos usque persecuta est, quoniam cuius virtutis magister esse debuerat, sanctitatis corruptor temptarat[10] exsistere.

12   Hoc movit C. Marium imperatorem, tum cum Lusium sororis suae filium, tribunum militum, a C. Plotio manipulari[11] milite iure caesum pronuntiavit, quia eum de stupro compellare ausus fuerat.

13   Sed ut eos quoque qui in vindicanda pudicitia dolore suo pro publica lege usi sunt strictim percurram, Sempronius Musca C. Gallium[12] deprehensum in adulterio flagellis cecidit, C. Memmius L. Octavium similiter deprehensum pernis[13] contudit, Carbo Attienus a Vibieno item Pontius a P. Cerennio deprehensi castrati sunt. Cn. etiam Furium Brocchum qui deprehenderat familiae stupran-

---

6 aeque similis* AL: aeque *Lipsius*   7 *add. Torr.*
8 *add. Halm ex* P
9 poenae *SB*[3]: naturae AL
10 temptarat *Halm*: -abat et AL: -abat A *corr.*, L *corr.*, G
11 manipulari *Kempf*: -rio AL: -re P
12 Gellium P
13 pernis* *sine causa suspectum*

buy luxuries at home with perils abroad.

To the punishment of a lustful Centurion succeeds the equally ignominious end of Military Tribune M. Laetorius Mergus. Tribune of the Plebs Cominius summoned him to trial before the people for having tried to seduce his adjutant. Laetorius could not bear his conscience in the matter, and before the trial date penalized himself, first by flight and then by suicide as well. He had fulfilled the limit of punishment, but after death was nonetheless convicted of unchastity by vote of the whole people.[12] The military standards, the sacred eagles, and the severe discipline of the camp, that surest guardian of Roman empire, pursued him even to the underworld, since he had tried to become corrupter of the purity of one of whose valour he should have been preceptor.

This counselled general C. Marius when he pronounced Military Tribune C. Lusius, his sister's son, justifiably killed by C. Plotius, a private soldier, because the Tribune had dared to solicit him sexually.[13]

But to run briefly over those who in avenging chastity made their own hurt stand for public law: Sempronius Musca scourged C. Gallius, whom he had caught in adultery, with lashes, C. Memmius[14] beat L. Octavius, similarly caught, with thigh bones, Carbo Attienus and Pontius were caught and castrated by Vibienus and P. Cerennius respectively, the man who caught Cn. Furius Brocchus gave him

---

[12] 292–290 (?): Broughton I.160. Dionysius (16.4) and the Suda give his praenomen as Gaius.

[13] 104: Cic. *Mil.* 9 etc.

[14] Divorced his wife Fausta, daughter of Sulla, in 55.

dum obiecit. quibus irae suae indulsisse fraudi non fuit.

ext. 1   Atque ut domesticis externa subnectam, Graeca femina, nomine Hippo, cum hostium classe esset excepta, in mare se, ut morte pudicitiam tueretur, abiecit. cuius corpus Erythraeo litori appulsum proxima undis humus sepulturae mandatum ad hoc tempus tumulo contegit: sanctitatis vero gloriam aeternae traditam memoriae Graecia laudibus suis celebrando cotidie florentiorem efficit.

ext. 2   Vehementius hoc, illud consideratius exemplum pudicitiae. exercitu et copiis Gallograecorum a Cn. Manlio consule in Olympo monte ex parte deletis, ex parte captis, Ortiagontis[14] reguli uxor mirae pulchritudinis a centurione, cui custodienda tradita erat, stuprum pati coacta, postquam ventum est in eum locum in quem centurio misso nuntio necessarios mulieris pretium quo eam redimerent adferre iusserat, aurum expendente centurione et in eius pondus animo oculisque intento, Gallograecis lingua gentis suae imperavit ut eum occiderent. interfecti deinde caput abscisum manibus retinens ad coniugem venit, abiectoque ante pedes eius iniuriae et ultionis suae ordinem exposuit. huius feminae quid aliud quisquam quam corpus in potestatem hostium venisse dicat? nam neque animus vinci nec pudicitia capi potuit.

ext. 3   Teutonorum vero coniuges Marium victorem orarunt ut ab eo virginibus Vestalibus dono mitterentur, adfirman-

---

14 Orti- *Briscoe*: Orgi- AL

---

15 Further information on these incidents is lacking.
16 Not found elsewhere.
17 189: Livy 38.24 etc.

to his slaves to be raped. None of these was penalized for indulging his anger.[15]

To attach external examples to domestic ones, a Greek woman named Hippo, captured by an enemy fleet, threw herself into the sea to protect her chastity by her death. The body was carried to the shore of Erythrae, delivered for burial; the ground next to the water covers it with a tomb to this day. But Greece has made the glory of her purity, consigned to eternal memory, flourish more every day by celebrating it with her praises.[16]

That is a more passionate example of chastity, this a more deliberate. The army and forces of the Galatians were partly destroyed, partly taken prisoner by Consul Cn. Manlius in Mount Olympus. The wife of the petty king Ortiago, a woman of extraordinary beauty, was forced to suffer rape by a Centurion to whose custody she had been consigned. When they came to the place to which the Centurion had told the woman's relations by messenger to bring the ransom money and the Centurion was weighing the gold, his mind and eyes intent on that operation, she commanded the Galatians in her native tongue to kill him. That done, she went to her husband with the severed head in her hands, threw it at his feet, and told him the story of her injury and vengeance.[17] Would anyone say that aught but the body of this woman came into the enemies' power? For her soul could not be vanquished nor her chastity captured.

The wives of the Teutones besought the victorious Marius to send them as a gift to the Vestal Virgins, declar-

tes aeque se atque illas virilis concubitus expertes futuras, eaque re non impetrata laqueis sibi nocte proxima spiritum eripuerunt. di melius, quod hunc animum viris earum in acie[15] non dederunt: nam si mulierum suarum virtutem imitari voluissent, incerta Teutonicae victoriae tropaea reddidissent.

2. LIBERE DICTA AUT FACTA

praef.

Libertatem autem vehementis spiritus dictis pariter et factis testatam ut non invitaverim, ita ultro venientem non excluserim. quae inter virtutem vitiumque posita, si salubri modo se temperavit, laudem, si quo non debuit profudit, reprehensionem meretur. ac vulgi sic auribus gratior quam sapientissimi cuiusque animo probabilior est, utpote frequentius aliena venia quam sua providentia tuta. sed quia humanae vitae partes persequi propositum est, nostra fide, propria aestimatione referatur.

1

Priverno capto interfectisque qui id oppidum ad rebellandum incitaverant, senatus indignatione accensus consilium agitabat quidnam sibi de reliquis quoque Privernatibus esset faciendum. ancipiti igitur casu salus eorum fluctuabatur, eodem tempore et victoribus et iratis subiecta. ceterum cum auxilium unicum in precibus restare animadverterent, ingenui et Italici sanguinis oblivisci non potuerunt: princeps enim eorum in curia interrogatus quam poenam mererentur, respondit 'quam merentur qui se dignos libertate iudicant.' verbis arma sumpserat exas-

---

[15] acie L *corr.*, G: -em AL

---

[18] 102: Flor. 1.38.17, Oros. 5.16.16–19.

ing that they would equally with the latter abstain from
sexual intercourse. Their plea not being granted, they took
their lives by hanging the following night. The gods be
thanked that they did not give such a spirit to their husbands in battle. For had these chosen to imitate the valour
of their wives, they would have cast into doubt the trophies
of Teutonic victory.[18]

2. FREELY SPOKEN OR
FREELY DONE

Though not inviting the freedom of a passionate spirit
attested in deeds and words alike, I would not exclude it
coming unasked. Located between virtue and vice, it deserves praise if it has tempered itself beneficially, blame if
it has launched out where it should not. It is rather pleasant
to the ears of the vulgar than approved in the minds of the
wisest, being more often protected by the indulgence of
others than by its own good sense. But since it is my purpose to go through the parts of human life, let it be recounted with good faith on my side and judgment as itself
deserves.

When Privernum was taken and those who had incited
that town to rebellion killed, the indignant senate deliberated on what to do with the rest of the inhabitants. So their
lives went up and down in the balance, subjected at the
same time to the victorious and the angry. However,
although they saw that their only remaining recourse lay
in entreaties, they could not forget their freeborn Italian
blood. For when their leader was asked in the senate
house what punishment they deserved to suffer, he replied: "That which men deserve who think they are worthy

15

VALERIUS MAXIMUS

peratosque patrum conscriptorum animos inflammaverat.
sed Plautius consul, favens Privernatium causae, regres-
sum animoso eius dicto obtulit, quaesivitque qualem cum
iis Romani pacem habituri essent impunitate donata. at is
constantissimo vultu 'si bonam dederitis' inquit, 'perpetuam, si malam, non diuturnam.' qua voce perfectum est
ut victis non solum venia sed etiam ius et beneficium
nostrae civitatis daretur.

2 Sic in senatu loqui Privernas ausus est: L. vero Philippus consul adversus eundem ordinem libertatem exercere
non dubitavit: nam segnitiam pro rostris exprobrans alio
sibi senatu opus esse dixit, tantumque a paenitentia dicti
afuit ut etiam L. Crasso, summae dignitatis atque eloquentiae viro, id in curia graviter ferenti manum inici iuberet. ille, reiecto lictore, 'non es' inquit 'mihi, Philippe,
consul, quia ne ego quidem tibi senator sum.'

3 Quid? populum ab incursu suo libertas tutum reliquit?
immo et similiter adgressa et aeque experta patientem est.
Cn. Carbo tribunus plebis, nuper sepultae Gracchanae
seditionis turbulentissimus vindex idemque orientium
civilium malorum fax ardentissima, P. Africanum, a Nu-
mantiae ruinis summo cum gloriae fulgore venientem, ab
ipsa paene porta in rostra perductum quid de Ti. Gracchi
morte, cuius sororem in matrimonio habebat, sentiret interrogavit, ut auctoritate clarissimi viri incohato iam in-
cendio multum incrementi adiceret, quia non dubitabat
quin propter tam artam adfinitatem aliquid pro memoria

1 329: Livy 8.21 etc.
2 91: Cic. *De orat.* 3.2–4.
3 Cf. VM 5.4.4.

16

of freedom." He had taken up arms with words and inflamed the Conscript Fathers' exasperated minds. But Consul Plautius, who favoured the cause of the Privernates, offered him a retreat from his bold saying, asking what sort of peace the Romans would have with them if they were granted impunity. With firm countenance he replied: "If you give us a good one, perpetual; if a bad, not for long." The result of his words was that the vanquished were not merely given pardon but also the right and benefit of our citizenship.[1]

Thus a man of Privernum dared to speak in the Roman senate. But Consul L. Philippus did not scruple to exercise freedom against the same body. For on the rostra, upbraiding their inertia, he said he needed another senate and so far from repenting of the saying he even ordered L. Crassus, a man of the highest standing and eloquence, to be arrested when he protested against it in the senate house. Crassus repulsed the lictor with the words: "Philippus, you are no Consul to me because I am no senator to you."[2]

Did freedom leave the people safe from her incursion? On the contrary, she attacked in similar fashion and was met with equal patience. Tribune of the Plebs Cn.[3] Carbo, a most aggressive avenger of the recently buried Gracchan sedition and a flaming firebrand of the rising civil calamities, led P. Africanus, who was returning from the ruins of Numantia in a blaze of glory, almost from the city gate to the rostra and asked him what he thought of the death of Ti. Gracchus, whose sister he had married. Carbo's purpose was by the prestige of an illustrious personage to add plenty of fuel to the fire already started, since he did not doubt that because of so close a connection Africanus would say something compassionate for the memory of his

17

interfecti necessarii miserabiliter esset locuturus. at is iure eum caesum videri respondit. cui dicto cum contio, tribunicio furore instincta, violenter succlamasset, 'taceant' inquit 'quibus Italia noverca est.' orto deinde murmure 'non efficietis' ait 'ut solutos verear quos alligatos adduxi.' universus populus ab uno iterum contumeliose correptus erat—quantus est honos virtutis!—et tacuit. recens ipsius victoria Numantina et patris Macedonica devictaeque Carthaginis avita spolia ac duorum regum Syphacis et Persei ante triumphales currus caten<at>ae[16] cervices totius tunc fori <ora>[17] clauserunt. nec timori datum est silentium, sed quia beneficio Aemiliae Corneliaeque gentis multi metus urbis atque Italiae finiti erant, plebs Romana libertati Scipionis libera non fuit.

4   Quapropter minus mirari debemus quod amplissima Cn. Pompeii auctoritas totiens cum libertate luctata est, nec sine magna laude, quoniam omnis generis hominum licentiae ludibrio esse quieta fronte tulit. Cn. Piso, cum Manilium Crispum reum ageret eumque evidenter nocentem gratia Pompeii eripi videret, iuvenili impetu ac studio accusationis provectus multa et gravia crimina praepotenti defensori obiecit. interrogatus deinde ab eo cur non se quoque accusaret, 'da' inquit 'praedes rei publicae te, si postulatus fueris, civile bellum non excitaturum, et iam de tuo prius quam de Manilii capite in consilium iudices mittam.' ita eodem iudicio duos sustinuit reos, accusatione

16 *add. Aldus*
17 *add. Kempf* (prementes ora A *corr.*)

---

4 Scipio belonged to the former by birth, the latter by adoption.   5 131/130: Cic. *De orat.* 2.106, Vell. 2.4.4 etc.

slain relative. He, however, replied that he thought Gracchus had been rightly killed. When the enraged assembly, incited by tribunician madness, clamoured violently against his words: "Let people to whom Italy is a stepmother hold their tongues," he said. Then as shouts went up, "You won't make me afraid of those I brought in chains now that they are loose." The whole people had been a second time insultingly chided by a single man and (such is the honour paid to virtue) held their peace. His own recent victory at Numantia, his father's in Macedonia, his grandfather's spoils of vanquished Carthage, and the chained necks of two kings, Syphax and Perseus, preceding triumphal cars stopped the mouths of the entire Forum. The silence was not a tribute to fear, but because many anxieties of Rome and Italy had been brought to an end thanks to the Aemilian and Cornelian clans,[4] the Roman populace was not free-spoken to Scipio's free speech.[5]

Therefore we ought the less to wonder that Cn. Pompeius' enormous authority so often struggled with such freedom, and not without great credit, since with unruffled countenance he let himself be a mockery to the license of all sorts of men. When Cn. Piso was prosecuting Manilius Crispus and saw that despite clear evidence of guilt he was being snatched from justice by Pompey's influence, carried away by youthful impetuosity and accusatory zeal, he made many grave charges against the over-powerful defender. Then asked by Pompey why he did not prosecute himself as well, he answered: "Give sureties to the commonwealth that if you are accused you will not start a civil war and I will now have a jury consider a capital indictment against you too ahead of Manilius." So in the same trial he coped with two defendants, Manilius by

Manilium, libertate Pompeium, et eorum alterum lege
peregit, alterum professione, qua solum poterat.

5   Quid ergo? libertas sine Catone? non magis quam Cato
sine libertate: nam cum in senatorem nocentem et infamem reum iudex sedisset, tabellaeque Cn. Pompeii lauda-
tionem eius continentes prolatae essent, procul dubio
efficaces futurae pro noxio, summovit eas e quaestione legem recitando, qua cautum erat ne senatoribus tali auxilio
uti liceret. huic facto persona admirationem adimit: nam
quae in alio audacia videretur, in Catone fiducia cognosci-
tur.

6   Cn. Lentulus Marcellinus consul, cum in contione de
Magni Pompeii nimia potentia quereretur, adsensusque ei
clara voce universus populus esset, 'acclamate' inquit,
'acclamate, Quirites, dum licet: iam enim vobis impune
facere non licebit.' pulsata tunc est eximii civis potentia
hinc invidiosa querella, hinc lamentatione miserabili.

7   Cui candida fascia crus alligatum habenti Favonius
'non refert' inquit 'qua in parte sit corporis diadema',
exigui panni cavillatione regias ei vires exprobrans. at is
neutra‹m› in parte‹m›[18] mutato vultu utrumque cavit, ne
aut hilari fronte libenter agnoscere potentiam aut ‹tristi
iram›[19] profiteri videretur, eaque patientia inferioris

[18] neutram in partem *Per.*: -ra in parte AL
[19] tristi iram *add.* A *corr.;* Br

---

[6] This prosecution will have taken place after Pompey's return
from the East in 62 or before he left Rome in 67. If Manilius was
the author of the lex Manilia in 66, only Valerius gives his cognomen. The prosecutor was Cn. Calpurnius Piso, Consul in 23, a
staunch republican in two civil wars.

prosecution, Pompey by unfettered speech. The former he dealt with by law, the latter by declaration, the only way open to him.[6]

What then? Freedom without Cato? No more than Cato without freedom. He was sitting on a jury trying a guilty senator and an infamous defendant. Tablets had been produced containing a testimonial by Cn. Pompeius which would doubtless have proved effective in favour of the offender. But Cato removed them from the case, reciting a law which prohibited the use of such assistance by senators.[7] The person deprived the act of admiration, for what would have seemed audacity in another man, in Cato is recognized as confidence.

Consul Cn. Lentulus Marcellinus was complaining at a public meeting of Magnus Pompeius' excessive power and the whole people loudly assented. "Applaud, citizens," he said, "applaud while you may; for soon you will not be able to do it with impunity." The power of an extraordinary citizen was assailed on that occasion, by invidious complaint on the one hand, by pathetic lamentation on the other.[8]

To Pompey, who was wearing a white bandage on his leg, Favonius said: "It makes no odds on what part of your body you have the diadem," quibbling at the tiny piece of cloth to reproach him with monarchical power. But Pompey's countenance did not change one way or the other. He was careful neither to seem to be gladly acknowledging his power by a cheerful look nor by a sour one to avow annoyance.[9] By such tolerance he gave even people of low birth

---

[7] 52: Plut. *Cat. min.* 48 etc. The law was Pompey's own (add *ipsius* after *legem*?).   [8] 56: cf. Dio 39.28.5.
[9] 60: cf. Cic. *Att.* 2.3.1, Amm. Marc. 17.11.4.

etiam generis et fortunae hominibus aditum adversus se
dedit: e quorum turba duos rettulisse abunde erit.

8   Helvius Mancia Formianus, libertini filius ultimae
senectutis, L. Libonem apud censores accusabat. in quo
certamine cum Pompeius Magnus humilitatem ei aeta-
temque exprobrans ab inferis illum ad accusandum remissum dixisset, 'non mentiris' inquit, 'Pompei: venio enim ab
inferis, in L. Libonem accusator venio. sed dum illic
moror, vidi cruentum Cn. Domitium Ahenobarbum
deflentem quod summo genere natus, integerrimae vitae,
amantissimus patriae in ipso iuventae flore tuo iussu esset
occisus. vidi pari claritate conspicuum M. Brutum ferro
laceratum, querentem id sibi prius perfidia, deinde etiam
crudelitate tua accidisse. vidi Cn. Carbonem, acerrimum
pueritiae tuae bonorumque patris tui defensorem, in tertio
consulatu catenis, quas tu ei inici iusseras, vinctum, obtes-
tantem se[20] adversus omne fas ac nefas, cum in summo
esset imperio, a te equite Romano trucidatum. vidi eodem
habitu et quiritatu praetorium virum Perpernam[21] saevitiam tuam exsecrantem, omnesque eos una voce indignan-
tes quod indemnati sub te adulescentulo carnifice occidis-
sent.' obducta iam vetustis cicatricibus bellorum civilium
vastissima vulnera municipali homini, servitutem pater-
nam redolenti, effrenatae temeritatis, intolerabilis spiritus, impune revocare[22] licuit. itaque eodem tempore et

[20] se *Kempf*: te AL   [21] Perpernam P: -pennam AL
[22] renovare *Lipsius*

[10] 55 (?). See Münzer in *RE* VIII.229.15. On Pompey's victims
see Broughton II.66 (Carbo), 77 (Domitius), 90 (Brutus), 120
(Perperna). Cf. VM 5.3.5.

22

and degree an opening against himself. It will be quite enough to mention two such out of the multitude.

Helvius Mancia of Formiae, son of a freedman and a very old man, was accusing L. Libo before the Censors. In the altercation Pompeius Magnus said that he had been sent back from the underworld to make his charge, casting his lowly station and old age in his teeth. "You do not lie, Pompey," he said. "Indeed I come from the underworld and I come as L. Libo's accuser. But while I was there, I saw Cn. Domitius Ahenobarbus all bloody, lamenting that he, a man of the noblest birth, life unstained, a sincere patriot, had been put to death by your order in the very flower of his youth. I saw M. Brutus, no less conspicuously distinguished, lacerated with steel, complaining that this happened to him first by your treachery, then too by your cruelty. I saw Cn. Carbo, the zealous defender of your boyhood and of your father's property, bound by the chains which you ordered placed upon him in his third Consulship, protesting that against all things lawful and unlawful he was slaughtered while holding highest authority by you, a Roman knight. I saw Perperna, an ex-Praetor, in the same guise and crying the same protest, cursing your savagery, all of them with one voice indignant that without judicial sentence they perished at your bidding, the stripling executioner."[10] A country townsman, smelling of his father's slavery, unbridled in his temerity, intolerable in his presumption, was allowed to recall with impunity the gaping wounds of the civil wars, now overlaid with shrivelled scars. So at that time it was at once very brave and very safe

fortissimum erat Cn. Pompeio maledicere et tutissimum.
sed non patitur nos hoc longiore querella prosequi per-
sonae insequentis aliquanto sors humilior.

9   Diphilus tragoedus, cum Apollinaribus ludis inter actum ad eum versum venisset in quo haec sententia conti-
netur 'miseria nostra magnus es,'[23] derectis in Pompeium
Magnum manibus pronuntiavit, revocatusque aliquotiens
a populo sine ulla cunctatione nimiae illum et intolerabilis
potentiae reum gestu perseveranter egit. eadem petulantia usus est in ea quoque parte 'virtutem istam veniet tempus cum graviter gemes.'

10   M. etiam Castricii libertate inflammatus animus. qui
cum Placentiae magistratum gereret, Cn. Carbone consule iubente decretum fieri quo sibi obsides a Placentinis
darentur, nec summo eius imperio obtemperavit nec maximis viribus cessit; atque etiam dicente multos se gladios
habere respondit 'et ego annos.' obstipuerunt tot legiones
tam robustas senectutis reliquias intuentes. Carbonis quoque ira, quia materiam saeviendi perquam exiguam habebat, parvulum vitae tempus ablatura, in se ipsa collapsa est.

11   Iam Ser. Galbae temeritatis plena postulatio, qui divum
Iulium consummatis victoriis in foro ius dicentem in hunc
modum interpellare sustinuit: 'C. Iuli Caesar, pro Cn.
Pompeio Magno, quondam genero tuo, in tertio eius
consulatu pecuniam spopondi, quo nomine nunc appellor.
quid agam? dependam?' palam atque aperte ei bonorum

---

[23] es *Per., coll. Cic.*: est AL

---

[11] 59: from Cic. *Att.* 2.19.3, with certain discrepancies, on
which see the introduction to my Cambridge edition, pp. 62f.

to insult Cn. Pompeius. But the considerably lowlier lot of the following individual does not permit me to deplore this at greater length.

Diphilus the tragic actor in the course of a performance at the Apollinarian games came to a verse containing the following sentiment: "To our misfortune art thou great." He declaimed it with hands pointing at Pompeius Magnus; recalled by the people several times, without any hesitation he persistently by gesture accused Pompey of excessive and intolerable power. He used the same effrontery in another passage: "But that same valour bitterly / in time to come shalt thou lament."[11]

The mind of M. Castricius too was fired by freedom. As a magistrate in Placentia, when Consul Cn. Carbo ordered a decree to be passed that the inhabitants give him hostages, Castricius neither obeyed his supreme authority nor yielded to his mighty power. And when Carbo said that he had many swords, Castricius replied "And I years." All those legions stood amazed as they beheld such sturdy remnants of old age. Carbo's ire having very little material on which to vent its fury, since it would take away but a very meagre life-space, collapsed upon itself.[12]

And now, Servius Galba's demand was full of temerity. As the divine Julius after the consummation of his victories was giving judgment in the Forum, Galba dared to interrupt him thus: "C. Julius Caesar, I pledged money for Cn. Pompeius Magnus, once your son-in-law, in his third Consulship. Now I am called upon for the amount. What shall I do? Pay?" Thus reproaching Caesar openly and with-

[12] 85: not found elsewhere, but cf. Cic. *Att.* 2.24.4 and my note there.

Pompeii venditionem exprobrando ut a tribunali sum-
moveretur meruerat. sed illud ipsa mansuetudine mitius
pectus aes alienum Pompeii ex suo fisco solvi iussit.

12   Age, Cascellius, vir iuris civilis scientia clarus, quam
periculose contumax! nullius enim aut gratia aut auctoritate compelli potuit ut de aliqua earum rerum quas triumviri ⟨dono⟩[24] dederant formulam componeret, hoc
animi iudicio universa victoriae[25] eorum beneficia extra
omnem ordinem legum ponens. idem cum multa de temporibus liberius loqueretur, amicique ne id faceret mone-
rent, duas res, quae hominibus amarissimae viderentur,
magnam sibi licentiam praebere respondit, senectutem et
orbitatem.

ext. 1   Inserit se tantis viris mulier alienigeni sanguinis, quae a
Philippo rege temulento immerens damnata, ⟨provocare
se iudicium vociferata est, eoque interrogante ad quem⟩[26]
provocaret,[27] 'ad Philippum' inquit, 'sed sobrium.' excussit
crapulam oscitanti, ac praesentia animi ebrium resipiscere
causaque diligentius inspecta iustiorem sententiam ferre
coegit. igitur aequitatem, quam impetrare non potuerat,
extorsit, potius praesidium a libertate quam ab innocentia
mutuata.

ext. 2   Iam illa non solum fortis sed etiam urbana libertas.
senectutis ultimae quaedam Syracusis, omnibus Dionysii
tyranni exitium propter nimiam morum acerbitatem et in-

---

[24] *add. coni. Briscoe*   [25] uni- vic- *Torr.*: uni- A: vic- LG
[26] *add.* P   [27] provocaret P: -rem AG: -re L

---

[13] 45: Cic. *Fam.* 6.18.3.
[14] 42: Not found elsewhere.

out concealment with the sale of Pompey's property, he deserved to be removed from the tribunal. But Caesar's heart, softer than gentleness itself, ordered that Pompey's debt be paid from his own treasury.[13]

Well then, Cascellius, a man famous for his knowledge of civil law, how perilously contumacious was he! By no man's favour or authority could he be constrained to compose a formula covering any of those items which the Triumvirs had donated; his judgment thus placed all the benefactions of their victory outside the course of law. The same often spoke freely about the times, and when his friends warned him not to do so, he answered that two things generally deemed eminently disagreeable gave him great licence, old age and childlessness.[14]

EXTERNAL

A woman of alien race inserts herself among these great men. Wrongfully condemned by king Philip when he was in liquor, she cried out that she appealed the judgment. When he asked whom she appealed to, "to Philip," she said, "but to Philip sober." She dissipated the fumes of wine as he yawned, and by her ready courage forced the drunkard to come to his senses and, after a more careful examination of the case, to render a juster verdict. Thus she extorted the equity which she could not get by asking, borrowing recourse from freedom rather than from innocence.[15]

The following freedom was not only brave but witty. In Syracuse, where everybody was praying for the destruction of the tyrant Dionysius because of his excessive harshness and the intolerable burdens he imposed, there was a

[15] Cf. Plut. *Moral.* 178F–179A, Stob. 3.13.49.

tolerabilia onera votis expetentibus, sola cotidie matutino
tempore deos ut incolumis ac sibi superstes esset orabat.
quod ubi is cognovit, non debitam sibi admiratus benivolentiam, arcessiit eam et quid ita hoc aut quo merito suo faceret interrogavit. tum illa 'certa est' inquit 'ratio propositi
mei: puella enim, cum gravem tyrannum haberemus, carere eo cupiebam. quo interfecto aliquanto taetrior arcem
occupavit. eius quoque finiri dominationem magni aesti-
mabam. tertium te superioribus importuniorem habere
coepimus rectorem. itaque ne, si tu fueris absumptus, de-
terior in locum tuum succedat, caput meum pro tua salute
devoveo.' tam facetam audaciam Dionysius punire erubuit.

ext. 3   Inter has et Theodorum Cyrenaeum quasi animosi spiritus coniugium esse potuit, virtute par, felicitate dissi-
mile:[28] is enim Lysimacho regi mortem sibi minitanti 'enimvero' inquit 'magnifica res tibi contigit, quia cantharidis
vim adsecutus es.' cumque hoc dicto accensus cruci eum
suffigi iussisset, 'terribilis' ait 'haec sit purpuratis tuis, mea
quidem nihil interest humine an sublime putrescam.'

3. DE SEVERITATE

praef.   Armet se duritia pectus necesse est, dum horridae ac
tristis severitatis acta narrantur, ut omni ‹miti›ore[29] cogi-

[28] parem ... dissimilem *coni. Briscoe*
[29] *add.* ⌐: omniore AL: mitiore G

---

[16] Not found elsewhere.
[17] Cic. *Tusc.* 1.102, 5.117, Sen. *Dial.* 9.14.3. Theodorus, called

very old woman who alone every morning implored the gods to grant that he live on and survive her. When Dionysius heard of it, he was amazed at the unmerited good will towards himself and summoning her asked why she did this and what he had done to deserve it. She replied: "I know exactly what I am doing. When I was a girl, we had an oppressive tyrant and I wanted to be rid of him. He was killed, and a considerably nastier individual seized the castle. I was anxious that his regime too should be brought to an end. Now we have you as our third ruler, crueller than your predecessors. For fear, therefore, that if you are liquidated a worse will come in your place, I devote my life for yours." Dionysius was ashamed to punish such amusing audacity.[16]

Between these ladies and Theodorus of Cyrene there could have been something like a marriage of courageous spirit, equal in valour, dissimilar in fortune. To king Lysimachus, who was threatening him with death, he said: "Indeed that's a fine thing you have there: you've gotten the power of the Spanish fly." Enraged by his words, the king ordered him crucified. "This cross," said he, "may terrify your courtiers. As for me, it's no matter whether I rot on the ground or above it."[17]

3. OF SEVERITY

The heart must arm itself with hardness while acts of harsh, grim Severity are related; setting aside all milder

"the atheist," is said to have been sent on an embassy to Lysimachus, one of Alexander's successors, but the date is unknown (*RE* VA.1826.30).

tatione seposita rebus auditu asperis vacet: ira⟨e⟩[30] enim destrictae et inexorabiles[31] vindictae et varia poenarum genera in medium procurrent, utilia quidem legum munimenta, sed minime in placido et quieto paginarum numero reponenda.

1a M. Manlius, unde Gallos depulerat, inde ipse praecipitatus est, quia fortiter defensam libertatem nefarie opprimere conatus fuerat. cuius iustae ultionis nimirum haec praefatio fuit: 'Manlius eras mihi, cum praecipites agebas Senonas: postquam imitari coepisti, unus factus es ex Senonibus.' huius supplicio aeternae memoriae nota inserta est: propter illum enim lege sanciri placuit ne quis patricius in arce aut Capitolio habitaret, quia domum eo loci habuerat ubi nunc aedem Monetae videmus.

1b Par indignatio civitatis adversus Sp. Cassium erupit, cui plus suspicio concupitae dominationis nocuit quam tres magnifici consulatus ac duo speciosissimi triumphi profuerunt: senatus enim populusque Romanus, non contentus capitali eum supplicio adficere, interempto domum superiecit, ut penatium quoque strage puniretur: in solo autem aedem Telluris fecit. itaque quod prius domicilium impotentis viri fuerat, nunc religiosae severitatis monumentum est.

1c Eadem ausum Sp. Maelium consimili exitu patria multavit. area vero domus eius, quo iustitia supplicii notior ad posteros perveniret, Aequimelii appellationem traxit.

---

[30] irae *Heraeus*: ira LG: ita A
[31] -iles L *corr.*: -ilis AL

---

[1] 384: Livy 6.20.13 etc.
[2] See VM 5.8.2.

thoughts, let it attend to matters rough in the hearing. Angers unsparing, retributions inexorable, punishments of various kinds shall come forth, useful defences of the laws to be sure, but by no means to be reckoned in the number of peaceful, tranquil pages.

M. Manlius was hurled from the place from which he had driven the Gauls because he had wickedly attempted to crush the liberty he had bravely defended. Her just vengeance will surely have been thus prefaced: "You were Manlius to me when you drove the Senones helter-skelter; now that you have turned to imitating them, you have become one of the Senones." By his punishment a stigma was put upon his memory for all time. For on his account it was decided to forbid by law that any patrician should dwell on the citadel or the Capitol, because Manlius had had a house where we now see the temple of Moneta.[1]

Equal wrath of the community broke out against Sp. Cassius. The suspicion of desiring to be ruler did him more harm than three magnificent Consulships and two splendid triumphs did him good. For the senate and people of Rome, not content with inflicting capital punishment upon him, cast his house upon his dead body, so that he was also punished by the destruction of his dwelling. On the site they built the temple of Tellus. So what was once the domicile of an over-ambitious man is now a monument of religious severity.[2]

His country punished Sp. Maelius, who made the same attempt with a similar outcome. The site of his house gained the name of Aequimelium, so that the justice of his punishment be better known to posterity.[3] Thus the men

---

[3] 439: Cic. *Dom.* 101, Livy 4.15.8–16.1 etc.

quantum ergo odii adversus hostes libertatis insitum animis antiqui haberent parietum ac tectorum in quibus versati fuerant ruinis testabantur. ideoque et M. Flacci et L. Saturnini seditiosissimorum civium corporibus trucidatis penates ab imis fundamentis eruti sunt. ceterum Flacciana area, cum diu[32] poenae nomine[33] vacua mansisset, a Q. Catulo Cimbricis spoliis adornata est.

1d   Viguit in nostra civitate Ti. et C. Gracchorum summa nobilitas ac spes amplissima. sed quia statum civitatis conati erant convellere, insepulta cadavera iacuerunt supremusque humanae condicionis honos filiis Gracchi et nepotibus Africani defuit. quin etiam familiares eorum, ne quis rei publicae inimicis amicus esse vellet, de Rupe[34] praecipitati sunt.

2   Idem sibi licere [tam][35] P. Mucius tribunus plebis quod[36] senatui et populo Romano credidit, qui omnes collegas suos, ‹qui›[37] duce Sp. Cassio id egerant ut magistratibus non subrogatis communis libertas in dubium vocaretur, vivos cremavit. nihil profecto hac severitate fidentius: unus enim tribunus eam poenam novem collegis inferre ausus est quam novem tribuni ab uno collega exigere perhorruissent.

3a   Libertatis adhuc custos et vindex Severitas, sed pro dignitate etiam ac pro disciplina aeque gravis: M. enim Claudium senatus Corsis, quia turpem cum iis pacem fece-

---

[32] diu A *corr.,* L: diis P

[33] poenae nomine *Kempf*: p(a)ene LG: penatibus A *corr.,* P; Br

[34] rupe A *corr.*: robore AL   [35] *del. Kempf*

[36] quod *Kempf*: quam AL idem ... Romano *intra cruces Briscoe*

[37] *add.* P

of old testified to the hatred implanted in their souls against enemies of liberty by the ruins of the walls and roofs that had been their homes. For that reason, when the bodies of those most seditious citizens M. Flaccus and L. Saturninus had been slaughtered, their houses were razed to their lowest foundations. After remaining empty for a long time by way of punishment, Flaccus' site was adorned by Q. Catulus with the spoils of the Cimbri.[4]

The exalted nobility and splendid promise of the Gracchi, Tiberius and Gaius, flourished in our community. But because they had tried to overthrow its constitution, their bodies lay unburied and the final honour of humanity was not accorded to the sons of Gracchus and the grandsons of Africanus. Even their friends were thrown from the Rock, so that no man should wish to be friend to enemies of the commonwealth.

Tribune of the Plebs P. Mucius too believed that he had the same licence as the senate and people. He burned alive all his colleagues, who under the leadership of Sp. Cassius had tried to endanger public freedom through the non-replacement of magistrates. Nothing for certain could be more self-assured than this severity. One Tribune dared to inflict on nine colleagues a retribution which nine Tribunes would have shuddered to exact from one colleague.[5]

Hitherto Severity is the guardian and avenger of freedom, but she is equally stern for dignity and discipline. The senate surrendered M. Claudius to the Corsi because he had made a dishonourable peace with them. When the

---

[4] 121: Saturninus' house is not mentioned in Cicero's list of such demolitions or elsewhere except here.

[5] 486 (?): on this problematical item see Broughton I.21 n.1.

rat, dedi‹di›t.[38] quem ab hostibus non acceptum in publica custodia necari iussit, semel laesa maiestate imperii quot modis irae pertinax vindex! factum eius rescidit, libertatem ademit, spiritum exstinxit, corpus contumelia carceris et detestanda Gemoniarum scalarum nota foedavit.

3b   Atque hic quidem senatus animadversionem meruerat: Cn. autem Cornelius Scipio Hispali filius prius quam mereri posset expertus est: nam cum ei Hispania provincia sorte obvenisset, ne illuc iret decrevit, adiecta causa quod recte facere nesciret. itaque Cornelius propter vitae inhonestum actum sine ullo provinciali ministerio tantum non repetundarum lege damnatus est.

3c   Ne in C. quidem Vettieno, qui ‹sibi›[39] sinistrae manus digitos, ne bello Italico militaret, absciderat, severitas senatus cessavit: publicatis enim bonis eius ipsum aeternis vinculis puniendum censuit, effecitque ut quem honeste spiritum profundere in acie noluerat, turpiter in catenis consumeret.

4   Id factum imitatus M'. Curius consul, cum dilectum subito edicere coactus esset et iuniorum nemo respondisset, coniectis in sortem omnibus tribubus, Polliae, quae prima exierat, primum nomen urna extractum citari iussit neque eo respondente bona adulescentis[40] hastae subiecit.

---

[38] add. ꜱ   [39] add. P   [40] delitescentis SB[1]

---

6 236. As Legate he was sent ahead to Corsica by his Consul: see Münzer in *RE* Claudius 115, Broughton I.223. Zonaras (8.18) gives him a cognomen, Clineas, and says he was banished; cf. VM 4.7.3, 6.9.13 on Caepio's fate.

7 139: Cn. Cornelius Scipio Hispanus (see VM 1.3.3) was Prae-

enemy would not take him, it ordered that he be put to death in the public gaol. The majesty of empire was violated once, but in how many ways did the senate persistently wreak its wrath! It undid his act, took away his liberty, extinguished his breath, maltreated his body with the contumely of prison and the abhorred stigma of the Gemonian Steps.[6]

He had earned the senate's censure. Cn. Cornelius Scipio, son of Hispalus, experienced it before he could earn it. When the province of Spain fell to him by lot, the senate decreed that he should not go there, giving as reason that he did not know how to do the right thing. So because he had led a discreditable life Cornelius was all but found guilty under the extortion law without any provincial service.[7]

Nor was the senate's severity idle in the case of C. Vettienus, who had cut off two fingers of his left hand to avoid service in the Italian War. It decreed that his property be confiscated and himself punished with chains in perpetuity. By its action he wore out disgracefully in bonds the life which he had not been willing to give honourably in battle.[8]

Consul M'. Curius imitated that action. He was obliged to proclaim a sudden levy, and none of the juniors answered. So he put all the tribes into a lottery and ordered that the first name in the Pollia, whose lot had come out first, should be drawn from the urn and called. When there was no answer, he put the young man's property up for auc-

tor. The name seems to be correct, *pace* Briscoe's index, but the rejection is hard to believe (see Münzer *RE* Cornelius 347, who ignores it).

[8] *Ca.* 90: the case is not recorded elsewhere.

quod ut illi nuntiatum est, ad consulis tribunal cucurrit collegiumque tribunorum appellavit. tunc M'. Curius, praefatus non opus esse eo cive rei publicae qui parere nesciret, et bona eius et ipsum vendidit.

5   Aeque tenax propositi L. Domitius: nam cum Siciliam praetor regeret et[41] ad eum eximiae magnitudinis aper allatus esset, adduci ad se pastorem cuius manu occisus erat iussit, interrogatumque qui eam bestiam confecisset, postquam comperit usum venabulo, cruci fixit, quia ipse ad exturbanda latrocinia, quibus provincia vastabatur, ne quis telum haberet edixerat. hoc aliquis in fine severitatis et saevitiae ponendum dixerit—disputatione enim utroque flecti potest: ceterum ratio publici imperii praetorem nimis asperum existimari non patitur.

6   Sic se in viris puniendis Severitas exercuit, sed ne in feminis quidem supplicio adficiendis segniorem egit. Horatius prius[42] proelio trium Curiatiorum, ‹tum ›[43] condicione pugnae omnium Albanorum victor, cum ex illa clarissima acie domum repetens sororem suam virginem Curiatii sponsi mortem profusius quam illa aetas debebat flentem vidisset, gladio, quo patriae rem bene gesserat, interemit, parum pudicas ratus lacrimas, quae praepropero amori dabantur. quem hoc nomine reum apud populum actum pater defendit. ita paulo propensior animus puellae

41 et A *corr.*: tum AL: cumque G
42 prius*: *secl. Kempf*
43 tum *add. SB*: ceterum A *corr.*

9 275: Varro *Menipp.* 195, Livy *Per.* 14.

tion. That being reported to the same, he ran to the Consul's tribunal and appealed to the board of Tribunes. Then M'. Curius sold both his property and himself, first observing that the commonwealth had no need of a citizen who did not know how to obey.[9]

Equally tenacious of purpose was L. Domitius. When Praetor[10] governing Sicily a boar of extraordinary size was brought to him. He ordered the shepherd by whose hand the animal had been killed to be led before him and asked how he had despatched it. When he learned that the man had used a hunting spear, he crucified him because he himself had published an edict forbidding the possession of weapons in order to get rid of the banditry which was ravaging the province. It might be said that this belongs on the borderline between severity and cruelty (it can be argued either way), but consideration of public authority does not allow us to regard the Praetor as too harsh.

Thus did Severity employ herself in penalizing men, but she displayed no less energy in the punishment of women. Horatius first defeated the three Curiatii in combat, next all the Albans by the terms of the fight. As he was coming home from that illustrious encounter, he saw his virgin sister weeping more profusely than became her years for the death of her affianced Curiatius. Opining that tears given to an over-hasty love smacked of unchastity, he killed her with the sword with which he had served his country well. Brought to trial before the people on that account, his father defended him. So the girl's rather too

[10] 97: Cic. *Verr.* 2.5.7. He was Proconsul or Propraetor, but "Praetor" sometimes simply means "governor" (of a province); cf. VM 9.14.ext.3.

ad memoriam futuri viri et fratrem ferocem vindicem et vindictae tam rigidae[44] adsensorem patrem habuit.

7 Consimili severitate senatus postea usus Sp. Postumio Albino Q. Marcio Philippo consulibus mandavit ut de iis quae sacris Bacchanalium inceste usae fuerant inquirerent. a quibus cum multae essent damnatae, in omnes cognati intra domos animadverterunt, lateque patens opprobrii deformitas severitate supplicii emendata est, quia quantum ruboris civitati nostrae mulieres turpiter se gerendo incusserant, tantum laudis graviter punitae attulerunt.

8 Publicia autem, quae Postumium Albinum consulem, item Licinia, quae Claudium Asellum viros suos veneno necaverant, propinquorum decreto strangulatae sunt: non enim putaverunt severissimi viri in tam evidenti scelere longum publicae quaestionis tempus exspectandum. itaque quarum innocentium defensores fuissent, sontium mature vindices exstiterunt.

9 Magno scelere horum severitas ad exigendam vindictam concitata est, Egnatii autem Mecennii[45] longe minore de causa, qui uxorem, quod vinum bibisset, fusti percussam interemit, idque factum non accusatore tantum sed etiam reprehensore caruit, unoquoque existimante optimo illam exemplo violatae Sobrietati poenas pependisse. et sane quaecumque femina vini usum immoderate appetit, omnibus et virtutibus ianuam claudit et delictis aperit.

---

44 rigidae Ꙅ: -dum AL
45 Mecenni *Kempf*: Metelli AL: Metenius (percussit) P

---

11 Livy 1.26 etc. The incident is placed in the reign of Hostilius Tullus.   12 186: Livy 39.18.6.   13 Or Publilia? See

partial memory of her husband that was to have been found a fierce chastiser in her brother and a father in agreement with so harsh a chastisement.[11]

With similar severity later on the senate commissioned Consuls Sp. Postumius Albinus and Q. Marcius Philippus to investigate women who had made impure use of Bacchanalian rites. Many were found guilty by them and all were executed in their homes by their kinsfolk. The disgrace of the scandal spread wide, but it was rectified by the severity of the retribution. The women brought as much credit to our community by their heavy punishment as they had put shame upon it by their misconduct.[12]

Publicia,[13] who had poisoned her husband, Consul Postumius Albinus, and Licinia, who had done the same to Claudius Asellus, were strangled by sentence of their kinsfolk. For those men of severity did not think that in so evident a crime they should await a lengthy public enquiry. So they made speed to punish the guilty ones, in whose defence they would have stood had they been innocent.[14]

Their severity was roused to exact punishment by a heinous crime, that of Egnatius Mecennius, by a much slighter cause. He cudgelled his wife to death because she had drunk wine. His action found none to prosecute or even to reprehend it. All agreed that the penalty she paid to injured Sobriety was an excellent precedent. And true it is that any female who seeks the use of wine past moderation closes the door to every virtue and opens it to every sin.[15]

Gundel, *RE* Publicia 26.   [14] 153: Livy *Per.* 48, Obsequens 17.

[15] In the reign of Romulus, by whom according to other sources he was tried and acquitted: Pliny *N.H.* 14.89 etc.

10   Horridum C. quoque Sulpicii Gali[46] maritale supercilium: nam uxorem dimisit quod eam capite aperto foris
versatam cognoverat, abscisa sententia, sed tamen aliqua
ratione mota: 'lex enim' inquit 'tibi meos tantum praefinit
oculos quibus formam tuam approbes. his decoris instru-
menta compara, his esto speciosa, horum te citeriori[47]
crede notitiae. ulterior tui conspectus supervacua irrita-
tione arcessitus in suspicione et crimine haereat necesse
est.'

11   Nec aliter sensit Q. Antistius Vetus repudiando uxorem
quod illam in publico cum quadam libertina vulgari secre-
to loquentem viderat: nam, ut ita dicam, incunabulis et
nutrimentis culpae, non ipsa commotus culpa citeriorem
delicto praebuit ultionem, ut potius caveret iniuriam quam
vindicaret.

12   Iungendus est his P. Sempronius Sophus, qui coniugem
repudii nota adfecit, nihil aliud quam se ignorante ludos
ausam spectare. ergo, dum sic olim feminis occurritur,
mens earum a delictis aberat.

ext. 1   Ceterum etsi Romanae severitatis exemplis totus terrarum orbis instrui potest, tamen externa summatim cog-
nosse fastidio non sit. Lacedaemonii libros Archilochi e
civitate sua exportari iusserunt, quod eorum parum vere-
cundam ac pudicam lectionem arbitrabantur: noluerunt
enim ea liberorum suorum animos imbui, ne plus moribus

---

[46] Gali *Briscoe*: Galli AL   [47] citeriori *Watt*[2]: certi- AL

---

[16] Cf. Plut. *Moral.* 267C, according to which Galus, Consul in
166, divorced his wife because he saw her with her dress pulled
over her head.

Rugged too was the marital brow of C. Sulpicius Galus. He divorced his wife because he learned that she had walked abroad with head uncovered. The sentence was abrupt, but there was reason behind it. "To have your good looks approved," says he, "the law limits you to my eyes only. For them assemble the tools of beauty, for them look your best, trust to *their* closer familiarity. Any further sight of you, summoned by needless incitement, has to be mired in suspicion and crimination."[16]

Nor did Q. Antistius Vetus feel otherwise. He divorced his wife because he had seen her in public talking tête-à-tête with a certain common freedwoman.[17] He was actuated by the cradle, so to speak, and aliments of guilt, not guilt itself, and furnished punishment in advance of offence, so as to guard against injury rather than avenge it.

To these is to be added P. Sempronius Sophus, who put the stigma of divorce upon his wife for no better reason than that she had dared to watch the games without his knowledge.[18] While women were thus checked in the old days, their minds stayed away from wrongdoings.

EXTERNAL

Now although the whole earth can be furnished with examples of Roman severity, let us not scorn to learn of external ones in brief. The Lacedaemonians ordered that the works of Archilochus be removed from their community because they thought them immodest and immoral reading. They did not wish their children's minds to be imbued with it, lest it do more harm to their character than good to

[17] I.e. a prostitute. Nothing further is known of this Antistius.
[18] 264 (?), cf. Münzer, *RE* Sempronius 86: Plut. *Moral.* 267C.

noceret quam ingeniis prodesset. itaque maximum poetam aut certe summo proximum, quia domum sibi invisam obscenis maledictis laceraverat, carminum exsilio multarunt.

ext. 2   Athenienses autem Timagoran, inter officium salutationis Dareum regem more gentis illius adulatum, capitali supplicio adfecerunt, unius civis humilibus blanditiis totius urbis suae decus Persicae dominationi summissum graviter ferentes.

ext. 3   Iam Cambyses inusitatae severitatis, qui mali cuiusdam iudicis e corpore pellem detractam sellae intendi in eaque filium eius iudicaturum considere iussit. ceterum et rex et barbarus atroci ac nova poena iudicis ne quis postea corrumpi iudex posset providit.

4. GRAVITER DICTA AUT FACTA

praef.   Magnam et bonam laudis partem in claris viris etiam illa vindicant quae aut ab iis dicta graviter aut facta pertinax memoria viribus aeternis comprehendit. quorum ex abundanti copia nec parca nimis nec rursus avida manu quod magis desiderio satisfaciat quam satietati redundet[48] hauriamus.

1a   Civitate nostra Cannensi clade perculsa, cum admodum tenui filo suspensa rei publicae salus ex sociorum fide penderet, ut eorum animi ad imperium Romanum tuen-

---

[48] redundet SB[3] (ad 3.8.ext.3): abu- AL

---

[19] Not attested elsewhere. The iambics by seventh-century Archilochus of Paros against his enemy Lycambes were notorious (cf. Hor. Epod. 6.13, Epist. 1.19.25).

their intelligence. So they punished with banishment the greatest, or at least the second greatest, of poets because he had lashed a family he hated with obscene insults.[19]

The Athenians inflicted capital punishment on Timagoras because in the ceremony of saluting king Darius he had followed the adulatory custom of that nation. They were indignant that the glory of their whole city should be humbled before Persian dominion by the crawling flattery of a single citizen.[20]

Cambyses'[21] severity was unusual. He flayed the skin from a certain corrupt judge and had it stretched over a chair on which he ordered the man's son to sit when passing judgment.[22] He was a king and a barbarian and by the horrible and novel punishment of a judge he sought to make sure that no judge could be bribed in the future.

4. IMPRESSIVE SAYINGS OR DOINGS

A great and good part of the glory of famous men is claimed by their impressive sayings or doings which pertinacious memory includes in her immortal power. From their abundant store let us draw, not with too sparing nor yet with too greedy a hand, enough to satisfy desire rather than to overflow satiety.

When our community was stricken by the disaster at Cannae, the survival of the commonwealth hung upon the loyalty of our allies, suspended by a very thin thread. To

[20] An envoy, in 367: Plut. *Artax.* 22.9–12. Cf. Xen. *Hellen.* 7.1.33–38 etc.   [21] Reigned 529–22.
[22] Herod. 5.25.

dum constantiores essent, maiori parti senatus principes
Latinorum in ordinem suum sublegi placebat. Annius
autem Campanus etiam consulem alterum Capua[49] creari
debere adseverabat: sic contusus et aeger Romani imperii
spiritus erat. tunc Manlius Torquatus, filius eius qui Lati-
nos apud Veserim inclita pugna fuderat, quam poterat
clara voce denuntiavit, si quis sociorum inter patres conscriptos sententiam dicere ausus esset, continuo eum inte-
rempturum. hae unius minae et Romanorum languentibus
animis calorem pristinum reddiderunt et Italiam ad ius
civitatis nobiscum exaequandum consurgere passae non
sunt: namque ut patris armis ita verbis filii fracta cessit.

1b   Par illius quoque Manlii gravitas, cui cum consulatus
omnium consensu deferretur eumque sub excusatione adversae valitudinis oculorum recusaret, instantibus cunctis
'alium' inquit, 'Quirites, quaerite ad quem hunc honorem
transferatis: nam si me gerere eum coegeritis, nec ego
mores vestros ferre nec vos meum imperium perpeti pote-
ritis.' privati tam ponderosa vox: quam graves fasces consulis exstitissent!

2a   Nihilo segnior Scipionis Aemiliani aut in curia aut in
contione gravitas. qui cum haberet consortem censurae
Mummium, ut nobilem ‹ducem›[50] ita enervis vitae, pro
rostris dixit se ex maiestate rei publicae omnia gesturum, si

49 Capua P: -ae AL
50 add. SB[1]

---

1 216: Livy 23.22.1–9. Times and persons are mixed up. This
Torquatus, Consul in 235 and 224, was not the son but the descendant of T. Manlius Imperiosus Torquatus, Consul for the third
time in 340 and victor of the Veseris.

make their minds steadier for the defence of Roman empire, the greater part of the senate favoured appointing the leading men of the Latins to their own order, and Annius the Campanian even declared that one of the Consuls should be elected from Capua. So battered and sick was the spirit of Roman empire. Then Manlius Torquatus, son of him who had routed the Latins at the Veseris in a famous battle, gave notice in a voice as loud as he could make it that if any of the allies dared to deliver an opinion among the Conscript Fathers, he would kill him forthwith. This threat from one individual restored their former fire to the languishing hearts of the Romans and did not let Italy rise up to gain equal rights of citizenship with us. She yielded, broken by the words of the son as by the arms of the father.[1]

Equally impressive was another Manlius. When offered the Consulship by universal consent, he refused with the excuse that he was suffering from a disease of the eyes. As they all insisted, he said: "Citizens, look for somebody else to whom you can transfer this office, for if you force me to undertake it, I shall not be able to put up with your ways nor you to endure my authority." So weighty a saying from a private citizen! How heavy would his consular fasces have proved![2]

No less strenuously impressive was Scipio Aemilianus, whether in senate house or assembly. As colleague in the Censorship he had Mummius, a distinguished general but slack in his manner of life. Scipio said from the rostra that he would do everything in accordance with the majesty of the commonwealth if his countrymen had either given him

[2] 211: Livy 26.22.2–9. Actually the same Manlius.

sibi cives vel dedissent collegam vel non dedissent.

2b   Idem, cum Ser. Sulpicius Galba et Aurelius ⟨Cotta⟩[51] consules in senatu contenderent uter adversus Viriathum in Hispaniam mitteretur, ac magna inter patres conscriptos dissensio esset, omnibus quonam eius sententia inclinaretur exspectantibus, 'neutrum' inquit 'mihi mitti placet, quia alter nihil habet, alteri nihil est satis', aeque malam licentis imperii magistram iudicans inopiam atque avaritiam. quo dicto ut neuter in provinciam mitteretur obtinuit.

3   C. vero Popillius a senatu legatus ad Antiochum missus, ut bello se quo Ptolomaeum lacessebat abstineret, cum ad eum venisset atque is prompto animo et amicissimo vultu dexteram ei porrexisset, invicem illi suam porrigere noluit, sed tabellas senatus consultum continentes tradidit. quas ut legit Antiochus, dixit se cum amicis collocuturum. indignatus Popillius quod aliquam moram interposuisset, virga solum quo insistebat denotavit, et 'prius' inquit 'quam hoc circulo excedas da responsum quod senatui referam.' non legatum locutum, sed ipsam curiam ante oculos positam crederes: continuo enim rex adfirmavit fore ne amplius de se Ptolomaeus quereretur, ac tum demum Popillius manum eius tamquam socii apprehendit. quam efficax est animi sermonisque abscisa gravitas! eodem momento Syriae regnum terruit, Aegypti texit.

4   P. autem Rutilii verba pluris an facta aestimem nescio: nam utrisque aeque admirabile inest robur. cum amici

[51] *add. Torr.*

---

[3] 142: Auct. vir. ill. 58.9.   [4] 144: not found elsewhere.
[5] 168: Livy 45.12.4–6 etc.

a colleague or not given him a colleague.[3]

Of the same Scipio: Consuls Ser. Sulpicius Galba and L. Aurelius Cotta were disputing in the senate which of them should be sent to Spain against Viriathus, and there was great dissension among the Conscript Fathers. As all waited to see which way Scipio's opinion tended, he said: "I do not think either one should be sent, because one of them has nothing and the other never has enough." He judged that poverty and greed were equally bad instructors for unfettered authority. By that saying he won his point that neither be sent to a province.[4]

C. Popillius was sent by the senate as envoy to Antiochus to make him hold off from the war with which he was harassing Ptolemy. On his arrival, Antiochus put his hand out promptly and with the friendliest countenance. Popillius would not put his hand out to him in return, but gave him the tablets containing the senate's decree. When Antiochus read it, he said he would consult with his friends. Popillius, angry that he should offer any delay, marked the ground on which he was standing with a stick and said: "Give me a reply to report to the senate before you leave this circle." One might have thought that it was not an envoy speaking but the senate house itself set before one's eyes. The king at once gave an assurance that Ptolemy would make no further complaint of him. Then and only then did Popillius clasp his hand as an ally's. How effective is a curt, impressive attitude and speech! At one and the same moment he intimidated the kingdom of Syria and protected the kingdom of Egypt.[5]

I do not know which to admire more, what P. Rutilius said or what he did. For both have a wonderful quality of strength. When he resisted an improper request by a

cuiusdam iniustae rogationi resisteret atque is per summam indignationem dixisset 'quid ergo mihi opus est amicitia tua, si quod rogo non facis?' respondit 'immo quid
mihi tua, si propter te aliquid inhoneste facturus sum?'
huic voci consentanea illa opera, quod magis ordinum dis-
sensione quam ulla culpa sua reus factus nec obsoletam
vestem induit, nec insignia senatoris deposuit, nec supplices ad genua iudicum manus tetendit, nec dixit quicquam
splendore praeteritorum annorum humilius, effecitque ut
periculum non impedimentum gravitatis eius esset, sed
experimentum. atque etiam cum ei reditum in patriam
Sullana victoria praestaret, in exsilio, ne quid adversus
leges faceret, remansit. quapropter felicitatis cognomen
iustius quis moribus gravissimi viri quam impotentis armis
adsignaverit: quod quidem Sulla rapuit, Rutilius meruit.

5   M. Brutus, suarum prius virtutum quam patriae parentis parricida—uno enim facto et illas in profundum praecipitavit et omnem nominis sui memoriam inexpiabili detes-
tatione perfudit—, ultimum proelium initurus, negantibus
quibusdam id committi oportere, 'fidenter' inquit 'in
aciem descendo: hodie enim aut recte erit aut nihil cura-
bo.' praesumpserat videlicet neque vivere se sine victoria
neque mori sine securitate posse.

ext. 1   Cuius mentio mihi subicit quod adversus D. Brutum in
Hispania graviter dictum est referre: nam cum ei se tota
paene Lusitania dedidisset ac sola gentis eius urbs Cingin-

---

6 Not found elsewhere.

7 92: see Münzer *RE* IA.1274–76.

8 Sen. *Ep.* 24.4, Quint. 11.1.13, Ov. *Ex P.* 1.3.63.

friend, the man flew into a violent rage and said, "What good is your friendship to me then if you don't do as I ask?" Rutilius replied: "On the contrary, what good is yours to me if I am to do something dishonourable on your account?"[6] His actions were consistent with that speech. Brought to trial through the strife of classes rather than any fault of his own, he did not put on shabby clothes or lay aside the emblems of senatorial rank or stretch hands in supplication to the knees of the jury or say anything below the lustre of his past years. He made his peril not a hindrance to his gravity but a test of it.[7] Even when Sulla's victory gave him the chance to return to his country, he remained in exile for fear of doing something illegal.[8] Therefore the surname of "Fortunate" would more fairly be assigned to the character of so impressive a man than to the arms of a lawless one. Sulla grabbed it, Rutilius deserved it.

M. Brutus murdered his own virtues before he murdered his country's father; for by a single act he hurled them into the abyss and drenched all memory of his name with inexpiable abhorrence. As he was going into his last battle, someone told him it should not be hazarded. "I go into battle with confidence," Brutus said. "Today either all will be well or I shall not be caring."[9] He must have made up his mind that he could neither live without victory nor die without freedom from anxiety.

EXTERNAL

Mention of him reminds me to relate a pithy saying against D. Brutus in Spain. Almost the whole of Lusitania had surrendered to him; Cinginnia was the only town of

9 42: cf. Plut. *Brut.* 40.

nia pertinaciter arma retineret, temptata redemptione propemodum uno ore legatis Bruti respondit ferrum sibi a maioribus quo urbem tuerentur, non aurum quo libertatem ab imperatore avaro emerent, relictum. melius sine dubio istud nostri sanguinis homines dixissent quam audissent.

ext. 2   Sed illos quidem Natura in haec gravitatis vestigia deduxit, Socrates autem, Graecae doctrinae clarissimum columen, cum Athenis causam diceret, defensionemque ei Lysias a se compositam, qua in iudicio uteretur, recitasset demissam et supplicem, imminenti procellae accommodatam, 'aufer' inquit 'quaeso istam: nam ego, si adduci possem ut eam in ultima Scythiae solitudine perorarem, tum me ipse morte multandum concederem.' spiritum contempsit ne careret gravitate, maluitque Socrates exstingui quam Lysias superesse.

ext. 3   Quantus hic in sapientia, tantus in armis Alexander illam vocem nobiliter edidit: Dareo enim uno iam et altero proelio virtutem eius experto atque ideo et partem regni Tauro tenus monte et filiam in matrimonium cum decies centum milibus talentum pollicente, cum Parmenion dixisset se, si Alexander esset, usurum ea condicione, respondit 'et ego uterer, si Parmenion essem.' vocem duabus victoriis respondentem dignamque cui tertia, sicut evenit, tribueretur.

ext. 4   Atque haec quidem et animi magnifici et prosperi status: illa vero, qua legati Lacedaemoniorum apud patrem eius miseram fortitudinis suae condicionem testati sunt, gloriosior quam optabilior: intolerabilibus enim oneribus

---

10 136: not found elsewhere.

that nation to remain obstinately in arms. To Brutus' envoys, who proposed a ransom, they replied almost with one voice that their ancestors had left them steel to defend their town, not gold to buy freedom from a greedy commander.[10] Words doubtless better said than heard by men of our race.

They indeed were led by Nature into these tracks of gravity. But when Socrates, most illustrious crown of Grecian learning, was pleading his case in Athens, Lysias read to him a defence composed by himself for his use at the trial. "Pray take this away," said Socrates. "If I could be persuaded to deliver it in the farthest wilderness of Scythia, I should admit myself that I deserved death."[11] He despised life lest it be without gravity and preferred extinction as Socrates to survival as Lysias.

Alexander, as great in arms as Socrates in wisdom, delivered himself of the following well-known utterance. After Darius had tried his mettle in a couple of battles and therefore promised him part of his kingdom as far as the Taurus mountain, also his daughter in marriage and a million talents, Parmenio said that if he were Alexander he would accept the offer. "And so should I accept it," retorted Alexander, "if I were Parmenio."[12] A saying in line with his two victories and worthy to be vouchsafed a third, as happened.

That utterance befitted a proud soul and a prosperous state of affairs. But this with which the Lacedaemonian envoys before Alexander's father testified to the sad plight of their bravery was more glorious than enviable. To his

[11] 399: Cic. *De orat.* 1.231 etc.
[12] 333: Plut. *Alex.* 29 etc.

civitatem eorum implicanti, si quid morte gravius imperare perseveraret, mortem se praelaturos responderunt.

ext. 5   Nec parum grave Spartani cuiusdam dictum, si quidem
nobilitate et sanctitate praestans, sed[52] in petitione magistratus victus, maximae sibi laetitiae esse praedicavit quod
aliquos patria sua se meliores viros haberet. quo sermone
repulsam honori adaequavit.

5. DE IUSTITIA

praef.   Tempus est Iustitiae quoque sancta penetralia adire, in
quibus semper aequi ac probi facti respectus religiosa cum
observatione versatur, et ubi studium verecundiae, cupiditas rationi cedit, nihilque utile, quod parum honestum
videri possit, ducitur. eius autem praecipuum et certissimum inter omnes gentes nostra civitas exemplum est.

1a   Camillo consule Falerios circumsedente, magister ludi
plurimos et nobilissimos inde pueros velut am‹bul›-
andi gratia eductos in castra Romanorum perduxit. quibus interceptis non erat dubium quin Falisci deposita belli
gerendi pertinacia tradituri se nostro imperatori essent. ea
re senatus censuit ut pueri vinctum magistrum virgis cae-
dentes in patriam remitterentur. qua iustitia animi eorum
sunt capti quorum moenia expugnari non poterant:
namque Falisci beneficio magis quam armis victi portas
Romanis aperuerunt.

[52] sed *Kempf*: et A: *om.* LG

---

[13] 338 (?): Cic. *Tusc.* 5.42 etc.
[14] Plut. *Moral.* 191F, 231B.

terms saddling their community with intolerable burdens
they answered that if he persisted in demanding something worse than death, they would prefer death.[13]

Not unimpressive is the saying of a certain Spartan.
Eminent in noble birth and purity of life but defeated in
his candidature for a magistracy, he said it was a great joy to
him that the country had some better men than himself.[14]
By that speech he made a rejection tantamount to an
honour.

5. OF JUSTICE

It is time also to approach the holy sanctuary of Justice,
where always dwells respect religiously observed for fair
and honest dealing and where partiality yields to modesty
and desire to reason, where nothing is judged expedient
that could seem less than honourable. The chief and surest
example of it among all nations is our community.

When Consul Camillus was laying siege to Falerii, a
schoolmaster led a large number of boys of the highest
birth as though for a walk out of the town to the Roman
camp. If they were taken, there was no doubt that the
Falisci would put aside their obstinate war-waging and surrender to our commander. In that situation the senate[1] decreed that the schoolmaster be bound and the boys sent
back to their town flogging him with rods. By such justice
the hearts of those whose walls could not be stormed were
taken captive. Vanquished by benefaction rather than by
arms, the Falisci opened their gates to the Romans.[2]

[1] All other sources give the credit to Camillus.
[2] 394: Livy 5.27 etc.

1b Eadem civitas aliquotiens rebellando ⟨pervicax⟩[53] semperque adversis contusa proeliis tandem se Q. Lutatio consuli dedere coacta est. adversum quam saevire cupiens populus Romanus, postquam a Papirio, cuius manu iubente consule verba deditionis scripta erant, doctus est Faliscos non potestati sed fidei se Romanorum commisisse, omnem iram placida mente deposuit, pariterque et viribus odii, non sane facile vinci adsuetis, et victoriae obsequio, quae promptissime licentiam sumministrat, ne iustitiae suae deesset obstitit.

1c Idem, cum P. Claudius Camerinos ductu atque auspiciis suis captos sub hasta vendidisset, etsi aerarium pecunia, fines agris auctos animadvertebat, tamen, quod parum liquida fide id gestum ab imperatore videbatur, maxima cura conquisitos redemit, iisque habitandi gratia locum in Aventino adsignavit et praedia restituit. pecuniam etiam non ad curiam sed sacraria aedificanda sacrificiaque facienda tribuit, iustitiaeque promptissimo tenore effecit ut exitio suo laetari possent, quia sic renati erant.

1d Moenibus nostris et finitimis regionibus ⟨inclusa⟩[54] quae adhuc rettuli; quod sequitur per totum terrarum orbem manavit. Timochares Ambraciensis Fabricio consuli

---

[53] *add. SB (cf. supra* belli gerendi pertinacia *et Flor.* 4.12.47 pertinax in rebellando) [54] *add. SB*[1]

---

[3] Perhaps C. Papirius Maso, Consul in 231. [4] 241: cf. Livy *Per.* 20 etc. [5] An unknown Claudius of early date (Broughton II.463). The name has been doubted (Münzer, *RE* Claudius 27), as has the identity of the defeated people.

[6] As explained by Badian, the Romans assigned the Camerini a site on the Aventine to dwell in and funds, not (indeed) for build-

The same community stubbornly renewed the fight a number of times but finally, buffeted by battles that always went against them, they were forced to surrender to Consul Q. Lutatius. The Roman people wished to take violent measures against them, but were instructed by Papirius,[3] by whose hand the words of the surrender were written at the Consul's order, that the Falisci had committed themselves not to Roman power but to Roman faith. Thus the people became calm, putting all anger aside. They resisted alike the power of hate, not wont to be easily overborne, and subservience to victory, which most readily affords licence, lest they fail the justice that was in them.[4]

P. Claudius[5] captured the inhabitants of Cameria under his leadership and auspices and sold them by auction. Because the general's good faith in this action seemed open to question, the same Roman people, though seeing that their treasury had been expanded with money and their boundaries with lands, made a very thorough search for them and redeemed them, giving them a place on the Aventine to dwell and restoring their properties. Money too they assigned, not to building a senate house but to erecting shrines and making sacrifices.[6] By the expeditious course of justice they made it possible for the Camerini to rejoice at their own destruction because they were thus reborn.

The actions I have thus far related were confined to our walls and the adjoining districts, what follows percolated through the whole earth. Timochares of Ambracia prom-

---

ing a senate house, but for building shrines and performing sacrifices. They got back their *sacra,* but were not restored as a civic community (SB[2]).

pollicitus est se Pyrrhum veneno per filium suum, qui potionibus eius praeerat, necaturum. ea res cum ad senatum
esset delata, missis legatis Pyrrhum monuit ut adversus
huius generis insidias cautius se gereret, memor urbem a
filio Martis conditam armis bella, non venenis gerere debere. Timocharis autem nomen suppressit, utroque modo
aequitatem amplexus, quia nec hostem malo exemplo tollere neque eum qui bene mereri paratus fuerat prodere
voluit.

2   Summa iustitia in quattuor quoque tribunis plebis eodem tempore conspecta est: nam cum L. Atratino, sub quo
duce aciem nostram apud Verruginem a Volscis inclinatam
cum ceteris equitibus correxerant, diem ad populum L.
Hortensius collega eorum dixisset, pro rostris iuraverunt
in squalore se esse[55] quoad imperator ipsorum reus esset
futuros:[56] non sustinuerunt enim egregii iuvenes, cuius armati periculum vulneribus et sanguine suo defenderant,
eius togati ultimum discrimen potestatis insignia retinen-
tes intueri. qua iustitia mota contio actione Hortensium
desistere coegit: nec se<cus se>[57] eo facto quod sequitur
exhibuit.

3   Cum Ti. Gracchus et C. Claudius ob nimis severe ges-
tam censuram maiorem partem civitatis exasperassent,
diem iis P. Popillius tribunus plebis perduellionis ad populum dixit, praeter communem consternationem privata
etiam ira accensus, quia necessarium eius Rutilium ex pu-

---

[55] se esse *intra cruces Briscoe*   [56] futuros ς: -rus AL
[57] *add. Kempf*: se* AL

---

[7] 278: Broughton I.194.
[8] 422: Livy 4.42.3–9.

ised Consul Fabricius that he would kill Pyrrhus by poison
through the agency of his son, who was in charge of the
king's beverages. The matter was brought before the
senate, which sent envoys to Pyrrhus with a warning to be
more on his guard against treachery of this nature. They
remembered that Rome was founded by a son of Mars
and should wage war by arms, not poisons. But they suppressed Timochares' name, embracing justice in two ways:
they were not willing to remove an enemy in a way that
would leave a bad precedent nor yet to betray a man who
had been ready to do them a service.[7]

Justice at its highest was seen also in four Tribunes of
the Plebs at the same time. L. Atratinus, under whose
command at Verrugo they, along with the rest of the horse,
had restored our line of battle when it was driven back by
the Volsci, was summoned to trial before the people by
their colleague L. Hortensius. The four took an oath standing on the rostra that so long as their commander was
under prosecution they would wear mourning. For these
excellent young men could not bear that he whose danger
under arms they had defended with their wounds and
blood should face ultimate peril in his gown before their
eyes while they still wore the emblems of power. The
assembly, stirred by such justice, forced Hortensius to give
up his suit.[8] Nor did they show themselves otherwise
minded in the act that follows.

Ti. Gracchus and C. Claudius had exasperated the ma-
jority of the community by over-severity in their exercise
of the Censorship. Tribune of the Plebs P. Popillius
summoned them before the people on a charge of treason.
Besides the general excitement he was privately angry
because they had ordered a kinsman of his, Rutilius, to de-

blico loco parietem demoliri iusserant. quo in iudicio primae classis permultae centuriae Claudium aperte damnabant, de Gracchi absolutione universae consentire videbantur. qui clara voce iuravit, si de collega suo gravius esset iudicatum, in factis se paribus eandem cum illo poenam exsilii subiturum, eaque iustitia tota illa tempestas ab utriusque fortunis et capite depulsa est: Claudium enim populus absolvit, Graccho causae dictionem Popillius remisit.

4   Magnam laudem et illud collegium tribunorum tulit, quod cum unus ex eo L. Cotta fiducia sacrosanctae potestatis creditoribus suis satis facere nollet, decrevit, si neque solveret pecuniam neque daret cum quo sponsio fieret, se appellantibus eum creditoribus auxilio futurum, iniquum ratum maiestatem publicam privatae perfidiae obtentu‹i›[58] esse. itaque Cottam in tribunatu quasi in aliquo sacrario latentem tribunicia inde iustitia extraxit.

5   Cuius ut ad alium aeque illustrem actum transgrediar, Cn. Domitius tribunus plebis M. Scaurum principem civitatis in iudicium populi devocavit, ut si Fortuna aspirasset, ruina, sin minus, certe ipsa obtrectatione amplissimi viri incrementum claritatis apprehenderet. cuius opprimendi cum summo studio flagraret, servus Scauri noctu ad eum pervenit, instructurum se eius accusationem multis et gravibus domini criminibus promittens. erat in eodem pectore ‹et›[59] inimicus [et Domitius][60] et dominus diversa aestimatione nefarium indicium perpen-

58 *add.* A *corr.*, G   59 *add. Gertz*   60 *del. Becker*

9 169: Livy 43.16 etc. (Broughton I.427 n.3). Popillius in the manuscripts will be Valerius' mistake for Rutilius (Livy).

molish a wall in a public place. In the trial many centuries of the first class were openly for condemning Claudius, whereas all of them seemed to agree on acquittal for Gracchus. But he took an oath in a loud voice that if judgment went against his colleague, he would undergo the same penalty of exile with Claudius, their actions being equal. By that justice the whole storm was averted from the fortunes and lives of both. For the people acquitted Claudius, and Popillius dropped the charge against Gracchus.[9]

Another board of Tribunes won great acclaim because when one of its members, L. Cotta, trusting in his sacrosanct power, refused to satisfy his creditors, they decreed that if he neither paid the money nor produced someone to stand surety, they would come to the aid of his creditors when they demanded their due. For they thought it unfair that public majesty should be a cover for private bad faith. So Cotta, hiding in the Tribunate as in some sanctuary, was pulled out by tribunician justice.[10]

To pass to another equally famous proceeding thereof, Tribune of the Plebs Cn. Domitius called M. Scaurus, the leading man of the community, to trial before the people, hoping to catch some enhancement of reputation by ruining a great man if Fortune was with him or, if not, at least by the mere detraction. He was thus in a fever of ambition to crush Scaurus, when a slave of Scaurus came to him one night, promising to furnish his prosecution with many serious charges against his master. In the same heart was an enemy and a master of slaves, weighing the wicked infor-

[10] Ca. 154: Lucil. 413–15.

dens. iustitia vicit odium: continuo enim, et suis auribus obseratis et indicis ore clauso, duci eum ad Scaurum iussit. accusatorem etiam reo suo, ne dicam diligendum, certe laudandum! quem populus cum propter alias virtutes tum hoc nomine libentius et consulem et censorem et pontificem maximum fecit.

6   Nec aliter ‹se›[61] L. Crassus in eodem iustitiae experimento gessit. Cn. Carbonis nomen infesto animo utpote inimicissimi sibi detulerat, sed tamen scrinium eius a servo allatum ad se, complura continens quibus facile opprimi posset, ut erat signatum cum servo catenato ad eum remisit. quo pacto igitur inter amicos viguisse tunc iustitiam credimus, cum inter accusatores quoque et reos tantum virium obtinuisse videamus?

7   Iam L. Sulla non se tam incolumem quam Sulpicium Rufum perditum voluit tribunicio furore eius sine ullo fine vexatus. ceterum cum eum proscriptum et in villa latentem a servo proditum comperisset, manumissum parricidam, ut fides edicti sui exstaret, praecipitari protinus saxo Tarpeio cum illo scelere parto pilleo iussit, victor alioquin insolens, hoc imperio iustissimus.

ext. 1   Verum ne alienigenae iustitiae obliti videamur, Pittacus Mitylenaeus, cuius aut meritis tantum cives debuerunt aut

[61] *add.* A *corr.*, G

---

[11] 104: cf. Cic. *Scaur.* fr. ap. Ascon. 21 Clark etc.
[12] 119: "Cn." should be "C."; cf. VM 3.7.6. Cicero often refers to the case (Broughton I.526), but Valerius is the only authority for this particular.
[13] 88: Livy *Per.* 77, Plut. *Sull.* 10.

mation in different scales. Justice got the better of hate. Straight away he shut his own ears and closed the informer's mouth, ordering that he be taken to Scaurus. A prosecutor to be praised at least, not to say loved, by his accused! Both for his other qualities and more gladly on account of this the people made him Consul and Censor and Chief Pontiff.[11]

In the same test of justice L. Crassus behaved no differently. He had launched a prosecution against Cn. Carbo in a spirit of hostility, for Carbo was his bitter enemy.[12] All the same, when a slave brought him a briefcase of Carbo's containing a quantity of material with which he could easily have been brought down, Crassus returned it to him sealed as it was along with the slave in chains. How then do we think justice flourished among friends in those days when we see it stood so strong between prosecutors and defendants?

L. Sulla wanted his own survival less than Sulpicius Rufus' ruin, endlessly harassed as he had been by the latter's tribunician frenzy. But when he learned that the proscribed Sulpicius had been betrayed by a slave as he was hiding in a country house, he freed the villain so that his edict should be seen to be faithfully observed but immediately afterwards ordered him to be hurled from the Tarpeian Rock along with the cap of liberty won by his crime.[13] In general an unbridled victor, Sulla in this order was a model of justice.

EXTERNAL

But lest we seem to have forgotten justice of alien origin, Pittacus of Mitylene, whose countrymen owed so much to his services or trusted so much to his character

moribus crediderunt ut ei s‹uis›[62] suffragiis tyrannidem deferrent, tam diu illud imperium sustinuit quam diu bellum de Sigeo cum Atheniensibus gerendum fuit. postquam autem pax victoria parta est, continuo reclamantibus Mitylenaeis deposuit, ne dominus civium ultra quam rei publicae necessitas exegerat permaneret. atque etiam cum recuperati agri dimidia pars consensu omnium offerretur, avertit animum ab eo munere, deforme iudicans virtutis gloriam magnitudine praedae minuere.

ext. 2   Alterius nunc mihi prudentia referenda est, ut alterius repraesentari iustitia possit. cum saluberrimo consilio Themistocles migrare Athenienses in classem coegisset, Xerxeque rege et copiis eius Graecia pulsis ruinas patriae in pristinum habitum reformaret et opes clandestinis molitionibus ad principatum Graeciae capessendum nutriret, in contione dixit habere se rem deliberatione sua provisam, quam si Fortuna ad effectum perduci passa esset, nihil maius aut potentius Atheniensi populo futurum, sed eam vulgari non oportere, postulavitque ut aliquis sibi cui illam tacite exponeret daretur. datus est Aristides. is postquam re‹m› cognovit,[63] classem illam Lacedaemoniorum, quae tota apud Gytheum subducta erat, velle incendere, ut ea consumpta dominatio maris ipsis cederet, processit ad cives et rettulit Themistoclen ut utile consilium ita minime iustum animo volvere. e vestigio universa contio quod aequum non videretur ne expedire quidem

---

[62] ei suis ⊂: eis AL
[63] rem cognovit *Madvig*: reco- AL

that they elected him into despotism, bore the weight of that power so long as war had to be waged with the Athenians about Sigeum. But after peace had been won by victory he immediately laid it down amid the protests of the Mitylenians, not wishing to remain master of his countrymen any longer than the necessity of the commonwealth demanded. Also when he was offered half of the recovered territory by universal consent, he turned his mind away from the gift, judging it unseemly to reduce the glory of valour by magnitude of plunder.[14]

I must now relate the shrewdness of one man to exhibit the justice of another. By his salutary advice Themistocles had made the Athenians migrate into their fleet. Now that king Xerxes and his forces had been driven from Greece, he was reshaping the ruins of his country into its former state and nourishing its power by secret machinations with a view to taking over the leadership of Greece. He said in the assembly that he had devised a plan whereby, if Fortune allowed it to go into effect, nothing would be greater or more powerful than the Athenian people, but it should not be made public; he therefore asked to be given someone to whom he could explain it in secret. He was given Aristides, who found that Themistocles wanted to set fire to the Lacedaemonian fleet, all of which was beached at Gytheum; with that burned up the mastery of the sea would thereby fall to Athens. Aristides went before the citizens and told them that the plan Themistocles was revolving in his mind was profitable but far from just. There and then the entire assembly cried out that what did not seem equitable was not expedient either and straightway

14 Early sixth century: cf. Strabo 617 etc.

proclamavit, ac protinus Themistoclen incepto iussit desistere.

ext. 3   Nihil illis etiam iustitiae exemplis fortius. Zaleucus, urbe Locrensium a se saluberrimis atque utilissimis legibus munita, cum filius eius adulterii crimine damnatus secundum ius ab ipso constitutum utroque oculo carere deberet ac tota civitas in honorem patris necessitatem poenae adulescentulo remitteret, aliquamdiu repugnavit. ad ultimum populi precibus evictus, suo prius, deinde filii oculo eruto usum videndi utrique reliquit. ita debitum supplicii modum legi reddidit aequitatis admirabili temperamento se inter misericordem patrem et iustum legis latorem partitus.

ext. 4   Sed aliquanto Charondae T<h>uri<n>i[64] praefractior et abscisior iustitia. ad vim et cruorem usque seditiosas contiones civium pacaverat lege cavendo ut, si quis eas cum ferro intrasset, continuo interficeretur. interiecto deinde tempore e longinquo rure gladio cinctus domum repetens, subito indicta contione sic ut erat in eam processit, ab eoque qui proxime constiterat solutae a se legis suae admonitus, 'idem' inquit 'ego illam sanciam', ac protinus ferro quod habebat destricto incubuit, cumque liceret culpam vel dissimulare vel errore defendere, poenam tamen repraesentare maluit, ne qua fraus iustitiae fieret.

[64] Thurini *Kempf*: Tyrii A *corr.,* LG

---

[15] 479: Cic. *Off.* 3.49 (based on a confusion? Cf. Plut. *Them.* 20 etc. and see A. R. Dyke ad Cic. loc., p. 554).

[16] A half-legendary lawgiver assigned by some to the seventh century: Aelian *Var. hist.* 13.24.

[17] Sixth century: Diodor. 12.19.

ordered Themistocles to give up his project.[15]

Nothing could be braver than the following examples of justice. Zaleucus[16] protected the city of Locri with very salutary and useful laws. His son was convicted on a charge of adultery and according to a law constituted by Zaleucus himself was due to lose both eyes. The whole community wished to spare the young man the necessity of punishment in honour of his father. For some time Zaleucus resisted, but in the end, overborne by the people's entreaties, he first gouged out one of his own eyes, then one of his son's, leaving the faculty of sight to them both. Thus he rendered to the law a due measure of retribution, by admirable balance of equity dividing himself between compassionate father and just lawgiver.

The justice of Charondas of Thurii was considerably harsher and more abrupt. He had pacified the assemblies of the citizens, which were strife-ridden to the point of violence and bloodshed, by making a law that anyone who came into them armed should immediately be put to death. Some time later he was coming home from a distant place in the country wearing his sword, when an assembly was suddenly announced. He went into it just as he was and was admonished by the person standing next to him that he had broken his own law. "And I shall ratify it too," he said, and forthwith drew the weapon he was carrying and fell upon it.[17] He might have concealed his fault or defended it as an error, but he preferred to pay the penalty outright, so that justice should not be compromised.

VALERIUS MAXIMUS

6. DE FIDE PUBLICA

praef.   Cuius imagine ante oculos posita venerabile Fidei numen dexteram suam, certissimum salutis humanae pignus, ostentat. quam semper in nostra civitate viguisse et omnes gentes senserunt et nos paucis exemplis recognoscamus.

1   Cum Ptolomaeus rex tutorem populum Romanum filio reliquisset, senatus M. Aemilium Lepidum, pontificem maximum, bis consulem, ad pueri tutelam gerendam Alexandriam misit, amplissimique et integerrimi viri sanctitatem rei publicae usibus et sacris operatam externae procurationi vacare voluit, ne fides civitatis nostrae frustra petita existimaretur. cuius beneficio regia incunabula conservata pariter ac decorata incertum Ptolomaeo reddiderunt patrisne fortuna magis an tutorum maiestate gloriari deberet.

2   Speciosa illa quoque Romana fides. ingenti Poenorum classe circa Siciliam devicta, duces eius fractis animis consilia petendae pacis agitabant. quorum Hamilcar ire se ad consules negabat audere, ne eodem modo catenae sibi inicerentur quo ab ipsis Cornelio Asinae consuli fuerant iniectae. Hanno autem, certior Romani animi aestimator, nihil tale timendum ratus, maxima cum fiducia ad coloquium eorum tetendit. apud quos cum de fine belli ageret et tribunus militum ei dixisset posse illi merito evenire quod Cornelio accidisset, uterque consul, tribuno tacere iusso, 'isto te' inquit 'metu, Hanno, fides civitatis nostrae

---

[1] 200: cf. Livy 31.2.3f. (Broughton I.321, 322 n.4).

[2] 256: Broughton I.208.

[3] 260: Livy *Per.* 17 etc. (Broughton I.205); cf. VM 6.9.11.

6. OF PUBLIC FAITH

When her image is set before our eyes the venerable divinity of Faith displays her right hand, the most certain pledge of human welfare. That she has always flourished in our community all nations have perceived; let us recall it with a few examples.

When king Ptolemy left the Roman people guardian to his son, the senate sent M. Aemilius Lepidus, Chief Pontiff and twice Consul, to Alexandria to look after the boy's tutelage, desiring that the probity of a very eminent and upright personage, versed in the usages and rituals of the commonwealth, should take time for an external charge, lest the faith of our community be thought to have been invoked in vain. By the senate's benefaction the royal cradle was both preserved and adorned, so that Ptolemy did not know whether he should be more proud of his father's fortune or of the majesty of his guardians.[1]

Splendid too is the following instance of Roman faith. After a huge Punic fleet had been defeated off the coast of Sicily,[2] its broken-spirited commanders were discussing how to sue for peace. One of them, Hamilcar, said he would not dare to go to the Consuls for fear of being put in chains in the same way as they themselves had put them on Consul Cornelius Asina.[3] But Hanno, a better judge of Roman mentality, thought there was nothing of that sort to be afraid of and went in full confidence for a conference with the Romans. While he was talking to them about ending the war, a Military Tribune said it would serve him right if what had befallen Cornelius were to happen to him. Thereupon both the Consuls told the Tribune to hold his tongue and said: "Hanno, the faith of our community frees

liberat.' claros illos fecerat tantum hostium ducem vincire potuisse, sed multo clariores fecit noluisse.

3   Adversus eosdem hostes parem fidem in iure legationis tuendo patres conscripti exhibuere: M. enim Aemilio Lepido L. Flaminio consulibus L. Minucium et L. Manlium Carthaginiensium legatis, quia manus his attulerant, per fetiales ⟨a M.⟩[65] Claudio praetore dedendos curaverunt. se tunc senatus, non eos quibus hoc praestabatur aspexit.

4   Cuius exemplum superior Africanus secutus, cum onustam multis et illustribus Carthaginiensium viris navem in suam potestatem redegisset, inviolatam dimisit, quia se legatos ad eum missos dicebant, tametsi manifestum erat illos vitandi praesentis periculi gratia falsum legationis nomen amplecti ut Romani imperatoris potius decepta fides quam frustra implorata iudicaretur.

5   Repraesentemus etiam illud senatus nullo modo praetermittendum opus. legatos ab urbe Apollonia Romam missos Q. Fabius Cn. Apronius aedilicii orta contentione pulsaverunt. quod ubi comperit, continuo eos per fetiales legatis dedidit, quaestoremque cum his Brundisium ire iussit, ne quam in itinere a cognatis deditorum iniuriam acciperent. illam curiam mortalium quis concilium ac non Fidei templum dixerit?

Quam ut civitas nostra semper benignam praestitit, ita

[65] *add.* P

---

4 187: Livy 38.42.7, Dio fr. 61.
5 203: Livy 30.25.9f. etc.
6 266: Livy *Per.* 15, Dio fr. 42.

you from any such apprehension." The power to have put in bonds so important an enemy general had made them famous, but their unwillingness to do so made them much more famous.

The Conscript Fathers showed equal faith in protecting ambassadorial rights in relation to the same enemies. In the Consulship of M. Aemilius Lepidus and L. Flaminius they had L. Minucius and L. Manlius surrendered by Praetor M. Claudius through Fetials to Carthaginian envoys because they had used violence against the same. The senate on that occasion looked at itself, not at those to whom it was making this amend.[4]

Following its example the elder Africanus dismissed unharmed many distinguished Carthaginians who were on board a ship which he had got into his power, because they said they had been sent to him as envoys; this, although it was obvious that they were embracing the false name of an embassy to avoid the danger they were in.[5] He preferred it thought that the faith of a Roman general had been imposed upon rather than that it had been appealed to in vain.

Let us also present another work of the senate, one by no means to be passed over. Q. Fabius and Cn. Apronius, former Aediles, struck some envoys sent to Rome from the city of Apollonia in a quarrel. When the senate learned of this, it immediately surrendered them through Fetials to the envoys and ordered a Quaestor to accompany the latter to Brundisium, so that no harm should come to them on the way from relatives of the persons surrendered.[6] Who would call that senate house a council of mortals and not a temple of Faith?

As our community has always rendered Faith abun-

in sociorum quoque animis constantem recognovit.

ext. 1   Post duorum in Hispania Scipionum totidemque Romani sanguinis exercituum miserabilem stragem, Saguntini victricibus Hannibalis armis intra moenia urbis suae compulsi, cum vim Punicam ulterius nequirent arcere, collatis in forum quae unicuique erant carissima atque undique circumdatis accensisque ignis nutrimentis, ne a societate nostra desisterent, publico et communi rogo semet ipsi superiecerunt. crediderim tunc ipsam Fidem, humana negotia speculantem, maestum gessisse vultum, perseverantissimum sui cultum iniquae Fortunae iudicio tam acerbo exitu damnatum cernentem.

ext. 2   Idem praestando Petelini eundem laudis honorem meruerunt. ab Hannibale, quia deficere a nostra amicitia noluerant, obsessi, legatos ad senatum auxilium implorantes miserunt. quibus propter recentem Cannensem cladem succurri non potuit. ceterum permissum est uti facerent quod utilissimum incolumitati ipsorum videretur. liberum ergo erat Carthaginiensium gratiam amplecti. illi tamen, feminis omnique aetate imbelli urbe egesta, quo diutius armati famem traherent, pertinacissime in muris constiterunt, exspiravitque prius eorum tota civitas quam ulla ex parte respectum Romanae societatis deposuit. itaque Hannibali non Peteliam, sed fidum Peteliae sepulcrum capere contigit.

---

7 In 211, whereas Hannibal captured Saguntum in 218. Valerius has excelled himself.

8 Livy 21.14, App. *Ib.* 12, Flor. 1.22.6.

9 216: Livy 23.20.4–10 etc.

dantly, so it has recognized its steadfast presence in the hearts of our allies.

After the pitiable slaughter of the two Scipios in Spain and as many armies of Roman race,[7] the Saguntines were driven by Hannibal's victorious arms inside the walls of their city. Unable to fend off the Punic power any longer, they collected into their forum all that each one of them held dearest and set inflammable substances around and ignited them. Then, rather than defect from our alliance, they threw themselves on top of the public and communal pyre.[8] I could believe that Faith herself on that occasion watching the affairs of men wore a face of sorrow as she saw her most persevering cult condemned by judgment of unkind Fortune in so bitter an outcome.

By the same performance the people of Petelia earned a like honourable acclaim. Invested by Hannibal because they refused to defect from our friendship, they sent envoys to the senate appealing for help. Because of the recent disaster at Cannae none could be given them. But they were authorized to do whatever they thought most expedient for their own safety, so they were free to embrace the favour of the Carthaginians. Instead, they emptied the town of women and all who were not of fighting age so that the men in arms could draw out their hunger the longer, and obstinately stood on their walls, so that their entire community perished before in any way discarding its respect for the Roman alliance. So Hannibal succeeded in taking, not Petelia, but Petelia's faithful tomb.[9]

7. DE FIDE UXORUM ERGA VIROS

1   Atque ut uxoriam quoque fidem attingamus, Tertia Aemilia, Africani prioris uxor, mater Corneliae Gracchorum, tantae fuit comitatis et patientiae ut cum sciret viro suo ancillulam ex suis gratam esse, dissimulaverit, ne domitorem orbis Africanum, femina magnum virum, impatientiae reum ageret, tantumque a vindicta mens eius afuit ut post mortem Africani manumissam ancillam in matrimonium liberto suo daret.

2   Q. Lucretium, proscriptum a triumviris, uxor Turia inter cameram et tectum cubiculi abditum una conscia ancillula ab imminente exitio non sine magno periculo suo tutum praestitit, singularique fide id egit ut cum ceteri proscripti in alienis et hostilibus regionibus per summos corporis et animi cruciatus vix evaderent, ille in cubiculo et in coniugis sinu salutem retineret.

3   Sulpicia autem, cum a matre Iulia diligentissime custodiretur, ne Lentulum Cruscellionem, virum suum proscriptum a triumviris, in Siciliam persequeretur, nihilo minus, famulari veste sumpta, cum duabus ancillis totidemque servis ad eum clandestina fuga pervenit, nec recusavit se ipsam proscribere ut ei fides sua in coniuge proscripto constaret.

7. OF THE FIDELITY OF WIVES
TOWARDS THEIR HUSBANDS

To touch also upon wifely fidelity, Tertia Aemilia, wife of the elder Africanus and mother of Cornelia of the Gracchi, was so accommodating and patient that although she knew that one of her slave girls had found favour with her husband, she pretended to be ignorant of it, lest she, a woman, charge a great man, world-conquering Africanus, with lack of self-control. And she was so far from any thought of revenge that after Africanus' death she freed the girl and gave her in marriage to one of her freedmen.[1]

Proscribed by the Triumvirs, Q. Lucretius was hidden by his wife Turia between the ceiling and the roof of their bedroom. So with one slave girl for accomplice she kept him safe from imminent death not without great risk to herself. When others of the proscribed barely escaped in alien and hostile regions at the price of cruel tortures of body and mind, he, thanks to her extraordinary fidelity, kept his life in his bedroom and the bosom of his spouse.[2]

Sulpicia was held in close custody by her mother Julia to prevent her following Lentulus Cruscellio, her husband proscribed by the Triumvirs, to Sicily. Nonetheless she reached him in a secret flight dressed as a servant along with two slave girls and as many slaves. She did not baulk at proscribing herself in order to maintain her fidelity to her proscribed husband.[3]

---

[1] Not found elsewhere. The elder Africanus died in 183.

[2] 43/42: App. *B.C.* 4.44. The famous inscription called Laudatio Turiae is now generally thought to refer to someone else.

[3] 43/42: App. *B.C.* 4.39.

8. DE FIDE SERVORUM

praef. Restat ut servorum etiam erga dominos quo minus ex-
spectatam hoc laudabiliorem fidem referamus.

1 M. Antonius, avorum nostrorum temporibus clarissimus orator, incesti reus agebatur. cuius in iudicio accusatores servum in quaestionem perseverantissime postula-
bant, quod ab eo, cum ad stuprum iret, lanternam
praelatam contenderent. erat autem is etiam tum imber-
bis, et stabat ⟨in⟩[66] corona,[67] videbatque rem ad suos
cruciatus pertinere, nec tamen eos fugitavit. ille vero, ut
domum quoque ventum est, Antonium hoc nomine vehementius confusum et sollicitum ultro est hortatus ut se
iudicibus torquendum traderet, adfirmans nullum ore suo
verbum exiturum quo causa eius laederetur, ac promissi
fidem mira patientia praestitit: plurimis etenim[68] laceratus
verberibus eculeoque impositus, candentibus etiam lam-
minis ustus, omnem vim accusationis custodita rei salute
subvertit. argui Fortuna merito potest quod tam pium et
tam fortem spiritum servili corpore[69] inclusit.

2 Consulem autem C. Marium Praenestinae obsidionis
miserabilem exitum sortitum, cuniculi latebris frustra evadere conatum, levique vulnere a Telesino, cum quo com-
mori destinaverat, perstrictum servus suus, ut Sullanae
crudelitatis expertem faceret, gladio traiectum interemit,
cum magna praemia sibi proposita videret si eum victoribus tradidisset. cuius dexterae tam opportunum ministe-

66 *add. Becker*
67 corona LG: -am A: coram A *corr.*
68 etenim *Lipsius*: etiam AL: enim ⌐
69 corpore *Watt*[1]: nomine AL

8. OF THE FIDELITY OF SLAVES

It remains to relate the fidelity of slaves towards their masters, the more praiseworthy as the less expected.

M. Antonius, a very famous orator in our forefathers' time, was accused of impurity. In his trial the prosecutors insistently demanded a slave for interrogation, contending that he carried a lantern in front of Antonius when he went to commit the crime. He was still beardless and stood there among the spectators realizing that the matter pertained to his own torture; yet he did not run away from it. When they got home, he spontaneously urged Antonius, who was much upset and worried on this account, to hand him over to the jury for torture, assuring him that no word would pass his lips detrimental to his master's case. And he kept his word with marvellous endurance. Lacerated with many stripes, put on the rack, burned with hot plates, he guarded the defendant's safety and destroyed all the force of the prosecution. Fortune can deservedly be blamed for enclosing so loyal and brave a spirit in the body of a slave.[1]

It was Consul C. Marius' fortune to be part of the pitiable outcome of the siege of Praeneste. He tried in vain to escape by hiding in a sewer and was lightly wounded by Telesinus, with whom he had determined to die. Then a slave of his ran him through with a sword and killed him to make him safe from Sulla's cruelty, though he saw that great rewards awaited him if he surrendered his master to the victors.[2] The timely service of his hand does not yield

---

[1] Cf. VM 3.7.9. The story of the slave is not found elsewhere.

[2] 82: Livy *Per.* 86–88 etc. (Broughton II.66).

rium nihil eorum pietati cedit a quibus salus dominorum protecta est, quia eo tempore Mario non vita sed mors in beneficio reposita erat.

3   Aeque illustre quod sequitur. C. Gracchus, ne in potestatem inimicorum perveniret, Philocrati servo suo cervices incidendas praebuit. quas cum celeri ictu abscidisset, gladium cruore domini manantem per sua egit praecordia. Euporum alii hunc vocitatum existimant; ego de nomine nihil disputo, famularis tantummodo fidei robur admiror. cuius si praesentiam animi generosus iuvenis imitatus foret, suo non servi beneficio imminentia supplicia vitasset: nunc commisit ut Philocratis quam Gracchi cadaver speciosius iaceret.

4   Alia nobilitas, alius furor, sed fidei par exemplum. Pindarus ‹C.›[70] Cassium Philippensi proelio victum, nuper ab eo manumissus, iussu ipsius obtruncatum insultationi hostium subtraxit, seque e conspectu hominum voluntaria morte abstulit, ita ut ne corpus quidem eius absumpti inveniretur. quis deorum, gravissimi sceleris ultor, illam dexteram, ‹quae›[71] in necem patriae parentis exarserat, tanto torpore illigavit ut se tremibunda Pindari genibus summitteret, ne publici parricidii quas merebatur poenas arbitrio piae victoriae exsolveret? tu profecto tunc, dive Iuli, caelestibus tuis vulneribus debitam exegisti vindictam, perfidum erga te caput sordidi auxilii supplex fieri cogendo, eo animi aestu compulsum ut neque retinere vitam vellet neque finire sua manu auderet.

---

[70] *add.* P   [71] *add.* A *corr.,* L *corr.*

---

3 121: Vell. 2.6.6 etc.   4 42: Vell. 2.70.2 etc.

to the loyalty of those who saved their masters' lives; for at that time not life but death was a kindness for Marius.

Equally celebrated is what follows. To avoid falling into the power of his enemies, C. Gracchus offered his neck for severance to his slave Philocrates. When the latter had beheaded him with a swift blow, he thrust the sword, dripping with his master's blood, through his own breast. Others think that his name was Euporus. I make no dispute about the name, I only admire the strength of the servant's fidelity.[3] If the nobly born young man had imitated his ready courage, he would have avoided the pains ahead thanks to himself, not his slave. As it was, he so managed it that Philocrates' dead body made a better showing than Gracchus'.

A different noble family, different frenzy, but an equal example of fidelity. When C. Cassius was defeated at the battle of Philippi, Pindarus, whom he had recently freed, killed him at his own orders and rescued him from the insults of his enemies. He then withdrew himself from the sight of men by voluntary death, so that even Cassius' body was not found after he was gone. Which of the gods avenging a most heinous crime tied that hand, which had flared up to kill the father of his country, with a numbness such that it lowered itself in trembling to the knees of Pindarus, lest at the arbitrament of pious victory it pay the penalty for public parricide as it deserved? Surely, divine Julius, you then wreaked the vengeance due to your celestial wounds, forcing your betrayer to go suppliant for ignominious aid, driven by such agitation of mind that he neither wished to retain his life nor dared to end it with his own hand.[4]

5   Adiunxit se his cladibus C. Plotius Plancus, Munatii Planci consularis et censorii frater. qui cum a triumviris proscriptus in regione Salernitana lateret, delicatiore vitae genere et odore unguenti occultam salutis custodiam detexit: istis enim vestigiis eorum qui miseros persequebantur sagax inducta cura abditum fugae eius cubile odorata est. a quibus comprehensi servi latentis multumque ac diu torti negabant se scire ubi dominus esset. non sustinuit deinde Plancus tam fideles tamque boni exempli servos ulterius cruciari, sed processit in medium iugulumque gladiis militum obiecit. quod certamen mutuae benivolentiae arduum dinosci facit utrum dignior dominus fuerit qui tam constantem servorum fidem experiretur, an servi qui tam iusta domini misericordia quaestionis saevitia liberarentur.

6   Quid? Urbinii Panapionis servus quam admirabilis fidei! cum ad dominum proscriptum occidendum domesticorum indicio certiores factos milites in Reatinam villam venisse cognosset, commutata cum eo veste, permutato etiam anulo, illum postico clam emisit, se autem in cubiculum ac lectulum recepit et ut Panapionem occidi passus est. brevis huius facti narratio, sed non parva materia laudationis: nam si quis ante oculos ponere velit subitum militum accursum, convulsa ianuae claustra, minacem vocem, truces vultus, fulgentia arma, rem vera aestimatione prosequetur, nec quam cito dicitur aliquem pro alio mori voluisse, tam id ex facili etiam fieri potuisse arbitrabitur. Panapio autem quantum servo deberet amplum ei faci-

---

5 43/42: Pliny *N.H.* 13.25, with the unsympathetic comment "who but would judge that the likes of him deserved to die?"

To these fatalities C. Plotius Plancus, brother of ex-Consul and Censor Munatius Plancus, added himself. Proscribed by the Triumvirs, he was hiding in the Salernum district, but his somewhat luxurious way of living and the odour of perfume uncovered his life's concealed safekeeping. For by these traces the keen attention of those in pursuit of such unfortunates was drawn and got wind of the secret lair of the fugitive. They arrested his slaves as he lay hidden and tortured them much and long, but they maintained ignorance of their master's whereabouts. Plancus could not bear that slaves so faithful and exemplary should be tormented further; he came out into the open and offered his throat to the soldiers' swords. Such a contest of mutual well-wishing makes it hard to determine which was the more deserving: the master to find such steadfast fidelity in his slaves or the slaves to be freed from the cruelty of interrogation by their master's just compassion.[5]

And then, how admirable the fidelity of Urbinius Panapio's slave! Learning that soldiers apprised by household informers had arrived at the country house near Reate to kill his proscribed master, he changed clothes with him, exchanged rings too, and let him secretly out by the back door. The slave then retired to the bedroom and the bed, and let himself be killed as Panapio. The act is short in the telling, but no small matter for praise. If we choose to imagine the sudden inrush of the soldiers, the door bolts forced, the threatening words, the fierce visages, the gleaming weapons, we shall make a true estimate of the case, nor think that in the time it takes to say that one man chose to die for another the thing could actually have been done so easily. Panapio acknowledged how much he owed

79

endo monumentum ac testimonium pietatis grato titulo reddendo confessus est.

7   Contentus essem huius exemplis generis, nisi unum me ⟨a⟩dicere[72] admiratio facti cogeret. Antius Restio, proscriptus a triumviris, cum omnes domesticos circa rapinam et praedam occupatos videret, quam maxime poterat dissimulata fuga se penatibus suis intempesta nocte subduxit. cuius furtivum egressum servus ab eo vinculorum poena coercitus, inexpiabilique litterarum nota per summam oris contumeliam inustus, curiosis speculatus oculis ac vestigia huc atque illuc errantia benivolo studio subsecutus, lateri voluntarius comes arrepsit. quo quidem tam exquisito tamque ancipiti officio perfectissimum ⟨in⟩exspectatae[73] pietatis cumulum expleverat: iis enim quorum felicior in domo status fuerat lucro intentis, ipse, nihil aliud quam umbra et imago suppliciorum suorum, maximum esse emolumentum eius a quo tam graviter punitus erat salutem iudicavit, cumque abunde foret iram remittere, adiecit etiam caritatem. nec hactenus benivolentia processit, sed in eo conservando mira quoque arte usus est: nam ut sensit cupidos sanguinis milites supervenire, amoto domino rogum exstruxit, eique egentem a se comprehensum et occisum senem superiecit. interrogantibus deinde militibus ubinam esset Antius, manum rogo intentans ibi illum datis sibi crudelitatis piaculis uri respondit. quia veri similia loquebatur, habita est voci fides. quo evenit ut Antius

---

[72] *add. Per.*   [73] *add. idem*

---

[6] 43/42: Sen. *Ben.* 3.25 etc.

to the slave by putting up a fine monument to him and testifying to his loyalty in a grateful inscription.[6]

I should rest content with my examples in this kind, were I not obliged to add one more by my admiration for the act. Antius Restio, proscribed by the Triumvirs, seeing all his household servants busy plundering and looting, stole out of his home in the dead of night in a flight as secret as he could make it. He had a slave whom he had put in chains and branded with inexpiable[7] letters on the face to his extreme indignity. This slave watched his furtive egress with curious eyes and, following his master's wandering footsteps with benevolent eagerness, crept up to his side as his voluntary companion. By such studied and dangerous service he had more than filled the most perfect measure of unlooked-for loyalty. While those whose condition in the house had been happier than his were intent on gain, he, who was nothing but the shadow and semblance of his punishments, saw his greatest profit in the life of one who had chastised him so severely. Where it would have been more than enough to forgive, he added affection. Nor did his will to help stop there; he also used a remarkable stratagem to save him. For when he saw that the bloodthirsty soldiers were upon them, he put his master out of the way and built a pyre, on which he threw an indigent old man whom he had seized and killed. When the soldiers asked where Antius was, he pointed to the pyre and answered that he was being burned there after having made atonement for the cruelty to himself. Since what he said sounded plausible, his words were believed. So it turned

---

[7] In effect "indelible." Cicero (*Rep.* 3.19) has *inexpiabiles poenae* for punishments which cannot be cancelled by expiation.

spatium <et>[74] quaerendae incolumitatis occasionem adsequeretur.

9. DE MUTATIONE MORUM AUT FORTUNAE

praef.　　Multum animis hominum et fiduciae adicere et sollicitudinis detrahere potest morum ac fortunae in claris viris recognita mutatio, sive nostros status sive proximorum ingenia contemplemur: nam cum aliorum fortunas spectando[75] ex condicione abiecta atque contempta emersisse claritatem videamus, quid aberit quin et ipsi meliora de nobis semper cogitemus, memores stultum esse perpetuae infelicitatis se praedamnare spemque, quae etiam incerta recte fovetur, interdum certam in desperationem convertere?

1　　Manlius Torquatus adeo hebetis atque obtusi cordis inter initia iuventae existimatus ut a patre L. Manlio, amplissimo viro, quia et domesticis et rei publicae usibus inutilis videbatur, rus relegatus agresti opere fatigaretur, postmodum patrem reum iudiciali periculo liberavit, filium victorem, quod adversus imperium suum cum hoste manum conseruerat, securi percussit, patriam Latino tumultu fessam speciosissimo triumpho recreavit, in hoc, credo, <malig>nae[76] Fortunae nubilo adulescentiae contemptu perfusus, quo senectutis eius decus lucidius enitesceret.

[74] spatium et *Watt*[1]: statum* AL
[75] spectando A *corr.*: et pectora* LG
[76] malignae ς: ne* AL

out that Antius gained time and opportunity to get out of danger.[8]

9. OF CHANGE OF CHARACTER OR FORTUNE

Recognition of change of character and fortune in famous men can add much confidence to our minds and take away much anxiety, whether we look at our own situations or those of our neighbours. For when in watching the fortunes of others we see how brilliance emerged from abjection and contempt, why shall we too not always have better thoughts about ourselves, mindful that it is foolish to sentence oneself in advance to perpetual infelicity and in the meanwhile convert hope, which it is right to foster even if uncertain, to certain despair?

Manlius Torquatus in the early stages of his adult life was supposed to be of so blunt and dull an intellect that his father L. Manlius, a man of the highest consequence, banished him to the country and wore him out with farm labour, because he appeared to be useless for both domestic and public employments. Later on he released his father, who was under prosecution, from the danger of a trial, he beheaded his victorious son for having fought with an enemy against his orders, and by a splendid triumph revived his country wearied with a Latin turmoil. Malignant Fortune's cloudy face, I suppose, doused him with contempt of his youth in order that the glory of his old age might shine the brighter.[1]

---

[8] 43/42: App. *B.C.* 4.43 etc.
[1] Cf. VM 2.7.6, 5.4.3.

2   Scipio autem Africanus superior, quem di immortales
nasci voluerunt ut esset in quo virtus se per omnes numeros hominibus efficaciter ostenderet, solutioris vitae pri-
mos adulescentiae annos egisse fertur, remotos quidem a
luxuriae crimine, sed tamen Punicis tropaeis, devictae
Carthaginis cervicibus imposito iugo teneriores.

3   C. quoque Valerius Flaccus secundi Punici belli temporibus luxu perditam adulescentiam incohavit. ceterum a
P. Licinio pontifice maximo flamen factus, quo facilius a
vitiis recederet, ad curam sacrorum et caerimoniarum
converso animo, usus duce frugalitatis religione, quantum
prius luxuriae fuerat exemplum, tantum postea modestiae
et sanctitatis specimen evasit.

4   Nihil Q. Fabio Maximo, qui Gallica victoria cognomen
Allobrogici sibimet ac posteris peperit, adulescente magis
infame, nihil eodem sene ornatius aut speciosius illo saeculo nostra civitas habuit.

5   Quis ignorat Q. Catuli auctoritatem in maximo clarissimorum virorum proventu excelsum gradum obtinuisse?
cuius si superior aetas revolvatur, multi lusus, multae
deliciae reperiantur. quae quidem ei impedimento non
fuerunt quo minus patriae princeps exsisteret, nomenque
eius in Capitolino fastigio fulgeret, ac virtute civile bellum
ingenti motu oriens sepeliret.

---

2 Gell. 7.8.5, citing Naevius.   3 In 209: Livy 27.8.4–10.

4 As Consul in 121. His earlier bad reputation is attested only
here, perhaps by confusion with his cousin by adoption Eburnus,
if Eburnus is indeed the Fabius Maximus of VM 2.7.3.

5 He was put in charge of the restoration of the Capitoline
temple of Jupiter in 78 and consecrated it in 68.

Scipio Africanus the elder, whom the immortal gods wished born so that there might be a man in whom virtue could effectively show herself to mankind in all her aspects, is said to have led a rather loose life in his first years as a young man; they were well removed to be sure from the reproach of dissipation but still not quite tough enough for the Punic trophies and the yoke planted on the neck of vanquished Carthage.[2]

C. Valerius Flaccus too at the time of the Second Punic War began with a youth of ruinous extravagance. But when he was made a Flamen by Chief Pontiff P. Licinius,[3] to withdraw from his vices the more easily he turned his mind to the care of sacred things and ceremonies, using religion as his guide to good conduct. Earlier an example of dissipation, he later became no less a pattern of propriety and purity.

Our community had no more disreputable member at that time than Q. Fabius Maximus in his young days, who by victory in Gaul[4] won for himself and his descendants the surname of Allobrogicus; and none in that era was more distinguished or respectable than the same in old age.

Everyone knows that Q. Catulus' reputation stood at a lofty level in a great plenty of illustrious men. If his earlier life were to be reviewed, many frolics and indulgences would be found. They did not hinder him from becoming the leading man in the country or prevent his name shining at the summit of the Capitol[5] or stop him from burying by his valour the mighty upheaval of a rising civil war.[6]

[6] Provoked by his colleague in the Consulship M. Lepidus in 78.

6   L. vero Sulla usque ad quaesturae suae comitia vitam
libidine, vino, ludicrae artis amore inquinatam perduxit.
quapropter C. Marius[77] consul moleste tulisse traditur
quod sibi asperrimum in Africa bellum gerenti tam delica-
tus quaestor sorte obvenisset. eiusdem virtus, quasi per-
ruptis et disiectis nequitiae qua obsidebatur claustris,
catenas Iugurthae manibus iniecit, Mithridatem compescuit, socialis belli fluctus repressit, Cinnae dominationem
fregit, eumque qui se in Africa quaestorem fastidierat
ipsam illam provinciam proscriptum et exsulem petere
coegit. quae tam diversa tamque inter se contraria si quis
apud animum suum attentiore comparatione expendere
velit, duos in uno homine Sullas fuisse crediderit, turpem
adulescentulum et virum dicerem fortem, nisi ipse se felicem appellari maluisset.

7   Atque ut nobilitati,[78] beneficio paenitentiae se ipsam
admonitae respicere, altiora modo suo sperare ausos sub-
texamus, T. Aufidius, cum Asiatici publici exiguam admodum particulam habuisset, postea totam Asiam proconsulari imperio obtinuit. nec indignati sunt socii eius parere
fascibus quem aliena tribunalia adulantem viderant. gessit
enim[79] se integerrime atque splendidissime. quo quidem[80] modo demonstravit pristinum quaestum suum Fortunae, praesens vero dignitatis incrementum moribus
ipsius imputari debere.

8   At P. Rupilius non publicanum in Sicilia egit, sed operas
publicanis dedit. idem ultimam inopiam suam auctorato

[77] Marius *Kempf*: -um AL
[78] nobilitati *Gronovius*: -tis AL
[79] enim *Damsté*: etiam AL
[80] quo quidem *Kempf*: quoque id AL

Down to his election as Quaestor[7] L. Sulla had led a life stained by lust, wine, and love of the theatre. Hence we are told that Consul C. Marius was displeased that so frivolous a Quaestor should have come his way by lot as he was conducting a very difficult war in Africa. But Sulla's ability, as though breaking and scattering the bars of profligacy by which it was confined, put chains on the hands of Jugurtha, subdued Mithridates, calmed the billows of the Social War, broke the domination of Cinna, and forced the man who had disdained him as Quaestor in Africa to resort to that very province as a proscribed exile. Whoever weighs such diversities and contradictions in his mind and compares them carefully might suppose that there were two Sullas in one person: the disreputable youth and the man whom I should call strong if he himself had not preferred to be styled fortunate.

To nobility, admonished by repentance to take heed to itself, let me attach those who dared to look higher than their measure. T. Aufidius, who had shared in a very small way in the Asian tax contracts, later governed the whole of Asia[8] with proconsular authority. Our allies were not aggrieved at obeying the fasces of a man they had seen fawning on other tribunals. For he behaved most uprightly and creditably, thereby proving that his former livelihood should be imputed to Fortune, but his present accession of dignity to his own character.

P. Rupilius was not a tax farmer in Sicily, he worked for the tax farmers. He also eked out his extreme poverty by

---

[7] In 108: cf. Plut. *Sull.* 1f., Sall. *Iug.* 95, Firm. *Math.* 1.7.28.
[8] The Roman province, probably in 65 (Broughton II.142 n.9). Cicero (*Brut.* 179) gives him a good character.

sociis officio sustentavit. ab hoc postmodum consule leges universi Siculi acceperunt, acerbissimoque praedonum ac fugitivorum bello liberati sunt. portus ipsos, si quis modo mutis rebus inest sensus, tantam in eodem homine varietatem status admiratos arbitror: quem enim diurnas capturas exigentem animadverterant, eundem iura dantem classesque et exercitus regentem viderunt.

9   Huic tanto incremento maius adiciam. Asculo capto Cn. Pompei‹us›,[81] Magni pater, P. Ventidium aetate ‹im›puberem[82] in triumpho suo populi oculis subiecit. hic est Ventidius qui postea Romae ex Parthis et per Parthos de Crassi manibus in hostili solo miserabiliter iacentibus triumphum duxit. ita qui captivus carcerem exhorruerat, victor Capitolium felicitate celebravit. in eodem etiam illud eximium, quod eodem anno praetor et consul est factus.

10   Casuum nunc contemplemur varietatem. L. Lentulus consularis lege Caecilia repetundarum crimine oppressus censor cum L. Censorino creatus est. quem quidem Fortuna inter ornamenta et dedecora alterna vice versavit, consulatu illius damnationem, damnationi censuram subiciendo, et neque bonis eum perpetuis frui neque malis aeternis ingemescere patiendo.

[81] *add. Pighius*
[82] *add. idem*

---

9 In 132 (Broughton I.498).

10 In 38. With questionable logic the avenging of Crassus' fate is regarded as a triumph over it. On Ventidius see sources in Briscoe.

hiring his services to the allies. Later the whole of Sicily accepted laws from him as Consul[9] and was freed from a very bitter war with pirates and runaway slaves. I think the very harbours, if dumb things have feelings, were astonished at such a variety of status in the same individual. They watched a man they had seen pulling in his daily takings sitting in judgment and commanding fleets and armies.

To this elevation, great as it was, I shall add a greater. When Asculum was captured, Cn. Pompeius, father of Magnus, subjected P. Ventidius, still a child, to the eyes of the people at his triumph. This is the Ventidius who later triumphed in Rome over the Parthians and through the Parthians over the shade of Crassus lying miserably on enemy soil.[10] So as a captive he had shuddered at the prison, as a victor he crowded the Capitol with his felicity. He was also extraordinary in having been made Praetor and Consul in the same year.

Let us now look at the variety of men's fortunes. L. Lentulus,[11] a Consular, after conviction on a charge of extortion under the Caecilian law,[12] was elected Censor[13] with L. Censorinus. Fortune turned him this way and that between honours and disgraces, following Consulship with conviction, conviction with Censorship, suffering him neither to enjoy lasting good nor bewail unchanging bad.

---

[11] Lupus, Consul in 156. His conviction, not elsewhere noticed, will have been in 154 or 153 after governorship of a province (Broughton I.451 n.2).

[12] A mistake for the *lex Calpurnia de repetundis* of 149, as often supposed. But the reference may be to an ad hoc court (Broughton).

[13] In 147.

11 Iisdem viribus uti voluit in Cn. Cornelio Scipione Asina.[83] qui consul a Poenis apud Liparas captus, cum belli iure omnia perdidisset, laetiore subinde vultu eius adiutus cuncta recuperavit, consul etiam iterum creatus est. quis crederet illum a duodecim securibus ad Carthaginiensium perventurum catenas? quis rursus existimaret a Punicis vinculis ad summi imperii perventurum insignia? sed tamen ex consule captivus et ex captivo consul est factus.

12 Quid? Crasso nonne pecuniae magnitudo locupletis nomen dedit? sed eidem postea inopia turpem decoctoris appellationem[84] inussit, si quidem bona eius a creditoribus, quia solidum praestare non poterat, venierunt. itaque qui ‹nimiis divitiis invisus fuerat›[85] amara suggillatione non caruit; cum egens ambularet, Dives ab occurrentibus salutabatur.

13 Crassum casus acerbitate Q. Caepio praecucurrit: is namque, praeturae splendore, triumphi claritate, consulatus decore, maximi pontificis sacerdotio ut senatus patronus diceretur adsecutus, in publicis vinculis spiritum deposuit, corpusque eius funesti‹s›[86] carnificis manibus laceratum in scalis Gemoniis iacens magno cum horrore totius fori Romani conspectum est.

14 Iam C. Marius maxima Fortunae luctatio est:[87] omnes enim eius impetus qua corporis qua animi robore fortis-

---

[83] Asina P: Nasica A: Naes- L

[84] appellationem *Lipsius*: superla- * AL

[85] *add. SB*[3]; Br   [86] *add. Gertz*   [87] maxima (G: -me A, -mae L) f- l- est L *corr.*: m- f- luctatione* A

---

[14] Cf. VM 6.6.2.

[15] Cic. *Tusc.* 1.81. The original Crassus Dives, Consul in 205,

She chose to use the same power in the case of Cn. Cornelius Scipio Asina, who as Consul was taken prisoner by the Carthaginians at Lipara. By the laws of war he had lost all, but aided anon by her more cheerful countenance he regained everything, and was even elected Consul a second time. Who would have believed that he would pass from the twelve axes to Carthaginian chains? Who again would have thought that he would pass from Punic bonds to the emblems of highest command? All the same, from Consul he became prisoner and from prisoner Consul.[14]

And Crassus? Did not the volume of his money give him the name of Rich? But later the lack of it branded him with the shameful appellation of bankrupt, when his property was sold by his creditors since he could not pay in full. And so he who had once been envied for his excessive wealth had to take a bitter insult: as a poor man, he was greeted as Mr. Rich by those who met him on the street.[15]

Q. Caepio surpassed Crassus in the harshness of his lot. By the distinction of his Praetorship, the brilliance of his triumph, the glory of his Consulship, the priesthood of Chief Pontiff, he won the title of Protector of the senate. But he breathed his last in public bonds and his body, torn by the dire hands of an executioner, was seen lying on the Gemonian Steps to the great consternation of the whole Roman Forum.[16]

Next is C. Marius, Fortune's greatest wrestle. For he stood up bravely to all her shocks by strength both of mind

had a descendant, Praetor in 57, who went bankrupt; cf. Cic. *Att.* 2.13.2 with commentary. Valerius and Pliny *N.H.* 33.133 confuse, as do moderns.

[16] See VM 4.7.3.

sime sustinuit. Arpinatibus honoribus iudicatus inferior, quaesturam Romae petere ausus est. patientia deinde repulsarum irrupit magis in curiam quam venit. in tribunatus quoque et aedilitatis petitione consimilem campi notam expertus, praeturae candidatus supremo in loco adhaesit,[88] quem tamen non sine periculo obtinuit: ambitus enim accusatus vix atque aegre absolutionem ab iudicibus impetravit. ex illo Mario, tam humili Arpini,[89] tam ignobili Romae, tam fastidiendo candidato, ille Marius evasit qui Africam subegit, qui Iugurtham regem ante currum egit, qui Teutonorum Cimbrorumque exercitus delevit, cuius bina tropaea in urbe spectantur, cuius septem in fastis consulatus leguntur, cui post exsilium consulem creari proscriptoque facere proscriptionem contigit. quid huius condicione inconstantius aut mutabilius? quem si inter miseros posueris, miserrimus, ‹si›[90] inter felices, felicissimus reperietur.

15   C. autem Caesar, cuius virtutes aditum sibi in caelum struxerunt,[91] inter primae iuventae initia privatus Asiam petens, a maritimis praedonibus circa insulam Pharmacussam[92] exceptus, quinquaginta se talentis redemit. parva igitur summa clarissimum mundi sidus in piratico myoparone rependi Fortuna voluit. quid est ergo quod amplius de ea queramur, si ne consortibus quidem divinitatis suae parcit? sed caeleste numen se ab iniuria vindicavit: continuo enim captos praedones crucibus adfixit.

[88] adh- *Gronovius*: ita h- AL
[89] Arpini G: -na AL: -nate A *corr.*
[90] si G: *om.* AL
[91] struxerunt A *corr.*: instr- AL
[92] Br

92

and body. Judged too humble for the honours of Arpinum, he ventured to stand for the Quaestorship in Rome. Then by his patience under rebuffs he did not so much enter the senate as break into it. In standing for the Tribunate and the Aedileship too he met with a similar electoral stigma, and as a candidate for the Praetorship hung on in the last place, which however he held not without risk; for accused of malpractice, he won an acquittal from the jury with the utmost difficulty. From that Marius, so lowly in Arpinum, so inglorious in Rome, so contemptible a candidate, emerged the Marius who subdued Africa, drove king Jugurtha before his chariot, destroyed the hosts of the Teutones and Cimbri, whose two trophies are seen in the city, whose seven Consulships are read in the Fasti, to whom it fell to become Consul after exile and to make a proscription after having been proscribed. What more unstable or changeable than his condition? If you put him among the wretched, he was wretched indeed; if among the fortunate, none will be found as fortunate as he.[17]

C. Caesar, whose virtues made their own road to heaven, in his earliest youth while travelling to Asia as a private citizen, was taken prisoner by sea robbers off the island of Pharmacussa and ransomed himself for fifty talents. So Fortune willed that the brightest star in the universe should be exchanged for a small sum in a pirate galley. So why should we complain of her any more if she does not spare even her partners in deity? But the celestial power avenged itself for the insult; for presently Caesar captured the pirates and crucified them.[18]

[17] See Weynand, *RE* suppl. VI.1363–1425.
[18] 74: Suet. *Iul.* 4 etc.

ext. 1   Attento studio nostra commemoravimus: remissiore
nunc animo aliena narrentur. perditae luxuriae Athenis
adulescens Polemo, neque illecebris eius tantummodo sed
etiam ipsa infamia gaudens, cum e convivio non post occa-
sum solis sed post ortum surrexisset domumque rediens
Xenocratis philosophi patentem ianuam vidisset, vino
gravis, unguentis delibutus, sertis capite redimito, perluci-
da veste amictus, refertam turba doctorum hominum
scholam eius intravit. nec contentus tam deformi introitu,
consedit etiam, ut clarissimum eloquium et prudentissima
praecepta temulentiae lasciviis elevaret. orta deinde, ut
par erat, omnium indignatione, Xenocrates vultum in eodem habitu continuit, omissaque re quam disserebat, de
modestia ac temperantia loqui coepit. cuius gravitate ser-
monis resipiscere coactus Polemo primum coronam capite
detractam proiecit, paulo post bracchium intra pallium
reduxit, procedente tempore oris convivalis hilaritatem
deposuit, ad ultimum totam luxuriam exuit, uniusque orationis saluberrima medicina sanatus ex infami ganeone
maximus philosophus evasit. peregrinatus est huius animus in nequitia, non habitavit.

ext. 2   Piget Themistoclis adulescentiam attingere, sive patrem aspiciam abdicationis iniungentem notam, sive matrem suspendio finire vitam propter filii turpitudinem
coactam, cum omnium postea Graii sanguinis virorum clarissimus exstiterit, mediumque Europae et Asiae vel spei
vel desperationis pignus fuerit: haec enim eum salutis suae

---

19 He succeeded Xenocrates as head of the Academy in
315/14. For his conversion see Hor. *Sat.* 2.3.254 etc.

With eager attention we have commemorated our own. Let alien examples be related more at our ease. There was a young man in Athens called Polemo, of a desperate profligacy, who rejoiced not only in its allurements but in the very infamy. Rising from a dinner party not after sunset but after sunrise and making his way home, he noticed that the door of the philosopher Xenocrates was wide open. Heavy with wine, drenched with perfumes, garlands on his head, dressed in transparent clothing, he entered Xenocrates' lecture hall which was filled with an assembly of learned men. Not content with so unseemly an entrance, he proceeded to sit down, intending to mock the splendid eloquence and wise precepts with tipsy fooleries. Naturally everyone waxed indignant, but Xenocrates without changing countenance dropped the topic on which he was discoursing and began to speak of modesty and temperance. The gravity of his words brought Polemo to his senses. First he took the garland from his head and threw it away, a little later drew his arm inside his cloak, as time went on put off the hilarity of his convivial face, finally stripped away luxury in its entirety and, healed by the salutary medicine of a single speech, from a notorious debauchee he ended up a great philosopher. His soul sojourned in vice, but vice was not its home.[19]

It irks me to touch upon the youth of Themistocles, whether I look at his father, who put upon him the stigma of repudiation, or his mother, who was driven to hang herself because of her son's infamy; although later he turned out the most famous of all the Grecian race and stood between Europe and Asia as the pledge of either hope or despair. For Europe had him as her life's protector, Asia

patronum habuit, illa vadem victoriae adsumpsit.

ext. 3   Cimonis vero incunabula opinione stultitiae fuerunt referta: eiusdem adulti[93] imperia salutaria Athenienses senserunt. itaque coegit eos stuporis semet ipsos damnare, qui eum stolidum crediderant.

ext. 4   Nam Alcibiaden quasi duae Fortunae partitae sunt, altera quae ei nobilitatem eximiam, abundantes divitias, formam praestantissimam, favorem civium propensum, summa imperia, praecipuas potentiae vires, flagrantissimum ingenium adsignaret, altera quae damnationem, exsilium, venditionem bonorum, inopiam, odium patriae, violentam mortem infligeret: nec aut haec aut illa universa, sed varia, perplexa, freto atque aestui similia.

ext. 5   Ad invidiam usque Polycratis, Samiorum tyranni, abundantissimis bonis conspicuus vitae fulgor excessit, nec sine causa: omnes enim conatus eius placido excipiebantur itinere, spes certum cupitae rei fructum apprehendebant, vota nuncupabantur simul et solvebantur, velle ac posse in aequo positum erat. semel dumtaxat vultum mutavit, perquam brevi tristitiae salebra succussum, tunc cum admodum gratum sibi anulum de industria in profundum, ne omnis incommodi expers esset, abiecit. quem tamen continuo recuperavit, capto pisce qui eum devoraverat. sed hunc, cuius felicitas semper plenis velis prosperum cursum tenuit, Orontes, Darei regis praefectus, in excelsissimo Mycalensis montis vertice cruci adfixit, e qua putres eius artus et tabido cruore manantia membra atque

93 adulti *Madvig*: stultitiae* AL

---

20 Born *ca.* 524: Nep. *Them.* 1.1f. etc.
21 Born *ca.* 510: Plut. *Cim.* 4.   22 Born mid-fifth century.

took him as her guarantor of victory.[20]

Cimon's beginnings were filled with a persuasion of stupidity; as a grown man, the Athenians found salvation in his commands. So he obliged those who had believed him a dullard to convict themselves of doltishness.[21]

As for Alcibiades,[22] two Fortunes as it were shared him between them. One assigned him outstanding nobility of birth, abundant riches, striking good looks, the ready favour of his countrymen, the highest commands, outstanding private power, an ardent intelligence; the other brought down upon him judicial condemnation, exile, sale of property, poverty, his country's hatred, a violent death. Nor did either part have a monopoly; they were variously intermingled, like the rough waters of a channel.[23]

The life of Polycrates, tyrant of the Samians, was brilliant to conspicuous excess and the arousing of envy by its abundance of blessings, as well it might. All his enterprises found an easy path to further them, his hopes seized assured enjoyment of the object desired, his vows were discharged as soon as taken, the wish and the power to attain it stood level. Only once did he change countenance, shaken by a very brief jolt of distress; that was when he deliberately flung a ring of which he was very fond into the sea, so that he should not be totally free of trouble. But presently he recovered it, when the fish that had swallowed it was caught. But this man, whose felicity always held its prosperous course full sail, was crucified by king Darius' viceroy Orontes on the highest peak of the mountain of Mycale. Up there Samos, long crushed in harsh servitude, saw with free and joyful eyes his rotting limbs, his

[23] Cf. Nep. *Alc.* 1, Plut. *Alc.* 2.

illam laevam, cui Neptunus anulum piscatoris manu resti-
tuerat, situ marcidam Samos, amara servitute aliquamdiu
pressa, liberis ac laetis oculis aspexit.

ext. 6 Dionysius autem, cum hereditatis nomine a patre Syracusanorum ac paene totius Siciliae tyrannidem accepisset,
maximarum opum dominus, exercituum dux, rector clas-
sium, equitatuum potens, propter inopiam litteras pueru-
los Corinthi docuit, eodemque tempore tanta mutatione
maiores natu ne quis nimis Fortunae crederet, magister
ludi factus ex tyranno, monuit.

ext. 7 Sequitur hunc Syphax rex, consimilem Fortunae iniquitatem expertus, quem amicum hinc Roma per Scipionem, illinc Carthago per Hasdrubalem ultro petitum ad
penates deos eius venerat. ceterum eo claritatis evectus ut
validissimorum populorum tantum non arbiter victoriae
exsisteret, parvi temporis interiecta mora catenatus a Lae-
lio legato ad Scipionem imperatorem pertractus est,
cuiusque dexteram regio insidens solio arroganti manu at-
tigerat, eius genibus supplex procubuit.

Caduca nimi<r>um[94] et fragilia puerilibusque consentanea crepundiis sunt ista quae vires atque opes humanae
vocantur. adfluunt subito, repente dilabuntur, nullo in
loco, nulla in persona stabilibus nixa radicibus consistunt,
sed incertissimo flatu Fortunae huc atque illuc acta quos
sublime extulerunt improviso recursu destitutos profundo

[94] *add.* ⌐

[24] 525: Herod. 3.39–42, 120–25 etc.
[25] He was expelled from Syracuse in 344: Cic. *Tusc.* 3.27 etc.

members dripping with putrescent gore, and his left hand, to which Neptune had restored the ring by the hand of a fisherman, drooping in decay.[24]

Dionysius had received as an inheritance from his father absolute rule over the Syracusans and almost the whole of Sicily. Lord of enormous wealth, commander of armies, ruler of fleets, master of cavalries, by reason of poverty he taught little boys their ABCs in Corinth; and at the same time he, a tyrant turned schoolmaster, admonished their elders by so signal a vicissitude not to trust too much in Fortune.[25]

King Syphax follows him, who experienced a similar unkindness of Fortune. Rome and Carthage in the persons of Scipio and Hasdrubal came to his dwelling unsummoned to seek his friendship. Yet, carried to such a height of renown that he became all but arbiter of victory between the mightiest peoples, after a short time's interval he was dragged in chains by the Legate Laelius to his commander Scipio and fell suppliant at the knees of the man whose hand he had arrogantly touched with his own as he sat upon his royal throne.[26]

Frail and fragile surely and like children's toys are the so-called power and wealth of humankind. Suddenly they stream in, abruptly they fall apart, in no place or person do they stand on fixed or stable roots, but driven hither and thither by Fortune's fickle breeze they forsake those they have raised aloft in unexpected withdrawal and lament-

---

"Dionysius in Corinth" was proverbial: on its meaning in Cic. *Att.* 9.9.1 see my commentary there.

[26] 203 and 206: Livy 28.17.10–18.12, 30.12.1–3, 13.1–7.

cladium miserabiliter immergunt. itaque neque existimari neque dici debent bona quae, ut inflictorum malorum amaritudine desiderium sui duplicent, ‹...›.[95]

95 *lacunam Pighius*

ably plunge them into an abyss of disaster. Therefore they should neither be thought nor called good things that in order to double the bitterness of inflicted evils by craving for their return * * *

LIBER SEPTIMUS

1. DE FELICITATE

praef. Volubilis Fortunae complura exempla rettulimus, constanter propitiae admodum pauca narrari possunt. quo patet eam adversas res cupido animo infligere, secundas parco tribuere. eadem, ubi malignitatis oblivisci sibi imperavit, non solum plurima ac maxima sed etiam perpetua bona congerit.

1 Videamus ergo quot gradibus beneficiorum Q. Metellum a primo originis die ad ultimum usque fati tempus numquam cessante indulgentia ad summum beatae vitae cumulum perduxerit. nasci eum in urbe terrarum principe voluit, parentes ei nobilissimos dedit, adiecit animi rarissimas dotes et corporis vires, ut sufficere laboribus posset, uxorem pudicitia et fecunditate conspicuam conciliavit, consulatus decus, imperatoriam potestatem, speciosissimi triumphi praetextum, largita est, fecit ut eodem tempore tres filios consulares, unum etiam censorium et triumphalem,[1] quartum praetorium videret utque tres filias nuptum daret earumque subolem sinu suo exciperet. tot partus, tot incunabula, tot viriles togae, tam multae nuptiales faces,

---

[1] et tr- *Kempf*: tr- et AL

BOOK VII

1. OF GOOD FORTUNE

We have recounted many examples of Fortune's volatility; of her steady favour very few can be narrated, from which it is evident that she loves to inflict adversity but only grudgingly vouchsafes prosperity. Yet once she has commanded herself to forget her malignity, she heaps blessings not only many and great but also enduring.

Let us see then by how many stages of benefaction she led Q. Metellus[1] from his first day of birth to his last day of death in never ceasing indulgence to the highest consummation of a happy life. She willed him born in the world's leading city; gave him the noblest of parents; added most unusual gifts of mind and strength of body so that he would be equal to his labours; furnished him with a wife conspicuous for her modesty and fecundity; lavished upon him the honour of the Consulship, the power of military command, the glory of a splendid triumph; granted him to see at the same time three sons ex-Consuls, one also an ex-Censor and triumphator, a fourth an ex-Praetor; allowed him to give three daughters in marriage and take their offspring in his lap. So many births, so many cradles, so many manly

[1] Macedonicus.

honorum imperiorum omnis denique gratulationis summa
abundantia, cum interim nullum funus, nullus gemitus,
nulla causa tristitiae. caelum contemplare, vix tamen ibi
talem statum reperies, quoniam quidem luctus et dolores
deorum quoque pectoribus a maximis vatibus adsignari
videmus. hunc vitae actum eius consentaneus finis excepit:
namque Metellum, ultimae senectutis spatio defunctum
lenique genere mortis inter oscula complexusque carissi-
morum pignorum exstinctum, filii et generi umeris suis
per urbem latum rogo imposuerunt.

2   Clara haec felicitas: obscurior illa, sed divino ‹ore regio›[2] splendori praeposita: cum enim Gyges, regno Lydiae
armis et divitiis abundantissimo inflatus, Apollinem Pythium sciscitatum venisset an aliquis mortalium se esset
felicior, deus, ex abdito sacrarii specu voce missa, Aglaum
Psophidium ei praetulit. is erat Arcadum pauperrimus et[3]
aetate iam senior terminos agelli sui numquam excesserat,
parvuli ruris fructibus [voluptatibus][4] contentus. verum
profecto beatae vitae finem Apollo, non adumbratum, oraculi sagacitate complexus est. quocirca insolenter fulgore
fortunae suae glorianti respondit magis se probare securitate ridens tugurium quam tristem curis et sollicitudinibus
aulam, paucasque glebas pavoris expertes quam pinguissima Lydiae arva metu referta, et unum aut alterum iugum
boum facilis tutelae quam exercitus et arma et equitatum

---

[2] *add. SB*[1]: divino splendori*(-re L) ALG
[3] et *Kempf*: sed AL   [4] *om.* P

---

[2] To the contrary cf. VM 7.5.4.
[3] 115: Cic. *Fin.* 5.82, *Tusc.* 1.85 etc.

gowns, so many marriage torches, superabundance of
offices, commands, every kind of satisfaction, and all the
while no funeral, no grieving, no cause for sadness.[2] Look
at heaven, you will hardly find there such a condition, since
we see mournings and sorrows assigned even to the hearts
of the gods by the greatest poets. This course of life was
followed by an end to match. Metellus passed through the
span of extreme old age and died a gentle death amid the
kisses and embraces of his dearest progeny, and his sons
and sons-in-law bore him through the city on their shoulders and placed him on the pyre.[3]

Metellus' good fortune is famous, the following is less
well-known but by divine utterance judged superior to
regal splendour. Gyges,[4] puffed up by the sovereignty of
Lydia abounding in arms and wealth, came to Pythian
Apollo to ask whether any mortal was more fortunate than
himself. From the hidden cavern of his sanctuary the god's
voice was given forth putting Aglaus of Psophis ahead of
him. Aglaus was the poorest man in Arcadia, and already
advanced in years he had never been outside the boundaries of his little farm, content with the produce of his
small holding. Surely Apollo by the keen insight of his oracle embraced the ultimate of happy living in truth, not
merely in outline. Accordingly he replied to the questioner
insolently glorying in the brilliance of his fortune that he
approved a hut smiling in security rather than a palace
glooming in cares and anxieties, a few clods free of fear
rather than the richest lands of Lydia replete with apprehension, one or two yokes of oxen easy to tend rather
than armies and weapons and cavalry burdensome with

[4] More or less legendary king of Lydia.

voracibus impensis onerosum, et usus necessarii horreolum nulli nimis appetendum quam thesauros omnium insidiis et cupiditatibus expositos. ita Gyges, dum adstipulatorem vanae opinionis deum habere concupiscit, ubinam solida et sincera esset felicitas didicit.

2. SAPIENTER DICTA AUT FACTA

praef.   Nunc id genus felicitatis explicabo quod totum in habitu animi, nec votis petitum[5] sed in pectoribus sapientia praeditis natum, dictis factisque prudentibus enitescit.

1   Ap. Claudium crebro solitum dicere accepimus negotium populo Romano melius quam otium committi, non quod ignoraret quam iucundus tranquillitatis status esset, sed quod animadverteret praepotentia imperia agitatione rerum ad virtutem capessendam excitari, nimia quiete in desidiam resolvi. et sane negotium nomine horridum civitatis nostrae mores in suo statu continuit, blandae appellationis quies plurimis vitiis respersit.

2   Scipio vero Africanus turpe esse aiebat in re militari dicere 'non putaram,' videlicet quia explorato et excusso consilio quae ferro aguntur administrari oportere arbitrabatur. summa ratione: inemendabilis est enim error qui violentiae Martis committitur. idem negabat aliter cum hoste confligi[6] debere quam aut si occasio obvenisset aut necessitas incidisset. aeque prudenter: nam et prospere

---

5 petitum *Kempf*: -tur AL   6 confligi ⊊: -gere AL

---

5 Pliny *N.H.* 7.151 etc.
1 Caecus, the Censor (312). The saying is not attested elsewhere.

voracious expenses, a little storehouse of necessities to be craved overmuch by none rather than treasure chambers open to the plots and cupidities of all and sundry. So Gyges, taking a fancy to have the god's backing for his illusion, learned where solid, sterling good fortune was to be found.[5]

2. THINGS WISELY SPOKEN OR DONE

I shall now set forth that species of good fortune which lies entirely in state of mind. It is not sought with prayers but born in hearts possessing wisdom and shines out in shrewd words and deeds.

We are told that Ap. Claudius used often to say that the Roman people were better trusted with trouble than with leisure.[1] Not that he was unaware of how pleasant is a state of tranquillity but because he saw that powerful empires are roused by disturbance to energetic action but lulled into sloth by excessive peace and quiet. And to be sure, trouble, rebarbative in name, has kept the morals of our community in position, whereas rest, bland in appellation, has spattered them with many a vice.

Scipio Africanus used to say that in warfare the words "I had not expected" disgraced the speaker,[2] thinking no doubt that military operations ought not to be conducted without a thoroughly researched and scrutinized plan. He was eminently right; for an error consigned to the violence of Mars is irreparable. Scipio also used to say that it was wrong to engage the enemy unless either an opportunity had cropped up or a necessity had arisen. No less wisely;

[2] Asellio ap. Gell. 13.3.6 etc. The saying is variously attributed.

gerendae rei facultatem omittere maxima dementia est et in angustias utique [pugnandi][7] compulsum abstinere se proelio pestiferae ignaviae adfert exitum, eorumque qui ista committunt alter beneficio Fortunae uti, alter iniuriae nescit resistere.

3   Q. quoque Metelli cum gravis tum etiam alta in senatu sententia, qui devicta Carthagine nescire se illa victoria bonine plus an mali rei publicae attulisset adseveravit, quoniam ut pacem restituendo profuisset, ita Hannibalem summovendo nonnihil nocuisset: eius enim transitu in Italiam dormientem iam populi Romani virtutem excitatam, metuique debere ne acri aemulo liberata in eundem somnum revolveretur. in aequo igitur malorum posuit uri tecta, vastari agros, exhauriri aerarium et prisci roboris nervos hebetari.

4   Quid? illud factum L. Fimbriae consularis quam sapiens! M. Lutatio Pinthiae, splendido equiti Romano, iudex addictus de sponsione, quam is cum adversario, quod vir bonus esset, fecerat, numquam id iudicium pronuntiatione sua finire voluit, ne aut probatum virum, si contra eum iudicasset, fama spoliaret, aut iuraret bonum esse, cum ea res innumerabilibus laudibus contineatur.

5   Forensibus haec, illa militaribus stipendiis prudentia exhibita. Papirius Cursor consul, cum Aquiloniam oppugnans proelium vellet committere, pullariusque non prosperantibus avibus optimum ei auspicium renuntiasset, de

[7] del. SB[1]

---

3 146: cf. App. *Lib.* 65.

4 This Fimbria, probably father of the Marian stalwart, was Consul in 104: cf. Cic. *Off.* 3.77.

for to neglect a chance of successful action is the height of folly, while to hold back from battle when forced unavoidably into a tight corner brings an outcome of disastrous inertia. Of those who make such mistakes, the one does not know how to use Fortune's kindness, the other how to resist her injury.

Q. Metellus too made a speech in the senate not only impressive but profound after the conquest of Carthage.[3] He affirmed that he knew not whether that victory had brought more good or more harm to the commonwealth; by restoring peace it had done good, but by removing Hannibal it had done some measure of harm. For by his passage into Italy the dormant energy of the Roman people had been aroused and it was to be feared that freed of its fierce rival it would sink again into the same slumber. Thus he placed the burning of houses, the laying waste of fields, the exhaustion of the treasury on an equal plane of evils with the slackening of the sinews of former strength.

And again, how wise that action of L. Fimbria,[4] the Consular! He was assigned as judge to M. Lutatius Pinthia, a distinguished Roman knight, concerning a wager he had made with his opponent "that he was a good man." Fimbria chose never to end that trial with a pronouncement on his part. He did not wish to rob a respected personage of reputation by finding against him nor yet to swear that he was a good man, that being something dependent on countless virtues.

That shrewdness was shown in campaigns of the Forum, what follows in those of the field. Consul Papirius Cursor was besieging Aquilonia. He wished to join battle and the keeper of the chickens reported excellent auspices, though the birds were in fact far from encouraging.

109

fallacia illius factus certior, sibi quidem et exercitui bonum omen datum credidit ac pugnam iniit, ceterum mendacem ante ipsam aciem constituit, ut haberent di cuius capite, si quid irae conceperant, expiarent. directum est autem sive casu sive etiam caelestis numinis providentia quod primum e contraria parte missum erat telum in ipsum pullarii pectus, eumque exanimem prostravit. id ut cognovit consul, fidente animo et invasit Aquiloniam et cepit. tam cito animadvertit quo pacto iniuria imperatoris vindicari deberet, quemadmodum violata religio expianda foret, qua ratione victoria apprehendi posset. egit virum severum, consulem religiosum, imperatorem strenuum, timoris modum, poenae genus, spei viam uno mentis impetu rapiendo.

6a   Nunc ad senatus acta transgrediar. cum adversus Hannibalem Claudium Neronem et Livium Salinatorem consules mitteret, eosque ut virtutibus pares ita inimicitiis acerrime inter se dissidentes videret, summo studio in gratiam reduxit, ne propter privatas dissensiones rem publicam parum utiliter administrarent, quia consimili[8] imperio nisi concordia inest, maior aliena opera interpellandi quam sua edendi cupiditas nascitur. ubi vero etiam pertinax intercedit odium, alter alteri quam uterque contrariis castris certior hostis proficiscitur.

    Eosdem senatus, cum ob nimis aspere actam censuram a Cn. Baebio tribuno plebis pro rostris agerentur rei, causae dictione decreto suo liberavit, vacuum omnis iudi-

---

[8] consulum *Wensky*

---

[5] 293: Livy 10.40.9–14, Oros. 3.22.3.   [6] Cf. VM 4.2.2.
[7] 204: Livy 29.37.17.

Informed of his deception, Papirius believed that for himself and his army a good omen had been given and began the fray. But he placed the liar right in front of the battle line, so that the gods might have someone on whose head to visit their anger, if angry they were. Whether by chance or the providence of divine power, the first missile discharged from the opposing side was guided right into the breast of the chicken keeper and laid him lifeless on the ground. When the Consul learned of it, he confidently invaded Aquilonia and took it. So quickly did he perceive how the insult to him as general ought to be avenged, how violated religion should be expiated, and how victory could be seized. He acted the man of severity, the religious Consul, the vigorous commander by catching in a single mental impulse the measure of fear, the method of punishment, and the path to hope.[5]

I shall now pass to the senate's proceedings. It sent Consuls Claudius Nero and Livius Salinator against Hannibal, but saw that while equal in their abilities they were enemies at bitter feud with one another. It therefore made a great point of reconciling them,[6] lest because of their private quarrel they manage public affairs to little advantage; for unless there is harmony between holders of similar authority, each becomes more concerned to interrupt the other's operations than to carry out his own. But where there is obdurate hate, each sets out as a more determined enemy to the other than both to the opposing camp.

When the same two were accused from the rostra by Tribune of the Plebs Cn. Baebius because of their unduly harsh exercise of the Censorship, the senate by its decree exempted them from answering the charge.[7] They made that office clear of any apprehension of judicial action; it

cii metu eum honorem reddendo qui exigere deberet[9] rationem, non reddere.

6b   Par illa sapientia senatus. Ti. Gracchum tribunum plebis, agrariam legem promulgare ausum, morte multavit. idem ut secundum legem eius per triumviros ager populo viritim divideretur egregie censuit, si quidem gravissimae seditionis eodem tempore et auctorem et causam sustulit.

6c   Quam deinde se prudenter in rege Masinissa gessit! nam cum promptissima et fidelissima eius opera adversus Carthaginienses usus esset, eumque in dilatando regno avidiorem cerneret, legem ferri iussit qua Masinissae ab imperio populi Romani solutam libertatem tribueret. quo facto cum optime meriti benivolentiam retinuit, tum Mauritaniae et Numidiae ceterarumque illius tractus gentium numquam fida pace quiescentem feritatem a valvis suis reppulit.

ext. 1a   Tempus deficiet domestica narrantem, quoniam imperium nostrum non tam robore corporum quam animorum vigore incrementum ac tutelam sui comprehendit. maiore itaque ex parte Romana prudentia in admiratione tacita reponatur, alienigenisque huius generis exemplis detur aditus.

Socrates, humanae sapientiae quasi quoddam terrestre oraculum, nihil ultra petendum a dis immortalibus arbitrabatur quam ut bona tribuerent, quia ii demum scirent quid unicuique esset utile, nos autem plerumque id votis experemus quod non impetrasse melius foret: etenim densissimis tenebris involuta mortalium mens, in quam late pa-

9 deberet ς: debent AL: debet G

should demand justification, not provide it.

The following is equally an example of the senate's wisdom. It punished with death Tribune of the Plebs Ti. Gracchus, who had dared to promulgate an agrarian law. The same senate commendably voted that land be divided individually among the people by a Board of Three according to Gracchus' law, removing at the same time both the cause of a very serious internal conflict and its instigator.[8]

And then how shrewdly it conducted itself with regard to king Masinissa! It had used his very ready and loyal service against the Carthaginians, and seeing him somewhat greedy in expanding his kingdom, it ordered that a law[9] be enacted giving Masinissa freedom independent of the Roman people's authority. Thereby it kept the good will of a deserving ally and thrust away from its own doors Mauritania and Numidia and the other nations of that region, whose savagery never rested in a trustworthy peace.

EXTERNAL

My time will run out as I relate domestic examples, for our empire takes its increase and maintenance from vigour of mind rather than strength of body. So let Roman shrewdness in greater part be put away in silent admiration and access given to alien-born instances of this kind.

Socrates, a sort of earthly oracle of human wisdom, thought that we should ask nothing of the immortal gods except that they give us good, because only they know what is expedient for each individual, whereas we often seek with vows something that were better not granted us.[10] For indeed, O mind of mortals enveloped in deepest darkness,

---

[8] 133: Broughton I.495.   [9] Not attested elsewhere.
[10] Cf. Plato II *Alc.* 142e–143a, Juv. *Sat.* 10.

tentem errorem caecas precationes tuas spargis! divitias appetis, quae multis exitio fuerunt; honores concupiscis, qui complures pessum dederunt; regna tecum ipsa volvis, quorum exitus saepenumero miserabiles cernuntur; splendidis coniugiis inicis manus: at haec ut aliquando illustrant, ita nonnumquam funditus domos evertunt. desine igitur stulta futuris malorum tuorum causis quasi felicissimis rebus inhiare, teque totam caelestium arbitrio permitte, quia qui tribuere bona ex facili solent, etiam eligere aptissime possunt.

ext. 1b   Idem expedita et compendiaria via eos ad gloriam pervenire dicebat qui id agerent ut quales videri vellent, tales etiam essent. qua quidem praedicatione aperte monebat ut homines ipsam potius virtutem haurirent quam umbram eius consectarentur.

ext. 1c   Idem, ab adulescentulo quodam consultus utrum uxorem duceret an se omni matrimonio abstineret, respondit utrum eorum fecisset, acturum paenitentiam. 'hinc te' inquit 'solitudo, hinc orbitas, hinc generis interitus, hinc heres alienus excipiet, illinc perpetua sollicitudo, contextus querellarum, dotis exprobratio, adfinium grave supercilium, garrula socrus lingua, subsessor alieni matrimonii, incertus liberorum eventus.' non passus est iuvenem in contextu rerum asperarum quasi laetae materiae facere dilectum.

ext. 1d   Idem, cum Atheniensium scelerata dementia tristem de capite eius sententiam tulisset, fortique animo et constanti vultu potionem veneni e manu carnificis accepisset,

---

11 Cic. *Off.* 2.43.
12 Diog. Laert. 2.33.

into how widespread a field of error do you scatter your blind prayers! You seek riches, that have destroyed many. You desire offices, that have brought to ruin not a few. You have visions of kingly powers, that are often seen to end in misery. You lay hold on brilliant marriages; but while they sometimes shed lustre on a house, at others they overthrow it utterly. So cease your foolish gaping after future causes of woe as though they were the luckiest of boons and trust yourself entirely to the will of the heavenly ones, for those who are wont to give blessings easily can also choose them most appropriately.

Socrates also used to say that a clear and short path to glory is taken by those who set out to be what they would wish to seem. By that pronouncement he plainly admonished mankind to drink in virtue itself rather than pursue its shadow.[11]

Socrates also, when consulted by a young fellow whether to take a wife or keep away from matrimony altogether, replied that whichever he did he would be sorry. "On the one hand," he said, "you will fall prey to loneliness and childlessness and the extinction of your line and an alien heir, on the other to perpetual anxiety, a tissue of complaints, harping on the dowry, the haughty frown of in-laws, the clacking tongue of your wife's mother, the stalker of other men's spouses, the doubtful outcome of children." He did not allow the young man in a context of disagreeables to think that he was making a choice of happiness.[12]

This too of Socrates: when the criminal folly of the Athenians condemned him to death and with stout heart and steady countenance he took the drink of poison from the executioner's hand and moved the cup to his lips, his

admoto iam labris poculo, uxore Xanthippe inter fletum et lamentationem vociferante innocentem eum periturum, 'quid ergo?' inquit; 'nocenti mihi mori satius esse duxisti?' immensam illam sapientiam, quae ne in ipso quidem vitae excessu oblivisci sui potuit!

ext. 2a   Age, quam prudenter Solo ⟨nemi⟩nem,[10] dum adhuc viveret, beatum dici debere arbitrabatur, quod ad ultimum usque fati diem ancipiti Fortunae subiecti essemus! felicitatis igitur humanae appellationem rogus consummat, qui se incursui malorum obicit.

ext. 2b   Idem, cum ex amicis quendam graviter maerentem videret, in arcem perduxit hortatusque est ut per omnes subiectorum aedificiorum partes oculos circumferret. quod ut factum animadvertit, 'cogita nunc tecum' inquit 'quam multi luctus sub his tectis et olim fuerint et hodieque versentur ⟨et⟩[11] insequentibus saeculis sint habituri, ac mitte mortalium incommoda tamquam propria deflere.' qua consolatione demonstravit urbes esse humanarum cladium consaepta miseranda. idem aiebat si in unum locum cuncti mala sua contulissent, futurum ut propria deportare domum quam ex communi miseriarum acervo portionem suam ferre mallent. quo colligebat non oportere nos quae fortuito patiamur praecipuae et intolerabilis amaritudinis iudicare.

ext. 3   Bias autem, cum patriam eius Prienen hostes invasissent, omnibus quos modo saevitia belli incolumes abire passa fuerat pretiosarum rerum pondere onustis fugienti-

---

[10] add. P   [11] add. P

---

[13] Diog. Laert. 2.35, Xen. Apol. 28 (the latter with Apollodorus instead of Xanthippe).

wife Xanthippe amid weeping and wailing cried out that he would die innocent. "What then," said he, "did you think it better for me to die guilty?" What immeasurable wisdom that in the very moment of departure from life could not forget itself![13]

Come then, how shrewdly did Solon deem that nobody while still alive should be called happy, because to the final day of our death we were subject to the hazards of Fortune![14] So the pyre puts the last touch on the name of human felicity, interposing itself against the onslaught of evils.

The same, seeing one of his friends plunged in grief, took him up to the citadel and told him to cast his eyes comprehensively around the buildings below. When he saw it was done, he said: "Now think to yourself how many mournings were under these roofs in times past and are in being today and shall dwell there in days to come; and stop bewailing the misfortunes of mortals as though they were peculiar to yourself." By that consolation he made it plain that cities are pitiful pens of human calamities. He also used to say that if all men took their woes to a single place, they would prefer to carry home their own rather than bear their portion from the common heap of miseries. From that he used to conclude that we should not consider what we happen to suffer as particularly and intolerably painful.[15]

When enemies had invaded Bias' city of Priene, as all whom the cruelty of war had suffered to get away unharmed were fleeing loaded with a weight of valuables, he was asked why he was not likewise bearing away any of his

---

[14] Herod. 1.32 etc.   [15] Not found elsewhere.

bus, interrogatus quid ita nihil ex bonis suis secum ferret
'ego vero' inquit 'bona mea mecum porto': pectore enim
illa gestabat non umeris, nec oculis visenda sed aestimanda
animo. quae domicilio mentis inclusa nec mortalium nec
deorum manibus labefactari queunt, et ut manentibus
praesto sunt ita fugientes non deserunt.

ext. 4   Iam Platonis verbis adstricta sed sensu praevalens sententia, qui tum demum beatum terrarum orbem futurum
praedicavit cum aut sapientes regnare aut reges sapere
coepissent.

ext. 5   Rex etiam ille subtilis iudicii, quem ferunt traditum sibi
diadema prius quam capiti imponeret retentum diu consi-
derasse ac dixisse 'o nobilem magis quam felicem pannum!
quem, si quis penitus cognoscat quam multis sollicitudinibus et periculis et miseriis sit refertus, ne humi quidem iacentem tollere velit.'

ext. 6   Quid? Xenocratis responsum quam laudabile! cum
maledico quorundam sermoni summo silentio interesset,
uno ex iis quaerente cur solus linguam suam cohiberet,
'quia dixisse me' inquit 'aliquando paenituit, tacuisse numquam.'

ext. 7   Aristophanis quoque altioris est prudentiae praeceptum, qui in comoedia introduxit remissum ab inferis ⟨prin-
cipem⟩[12] Atheniensium Periclen vaticinantem non opor-

---

[12] add. Kapp (Ath- intra cruces Briscoe)

---

[16] Priene was taken and burnt by the Persians after the battle
of Lade (495). The wise man of the anecdote is Bias in Cic. Parad.
8, but the fourth-century philosopher Stilpo in later sources (Sen.
Dial. 2.5.6 etc.).

[17] Plato Rep. 473d, Cic. Q.fr. 1.1.29.

goods. "On the contrary," he said, "I carry my goods with myself."[16] For he bore them in his heart, not on his shoulders; not for the sight of the eyes but for the judgment of the mind. Included in the mind's habitation, they cannot be shaken by the hand of god or man; and as they are present to us when we stay, so they do not forsake us when we flee.

Then we have Plato's pronouncement, concise in word but powerful in sense; he declared that the world would be happy when and only when wise men started to rule or rulers to be wise.[17]

That king had nice judgment of whom they say that when handed a diadem, before placing it on his head, he held it a long time and considered it and said: "A noble rag, but not a happy one. If someone really knew how full it is of cares and dangers and miseries, he wouldn't want to pick it up if he saw it lying on the ground."[18]

And again, how laudable was that answer of Xenocrates! Being present at a backbiting conversation between certain persons, he said absolutely nothing. When one of them asked why he alone held his tongue, he said: "Because I have sometimes been sorry I spoke, never that I kept silent."[19]

Deeply shrewd is Aristophanes' advice. He put the Athenian leader Pericles into a comedy, brought back from the underworld and giving a prophetic warning:[20] "Don't

---

[18] Ascribed to Antigonus (which Antigonus not stated) in Stobaeus (4.8.20).   [19] Attributed to Simonides in Plut. *Moral.* 125D and Stob. 3.2.41, 33.12.

[20] Not Pericles but Aeschylus (*Frogs* 1431f.), with reference to Alcibiades.

tere in urbe nutriri leonem: sin autem sit altus, obsequi ei
convenire: monet enim ut praecipuae nobilitatis et concitati ingenii iuvenes refrenentur, nimio vero favore ac pro-
fusa indulgentia pasti quo minus potentiam obtineant ne
impediantur, quod stultum et inutile sit eas obtrectare
vires quas ipse foveris.

ext. 8   Mirifice etiam Thales: nam interrogatus an facta hominum deos fallerent 'ne⟨c⟩[13] cogitata' inquit, ut non solum
manus sed etiam mentes puras habere vellemus, cum se-
cretis cogitationibus nostris caeleste numen adesse credi-
dissemus.

ext. 9   Ac ne quod sequitur quidem minus sapiens. unicae
filiae pater Themistoclen consulebat utrum eam pauperi
sed ornato an locupleti parum probato collocaret. cui is
'malo' inquit 'virum pecunia quam pecuniam viro indigen-
tem.' quo dicto stultum monuit ut generum potius quam
divitias generi legeret.

ext. 10   Age, Philippi quam probabilis epistula, in qua Alexandrum quorundam Macedonum benivolentiam largitione
ad se adtrahere conatum sic increpuit! 'quae te, fili, ratio in
hanc tam vanam spem induxit, ut eos tibi fideles futuros
existimares quos pecunia ad amorem tui compulisses?' a
caritate istud pater, ab usu[14] Philippus, maiore ex parte
mercator Graeciae quam victor.

ext. 11a   Aristoteles autem, Callisthenen, auditorem suum, ad
Alexandrum dimittens, monuit cum eo aut quam rarissime

---

[13] nec G *corr.*: ne AL: ne (... quidem) P
[14] ab usu *Madvig*: avus o AL; Br

---

[21] Diog. Laert. 1.36.   [22] Cic. *Off.* 2.71 etc.
[23] Cic. *Off.* 2.53.

rear a lion in the city, but if one is raised, best do what it wants." He is telling them that young men of exalted birth and lively turn should be reined in, but if fed on overmuch popularity and lavish indulgence they should not be hindered from holding power; for it is foolish and useless to carp at forces which you yourself have encouraged.

A wonderful saying too, this of Thales. Asked whether men's actions went unnoticed by the gods, he said: "No, not even their thoughts." He meant that we should try to keep not only our hands clean but our minds as well, and believe that a divine power is present at our secret cogitations.[21]

What follows is no less wise. The father of an only daughter asked Themistocles' advice: should he give her to a poor man of high standing or a rich man of none too good repute. Themistocles answered: "I would rather have a man in need of money than money in need of a man." With that saying he told the silly fellow that he should choose a son-in-law rather than a son-in-law's riches.[22]

Come then, what a commendable letter that was of Philip's in which he reproved Alexander for trying to attract the good will of certain Macedonians by giving them money! "My son, whatever line of reasoning gave you this idle expectation to make you think that people whose love you forced with money would be loyal to you?"[23] As a father he wrote this from affection, as Philip from experience—Philip, who bought more of Greece than he conquered.

When Aristotle send his auditor Callisthenes to Alexander, he counselled him to talk with the king either as seldom or as agreeably as possible, to the end evidently that

aut quam iucundissime loqueretur, quo scilicet apud
regias aures vel silentio tutior vel sermone esset acceptior.
at ille, dum Alexandrum Persica Macedonem salutatione
gaudentem obiurgat et ad Macedonicos mores invitum
revocare benivole perseverat, spiritu carere iussus seram
neglecti salubris consilii paenitentiam egit.

ext. 11b   Idem Aristoteles de semet ipso‹s›[15] in neutram partem
loqui debere praedicabat, quoniam laudare se vani, vituperare stulti esset. eiusdem est utilissimum praeceptum ut
voluptates abeuntes consideremus. quas quidem sic osten-
dendo minui:[16] fessis enim paenitentiaeque plenis[17] animis nostris subici,[18] quo minus cupide repetantur.

ext. 12   Nec parum prudenter Anaxagoras interroganti cuidam
quisnam esset beatus 'nemo' inquit 'ex iis quos tu felices
existimas, sed eum in illo numero reperies qui a te ex miseris[19] constare creditur.' non erit ille divitiis et honoribus
abundans, sed aut exigui ruris aut non ambitiosae doctrinae fidelis ac pertinax cultor, in recessu[20] quam in fronte
beatior.

ext. 13   Demadis quoque dictum sapiens: nolentibus enim
Atheniensibus divinos honores Alexandro decernere, 'vi-
dete' inquit 'ne dum caelum custoditis, terram amittatis.'

ext. 14   Quam porro subtiliter Anarcharsis leges araneorum
telis comparabat! nam ut illas infirmiora animalia retinere,

---

[15] de semet ipsos *Kempf*: s- i- P: de s- ipso AL   [16] minui
SB: -uit AL   [17] fessis ... plenis *Gertz*: -sas ... -nas AL
[18] subici *SB*: -cit AL   [19] miseris Ⴠ: -riis AL
[20] recessu *Pighius*: sec- AL

---

[24] Diog. Laert. 5.4f. Alexander put him to death in 327; cf. VM
9.3.ext.1.

his silence should be the safer or his conversation the more acceptable in the royal ears. But Callisthenes used to scold Alexander as a Macedonian for liking the Persian mode of salutation and in all good will persisted in trying to bring him back against his inclination to Macedonian ways. Told to take leave of his life, he regretted too late his neglect of salutary advice.[24]

The same Aristotle used to say that a man should speak neither well nor ill of himself, since self-praise smacked of vanity and self-censure of stupidity. He also gave the excellent advice to think of pleasures as they are when they are leaving us; for that by being shown in that light they are reduced, presented to minds weary and full of regret so that we may be less eager to seek them afresh.[25]

Shrewdly enough too said Anaxagoras to somebody who asked him who was the happy man: "None of those whom you think fortunate. You will find him in the number which you think to be made up of miserables."[26] He will not abound in riches and offices, he will be a faithful, persevering cultivator of a small holding or of unpretentious learning, happier in the back row than the front.

Demades too had a wise saying. When the Athenians were unwilling to decree divine honours to Alexander, "Take care," he said, "that in guarding the heavens you don't lose the earth."[27]

And then how neatly Anacharsis used to compare laws to spiders' webs! He used to say that just as they kept the

[25] Neither saying is reported elsewhere.
[26] Not found elsewhere.
[27] Cf. Aelian *Var. hist.* 5.12.

valentiora transmittere, ita his humiles et pauperes constringi, divites et praepotentes non alligari.

ext. 15 Nihil etiam Agesilai facto sapientius, si quidem cum adversus rem publicam Lacedaemoniorum conspirationem ortam noctu comperisset, leges Lycurgi continuo abrogavit, quae de indemnatis supplicium sumi vetabant: comprehensis autem et interfectis sontibus, e vestigio restituit atque utrumque simul providit, ne salutaris animadversio vel iniusta esset vel iure impediretur. itaque, ut semper esse possent, aliquando non fuerunt.

ext. 16 Sed nescio an Hannonis excellentissimae prudentiae consilium: Magone enim Cannensis pugnae exitum senatui Poenorum nuntiante, inque tanti successus fidem anulos aureos trium modiorum mensuram explentes fundente, qui interfectis nostris civibus detracti erant, quaesivit an aliquis sociorum post tantam cladem a Romanis defecisset, atque ut audivit neminem ad Hannibalem transisse, suasit protinus ut legati Romam, per quos de pace ageretur, mitterentur. cuius si sententia valuisset, neque secundo Punico bello victa Carthago neque tertio deleta foret.

ext. 17 Ne Samnites quidem parvas poenas consimilis erroris pependerunt, quod Herennii Pontii salutare consilium neglexerant. qui auctoritate et prudentia ceteros praestans, ab exercitu et duce eius filio suo consultus quidnam fieri de legionibus Romanis apud furcas Caudinas inclusis deberet, inviolatas dimittendas respondit. postero die eadem de re interrogatus, deleri eas oportere dixit, ut aut maximo

---

28 Plut. *Solon* 5.
29 Plut. *Ages.* 30 etc.
30 216: Livy 23.11.7–13.5.

weaker animals but let the stronger ones through, so the laws tied up the humble and the poor, but did not bind the rich and powerful.[28]

Nothing too could be wiser than an action of Agesilaus. Learning one night that a conspiracy was afoot against the Lacedaemonian commonwealth, he immediately abrogated the laws of Lycurgus which forbade the taking of punitive measures against persons not convicted of offence. Then, having arrested and executed the guilty, he promptly restored the laws.[29] Thus he provided for two things at once, that salutary punishment should be neither unlawful nor hindered by law. So that the laws should exist for always, they ceased to exist temporarily.

But perhaps Hanno's advice was quite outstandingly shrewd. When Mago reported the result of the battle of Cannae to the Carthaginian senate and in proof of this great success poured out gold rings taken from the fingers of our slain countrymen to the quantity of three pecks, Hanno asked whether any of the Roman allies had defected after so great a disaster. Hearing that none had gone over to Hannibal, he urged that envoys be sent immediately to Rome to negotiate peace.[30] Had his view prevailed, Carthage would not have been defeated in the Second Punic War and destroyed in the Third.

The Samnites too paid no small price for a similar mistake in that they neglected the salutary counsel of Herennius Pontius. Preeminent in authority and shrewdness, he was consulted by the army and its leader, his own son, on what should be done about the Roman legions which had been shut in at the Caudine Forks. He replied that they should be dismissed unharmed. The next day, asked the same question, he said they should be wiped out, so that

beneficio gratia hostium emeretur aut gravissima iactura vires confringerentur. sed improvida temeritas victorum, dum utramque partem spernit utilitatis, sub iugum missas in perniciem suam accendit.

ext. 18   Multis et magnis sapientiae exemplis parvulum adiciam. Cretes, cum acerbissima exsecratione adversus eos quos vehementer oderunt uti volunt, ut mala consuetudine delectentur optant, modestoque voti genere efficacissimum ultionis eventum reperiunt: inutiliter enim aliquid concupiscere et in eo perseveranter morari, exitio ea vicina dulcedo est.

3. VAFRE DICTA AUT FACTA

praef.   Est aliud factorum dictorumque genus, a sapientia proximo deflexu ad vafri<ti>ae[21] nomen progressum, quod, nisi <a>[22] fallacia vires adsumpsit, finem[23] propositi non invenit, laudemque occulto magis tramite quam aperta via petit.

1   Servio Tullio regnante cuidam patri familiae in agro Sabino praecipuae magnitudinis et eximiae formae vacca nata est. quam oraculorum certissimi auctores in hoc a dis immortalibus editam responderunt, ut quisquis eam Aventinensi Dianae immolasset, eius patria totius terrarum orbis imperium obtineret. laetus eo dominus bovem summa cum festinatione Romam actam in Aventino ante aram

---

[21] *add. Vorst*
[22] *add. Torr.*
[23] finem *Per.*: fidem AL

either the favour of the enemy should be earned by a grand benefaction or their strength broken by a crushing loss. But the thoughtless rashness of the victors spurned either course of expediency. Sending the legions under the yoke, it fired them to its own destruction.[31]

To many major examples of wisdom I will add a minor one. When the Cretans want to pronounce their most bitter curse upon objects of their violent hatred, they pray that these delight in their evil courses. So by a moderate sort of prayer they find the most effectively revengeful issue. For to take a fancy to something contrary to expediency and obstinately persist in it is a pleasure that borders on destruction.[32]

3. THINGS CRAFTILY SAID OR DONE

There is another kind of doings and sayings that by an easy deflexion moves from wisdom to the name of craftiness. It does not achieve its object unless it borrows strength from deceit and it seeks acclaim by hidden track rather than open highway.

In the reign of Servius Tullius a certain paterfamilias in the Sabine district had a cow of unusual size and remarkable beauty born on his farm. The most reliable oraclemongers answered on enquiry that the animal had been sent by the immortal gods so that whoever sacrificed her to Diana of the Aventine, his country would gain the empire of the whole world. The owner was delighted and in hot haste drove the cow to Rome and set her before Diana's

[31] 321: Livy 9.3.4–13, Flor. 1.11.10.
[32] Not found elsewhere.

Dianae constituit, sacrificio Sabinis regimen humani generis daturus. de qua re antistes templi certior factus religionem hospiti intulit, ne prius victimam caederet quam proximi am‹nis se ›[24] aqua abluisset, eoque alveum Tiberis petente vaccam ipse immolavit, et urbem nostram tot civitatium, tot gentium dominam pio sacrificii furto reddidit.

2   Quo in genere acuminis in primis Iunius Brutus referendus est: nam cum a rege Tarquinio, avunculo suo, omnem nobilitatis indolem excerpi, interque ceteros etiam fratrem suum, quod vegetioris ingenii erat, interfectum animadverteret, obtunsi se cordis esse simulavit, eaque fallacia maximas virtutes suas texit. profectus etiam Delphos cum Tarquinii filiis, quos is ad Apollinem Pythium muneribus ‹et›[25] sacrificiis honorandum miserat, aurum deo nomine doni clam cavato baculo inclusum tulit, quia timebat ne sibi caeleste numen aperta liberalitate venerari tutum non esset. peractis deinde mandatis patris, Apollinem iuvenes consuluerunt quisnam ex ipsis Romae regnaturus videretur. at is penes eum summam urbis nostrae potestatem futuram respondit qui ante omnes matri osculum dedisset. tum Brutus, perinde atque casu prolapsus, de industria se abiecit, terramque, communem omnium matrem existimans, osculatus est. quod tam vafre Telluri impressum osculum urbi libertatem, Bruto primum in fastis locum tribuit.

3   Scipio quoque superior praesidium calliditatis amplexus est: ex Sicilia enim petens Africam, cum e fortissi-

---

[24] *add. Kempf:* se pr- am- aqua P, A *corr.:* proximiamaquam L; Br
[25] *add.* L *corr.*

---

[1] Livy 1.45.4–7 etc.   [2] Otherwise in Livy.

altar on the Aventine, intending to give the Sabines the rule of mankind by her sacrifice. Informed of this, the temple priest put a religious impediment in the stranger's way, telling him that he must not kill the victim until he had washed in the water of the river nearby. Then, as he made for the channel of the Tiber, the priest immolated the cow himself and by this pious sacrificial trick made our city mistress of so many communities and nations.[1]

In this sort of sharpness Junius Brutus deserves particular mention. He noticed that his uncle king Tarquin was picking out all men of promise among the nobility and that among others his own brother had been put to death because of his lively intelligence. He therefore pretended to be dull of intellect and veiled his great abilities by that deception. Leaving too for Delphi with Tarquin's sons, whom the king had sent to honour Pythian Apollo with gifts and sacrifices, he took some gold for the god as a gift secretly hidden in a hollow stick, fearing that it would not be safe for him to venerate the heavenly deity with an open donation.[2] After attending to their father's commissions, the young men consulted Apollo as to which among them seemed likely to be king in Rome. The god replied that supreme power in our city would lie with him who was the first to give his mother a kiss. Then Brutus purposely threw himself on the ground as though by an accidental stumble and kissed it, reckoning it to be the common mother of all kings. That kiss so craftily impressed on Earth gave freedom to the city and the first place in the Fasti to Brutus.[3]

The elder Scipio too embraced the help of cunning. As he was heading for Africa from Sicily, he wanted to make

[3] Livy 1.56.7–12 etc.

mis peditibus Romanis trecentorum equitum numerum
complere vellet neque tam subito eos posset instruere,
quod temporis angustiae negabant sagacitate consilii adsecutus est: namque ex iis iuvenibus quos secum tota ex
Sicilia nobilissimos et divitissimos sed inermes habebat,
trecentos speciosa arma et electos equos quam celerrime
expedire iussit, velut eos continuo secum ad oppugnan-
dam Carthaginem avecturus. qui cum imperio ut celeriter
ita longinqui et periculosi belli respectu sollicitis animis
paruissent, remittere se ⟨eis⟩[26] Scipio illam expeditionem,
si arma et equos militibus suis tradere voluissent, edixit.
rapuit condicionem imbellis ac timida iuventus instru-
mentoque suo cupide nostris cessit. ergo calliditas ducis
providit ut quod, si protinus imperaretur, gra⟨ve fuisset, id
inten⟩to[27] prius, deinde remisso militiae metu maximum
beneficium fieret.

4a   Quod sequitur ⟨invito, sed⟩[28] narrandum[29] est. Q. Fabius Labeo, arbiter a senatu finium constituendorum inter
Nolanos ac Neapolitanos datus, cum in rem praesentem
venisset, utrosque separatim monuit ut omissa cupiditate
regredi a nodo controversia⟨e⟩[30] quam progredi mallent.
idque cum utraque pars auctoritate viri mota fecisset, aliquantum in medio vacui agri relictum est. constitutis
deinde finibus ut ipsi terminaverant, quidquid reliqui soli
fuit populo Romano adiudicavit. ceterum etsi circumventi
Nolani ac Neapolitani queri nihil potuerunt, secundum ip-

---

[26] *add.* P   [27] *sic Halm*: si quod ... grato* AL
[28] *add. SB* (invito *Gertz*); Br
[29] narrandum *intra cruces Briscoe*   [30] a *(Torr.)* nodo -siae
SB³: modo -sia AL: de modo -siae *Halm;* Br

up a troop of three hundred horse from the bravest Roman
footmen but could not equip them at such short notice. So
what the shortage of time denied, he achieved by sagacity
of counsel. He had with him the noblest and richest young
men from the whole of Sicily, but they were unarmed. He
ordered three hundred of them to make ready handsome
arms and picked horses as soon as possible, as though he
intended to take them with him at once to the siege of
Carthage. They obeyed the command promptly but also
with anxiety at the prospect of a distant and dangerous
campaign. Scipio then announced that he would let them
off the expedition provided they were willing to hand over
the arms and horses to his soldiers. The unwarlike and
timid young men caught at the offer and eagerly yielded
their equipment to our men. Thus the cunning of our commander so managed that what would have been a burden
if demanded outright became a great concession when
the threat of military service was first made and then re-
mitted.[4]

What follows also has to be told, with whatever reluc-
tance. Q. Fabius Labeo was appointed by the senate as
arbiter to fix boundaries between Nola and Neapolis. Arriving at the scene, he advised both separately not to be
greedy but to go backwards from the nodal point of the
dispute rather than forwards. Both sides did accordingly,
swayed by his authority, leaving a tract of unclaimed land
in the middle. Then having fixed the boundaries as the
parties themselves had determined them, he awarded
whatever ground remained to the Roman people. Though
tricked, the Nolans and Neapolitans could make no com-

4 205: Livy 29.1.2–10, App. *Lib.* 8.

sorum demonstrationem dicta sententia, improbo tamen praestigiarum genere novum civitati nostrae vectigal accessit.

4b   Eundem ferunt, cum a rege Antiocho, quem bello superaverat, ex foedere icto dimidiam partem navium accipere deberet, medias omnes secuisse, ut eum tota classe privaret.

5   Nam M. Antonio remittendum convicium est, qui idcirco se aiebat nullam orationem scripsisse, ut si quid superiore iudicio actum ei[31] quem postea defensurus esset nociturum foret, non dictum a se adfirmare posset, quia facti vix pudentis causam tolerabilem habuit: pro periclitantium enim capite non solum eloquentia sua uti, sed etiam verecundia abuti erat paratus.

6   Sertorius vero, corporis robore atque animi consilio parem Naturae indulgentiam expertus, proscriptione Sullana dux Lusitanorum fieri coactus, cum eos oratione flectere non posset ne cum Romanis universa acie configere vellent, vafro consilio ad suam sententiam perduxit: duos enim in conspectu eorum constituit equos, validissimum alterum, ‹alterum›[32] infirmissimum, ac deinde validi caudam ab imbecillo sene paulatim carpi, infirmi a iuvene eximiarum virium universam convelli iussit. obtemperatum imperio est. sed dum adulescentis dextera irrito se labore fatigat, senio confecta manus ministerium exsecuta est. tunc barbarae contioni, quorsum ea res tenderet cognos-

[31] ei P (*de* AL *non liquet*)
[32] *add.* P

---

5 Labeo was Consul in 183: Cic. *Off.* 1.33.

plaint since the decision had been pronounced in accordance with their own showing; all the same a new revenue accrued to our city by a species of shameless chicanery.[5]

It is said of the same person that when according to a treaty made with king Antiochus, whom he had defeated in war, he should have taken half the king's ships, he cut all of them down the middle so as to deprive him of his entire fleet.[6]

We have to remit our censure of M. Antonius, who used to say that he never put a speech in writing so that if something said at an earlier trial would damage a subsequent client he could deny having said it. He had a tolerable excuse for a scarcely honourable proceeding, for on behalf of men in jeopardy he was ready not only to use his eloquence but even to abuse his sense of decency.[7]

Sertorius met with Nature's indulgence equally in strength of body and shrewdness of mind. Forced by the Sullan proscription to become leader of the Lusitanians, he could not turn them by words from their desire to engage the Romans with their entire force, so he brought them to his opinion by a crafty device. He put two horses in front of them, one very powerful, the other very weak. Then he ordered the tail of the powerful horse to be plucked gradually by a feeble old man and the tail of the weak horse to be torn off whole by a young man of exceptional strength. His command was obeyed. But while the young man's hand tired itself in fruitless effort, the hand enfeebled by old age executed its service. Then he put it to the assembly of barbarians, who wanted to know where

6 188: cf. Livy 38.39.3.
7 Cic. *Cluent.* 140.

cere cupienti, subicit equi caudae consimilem esse nostrum exercitum, cuius partes aliquis adgrediens opprimere possit, universum conatus prosternere celerius
tradiderit victoriam quam occupaverit. ita gens barbara,
aspera et regi difficilis, in exitium suum ruens, quam utilitatem auribus respuerat, oculis pervidit.

7   Fabius autem Maximus, cui[33] non dimicare vincere
fuit, cum praecipuae fortitudinis Nolanum peditem dubia
fide suspectum et strenuae operae Lucanum equitem
amore scorti deperditum in castris haberet, ut utroque
potius bono milite uteretur quam in utrumque animadverteret, alteri suspicionem suam dissimulavit, in altero disciplinam paululum a recto tenore deflexit: namque illum
plene pro tribunali laudando omnique genere honoris prosequendo animum suum a Poenis ad Romanos coegit revocare, et hunc clam meretricem redimere passus paratissimum pro nobis ‹acriorem›[34] excussioremque reddidit.

8   Veniam nunc ad eos quibus salus astutia quaesita est.
M. Volusius, aedilis plebis proscriptus, adsumpto Isiaci habitu per itinera viasque publicas stipem petens, quisnam
re vera esset occurrentes dinoscere passus non est, eoque
fallaciae genere tectus in M. Bruti castra pervenit. quid illa
necessitate miserius, quae magistratum populi Romani
abiecto honoris praetexto alienigenae religionis obscuratum insignibus per urbem iussit incedere? o nimis aut hi
suae vitae aut illi alienae mortis cupidi, qui talia vel ipsi

[33] cui *Madvig*: cuius AL   [34] *add. SB*[3]

[8] 80–72: Front. *Strat.* 1.10.1, Pliny *Ep.* 3.9.11, Plut. *Sert.* 16.

this was tending, that the Roman army was like a horse's tail: anyone who attacked its parts could overcome it, but if he tried to floor the whole of it, he would more likely give the victory than gain it. Thus the barbarian nation, rough and hard to govern, as it rushed upon its undoing, saw with eyes the expediency which it had scorned with ears.[8]

Fabius Maximus, for whom not to fight was to win, had in his army an infantryman from Nola, outstandingly brave but suspected of doubtful loyalty, and a Lucanian trooper, smart in the service but desperately in love with a whore. Wishing to use both as good soldiers rather than punish them, he disguised his suspicions of the one and bent discipline a little from the straight in the case of the other. By generously praising the former from his tribunal and giving him all manner of decorations he made him turn his mind away from the Carthaginians back to the Romans. The latter he allowed to buy the girl secretly out of prostitution and thus, very ready as he already was to fight for us, made him all the keener and livelier.[9]

I come now to those who saved their lives by their cleverness. Aedile of the Plebs M. Volusius was proscribed. Putting on the garb of a priest of Isis and begging his way through the streets and highways, he did not let those he met recognize who he really was, and covered by that mode of deception, he reached M. Brutus' camp.[10] A pitiful necessity indeed that bade a magistrate of the Roman people throw aside his glory of office and walk through the city disguised by the emblems of a foreign cult. Too loving of their lives or of others' deaths were they who either bore

9 216 (?): Plut. *Fab.* 20, Auct. vir. ill. 43.4; cf. Livy 23.15.7–16.1.
10 43/42: App. *B.C.* 4.47.

sustinuerunt vel alios perpeti coegerunt!

9   Aliquanto speciosius Sentii Saturnini Vetulonis in
eodem genere casus ultimae sortis auxilium. qui cum a
triumviris inter proscriptos nomen suum propositum
audisset, continuo praeturae insignia invasit, praeceden-
tibusque in modum lictorum et apparitorum et servorum
publicorum subornatis vehicula comprehendit, hospitia
occupavit, obvios summovit, ac tam audaci usurpatione
imperii in maxima luce densissimas hostilibus oculis tenebras offudit. idem ut Puteolos venit, perinde ac publicum
ministerium agens, summa cum licentia correptis navibus
in Siciliam, certissimum tunc proscriptorum perfugium,
penetravit.

10   His uno adiecto levioris notae exemplo ad externa
devertar. amantissimus quidam filii, cum eum inconcessis
ac periculosis facibus accensum ab insana cupiditate [pa-
ter][35] inhibere vellet, salubri consilio patriam indulgentiam temperavit: petiit enim ut prius quam ad eam quam
diligebat iret, vulgari et permissa venere uteretur. cuius
precibus obsecutus adulescens, infelicis animi impetum,
satietate licentis concubitus resolutum, ad id quod non
licebat tardiorem pigrioremque adferens, paulatim deposuit.

ext. 1   Cum Alexander Macedonum rex, sorte monitus ut eum
qui sibi porta egresso primus occurrisset interfici iuberet,
asinarium forte ‹ante›[36] omnes obviam factum ad mortem

---

35 *del.* A *corr.*
36 *add.* A *corr.*

such things themselves or forced others to endure them.

Somewhat more seemly was Sentius Saturninus Vetulo's[11] recourse of last resort in the same sort of predicament. When he heard that his name had been published among the proscribed by the Triumvirs, he at once usurped the insignia of the Praetorship and with hirelings walking in front of him like lictors and orderlies and public slaves, he seized vehicles, took possession of hospices, removed persons coming his way, and by so bold an assumption of authority in broad daylight he plunged hostile eyes in deepest darkness. When he got to Puteoli, he commandeered ships with absolute license as in the course of public duty and made his way to Sicily, then the safest refuge for the proscribed.[12]

To these examples I will add one of lesser note and then return to external ones. A very fond father, seeing his son aflame with an illicit and dangerous passion and wishing to restrain him from his infatuation, tempered paternal indulgence with salutary counsel. He asked his son, before he went to his beloved, to engage in common, permitted sexual intercourse. The young man yielded to his urgings. He brought the drive of his unhappy soul, slackened by the satiety of licensed sex, more slow and sluggish to the forbidden practice and gradually laid it aside.[13]

EXTERNAL

Alexander, king of the Macedonians, was warned by an oracle to order the first person he met after he went out of the gate to be killed. As it chanced, he met a donkey man and commanded him to be hauled off to his death. When

---

[11] Cf. VM 9.1.8 n. 9.

[12] 43/42: App. *B.C.* 4.45.   [13] Not found elsewhere.

abripi imperasset, eoque quaerente quidnam se immeren-
tem capitali supplicio innocentemque addiceret, cum ad
excusandum factum suum oraculi praeceptum rettulisset,
asinarius, 'si ita est' inquit, 'rex, alium sors huic morti desti-
navit: nam asellus, quem ego ante me agebam, prior tibi
occurrit.' delectatus Alexander et illius tam callido dicto et
quod ipse ab errore revocatus erat, occasionem in aliquanto viliore animali expiandae religionis rapuit. summa in
hoc [mansuetudo calliditas],[37] ⟨par⟩[38] in alterius regis
equisone calliditas.

ext. 2   Sordida magorum dominatione oppressa, Dareus, sex
adiutoribus eiusdem dignitatis adsumptis, pactum cum
praeclari operis consortibus fecit ut equis insidentes solis
ortu cursum in quendam locum dirigerent, isque regno
potiretur cuius equus in eo primus hinnisset. ceterum
maximae mercedis competitoribus Fortunae beneficium
exspectantibus, solus acumine equisonis sui Oebaris prosperum exoptatae rei effectum adsecutus est, qui in equae
genitalem partem demissam manum, cum ad eum locum
ventum esset, naribus equi admovit. quo odore irritatus
ante omnes hinnitum edidit, auditoque eo sex reliqui
summae potestatis candidati continuo equis delapsi, ut est
mos Persarum, humi prostratis corporibus Dareum regem
salutaverunt. quantum imperium quam parvo interceptum est vaframento!

ext. 3   Bias autem, cuius sapientia diuturnior inter homines
est quam patria Priene fuit, si quidem haec etiam nunc spi-

---

[37] *secl. SB* (call-*del. Kempf*)   man- call-*intra cruces Briscoe*
[38] *add. SB*

the man asked why he should be sentenced to capital punishment, undeserving as he was and innocent, Alexander in excuse of his action related the oracle's advice. "If that's how it is, your majesty," said the donkey man, "the oracle meant for another to die; for the donkey that I was driving in front of me met you before I did." Alexander was pleased with his cunning speech and pleased to be called back from a blunder, so he seized the opportunity to satisfy the religious requirement by the sacrifice of a somewhat cheaper life.[14] Great was his cunning; and equal the cunning of another monarch's groom.

After the degrading rule of the magi had been crushed, Darius, who had enlisted six assistants of the same rank as himself, made a pact with his accomplices in the splendid exploit: mounted on their horses at sunrise they would ride to a place appointed and he whose horse was the first to neigh there would have the kingdom. Darius' competitors for the great prize awaited the gift of Fortune, he alone succeeded in gaining the object of his desire by the wit of his groom Oebaris, who plunged his hand into the genitals of a mare and, when they arrived at the place, put it to the nostrils of his stallion. Stimulated by the odour, the horse let loose a neigh in front of them all. When they heard it, the other six candidates for supreme power at once dismounted and, prostrating their bodies on the ground, as is the Persian custom, saluted Darius as king. How mighty a power was stolen by how small an artifice![15]

Bias' wisdom has lasted longer among men than his country, Priene. The former breathes even now, but the

---

[14] Not found elsewhere.
[15] 522: Herod. 3.85–87, Justin 1.10.

rat, illius perinde atque exstinctae vestigia tantummodo
exstant, ita aiebat oportere homines in usu amicitiae versa-
ri ut meminissent eam ad gravissimas inimicitias posse
converti. quod quidem praeceptum prima specie nimis
fortasse callidum videatur inimicumque simplicitati, qua
praecipue familiaritas gaudet, sed si altius in ⟨abd⟩ita
⟨a⟩nimi[39] cogitatio demissa fuerit, perquam utile reperietur.

ext. 4 Lampsacenae vero urbis salus unius vaframenti beneficio constitit: nam cum ad excidium eius summo studio
Alexander ferretur, progressumque extra moenia Anaxi-
menen, praeceptorem suum, vidisset, quia manifestum
erat futurum ut preces suas irae eius opponeret, non factu-
rum se quod petisset iuravit. tunc Anaximenes 'peto' inquit 'ut Lampsacum diruas.' haec velocitas sagacitatis oppidum vetusta nobilitate inclitum exitio, cui destinatum
erat, subtraxit.

ext. 5 Demosthenis quoque astutia mirifice cuidam aniculae[40] succursum est, quae pecuniam depositi nomine a
duobus hospitibus acceperat ea condicione ut illam simul
utrisque redderet. quorum alter interiecto tempore, tamquam mortuo socio squalore obsitus, deceptae omnes
nummos abstulit. supervenit deinde alter et depositum
petere coepit. haerebat misera [et][41] in maxima pariter et
pecuniae et defensionis penuria, iamque de laqueo et suspendio cogitabat: sed opportune Demosthenes ei patronus adfulsit. qui, ut ⟨in⟩[42] advocationem venit, 'mulier'
inquit 'parata est depositi se fide solvere, sed nisi socium
adduxeris, id facere non potest, quoniam, ut ipse vocifera-

---

[39] *sic SB*[1]: altiori nitamini* AL [40] aniculae *Kempf ex* P:
ancillae AL [41] *del.* A *corr.*, G [42] *add.* P

latter is as good as extinct, only vestiges survive. He used to
say that in the practice of friendship we should remember
that it can change to the direst enmity.[16] Perhaps at first
sight this precept may seem too calculating, at variance
with the guilelessness in which familiarity especially de-
lights. But if reflection be plunged deeper into the hidden
places of the mind, it will be found very useful indeed.

The survival of the city of Lampsacus was thanks to a
single stroke of craft. Alexander was earnestly bent on its
destruction. Seeing his teacher Anaximenes come outside
the walls obviously about to oppose his entreaties to his
own wrath, Alexander swore that he would not do what he
asked. Then said Anaximenes: "I ask that you destroy
Lampsacus." His swift sagacity rescued a town famous in
historic renown from the ruin to which it had been destined.[17]

Demosthenes' cleverness too came marvellously to the
aid of a certain old woman. She had taken money as a deposit from two guests on the condition that she return it to
both at the same time. After a while one of the two came
dressed in mourning as though his partner was dead and so
deceived the woman and took away the whole sum. Then
the other came along and proceeded to ask for his deposit.
The unhappy woman was in a quandary; as poorly off for
money as for defence, she was already thinking of a rope to
hang herself when in the nick of time Demosthenes appeared to the rescue as her advocate. When he came to
plead he said: "The woman is ready to discharge her trust
as depositary, but unless you bring your partner she cannot

[16] Aristot. *Rhet.* 2.13.4, Cic. *Amic.* 59 etc.
[17] 334: Pausan. 6.18.2–4.

141

ris, haec dicta est lex, ne pecunia alteri sine altero numera-
retur.'

ext. 6   Ac ne illud quidem parum prudenter. quidam Athenis
universo populo invisus, causam apud eum capitali crimine dicturus, maximum honorem subito petere coepit,
non quod speraret se illum consequi posse, sed ut haberent homines ubi procursum irae, qui acerrimus esse solet,
effunderent. neque eum haec tam callida consilii ratio
fefellit: comitiis enim clamore infesto et crebris totius
contionis sibilis vexatus, nota etiam denegati honoris per-
strictus, eiusdem plebis paulo post in discrimine vitae
clementissima suffragia expertus est. quod si adhuc ei
ultionem sitienti capitis sui periculum obiecisset, nullam
partem defensionis odio obseratae aures reciperent.

ext. 7   Huic vaframento consimilis illa calliditas. superior
Hannibal a Duilio[43] consule navali proelio victus timens-
que classis amissae poenas dare, offensam astutia m⟨ire⟩[44]
avertit: nam ex illa infelici pugna prius quam cladis nuntius
domum perveniret quendam ex amicis compositum et formatum[45] Carthaginem misit. qui postquam civitatis eius
curiam intravit, 'consulit vos' inquit 'Hannibal, cum dux
Romanorum magnas secum maritimas trahens copias
advenerit, an cum eo confligere debeat.' acclamavit universus senatus non esse dubium quin oporteret. tum ille
'conflixit' inquit 'et superatus est.' ita liberum iis non reli-

---

43 Duilio P: Iulio LG: *silet* A
44 *add.* P
45 formatum AL: or- G: subor- P

---

18 This and the following are not found elsewhere.
19 260: Diodor. 23.10 etc.

do it, since as you yourself proclaim, the terms were that the money should not be paid to one without the other."[18]

The following too was quite shrewdly done. A certain person in Athens, who was universally disliked, was to plead his case before the people on a capital charge. He suddenly set up as a candidate for a very high office, not because he hoped he could get it, but to give people a means of discharging their first rush of anger, which is generally the most violent. Nor did this cunning calculation let him down. At the election he was assailed with hostile shouts and frequent hisses from the whole assembly and wounded with the stigma of office denied. A little later, when his life was at stake, he found the votes of the same populace most merciful. But if he had put his mortal danger before them as they were still thirsting for vengeance, ears stopped by hatred would have admitted no part of his defence.

This stratagem is paralleled by the following piece of cunning. An earlier Hannibal, defeated by Consul Duilius in a naval battle, was afraid he would be punished for losing his fleet and turned the resentment aside with a wonderful stroke of cleverness. Before a report of the disaster reached home from that unlucky battle, he sent one of his friends, properly set up and primed, to Carthage. On entering the senate of that community, the emissary said: "Hannibal wants your advice. When the Roman commander arrives bringing a large naval force along with him, ought he to join battle?" The entire senate cried out that he certainly ought. Then said the messenger: "He did join battle and was defeated."[19] So he left them no freedom to

quit id factum damnare quod ipsi fieri debuisse iudicaverant.

ext. 8   Alter[46] Hannibal Fabium Maximum, invictam armorum suorum vim saluberrimis cunctationibus pugnae ludificantem, ut aliqua suspicione trahendi belli respergeret, totius Italiae agros ferro atque igni vastando unius eius fundum immunem ab hoc iniuriae genere reliquit. profecisset aliquid tanti beneficii insidiosa adumbratio eius, nisi Romanae urbi et Fabii pietas et Hannibalis vafri mores fuissent notissimi.

ext. 9   Tusculanis etiam acumine consilii incolumitas parta est. cum enim crebris rebellationibus meruissent ut eorum urbem funditus Romani evertere vellent atque ad id exsequendum Furius Camillus, maximus dux, validissimo instructus exercitu venisset, universi ei togati obviam processerunt, commeatusque et cetera pacis munia benignissime praestiterunt, armatum etiam intrare moenia passi sunt, nec vultu nec habitu mutato. qua constantia tranquillitatis non solum ad amicitiae nostrae ius sed etiam ad communionem civitatis usque penetrarunt, sagaci hercule usi simplicitate, quoniam aptius esse intellexerant metum officiis dissimulare quam armis protegere.

ext. 10   At Volscorum ducis Tulli exsecrabile consilium. qui ad bellum inferendum Romanis maxima cupiditate accensus, cum aliquot adversis proeliis contusos animos suorum et ob id paci proniores animadverteret, insidiosa ratione quo volebat compulit: nam cum spectandorum ludorum gratia magna Volscorum multitudo Romam convenisset, consuli-

---

[46] alter *SB*: item AL: alter item ⊊

condemn an action which they themselves had approved.

The other Hannibal was ravaging the lands of all Italy with fire and sword. Wishing to cast some suspicion of dragging out the war upon Fabius Maximus, who with salutary deferments of battle was mocking the unconquered violence of his arms, he left his farm, and his only, immune from attack. His insidious pretence of so great a favour would have had some effect if the city of Rome had not been well aware of Fabius' patriotism and Hannibal's crafty ways.[20]

The Tusculans too were saved by sharp policy. By their repeated resumptions of arms they had deserved that the Romans should decide to raze their city to the ground and Furius Camillus, the great commander, had come for that purpose at the head of a very powerful army. All the inhabitants came out to meet him wearing gowns and supplied provisions and other peaceful gifts most liberally. They even let him enter their walls armed without changing countenance or dress. This persevering calm won them admission not only to our friendship but even to common citizenship. They practised an artlessness truly sagacious, since they realised that it answered better to disguise their fears with good offices than to protect them with arms.[21]

But the device of Tullus, the Volscian chief, was abominable. Afire with passionate eagerness to fight the Romans, he saw that his men were dispirited by a number of adverse battles and therefore more inclined to peace. So he chose a treacherous method of pushing them in the direction he wanted. A great multitude of Volsci had flocked to Rome to watch the games. Tullus told the Consuls that he was

[20] 217: Livy 22.23.4 etc.   [21] 381: Livy 6.25.6–26.8 etc.

145

bus dixit vehementer se timere ne quid hostile subito moli-
rentur, monuitque ut essent cautiores, et protinus ipse
urbe egressus est. quam rem consules ad senatum detule-
runt. qui, tametsi nulla suspicio suberat, auctoritate tamen
Tulli commotus ut ante noctem Volsci abirent decrevit.
qua contumelia irritati facile impelli potuerunt ad rebellandum. ita mendacium versuti ducis simulatione benivolentiae involutum duos simul populos fefellit, Romanum
ut insontes notaret, Volscum ut deceptis irasceretur.

4. STRATEGEMATA

praef. Illa vero pars calliditatis egregia et ab omni reprehensione procul remota, cuius opera, quia appellatione ‹ Latina ›[47] vix apte exprimi possunt, Graeca pronuntiatione
strategemata dicantur.

1 Omnibus militaribus copiis Tullus Hostilius Fidenas
adgressus, quae surgentis imperii nostri incunabula crebris rebellationibus torpere passae non sunt, finitimisque
tropaeis ac triumphis alitam virtutem eius spes suas ulterius promovere docuerunt. Mettius Fufetius, dux Albanorum, dubiam et suspectam semper societatis suae fidem
repente in ipsa acie detexit: nudato[48] enim Romani exercitus latere in proximo colle consedit, pro adiutore specula-
tor pugnae futurus, ut aut victis insultaret aut victores fessos adgrederetur. non erat dubium quin ea res militum
nostrorum animos debilitata esset, cum eodem tempore

[47] add. ς; Br
[48] nudato coni. Briscoe: detecto AL: deserto Halm ex P

[22] 491: Livy 2.37 etc.

greatly afraid they might make some sudden hostile attempt and warned them to be more on their guard. He himself left the city forthwith. The Consuls brought the matter to the senate, which decreed that the Volsci should leave before nightfall, swayed by Tullus' authority although there was no suspicion. Provoked by the insult, the Volsci could easily be pushed into taking up arms again. So it was that the lie of a wily chieftain, wrapped in a pretence of good will, duped two peoples at once, making the Romans put a stigma on the innocent and angering the Volsci against those he had misled.[22]

4. STRATAGEMS

Here is a laudable part of cunning far removed from all censure. Its performances can hardly be properly expressed by a Latin name, so let them be called in Greek parlance "stratagems."

Tullus Hostilius with all his armed forces attacked Fidenae, which with frequent resumptions of conflict did not suffer the cradle of our rising empire to rest inactive, and taught valour nourished on border trophies and triumphs to advance its hopes further afield. Mettius Fufetius, leader of the Albans, suddenly in the midst of battle unmasked his always dubious and suspect loyalty as an ally. For laying bare the flank of the Roman army, he took up a position on a neighbouring hill, intending to be a spectator of the fight rather than an assistant, so that he should either spring upon the losers or attack the weary victors. It was not to be doubted that this would weaken the morale of our soldiers, when they saw the enemy closing with them at the

147

et hostes confligere et auxilia deficere cernerent. itaque ne id fieret Tullus providit: concitato enim equo omnes pugnantium globos percucurrit, praedicans suo iussu secessisse Mettium, eumque, cum ipse signum dedisset, invasurum Fidenatium terga. quo imperatoriae artis consilio metum fiducia mutavit, proque trepidatione alacritate suorum pectora replevit.

2   Et ne continuo a nostris regibus recedam, Sex. Tarquinius, Tarquinii filius, indigne ferens quod patris viribus expugnari Gabii nequirent, valentiorem armis excogitavit rationem qua interceptum illud oppidum Romano imperio adiceret: subito namque se ad Gabinos contulit tamquam parentis saevitiam et verbera, quae voluntate sua perpessus erat, fugiens, ac paulatim uniuscuiusque fictis et compositis blanditiis alliciendo benivolentiam, ut apud omnes plurimum posset, consecutus, familiarem suum ad patrem misit, indicaturum quemadmodum cuncta in sua manu haberet et quaesiturum quidnam fieri vellet. iuvenili calliditati senilis astutia respondit, si quidem re eximia delectatus Tarquinius, fidei autem nuntii parum ⟨credens⟩,[49] nihil respondit, sed seducto eo in hortum maxima et altissima papaverum capita baculo decussit. cognito adulescens silentio simul ac patris facto, causam alterius, ⟨alterius⟩[50] argumentum pervidit, nec ignoravit praecipi sibi ut excellentissimum quemque Gabinorum aut exsilio summoveret aut morte consumeret. ergo spoliatam bonis propugnatoribus civitatem tantum non vinctis manibus ei tradidit.

[49] *add.* P   [50] *add. Kempf*

---

[1] Livy 1.27.3–9 etc.
[2] Livy 1.53.4–54.10 etc.

same time as their supports were defecting. Therefore
Tullus took measures to prevent that. Spurring his horse,
he rode through all the knots of combatants calling out that
Mettius had withdrawn on his orders and would attack the
rear of the Fidenates when he himself gave the signal. By
this device of generalship he changed fear into confidence
and filled the hearts of his men with eagerness instead of
terror.[1]

And not to leave our kings just yet, Sex. Tarquinius, son
of Tarquin, took it hard that Gabii could not be stormed by
his father's power. So he thought of a method stronger than
arms whereby to capture the town and add it to Roman
empire. He suddenly betook himself to the Gabini as
though fleeing from his parent's cruelty and stripes, which
he had suffered of his own accord. Step by step, with false,
manufactured blandishments he won the good will of each
individual so as to become highly influential with them all.
He then sent a comrade to his father to tell him how he had
everything in his own hands and to ask what he wished
done. The old man's astuteness matched the young man's
cunning. Tarquin was highly delighted by the message, but
not altogether trusting the honesty of the messenger he
gave no answer but drew him aside into the garden and
there with his stick struck down the heads of the largest
and tallest poppies. Young Sextus, hearing of his father's silence and of what he did, understood the reason for the
one and the meaning of the other, not failing to realise that
he was being advised to get rid of the most prominent citizens of Gabii by banishment or liquidate them by death. So
he virtually handed over the community with hands bound
to Tarquin, stripped of its loyal defenders.[2]

3   Illud quoque maioribus et consilio prudenter et exitu
feliciter provisum: cum enim urbe capta Galli Capitolium
obsiderent, solamque potiendi eius spem in fame eorum
repositam animadverterent, perquam callido genere consilii unico perseverantiae irritamento victores spoliave-
runt: panes enim iacere compluribus e locis coeperunt.
quo spectaculo obstupefactos, infinitamque frumenti
abundantiam nostris superesse credentes, ad pactionem
omittendae obsidionis compulerunt. misertus est tunc
profecto Iuppiter Romanae virtutis, praesidium ab astutia
mutuantis, cum summa alimentorum inopia proici praesidia inopiae cerneret. igitur ut vafro ita periculoso consilio
salutarem exitum dedit.

4   Idemque Iuppiter postea praestantissimorum ducum
nostrorum sagacibus consiliis propitius aspiravit: nam cum
alterum Italiae latus Hannibal laceraret, alterum invasis-
set Hasdrubal, ne duorum fratrum iunctae copiae intolerabili onere fessas simul nostras urguerent, hinc Claudii
Neronis vegetum consilium, illinc Livii Salinatoris inclita
providentia effecit: Nero enim, compresso a se in Lucanis
Hannibale, praesentiam suam, quoniam ita ratio belli desi-
derabat, mentitus hosti, ad opem collegae ferendam per
longum iter celeritate mira tetendit. Salinator, in Umbria
apud Metaurum flumen proximo die dimicaturus, summa
cum dissimulatione Neronem castris noctu recepit: tribunos enim a tribunis, centuriones a centurionibus, equites
ab equitibus, pedites a peditibus excipi iussit, ac sine ulla

---

3 390: Livy 5.48.4 etc.

The following measure too of our ancestors was shrewd in the conception and fortunate in the result. After capturing the city the Gauls besieged the Capitol and saw that their only hope of taking it lay in starving out the defenders. So by a very cunning kind of ruse the latter stripped the victors of their only incentive to persevere: they started to throw loaves of bread from various points. The Gauls were amazed at the sight and in the belief that our men still had an endless abundance of grain they were driven to come to an agreement to raise the siege. Surely Jupiter took pity then on Roman valour, as it borrowed aid from cunning, when he saw the defences against want thrown out though food was scarce in the extreme. And so he gave a salutary result to the crafty but equally dangerous expedient.[3]

The same Jupiter later propitiously favoured the sagacious counsels of our foremost generals. Hannibal was tearing at one side of Italy, Hasdrubal had invaded the other. On one the vigorous policy of Claudius Nero, on the other the celebrated foresight of Livius Salinator prevented the junction of the forces of the two brothers, which together would have placed an intolerable load on Rome's weary back. Nero had Hannibal cooped up in Lucania. Falsely pretending to the enemy that he was on the spot, he marched with extraordinary speed over the long route to bring aid to his colleague, since that was what war's logic called for. Salinator was in Umbria at the river Metaurus, intending to give battle the following day. With the utmost concealment he took Nero into his camp during the night. For he ordered Tribunes to take in Tribunes, Centurions Centurions, horsemen horsemen, footmen footmen, and without any confusion put another army

tumultuatione solo vix unum exercitum capienti alterum inseruit. quo evenit ne Hasdrubal cum duobus se consulibus proeliaturum prius sciret quam utriusque virtute prosterneretur. ita illa toto terrarum orbe infamis Punica calliditas, Romana elusa prudentia, Hannibalem Neroni, Hasdrubalem Salinatori decipiendum tradidit.

5   Memorabilis etiam consilii Q. Metellus. qui cum pro consule bellum in Hispania adversus Celtiberos gereret, urbemque Contrebiam caput eius gentis viribus expugnare non posset, intra pectus suum multum ac diu consiliis agitatis, viam repperit qua propositum ad exitum perduceret. itinera magno impetu ingrediebatur, deinde alias atque alias regiones petebat: hos obsidebat montes, paulo post ad illos transgrediebatur, cum interim tam suis omnibus quam ipsis hostibus ignota erat causa inopinatae eius ac subitae fluctuationis. interrogatus quoque a quodam amicissimo sibi quid ita sparsum et incertum militiae genus sequeretur, 'absiste' inquit 'istud quaerere: nam si huius consilii mei interiorem tunicam consciam esse sensero, continuo eam cremari iubebo.' quorsum igitur ea dissimulatio erupit aut quem finem habuit? postquam vero et exercitum suum ignorantia et totam Celtiberiam errore implicavit, cum alio cursum derexisset, subito ad Contrebiam reflexit eamque inopinatam et attonitam oppressit. ergo nisi mentem suam dolos scrutari coegisset, ad ultimam ei senectutem apud moenia Contrebiae armato sedendum foret.

onto ground that was hardly big enough for one. As a result Hasdrubal did not know that he would be fighting with two Consuls until after the valour of them both had laid him low. Thus that Punic cunning, infamous the world over, was outwitted by Roman shrewdness. It gave Hannibal to Nero and Hasdrubal to Livius to be duped.[4]

Memorable also was the policy of Q. Metellus. He was waging war as Proconsul in Spain against the Celtiberi and was unable to take the city of Contrebia, the capital of that nation, by force. After much and lengthy turning over of plans in his mind, he found a way to bring his purpose to fruition. With great energy he set about marches, then headed for this region and that. He would occupy mountains only to pass over to other mountains a little later; and all the while the reason for his unlooked-for, sudden restlessness was as unknown to all his own men as it was to the enemy themselves. Questioned by a close friend why he was prosecuting so desultory and fidgety a campaign, he replied: "Don't ask. For if I find that my shirt knows about this plan of mine, I shall have it burned immediately." What then was the upshot of this masquerade, how did it end? Having involved his own army in ignorance and the whole of Celtiberia in his wandering, he took a different direction, then suddenly turned back on Contrebia, and catching the place unsuspecting and surprised, took it. So if he had not forced his mind to examine trickery, he would have had to go on sitting in arms at the walls of Contrebia into ultimate old age.[5]

4 207: Livy 27.46.1f. etc.
5 142: Plut. *Moral.* 202A, 506D, Front. *Strat.* 1.1.12, Auct. vir. ill. 61.5.

ext. 1 Agathocles autem Syracusarum rex audaciter callidus: cum enim urbem eius maiore ex parte Carthaginienses occupassent, exercitum suum in Africam traiecit ut metum metu, vim vi discuteret, nec sine effectu: nam repentino eius adventu perculsi Poeni libenter incolumitatem suam salute hostium redemerunt, pactique sunt ut eodem tempore et Africa Siculis et Sicilia Punicis armis liberaretur. at[51] si Syracusarum moenia tueri perseverasset, ‹Sic›ilia[52] belli malis urgueretur, bona pacis fruenda securae Carthagini reliquisset. nunc inferendo quae patiebatur, dum alienas potius lacessit opes quam suas tuetur, quo aequiore animo regnum deseruit, eo tutius recepit.

ext. 2 Quid? Hannibal Cannensem populi Romani aciem nonne prius quam ad dimicandum descenderet compluribus astutiae copulatam laqueis ad tam miserabilem perduxit exitum? ante omnia enim providit ut et solem et pulverem, qui ibi vento multus ex‹ci›tari[53] solet, adversum haberet. deinde partem copiarum suarum inter ipsum proelii tempus de industria fugere iussit; quam cum a reliquo exercitu abrupta legio Romana sequeretur, trucidandam eam ab iis quos ‹in›[54] insidiis collocaverat curavit. postremo quadringentos equites subornavit qui simulata transitione petierunt consulem; a quo iussi more transfugarum depositis armis in ultimam pugnae partem secedere, destrictis gladiis, quos inter tunicas et loricas abdide-

---

[51] at A corr.: age AL   [52] Sicilia Halm: illa* AL
[53] add. G   [54] add. A corr., G

---

[6] 310–307: Diodor. 20.3, Justin 22.4.1f.
[7] 216: Livy 22.46.8f., 48 etc.

BOOK VII.4

EXTERNAL

Agathocles, king of Syracuse, was adventurously cunning. When the Carthaginians had captured the greater part of his city, he took his army over to Africa, in order to dissipate fear by fear and force by force; and not without effect. Shocked by his sudden arrival, the Carthaginians gladly bought their own safety at the price of their enemies' and agreed that Africa should be freed from Sicilian arms and Sicily from Carthaginian simultaneously.[6] But if he had kept on defending the walls of Syracuse, Sicily would have been afflicted by the evils of war and he would have left the blessings of peace to be enjoyed by Carthage in security. As it was, he imposed what he suffered, challenging alien power rather than protecting his own, and the more coolly he deserted his kingdom, the safer he recovered it.

What of Hannibal? Did he not bring the army of the Roman people at Cannae to so miserable an end after entangling it in many nooses of cunning before he went into battle?[7] To begin with, he made sure that they should have their faces to the sun and the dust, which is commonly raised there in large quantities by the wind. Then he ordered part of his forces to take to flight deliberately while the battle was actually in progress; when they were separated from the rest of the army and a Roman legion pursued them, he saw to it that the legion was slaughtered by men whom he had placed in ambush. Lastly, he set up four hundred horsemen, who went to the Consul pretending to be deserters. The Consul ordered them as such to lay down their arms and retire to the furthest part of the battle, as deserters are wont to do. Drawing swords which they had secreted between their tunics and breastplates, they ham-

155

rant, poplites pugnantium Romanorum ceciderunt. haec
fuit Punica fortitudo, dolis et insidiis et fallacia instructa.
quae nunc certissima circumventae virtutis nostrae excusatio est, quoniam decepti magis quam victi sumus.

5. DE REPULSIS

praef.   Campi quoque repraesentata condicio ambitiosam in-
gredientes viam ad fortius sustinendos parum prosperos
comitiorum eventus utiliter instruxerit, quia propositis
ante oculos clarissimorum virorum repulsis ut non minore
cum spe honores ita prudentiore cum animi iudicio petent,
meminerintque nefas non esse aliquid ab omnibus uni ne-
gari, cum saepenumero singuli cunctorum voluntatibus
resistere fas esse duxerint, scientes etiam patientia quaeri
debere quod gratia impetrari nequierit.

1   Q. Aelius Tubero, a Q. Fabio Maximo epulum populo
nomine P. Africani patrui sui dante rogatus ut triclinium
sterneret, lectulos Punicanos pellibus haedinis stravit et
pro argenteis vasis Samia exposuit. cuius rei deformitas sic
homines offendit ut cum alioqui vir egregius haberetur,
comitiisque praetoriis candidatus in campum L. Paullo
avo et P. Africano avunculo nixus descendisset, repulsa
inde abiret notatus: nam ut privatim semper continentiam
probabant ita publice maxima cura splendoris habita est.
quocirca urbs, non unius convivii numerum sed totam se
in illis pelliculis iacuisse credens, ruborem epuli suffragiis
suis vindicavit.

---

[1] Allobrogicus, whose adoptive father Q. Fabius Maximus
Aemilianus was the younger Africanus' natural brother. Tubero's
mother was Africanus' sister.

[2] 129 (?): Cic. *Mur.* 75f., Sen. *Ep.* 95.72.

strung the fighting Romans. Such was Punic bravery, equipped with tricks and treacheries and deceit. That is now the surest excuse for our hoodwinked valour, since we were deceived rather than vanquished.

5. OF ELECTORAL DEFEATS

A presentation of what happens on the Campus will be a useful preparation for those entering on the path of public office. It will help them bear adverse election results with more fortitude, for when rejections of men of great renown are placed in front of them, they will seek offices not with less hope but with shrewder judgment. They will bear in mind that there is no sin in the denial of something to an individual by the community, since individuals have often thought it right to resist the wishes of the generality. They will know too that what cannot be won by favour should be sought by patience.

Q. Aelius Tubero was asked by Q. Fabius Maximus,[1] who was giving a feast to the people in the name of his uncle P. Africanus, to fit out a dining room. He spread Punic couches with goatskins and put out Samian utensils instead of silver. This shabby proceeding gave such offence that although he otherwise passed for an excellent person and went down to the Campus as a candidate at the praetorian elections relying on his grandfather L. Paullus and his maternal uncle P. Africanus, he left it with the stigma of rejection. For while they always approved of private frugality, publicly they set much store on a handsome show. So the city felt that its whole entity, not just the complement of one dinner party, had lain on those skins and by its votes took its revenge for the shame of the banquet.[2]

2   P. autem Scipio Nasica, togatae potentiae clarissimum lumen, qui consul Iugurthae bellum indixit, qui Matrem Idaeam e Phrygiis sedibus ad nostras aras focosque migrantem sanctissimis manibus excepit, qui multas et pestiferas seditiones auctoritatis suae robore oppressit, quo principe senatus per aliquot annos gloriatus est, cum aedilitatem curulem adulescens peteret manumque cuiusdam rustico opere duratam more candidatorum tenacius apprehendisset, ioci gratia interrogavit eum num manibus solitus esset ambulare. quod dictum a circumstantibus exceptum ad populum manavit, causamque repulsae Scipioni attulit: omnes namque rusticae tribus, paupertatem sibi ab eo exprobratam iudicantes, iram suam adversus contumeliosam eius urbanitatem destrinxerunt. igitur civitas nostra nobilium iuvenum ingenia ab insolentia revocando magnos et utiles cives fecit, honoribusque non patiendo eos a securis peti debitum auctoritatis pondus adiecit.

3   Nullus error talis in L. Aemilio Paullo conspectus est, sed tamen aliquotiens frustra consulatum petiit, idemque, cum iam campum repulsis suis fatigasset, bis consul et censor factus amplissimum etiam dignitatis gradum obtinuit. cuius virtutem iniuriae non fregerunt sed acuerunt, quoniam quidem ipsa nota accensam cupiditatem summi honoris ardentiorem ad comitia detulit, ut populum, quia

---

³ *Ca.* 145: cf. Cic. *Planc.* 51, whose reference *quo cive neminem statuo in hac re publica fortiorem* points firmly to the Consul of 138, slayer of Ti. Gracchus. Valerius here conflates four generations of Scipiones Nasicae (Münzer, *RE* IV.1494f.; Briscoe in *Sileno* 1993, p. 407).

⁴ Briscoe after Kempf reads *a scurris* ("by wags," a fifteenth-century conjecture) for *a securis*, which latter however

P. Scipio Nasica was a brilliant luminary of civilian power. As Consul he declared war on Jugurtha; he received in purest hands the Idaean Mother as she migrated from her Phrygian seat to our altars and hearths; by the strength of his authority he suppressed many noxious turmoils; for some years the senate gloried in him as their Leader. Standing for the Curule Aedileship[3] as a young man, after the manner of candidates he gripped somebody's hand, which had been hardened by farm labour, rather tightly, and asked him as a joke whether he was by way of walking on his hands. Bystanders caught the remark and it spread to the public and caused Scipio's defeat. For all the rustic tribes thought he had taunted them with poverty and vented their anger against his insulting wit. So our community by restraining the minds of young nobles from insolence made them great and useful citizens, and added to offices their due weight of authority by not letting election be taken for granted.[4]

No such blunder was seen in L. Aemilius Paullus' case and yet he several times stood for the Consulship without success. But after he had tired the Campus out with his rejections,[5] he was elected Consul twice and Censor and enjoyed a standing second to none. Rebuffs did not break his manly spirit but sharpened it. He brought a more ardent desire for the highest office to the voters, fired by the very

makes good sense. And would Valerius have used the former of this admired figure even by implication?

5 Cf. Livy 39.32.6. Paullus' first Consulship was in 182. Plutarch in his Life says nothing about previous failures and Livy does not necessarily imply more than one—another Valerian exaggeration.

nobilitatis splendore et animi bonis movere non potuerat,
pertinacia vinceret.

4 Q. autem Caecilium Metellum pauci et maesti amici
consulatus repulsa adflictum, tristitia ac rubore plenum,
domum reduxerunt. eundem de Pseudophilippo trium-
phantem universus senatus laetum et alacrem in Capitolium prosecutus est. Achaici etiam belli, cui summam
manum L. Mummius adiecit, maxima pars ab hoc viro
profligata est. eine ergo populus consulatum negare potuit
cui mox duas clarissimas provincias aut daturus erat aut
debiturus, Achaiam ac Macedoniam? et quidem hoc facto
meliore eo cive usus est: intellexit enim quam industrie
sibi gerendus esset consulatus quem tanto labore impetrari senserat.

5 Quid tam excellens, quid tam opulentum quam L. Sulla? divitias imperia largitus est, leges vetustas abrogavit,
novas tulit. hic quoque in eo campo cuius postea dominus
exstitit repulsa praeturae suggillatus est, omnia loca petiti
honoris, si quis modo deorum formam et imaginem
futurae eius potentiae populo Romano repraesentasset,
impetraturus.

6 Sed ut comitiorum maximum crimen referam, M. Porcius Cato, plus moribus suis praeturae decoris adiecturus
quam praetexto eius splendoris ipse laturus, consequi
illam a populo aliquando non potuit. proxima dementiae
suffragia, quae quidem satis graves poenas erroris sui pe-

---

[6] Two defeats, according to Auct. vir. ill. 61.3. Metellus
(Macedonicus) was Praetor in 148 and Consul in 143.

[7] As though his exploits in Macedonia and Achaea in 148–46
had come after the rejection instead of the other way round.

stigma, so that by pertinacity he vanquished the public since he had not been able to move them by splendour of birth and mental gifts.

A few sorrowful friends accompanied Q. Caecilius Metellus home, dashed by his defeat in an election for the Consulship,[6] full of gloom and embarrassment; the same Metellus was escorted to the Capitol by the whole senate in joyous and cheerful mood at his triumph over False Philip. The greater part of the Achaean War, too, to which L. Mummius gave the finishing touch, was accomplished by the same personage. Could the people deny the Consulship to one to whom they were soon about either to give or to owe two splendid provinces, Achaea and Macedonia?[7] And indeed by that action they made him a better citizen for their service; for he realised what diligence he had to show in his conduct of the Consulship, which he had found it so much trouble to procure.

Outstanding and powerful as none other was L. Sulla. He lavished riches and commands, abrogated old laws, carried new. He too, in that Campus of which he later became lord, was affronted by a rejection for the Praetorship.[8] But if some god had shown the Roman people the shape and semblance of his future power, he would have gained all places for the office he sought.

But to relate the worst blot on the elections, M. Porcius Cato, who by his character would have conferred more distinction on the Praetorship than he would himself have gained splendour by its glory, at one time failed to obtain it from the people. Those votes come close to lunacy, and they paid dearly enough for their blunder, since they were

[8] 94: Plut. *Sull.* 5, Firm. *Math.* 1.7.28.

penderunt, quoniam quem honorem Catoni negaverant
Vatinio dare coacti sunt. ergo, si vere aestimare volumus,
non Catoni tunc praetura sed praeturae Cato negatus est.

6. DE NECESSITATE

praef.   Abominandae quoque necessitatis amarissimae leges
et truculentissima imperia cum urbem nostram tum etiam
exteras gentes multa non intellectu tantum sed etiam auditu gravia perpeti coegerunt.

1a   Nam aliquot adversis proeliis secundo Punico bello ex-
hausta militari iuventute Romana, senatus auctore Ti.
Graccho consule censuit uti publice servi ad usum ⟨belli
et ad⟩ propulsandum[55] hostium impetum[56] emerentur,
eaque de re per tribunos plebis ad populum lata rogatione
tres creati sunt viri, qui quattuor et viginti milia servorum
comparaverunt, adactosque iure iurando strenuam se for-
temque operam daturos, ⟨et⟩[57] quoad Poeni essent in Italia laturos arma,[58] in castra miserunt. ex Apulia etiam [et]
a[59] Paediculis septuaginta atque ducenti ad supplemen-
tum equitatus sunt empti. quanta violentia est casus acer-
bi! quae civitas ad id tempus ingenuae quoque originis
capite censos habere milites fastidierat, eadem cellis servilibus extracta corpora et a pastoralibus casis collecta mancipia velut praecipuum firmamentum exercitui suo adiecit.

[55] belli ... propulsandum *SB*[1]: -dorum AL
[56] impetum *om.* P   [57] *add.* ϛ
[58] laturos arma A *corr.*: datura arma A: daturam L
[59] a *Briscoe*: et a AL: e P

obliged to grant Vatinius the office they had denied to Cato. So if we want to reckon aright, the Praetorship was not denied to Cato on that occasion but Cato to the Praetorship.[9]

6. OF NECESSITY

The bitter laws and cruel commands of odious necessity have forced our city and foreign nations too to suffer many things grievous not only to understand but even to hear.

In the Second Punic War, when Rome's manpower was exhausted by several adverse battles, the senate on the motion of Consul Ti. Gracchus decreed that slaves be purchased publicly for use in war and to repel the onset of the enemy. Concerning this matter three commissioners were appointed by a bill introduced by the Tribunes of the Plebs in the popular assembly; they collected 24,000 slaves. Bound by an oath to give strenuous and brave service and to bear arms as long as the Carthaginians were in Italy, they were sent to camp.[1] Moreover, 270 were bought from Apulia, from the Paediculi,[2] as cavalry reinforcements. How great is the violence of sour chance! The community that until then had scorned to have *capite censi* even of free birth as soldiers added bodies drawn from servants' attics and slaves collected from shepherds' huts to its

9 55: Livy *Per.* 105, Plut. *Cat. min.* 42 etc.

1 216: Livy 22.57.11f. etc. Gracchus was Consul in 215 and the slaves were put under his command.

2 Or Poediculi (cf. *RE*) = Peucetii, a tribe of Illyrian origin (Livy 23.32.1). Nothing else is known of this transaction.

cedit ergo interdum generosus spiritus utilitati et Fortunae viribus succumbit, ubi, nisi tutiora consilia legeris, speciosa sequenti concidendum est.

1b   Cannensis autem clades adeo urbem nostram vehementer confudit ut M. Iunio Pera dictatore rem publicam administrante spolia hostium adfixa templis, deorum numini consecrata, instrumento militiae futura convellerentur, ac praetextati pueri arma induerent, addictorum etiam et capitali crimine damnatorum sex milia conscriberentur. quae si per se aspiciantur, aliquid ruboris habeant, si autem admotis necessitatis viribus ponderentur, saevitiae temporis convenientia praesidia videantur.

1c   Propter eandem cladem senatus Otacilio, qui Siciliam, Cornelio Mammulae, qui Sardiniam pro praetoribus obtinebant, querentibus quod neque stipendium neque frumentum classibus eorum et exercitibus socii praeberent, adfirmantibus etiam ne habere quidem eos unde id praestare possent, rescripsit aerarium longinquis impensis non sufficere: proinde quo pacto tantae inopiae succurrendum esset ipsi viderent. his litteris quid aliud quam imperii sui gubernacula e manibus abiecit, Siciliamque et Sardiniam, benignissimas urbis nostrae nutrices, gradus <et>[60] stabilimenta bellorum, tam multo sudore et sanguine in potestatem redactas, paucis verbis, te scilicet, Necessitas, iubente, dimisit.

2   Eadem Casilinates, obsidione Hannibalis clausos alimentorumque facultate defectos, lora necessariis vinculorum usibus subducta eque scutis detractas pelles ferventi

[60] *add.* ⌐

---

[3] 216: Livy 23.14.2f. etc.   [4] 216: Livy 23.21.1–4.

army as special strengthening. So sometimes a noble spirit yields to expediency and bows to the power of Fortune in cases where unless we choose counsels of safety those of handsome show lead to collapse.

The disaster at Cannae threw our city into such confusion that when Dictator M. Junius Pera was in charge of the commonwealth, enemy spoils fixed to temples and consecrated to divine power were torn down to be used as instruments of war, boys still in boys' gowns put on armour, 6,000 assigned debtors and men convicted on capital charges were enlisted.[3] Looked at by themselves, these measures would carry some disgrace, but weighed along with the added force of necessity, they would appear as recourses suited to the cruelty of the hour.

On account of the same disaster the senate gave their reply to Otacilius and Cornelius Mammula, respectively governing Sicily and Sardinia as Propraetors, who had complained that the allies were not furnishing pay and grain for their fleets and armies and affirmed that they did not even have the wherewithal so to provide. The senate wrote in reply that the treasury could not cover distant expenses; they must decide for themselves how to cope with so large a deficit.[4] By these letters did they not drop from their hands the rudder of their empire? In a few words, at your command to be sure, O Necessity, they dismissed Sicily and Sardinia, those generous foster mothers of our city, stepping-stones and stabilizers of wars, brought under our power with so much sweat and blood.

You also caused the citizens of Casilinum, shut in by Hannibal's siege and running out of food, to take straps from their function as binders and leather stripped from

resolutas aqua mandere voluisti. quid illis, si acerbitatem
casus intueare, miserius, si constantiam respicias, fidelius?
qui ne a Romanis desciscerent, tali uti cibi genere sustinuerunt, cum pinguissima arva sua fertilissimosque campos moenibus suis subiectos intuerentur. itaque Capuae[61]
urbis, quae Punicam feritatem deliciis suis cupide fovit, in
propinquo situm Casilinum, incolarum[62] virtute clarum,
perseverantis amicitiae pignore impios oculos verberavit.

3   In illa obsidione et fide cum trecenti Praenestini per-
manerent, evenit ut ex iis quidam murem captum ducentis
potius denariis vendere quam ipse leniendae famis gratia
consumere mallet. sed, credo, deorum providentia [effec-
tum][63] et venditori et emptori quem uterque merebatur
exitum attribuit: avaro enim [et][64] fame consumpto manubiis sordium suarum frui non licuit, aequi animi vir ad salutarem impensam faciendam, care quidem verum necessa-
rie comparato cibo, vixit.

4   C. autem Mario Cn. Carbone consulibus civili bello
cum L. Sulla dissidentibus, quo tempore non rei publicae
victoria quaerebatur sed praemium victoriae res erat publica, senatus consulto aurea atque argentea templorum
ornamenta, ne militibus stipendia deessent, conflata sunt:
digna enim causa erat, hinc an illi crudelitatem suam proscriptione civium satiarent, ut di immortales spoliarentur!

[61] Capuae *SB*[1]: Campanae AL
[62] incolarum *Foertsch*: moderarum* AL
[63] *del.* A *corr.*
[64] *om.* ⌐

[5] 216: Livy 23.19.13.   [6] 216: as part of the garrison.
[7] Strabo 249, Pliny *N.H.* 8.222, [Front.] *Strat.* 4.5.20; cf. Livy

shields and chew them macerated in boiling water.[5] What unhappy folk if you consider the cruelty of their plight, what faithful folk if you look at their steadfastness! Such food did they bring themselves to eat rather than defect from Rome while they looked at their fat fields and fertile plains spread out below their walls! So Casilinum, illustrious by the courage of her inhabitants, scourged with the pledge of steadfast friendship the impious eyes of her neighbour Capua, that eagerly pampered Punic savagery with her luxuries.

Three hundred men of Praeneste held fast[6] in that siege and that fidelity. It happened that one of them captured a rat and preferred to sell it for two hundred denarii rather than consume it himself to assuage his hunger. But divine providence, I think, gave both seller and buyer the outcome they deserved. The money-grubber perished of starvation and so could not enjoy the spoils of his avarice; whereas he who resigned himself to a salutary expense lived by the food he had procured, at a high price to be sure, but of necessity.[7]

When Consuls C. Marius[8] and Cn. Carbo were contending with L. Sulla in civil war, a war not fought for the victory of the commonwealth but with the commonwealth as victory's reward, gold and silver temple ornaments were melted down by decree of the senate to provide pay for the troops. To be sure it was a worthy cause to despoil the immortal gods: for one side or the other to glut their cruelty by proscription of their fellow countrymen! It was not the

23.19.13–17. Strabo's text has a medimnus (bushel and a half) of corn instead of the rat, but Livy supports the latter.

   [8] The younger, in 82. The decree is not recorded elsewhere.

non ergo patrum conscriptorum voluntas sed taeterrimae necessitatis truculenta manus illi consulto stilum suum impressit.

5 Divi Iulii exercitus, id est invicti ducis invicta dextera, cum armis Mundam clausisset aggerique exstruendo materia deficeretur, congerie hostilium cadaverum quam desideraverat altitudinem instruxit, eamque tragulis et pilis, quia roboreae sudes deerant, magistra novae molitionis necessitate usus, vallavit.

6 Atque ut divi iam[65] filii mentionem caelesti patris recordationi subnectam, cum effusurus se in nostras provincias Parthorum rex Phraates videretur, vicinaeque imperio eius regiones subito indicti tumultus denuntiatione quaterentur, tanta in Bosporano tractu commeatus penuria incessit uti sex milibus denariis singula vasa olei, frumentique modiis totidem mancipia permutarentur. sed amarissimam tempestatem Augusti cura, tutelae tunc terrarum vacans, dispulit.

ext. 1 Cretensibus nihil tale praesidii adfulsit, qui, obsidione Metelli ad ultimam penuriam compulsi, sua iumentorumque suorum urina sitim torserunt iustius dixerim quam sustentarunt, quia dum vinci timent, id passi sunt quod eos ne victor quidem pati coegisset.

ext. 2 Numantini autem, a Scipione vallo et aggere circumdati cum omnia quae famem eorum trahere poterant

[65] divi iam *Per.*: divinam AL

9 45: *Bell. Hisp.* 32.1 etc.
10 IV, reigned 38/37–2 B.C. No further information.
11 The Crimea: a long way from Parthia; but the Bosporan

will of the Conscript Fathers, therefore, that pressed its pen on that decree but the savage hand of an appalling necessity.

When the divine Julius' army, that is, the unconquered right hand of the unconquered general, had invested Munda with arms and ran short of timber to construct a rampart, they built one to the desired height with a mass of enemy corpses and palisaded it with spears and javelins for lack of wooden stakes, using necessity to teach them a new construction technique.[9]

And to follow up recollection of the celestial father with mention of the divine son, when Phraates,[10] king of the Parthians, seemed about to let himself loose upon our provinces, and the regions close to his empire were shaken by the suddenly declared threat of a tumult, such a dearth of provisions ensued in the Bosporan area[11] that a flask of oil sold for six thousand denarii and slaves were exchanged for pecks of grain one for one. But the care of Augustus, which then had time to spare for the wardship of earth, dispelled the grievous crisis.

EXTERNAL

No such light of protection shone for the Cretans. Driven to extremity of want by Metellus' siege, they tortured (a more fitting word than "slaked") their thirst with their own urine and that of their pack animals; for fearing to be vanquished, they suffered a thing that even a victor would not have made them suffer.[12]

Encircled by Scipio with palisade and mound, the Numantines consumed everything that could prolong

kingdom was the main source of food supplies for northern Asia Minor and the Aegean area.   [12] 67: not found elsewhere.

consumpsissent, ad ultimum humanorum corporum dapibus usi sunt. quapropter capta iam urbe complures inventi sunt artus et membra trucidatorum corporum sinu suo gestantes. nulla est in his necessitatis excusatio: nam quibus mori licuit, sic vivere necesse non fuit.

ext. 3   Horum trucem pertinaciam in consimili facinore Calagurritanorum exsecrabilis impietas supergressa est. qui quo perseverantius interempti Sertorii cineribus, obsidionem Cn. Pompeii frustrantes, fidem praestarent, quia nullum iam aliud in urbe eorum supererat animal, uxores suas natosque ad usum nefariae dapis verterunt: quoque diutius armata iuventus viscera sua visceribus suis aleret, infelices cadaverum reliquias sallire non dubitavit. en quam aliquis in acie hortaretur ut pro salute coniugum et liberorum fortiter dimicaret! ex hoc nimirum hoste tanto duci poena magis quam victoria petenda fuit, quia plus vindicatus gravitatis[66] quam victus gloriae adferre potuit, cum omne serpentum ac ferarum genus comparatione sui titulo feritatis superarit: nam quae illis dulcia vitae pignora proprio spiritu cariora sunt, ea Calagurritanis prandia atque cenae exstiterunt.

7. DE TESTAMENTIS QUAE ⟨RE⟩SCISSA[67] SUNT

praef.   Vacemus nunc negotio quod actorum hominis et praecipuae curae et ultimi est temporis, consideremusque

---

[66] gravitatis *SB*[1]: libertatis* AL: *del. Per.*   [67] *add.* G *corr.*

---

13 133: App. *Ib.* 96, Flor. 1.34.14.   14 72/71: Sall. *Hist.* 3.86f. Maurenbrecher, Juv. 15.93f., Oros. 5.23.14.

their hunger until finally they fed on the flesh of human bodies. For that reason when the city was captured many were found carrying in their garments the limbs and members of slaughtered bodies. Here necessity is no excuse. For people who were free to die, it was not necessary to live thus.[13]

Their savage obstinacy was surpassed by the detestable impiety of the people of Calagurris in a similar crime. The more obstinately to keep their word to the ashes of the slain Sertorius in frustration of Cn. Pompeius' siege, since there was no longer any other living thing left in the town, they turned their wives and children to use in a nefarious meal; and the longer to nourish flesh with flesh, both their own, the armed warriors did not scruple to salt the hapless remnants of the corpses.[14] A fine set for somebody to exhort in battle to fight bravely for their wives and families! Surely so great a general should have sought retribution rather than victory against these enemies, since their punishment could bring him more respect than their conquest could bring him glory, for they outdid in savagery every species of reptile and wild beast you might compare them with. To those creatures the sweet pledges of life are more dear than their own breath; to the men of Calagurris they became lunch and dinner.

7. OF WILLS THAT WERE RESCINDED

Now let us spare time for a business which among a man's activities claims special care and his final hours, and

quae testamenta aut rescissa sunt legitime facta, aut cum
merito rescindi possent, rata manserunt, quaeve ad alios
quam qui exspectabant honorem hereditatis transtulerunt:
atque ita ut ea ordine quo proposui exsequar.

1   Militantis cuiusdam pater, cum de morte filii falsum e
castris nuntium accepisset, [qui erat falsus][68] aliis heredibus scriptis decessit. peractis deinde stipendiis adulescens
domum petiit. errore patris, impudentia amicorum[69] domum sibi clausam repperit: quid enim illis inverecundius?
florem iuventae pro re publica absumpserat, maximos
labores ac plurima pericula toleraverat, adverso corpore
exceptas ostendebat cicatrices: et postulaba<n >t[70] ut avitos
eius lares otiosa ipsi urbi onera possiderent. itaque depositis armis coactus est in foro togatam ingredi militiam
[acerve]:[71] cum improbissimis enim heredibus de paternis
bonis apud centumviros contendit. omnibusque non solum consiliis sed etiam sententiis superior discessit.

2   Item M. Anneii Carseolani, splendidissimi equitis
Romani, filius, a Sufenate avunculo suo adoptatus, testamentum naturalis patris, quo praeteritus erat, apud centumviros rescidit, cum in eo Tullianus, Pompeii Magni
familiaris, ipso quidem Pompeio signatore heres scriptus
esset. itaque illi in iudicio plus cum excellentissimi viri
gratia quam cum parentis cineribus negotii fuit. ceterum

68 *del.* A *corr.*; Br
69 amicorum *intra cruces Briscoe*
70 *add. Halm*
71 acerbe A *corr.*, L *corr.*, G: *del.* SB[1]

1 Cic. *De orat.* 1.175 (the wording *illius militis* shows that the
case was well known). Pliny the younger (*Ep.* 6.33.5) pleaded a

consider wills: wills which lawfully made were rescinded, or which, when they might properly have been rescinded, remained valid, or which transferred the honour of inheritance to others than those who were expecting it. I shall proceed in the order stated.

The father of a serving soldier received from the army a false report of his son's death and died after naming other heirs in his will. Then the young man finished his years of service and came home. He found the house closed to him by his father's error and the effrontery of their friends. For what could be more brazen than they? He had spent the flower of his youth on behalf of the commonwealth, had endured great fatigues and many dangers, showed scars received in the front of his body: and they, idle burdens upon the city, demanded possession of his ancestral home. So, weapons laid down, he was obliged to embark on a civilian campaign in the Forum, for he contended with the unscrupulous heirs about his father's estate in the Court of a Hundred; and he left the winner, not only by all the juries but by all the votes.[1]

Likewise the son of M. Anneius of Carseoli, a distinguished Roman knight, who had been adopted by his uncle Sufenas, got the will of his natural father, in which he had been passed over, rescinded in the Court of a Hundred, although Tullianus, a close friend of Pompeius Magnus, had been named heir in it, with Pompey himself as witness. So in the trial he had more trouble with the influence of a pre-eminent individual than with his parent's ashes. But al-

---

case before the Court of a Hundred in which four juries voted separately (*duobus consiliis vicimus, totidem victi sumus*), but little is known about the procedure.

quamvis utraque haec adversus nitebantur, tamen paterna
bona obtinuit: nam L. quidem Sextilius et P. Popillius, quos
M. Anneius sanguine sibi coniunctos eadem ex parte qua
Tullianum heredes fecerat, sacramento cum adulescentulo contendere ausi non sunt, tametsi praecipuis eo tempore Magni viribus ad defendendas tabulas testamenti
invitari poterant et aliquantum adiuvabat heredes quod
M. Anneius in Sufenatis familiam ac sacra transierat. sed
artissimum inter homines procreationis vinculum patris
simul voluntatem et principis auctoritatem superavit.

3   C. autem Tettium a patre infantem exheredatum,
Petronia matre, quam Tettius, quoad vixit, in matrimonio
habuerat, natum, divus Augustus in bona paterna ire decreto suo iussit, patris patriae animo usus, quoniam Tettius
in proprio iure[72] procreato filio summa cum iniquitate
paternum nomen abrogaverat.

4   Septicia quoque, mater Trachalorum Ariminensium,
irata filiis, in contumeliam eorum, cum iam parere non
posset, Publicio seni admodum nupsit, testamento etiam
utrumque[73] praeteriit.[74] a quibus aditus divus Augustus et
nuptias mulieris et suprema iudicia improbavit: nam hereditatem maternam filios habere iussit, dotem, quia non
creandorum liberorum causa coniugium intercesserat, vi-

---

[72] iure A *corr.,* LG: lare *Madvig*   [73] utrumque LGP:
utroque A *corr.*   [74] praeteriit P: -rito A *corr.,* LG

---

[2] This and the following five items are not on record elsewhere.

[3] Briscoe reads *lare* (Madvig) for *iure,* but a son begotten in
the father's home is not necessarily legitimate. I suspect that *in
proprio iure* is a legal phrase (otherwise why not *suo*?), meaning

though both strove against him, he nonetheless obtained his father's goods. As for L. Sextilius and P. Popillius, blood relations of M. Anneius whom he had made his heirs equally with Tullianus, they did not dare to contend with the young man by oath, although Magnus' paramount power at that time might have invited them to defend the will, and the heirs were somewhat helped by M. Anneius' transition into the family and family rites of Sufenas. But the bond of procreation, the most binding between human beings, overbore a father's wishes and a great man's authority at the same time.[2]

C. Tettius was disinherited in infancy by his father, who had taken his mother Petronia in wedlock during her lifetime. The divine Augustus ordered him by his personal fiat to take possession of his father's goods, acting in the spirit of the Fatherland's father. For it was quite unjust of Tettius to cancel his name of father in the case of a son whom he had begotten as of personal right.[3]

Septicia too, mother of the Trachali of Ariminum,[4] got angry with her sons and to insult them, being no longer capable of bearing children, she married Publicius, quite an old man, and also left both of them out of her will. They approached the divine Augustus, who reprobated both the woman's marriage and her last dispositions. For he gave the sons possession of their mother's inheritance and forbade the husband to keep her dowry, since the marriage had not been for the purpose of procreating children. If

that the author of an action was exclusively entitled to perform it.

4 Festus (504 L) mentions the Trachali of Ariminum, *maritimi homines,* with cognomen from Τράχηλος ('neck') meaning the upper part of dye-bearing shellfish.

175

rum retinere vetuit. si ipsa Aequitas hac de re cognosceret, potuitne iustius aut gravius pronuntiare? spernis quos genuisti, nubis effeta, testamenti ordinem malevolo[75] animo confundis, neque erubescis ei totum patrimonium addicere cuius pollincto iam corpori marcidam senectutem tuam substravisti. ergo dum sic te geris, ad inferos usque caelesti fulmine adflata es.

5   Egregia C. quoque Calpurnii Pisonis praetoris urbani constitutio: cum enim ad eum Terentius ex octo filiis, quos in adulescentiam perduxerat, ab uno in adoptionem dato exheredatum se querellam detulisset, bonorum adulescentis possessionem ei dedit, heredesque lege agere passus non est. movit profecto Pisonem patria maiestas, donum vitae, beneficium educationis, sed aliquid etiam flexit circumstantium liberorum numerus, quia cum patre septem fratres impie exheredatos videbat.

6   Quid? Mamerci Aemilii Lepidi consulis quam grave decretum! Genucius quidam, Matris Magnae Gallus, a Cn. Oreste praetore urbano impetraverat ut restitui se in bona Naevii Ani[76] iuberet, quorum possessionem secundum tabulas testamenti ab ipso acceperat. appellatus Mamercus a Surdino, cuius libertus Genucium heredem fecerat, praetoriam iurisdictionem abrogavit, quod diceret Genucium amputatis sua[77] ipsius sponte genitalibus corporis partibus neque virorum neque mulierum numero haberi debere.

---

[75] malevolo *Watt*[3]: violento AL
[76] Naevii Anii A *corr.*: Naeviani AL
[77] sua *Heraeus*: sui AL

Equity herself had taken cognizance of this matter, could she have given a juster or weightier decision? You spurn those to whom you gave birth, sterile you marry, you confound testamentary order by your malevolence, and you are not ashamed to assign your whole estate to the man beneath whose body, already laid out for burial, you spread your withered senility. So thus conducting yourself, even down in the underworld you were blasted by a celestial thunderbolt.

Excellent too was the ruling of City Praetor[5] C. Calpurnius Piso. Terentius made complaint to him that of eight sons whom he had raised to young manhood one, whom he had given in adoption, had disinherited him. Piso gave him possession of the estate and would not allow the heirs to go to law. No doubt Piso was influenced by paternal majesty, the gift of life, the benefaction of an upbringing, but also the number of the surrounding children swayed him to some extent, the seven brothers whom he saw impiously disinherited along with their father.

And now, how weighty the judgment of Consul[6] Mamercus Aemilius Lepidus! A certain Genucius, a eunuch priest of the Great Mother, had obtained an order from City Praetor Cn. Orestes restoring to him the property of Naevius Anus, of which he had received possession from the Praetor himself according to the will. Surdinus, whose freedman had made Genucius his heir, appealed to Mamercus, who cancelled the Praetor's ruling, saying that Genucius, whose genital parts had been amputated by his own choice, should not be reckoned among either men or

conveniens Mamerco, conveniens principi senatus decretum, quo provisum est ne obscena Genucii praesentia
inquinataque voce tribunalia magistratuum sub specie
petiti iuris polluerentur.

7   Multo Q. Metellus praetorem urbanum severiorem
egit quam Orestes gesserat. qui Vecilio lenoni, bonorum
Vibieni possessionem secundum tabulas testamenti ‹pe-
tenti›,[78] non dedit, quia vir nobilissimus et gravissimus
fori ac lupanaris separandam condicionem existimavit,
nec aut factum illius comprobare voluit, qui fortunas suas
in stabulum contaminatum proiecerat aut huic tamquam
integro civi iura reddere, qui se ab omni honesto vitae
genere abruperat.

8. QUAE RATA MANSERUNT CUM
CAUSAS HABERENT CUR
RESCINDI POSSENT

praef.   His rescissorum testamentorum exemplis contenti, attingamus ea quae rata manserunt, cum causas haberent
propter quas rescindi possent.

1   Quam certae, quam etiam notae insaniae Tuditanus!
utpote qui populo nummos sparserit, togamque velut tra-
gicam vestem in foro trahens maximo cum hominum risu

[78] *add.* P

---

[7] Archaic form of Marcus, redolent of old-time manners, perhaps assumed by himself.

[8] Probably Creticus, Consul in 69, Praetor in 74 or a year or
two later (cf. Broughton II.108 n.3).

women. A judgment appropriate to a Mamercus,[7] appropriate to a Leader of the Senate; it provided that magistrates' tribunals should not be defiled by Genucius' obscene presence and tainted voice under the pretext of seeking justice.

Q. Metellus[8] took his function of City Praetor much more stringently than Orestes had done. He refused to grant Vecilius the pimp possession of Vibienus' estate as claimed under his will. A gentleman of the highest birth and repute, Metellus considered that the status of Forum and brothel should be kept separate. He was unwilling to approve the act of a man who had cast his wealth into a filthy whorehouse or to render judgment to one who had broken away from every respectable kind of life as though to a citizen in good standing.

8. OF THOSE THAT REMAINED VALID, THOUGH WITH REASONS FOR WHICH THEY MIGHT HAVE BEEN RESCINDED

Content with these examples of wills rescinded, let us touch upon those that remained valid, though having reasons for which they might have been rescinded.

How certain, how notorious even, was the insanity of Tuditanus![1] He scattered coins among the people, he trailed his gown like a tragic robe in the Forum amid the

---

[1] Cf. Cic. *Acad.* 2.89, *Phil.* 3.16. He will have died in the first quarter of the first century, leaving a daughter, mother of the famous Fulvia, and so far as is known, no son. That in itself should protect *filiam* in a context of legal and other uncertainties.

conspectus fuerit, ac multa his consentanea fecerit. testamento filiam[79] instituit heredem, quod Ti. Longus sanguine ei proximus hastae iudicio subvertere frustra conatus est: magis enim centumviri quid scriptum esset in tabulis quam quis eas scripsisset considerandum existimaverunt.

2   Vita Tuditani demens, Aebutiae autem, quae L. Menenii Agrippae uxor fuerat, tabulae testamenti plenae furoris: nam cum haberet duas simillimae probitatis filias, Plaetoriam et Afroniam, animi sui potius inclinatione provecta quam ullis alter‹ut›rius[80] iniuriis aut officiis commota, Plaetoriam tantummodo heredem instituit; filiis etiam Afroniae ex admodum amplo patrimonio viginti milia nummum legavit. Afronia tamen cum sorore sacramento contendere noluit, testamentumque matris patientia honorare quam iudicio convellere satius esse duxit, eo se ipso indigniorem iniuria ostendens quo eam aequiore animo sustinebat.

3   Minus mirandum errorem muliebrem Q. Metellus fecit: is namque, plurimis et celeberrimis eiusdem nominis viris in urbe nostra vigentibus, Claudiorum etiam familia, quam artissimo sanguinis vinculo contingebat, florente, Carrinatem solum heredem reliquit, nec hac re testamentum eius quisquam attemptavit.

4   Item Pompeius Reginus, vir transalpinae regionis, cum testamento fratris praeteritus esset et ad coarguendam ini-

---

---

2 Nepos, Consul in 57, died a few years later.

guffaws of onlookers, he committed many similar extravagances. By his will he made his daughter his heir, which Ti. Longus, his nearest of kin, tried unsuccessfully to cancel in the Court of a Hundred. For the Hundred thought that what was written in the will ought to be considered rather than who wrote it.

Tuditanus' life was crazy; Aebutia's will (she had been the wife of L. Menenius Agrippa) was full of insanity. She had two daughters, Pletonia and Afronia, of equally blameless character. Induced by personal inclination rather than swayed by any injuries or good offices of one or the other, she made Pletonia her only heir, also leaving 20,000 sesterces from a very large estate as a legacy to Afronia's children. Afronia, however, chose not to go to law with her sister and thought it better to honour her mother's will with patience rather than to overturn it in court. By bearing the injury with resignation she showed herself all the more undeserving of it.

Q. Metellus[2] made a feminine aberration less surprising. Many very well-known men of the same name were flourishing in our city and the family of the Claudii too, with which he was connected by a close tie of blood,[3] was thriving, but he left Carrinas[4] his sole heir. And no one challenged his will on that account.

Likewise Pompeius Reginus, a man of the Transalpine country, was passed over in his brother's will. To expose the

---

[3] P. Clodius Pulcher and his brothers were half-brothers of this Metellus. Prominent Metelli when Nepos died were Scipio, Consul in 52, and Creticus, if he was still alive which is doubtful, neither closely related to him.

[4] Son of a proscribed Marian, probably Consul Suffect in 43.

quitatem eius binas tabulas testamentorum suorum in co-
mitio incisas, adhibita[81] utriusque ordinis maxima fre-
quentia, recitasset, in quibus magna ex parte heres frater
erat scriptus, praelegabaturque ei centies et quinquagies sestertium, multum ac diu inter adsentientes indig-
nationi suae amicos questus, quod ad hastae iudicium attinuit, cineres fratris quietos esse passus est. et erant ab eo
instituti heredes neque sanguine Regino pares neque
proximi, sed alieni et humiles, ut non solum flagitiosum silentium sed etiam praelatio contumeliosa videri posset.

5   Aeque felicis impunitatis sed nescio an taetrioris haec
delicti testamenta.

QUAE ADVERSUS OPINIONES HOMINUM
HEREDES HABUERUNT

Q. Caecilius, L. Luculli promptissimo studio maxi-
maque liberalitate et honestum dignitatis gradum et amplissimum patrimonium consecutus, cum prae se semper
tulisset unum illum sibi esse heredem, moriens etiam anulos ei suos tradidisset, Pomponium Atticum testamento
adoptavit omniumque bonorum ‹heredem›[82] reliquit. sed
fallacis et insidiosi cadaver populus Romanus, cervicibus
reste circumdatis,[83] per vias traxit. itaque nefarius homo
filium quidem et heredem habuit quem voluit, funus
autem et exsequias quales meruit.

[81] adhibita *Cornelissen*: hab- AL
[82] *hic* G, *post* reliquit A *corr.*: *om.* AL
[83] circumdatis *Gertz*: -tum AL

latter's injustice, he unsealed the two tablets of his own will in the place of assembly and read them aloud before a large gathering of both orders; in them his brother was named heir in large part and further bequeathed fifteen million sesterces. He complained much and long among friends who sympathized with his indignation, but as for carrying the case to the Court of a Hundred, he let his brother's ashes rest in peace. Moreover, the heirs appointed by his brother were neither related as nearly as Reginus nor next after him, but outsiders of humble status, so that not only might his silence seem outrageous but his preference insulting.[5]

The following wills were equally lucky in their immunity, but perhaps more shockingly immoral.

THOSE THAT HAD HEIRS CONTRARY
TO GENERAL EXPECTATION

Q. Caecilius had attained a respectable status and ample wealth by the ready patronage and unstinted generosity of L. Lucullus. He had always given out that Lucullus was his sole heir and on his deathbed gave him his signet rings. In his will, however, he adopted Pomponius Atticus and left him heir to all he possessed. But the Roman people put a rope round the neck of the treacherous deceiver and dragged his corpse through the streets. So the villain had the son and heir he wanted, but funeral obsequies such as he deserved.[6]

---

[5] Nothing else known.

[6] 58: cf. Nep. *Att.* 5f., who calls him a friend of Lucullus, but says nothing about any scandal; neither is there any hint of it in Cicero's letter of congratulation to Atticus (*Att.* 3.10). Valerius' story looks like exaggeration if not fiction.

6   Neque aliis dignus fuit T. Marius Urbinas, qui ab infimo militiae loco beneficiis divi Augusti imperatoris ad summos castrenses honores perductus eorumque uberrimis quaestibus locuples factus, non solum ceteris vitae temporibus ei se fortunas suas relinquere a quo acceperat praedicavit, sed etiam pridie quam exspiraret idem istud ipsi Augusto dixit, cum interim ne nomen quidem eius tabulis testamenti adiecit.

7   L. autem Valerius, cui cognomen Heptachordo fuit, togatum hostem Cornelium Balbum expertus, utpote ope⟨ra⟩ eius et consilio compluribus privatis litibus vexatus, ad ultimumque subiecto accusatore capitali crimine accusatus, praeteritis advocatis et patronis suis solum heredem reliquit. nimirum consternatio quae⟨dam⟩[84] animum eius transversum egit: amavit enim sordes suas et dilexit pericula et damnationem votis expetivit, auctorem harum rerum benivolentia, propulsatores[85] odio insecutus.

8   T. Barrus Lentulo Spintheri, cuius amantissimum animum liberalissimamque amicitiam senserat, decedens anulos suos perinde atque unico heredi tradidit, quem nulla ex parte heredem relinquebat. quantum illo momento temporis conscientia, si modo vires quas habere creditur possidet, a taeterrimo homine supplicium exegit! inter ip-

---

[84] *add.* * *Madvig*
[85] -res *Pighius*: -rum AL: -rem A *corr.,* G

---

[7] Not found elsewhere.

[8] The surname Heptachordus is otherwise unknown, but this Valerius is identified by Münzer (*RE* IV.1262f., VIII A 35f.) with

Nor did T. Marius of Urbinum deserve better. From the lowest rank in the army he was raised by the favour of the divine Augustus as Commander in Chief to the highest military posts and became rich with the abundant profits they yielded. Not only did he at other times of his life give out that he was leaving his wealth to the one from whom he had received it, but the day before he died he told Augustus himself the same thing. And all the while he did not even put Augustus' name in his will.[7]

L. Valerius surnamed Heptachordus found himself at civilian war with Cornelius Balbus, by whose agency and devices he was harassed with a number of private lawsuits and finally accused of a capital offence by a prosecutor whom Balbus had put up. Yet he left Balbus his sole heir, passing over his supporters and advocates. Surely some confusion drove his mind off track. For he loved his garb of woe and delighted in his perils and prayed to be found guilty, pursuing the instigator of these things with good will and their rebutters with hatred.[8]

T. Barrus on his death bed gave his rings to Lentulus Spinther,[9] whom he had found a very affectionate and generous friend, as if to his sole heir. But he was leaving him heir to nothing. At that moment of time what a retribution did his conscience exact from the foul wretch, if conscience possesses the power ascribed to it! For he

L. Valerius Flaccus, defended by Cicero in 59; Briscoe (index) agrees. A L. Balbus was assistant prosecutor (Schol. Bob. 93 Stahl). This may well be right, but one must not forget L. Herennius Balbus, who appeared against Cicero as assistant-prosecutor of Caelius Rufus.

[9] Consul in 57. Nothing else is known of this or the next item.

sam enim fallacis et ingratae culpae cogitationem spiritum posuit, quasi tortore aliquo mentem eius intus cruciante, quod animadvertebat e vita ad mortem transitum suum et superis dis invisum esse et inferis detestabilem futurum.

9   M. vero Popillius senatorii ordinis Oppium Gallum, ab ineunte aetate familiarissimum sibi, moriens pro vetusto iure amicitiae et vultu benigno respexit et verbis magnum prae se amorem ferentibus prosecutus est, unum etiam de multis qui adsidebant ultimo complexu et osculo dignum iudicavit; super quae[86] anulos quoque suos ei tradidit, videlicet ne quid ex ea hereditate quam non erat aditurus amitteret. quos Oppius, vir ⟨suorum⟩[87] diligens sed morientis amici plenum contumeliae ludibrium, in locellum repositos et a praesentibus adsignatos diligentissime heredibus illius exheres ipse reddidit. quid hoc ioco[88] inhonestius aut quid intempestivius? senator populi Romani curia egressus, homo vitae fructibus continuo cariturus, sanctissima iura familiaritatis, morte pressis oculis et spiritu supremos anhelitus reddente, scurrili lusu suggillanda sibi desumpsit.

[86] super quae G: superque A: suque L: insuperque *Aldus*
[87] *add.* SB[3]
[88] ioco *Lipsius*: loco AL

breathed his last just as he was meditating upon his wicked deceit and ingratitude. It was like a torturer tormenting his mind within, as he saw that his passage from life to death was hateful to the gods above and would be detestable to those below.

M. Popillius, a man of senatorial rank, had a close friend from boyhood, Oppius Gallus. While he lay dying, as befitted their longstanding bond of amity, he looked at Gallus lovingly and spoke to him in words evincive of great affection. Of many who were present he judged Gallus alone worthy of his last embrace and kiss. Furthermore, he gave Gallus his rings, presumably to make sure he lost nothing of that inheritance which he was not about to receive. Gallus, one who loved those close to him but the object of his dying friend's contumelious mockery, put them in a purse, had them sealed by those present, and gave them with all care to Popillius' heirs, of whom he was not one. A most shabby and untimely jest! A senator of the Roman people, just out of the senate house, a man presently to lose life's enjoyments, chose the sacred ties of friendship as something to abuse with a scurrilous jape, even as death weighed upon his eyelids and his breath gave its final gasps.

LIBER OCTAVUS

1. INFAMES REI QUIBUS DE CAUSIS
ABSOLUTI AUT DAMNATI SINT

praef.   Nunc, quo aequiore animo ancipites iudiciorum motus
tolerentur, recordemur invidia laborantes pro quibus causis aut absoluti sint aut damnati.

absol. 1   M. Horatius, interfectae sororis crimine a Tullo rege
damnatus, ad populum provocato iudicio absolutus est.
quorum alterum atrocitas necis movit, alterum causa
flexit, quia immaturum virginis amorem severe magis
quam impie punitum existimabat. itaque forti<s facti>[1]
punitione liberata fratris dextera tantum consanguineo
quantum hostili cruore gloriae haurire potuit.

absol. 2   Acrem se tunc pudicitiae custodem populus Romanus,
postea plus iusto placidum iudicem praestitit. cum a
Libone tribuno plebis Ser. Galba pro rostris vehementer
increparetur, quod Lusitanorum magnam manum interposita fide praetor in Hispania interemisset, actionique
tribuniciae M. Cato ultimae senectutis oratione sua, quam

<hr>

[1] *add.* SB[3]

<hr>

[1] See VM 6.3.6.

BOOK VIII

1. FOR WHAT REASONS ILL-FAMED DEFENDANTS WERE ACQUITTED OR CONDEMNED

Now, so that the uncertain operations of trials may be borne with equanimity, let us record for what reasons persons labouring under unpopularity were either acquitted or condemned.

ACQUITTED

M. Horatius was convicted of his sister's murder by king Tullus, but appealed to the people for trial and was acquitted. The king was moved by the atrocity of the killing; the people were swayed by the reason for it, reckoning that the girl's precocious passion had been punished severely rather than impiously. So the brother's right hand, freed of punishment for its brave deed, could draw as much glory from kindred as from enemy blood.[1]

The Roman people showed itself on that occasion a fierce guardian of chastity, but later on an unduly lenient judge. Ser. Galba was vehemently attacked from the rostra by Tribune of the Plebs Libo for killing as Praetor in Spain a large body of Lusitanians with whom he had made a treaty, and M. Cato supported the Tribune's proceeding in

in Origines rettulit, subscriberet, reus, pro se iam nihil recusans, parvulos liberos suos et Gali[2] sanguine sibi coniunctum filium flens commendare coepit, eoque facto mitigata contione qui omnium consensu periturus erat paene nullum triste suffragium habuit. misericordia ergo illam quaestionem, non aequitas rexit, quoniam quae innocentiae tribui nequierat absolutio, respectui puerorum data est.

absol. 3   Consentaneum quod sequitur. A. Gabinius in maximo infamiae suae ardore suffragiis populi ⟨C.⟩[3] Memmio accusatore subiectus, abruptae esse spei videbatur, quoniam et accusatio partes suas plene exhibebat et defensionis praesidia invalida fide nitebantur et qui iudicabant ira praecipiti[4] poenam hominis cupide expetebant. igitur viator et carcer ante oculos obversabantur, cum interim omnia ista propitiae Fortunae interventu dispulsa sunt: filius namque Gabinii Sisenna consternationis impulsu ad pedes se Memmii supplex prostravit, inde aliquod fomentum procellae petens unde totus impetus tempestatis eruperat. quem truci vultu a se victor insolens repulsum, excusso e manu anulo, humi iacere aliquamdiu passus est. quod spectaculum fecit ut Laelius tribunus plebis approbantibus cunctis Gabinium dimitti iuberet, ac documentum daretur neque secundarum rerum proventu insolenter abuti neque adversis ⟨prae⟩propere[5] debilitari oportere:

2 Gali *Briscoe*: Galli AL: C. Galli *Halm*
3 *add.* P
4 praecipiti A *corr.*, L. *corr.*, G: perc- AL: perciti Ϛ
5 *add. Halm*

a speech of his extreme old age which he put into his *Origins*. The accused declared his readiness to accept any punishment for himself, but began to commend with tears his little children and Galus' son, who was his blood relation. By so doing he softened the hearts of the assembly and, doomed as he had been by universal consent, he received hardly a single vote of guilty. So pity, not justice, governed that trial, since the acquittal which could not have been vouchsafed to innocence was granted to compassion for the boys.[2]

What follows is in like vein. A. Gabinius was in a mighty blaze of infamy when he was subjected to the votes of the people, C. Memmius prosecuting. His case was thought hopeless, for the prosecution was amply fulfilling its role, the support on which the defence counted[3] was untrustworthy, and the jury in hasty anger was eager for the man's punishment. So constable and prison loomed before his eyes, when all such presentiments were dispelled by an intervention of propitious Fortune. For Gabinius' son Sisenna[4] in an impulse of distraction threw himself as a suppliant at Memmius' feet, seeking some alleviation of the storm in the quarter from which its entire fury had broken. The insolent victor repulsed him with a grim look and let him lie on the ground for some time—even his ring was shaken off his hand. The spectacle caused Tribune of the Plebs Laelius to order amid general approval that Gabinius be discharged—a lesson not to abuse insolently a harvest of success or to be prematurely enfeebled by its

---

[2] 149: Cic. *Brut.* 80 and 89 etc. (Münzer *RE* IV A. 762–63).

[3] I.e. Pompey.

[4] A Cornelius (?) Sisenna adopted by Gabinius.

191

idque proximo exemplo aeque patet.

absol. 4   Ap. Claudius, nescio religionis maior an patriae iniuria, si quidem illius vetustissimum morem neglexit, huius pulcherrimam classem amisit, infesto populo obiectus, cum effugere debitam poenam nullo modo posse crederetur, subito coorti imbris beneficio tutus fuit a damnatione: discussa enim quaestione aliam velut dis interpellantibus de integro instaurari non placuit. ita cui maritima tempestas causae dictionem contraxerat, caelestis salutem attulit.

absol. 5   Eodem auxilii genere Tucciae virginis Vestalis, incesti criminis reae, castitas infamiae nube obscurata emersit. quae conscientia certa sinceritatis suae spem salutis ancipiti argumento ausa petere est: arrepto enim cribro 'Vesta' inquit, 'si sacris tuis castas semper admovi manus, effice ut hoc hauriam e Tiberi aquam et in aedem tuam perferam.' audaciter et temere iactis votis sacerdotis Rerum ipsa Natura cessit.

absol. 6   Item L. Piso a C.[6] Claudio Pulchro accusatus, quod graves et intolerabiles iniurias sociis intulisset, haud dubiae ruinae metum fortuito auxilio vitavit: namque per id ipsum tempus quo tristes de eo sententiae ferebantur, repentina vis nimbi incidit, cumque prostratus humi pedes iudicum oscularetur, os suum caeno replevit. quod

---

[6] C. *Briscoe*: L. AG: B. L

---

[5] 54: Gabinius was convicted on a charge of extortion, Cicero defending (Dio 46.8.1), and went into exile. Valerius' story seems to refer to a previous trial before the people (*iudicium populi*), not known from other sources: see E. Fantham in *Historia* 24 (1975).433f.   [6] A mistake for P., also found in later authors.

[7] 249: Livy *Per.* 19 etc.; cf. VM 1.4.3, 8.1.damn.4.

opposite.[5] And that is no less apparent from the next example.

Whether Ap.[6] Claudius was a greater affront to religion or to his country I know not, seeing that he neglected the time-honoured usage of the one and lost a splendid fleet of the other.[7] Exposed to a hostile public, it seemed as though he could not possibly escape the punishment he deserved, when he was saved from conviction thanks to a sudden rainstorm. For the proceedings were disrupted and it was decided not to repeat them afresh; the gods, it was felt, had intervened. A storm at sea had caused his trial, a storm from the sky brought him salvation.[8]

Through the same sort of aid, the chastity of the Vestal Virgin Tuccia, charged with impurity, emerged from an obscuring cloud of ill fame. In the certain knowledge of her innocence she dared to seek hope of salvation with an argument of doubtful issue. Seizing hold of a sieve, "Vesta," she said, "if I have always brought pure hands to your sacred service, make it so that with this I draw water from the Tiber and bring it to your temple." To the priestess' prayer thrown out boldly and rashly the Nature of Things gave way.[9]

Likewise L. Piso, prosecuted by C. Claudius Pulcher for the grievous and intolerable injuries he had inflicted on our allies, avoided the threat of certain ruin by fortuitous aid. For at the very moment when votes of guilty were being cast at his trial, a sudden storm of rain fell, and as he was prostrate on the ground kissing the jury's feet, he filled his mouth with mud. The sight turned the whole court

---

8 But see Münzer *RE* Claudius 304.
9 230 (?): Livy *Per.* 20 etc. (Broughton I.227).

conspectum totam quaestionem a severitate ad clemen-
tiam et mansuetudinem transtulit, quia satis iam graves
eum poenas sociis dedisse arbitrati sunt, huc deductum
necessitatis ut abicere se tam suppliciter et[7] attollere tam
deformiter cogeretur.

absol. 7 Subnectam duos accusatorum suorum culpa absolutos.
Q. Flavius a C. Valerio aedile apud populum reus actus,
cum quattuordecim tribuum suffragiis damnatus esset,
proclamavit se innocentem opprimi. cui Valerius aeque
clara voce respondit nihil sua interesse nocensne an
innoxius periret, dummodo periret. qua violentia dicti reli-
quas tribus adversario donavit. abiecerat inimicum, eundem, dum pro certo pessum datum credidit, erexit, victoriamque in ipsa victoria perdidit.

absol. 8 C. etiam Cosconium Servilia lege reum, propter plurima et evidentissima facinora sine ulla dubitatione nocentem, Valerii Valentini accusatoris eius recitatum in iudicio
carmen, quo puerum praetextatum et ingenuam virginem
a se corruptam poetico ioco significaverat, erexit, si quidem iudices iniquum rati sunt eum victorem dimittere qui
palmam non ex alio ferre, sed de se dare merebatur. magis
vero Valerius in Cosconii absolutione damnatus quam
Cosconius in sua causa liberatus est.

absol. 9 Attingam eos quoque quorum salus propriis obruta cri-

7 et *Foertsch*: aut AL

10 110 (?): Cic. *De orat.* 2.265. See SB *Onomasticon to Cicero's
Treatises* (Teubner, 1996), 21f.

11 Evidence indicates that the defendant was M. Flavius of
Livy 8.22.2–4, accused by Aediles of a sexual offence in 328 or

from severity to mercy and leniency, since they thought he had already paid our allies penalty enough, brought to the necessity of casting himself down in such supplication and picking himself up in such unseemliness.[10]

I shall add two persons acquitted through the fault of their accusers. Q. Flavius was brought to trial before the people by Aedile C. Valerius. Found guilty by the votes of fourteen tribes, he cried out that he was being condemned an innocent man. Valerius replied no less loudly that he did not care whether Flavius perished innocent or guilty so long as he perished. By the violence of that utterance he made his opponent a present of the remaining tribes.[11] He had cast his enemy down, but believing him ruined for certain he raised him up and lost victory in the very winning.

C. Cosconius was charged under the Servilian law, guilty beyond a doubt by reason of many fully evident criminal acts. He was put on his feet by a poem of his prosecutor Valerius Valentinus recited in court, in which by way of a literary joke Valerius had intimated that a boy under age and a free-born girl had been seduced by himself. The jury thought it improper to send away victorious a man who deserved not to win victory over somebody else but to yield the same over himself. However, Valerius was condemned in Cosconius' acquittal rather than Cosconius acquitted in his own case.[12]

I shall also touch upon persons overwhelmed by charges against themselves who owed their survival to the

slightly earlier, and the prosecuter C. Valerius Potitus, Consul in 331 (Münzer, *RE* Flavius 19).

[12] A Valerius Valentinus, author of a literary joke, was mentioned by Lucilius; cf. *RE* Valerius 372.

minibus proximorum claritati donata est. A. Atilium Calatinum, Soranorum oppidi proditione reum admodum infamem, imminentis damnationis periculo pauca verba Q. Maximi soceri subtraxerunt, quibus adfirmavit si in eo crimine sontem illum ipse comperisset, dirempturum se fuisse adfinitatem: continuo enim populus paene iam exploratam sententiam suam unius iudicio concessit, indignum ratus eius testimonio non credere cui difficillimis rei publicae temporibus bene se exercitus credidisse meminerat.

absol. 10   M. quoque Aemilius Scaurus, repetundarum reus, adeo perditam et comploratam defensionem in iudicium attulit ut, cum accusator diceret lege sibi centum atque viginti hominibus denuntiare testimonium licere, seque non recusare quominus absolveretur, si totidem nominasset quibus in provincia nihil abstulisset, tam bona condicione uti non potuerit. tamen propter vetustissimam nobilitatem et recentem memoriam patris absolutus est.

absol. 11   Sed quemadmodum splendor amplissimorum virorum in protegendis reis plurimum valuit, ita ‹in›[8] opprimendis non sane multum potuit; quin etiam evidenter noxiis, dum eos acrius impugnat, profuit. P. Scipio Aemilianus ‹L.›[9] Cottam apud populum accusavit. cuius causa, quamquam gravissimis criminibus erat confessa, septies ampliata et ad ultimum octavo iudicio absoluta est, quia

---

[8] *add.* A *corr.*   [9] *add. Pighius*

---

[13] Sora, a Latin colony, defected to the Samnites in 315 and was retaken by the Romans, then fell again to the Samnites in 306: Livy 9.23f. and 43.1, Diodor. 20.80 and 90. Q. Maximus will be Rullianus.

fame of their kin. A. Atilius Calatinus was on trial for the betrayal of the town of Sora (?).[13] He was very badly regarded, but a few words from his father-in-law Q. Maximus rescued him from the peril of imminent conviction. Maximus affirmed that if he himself had found Atilius to be guilty on that charge, he would have broken off their connection. The people at once surrendered their verdict, already almost cut and dried, to the judgment of one individual, thinking it wrong not to trust the testimony of a man to whom it remembered having entrusted its armies with good results at a time of the gravest national crisis.

M. Aemilius Scaurus too, on trial for extortion, brought an utterly hopeless defence into court. So much so that when the prosecutor said that under the law he could call one hundred and twenty witnesses and that he would not object to an acquittal if Scaurus named that number of persons in the province from whom he had taken nothing, Scaurus was unable to take advantage of so fair an offer. All the same he was acquitted because of his age-old nobility and the recent memory of his father.[14]

While the distinction of eminent men has counted heavily in protecting the accused, it has had no very great influence in convicting them. Indeed it has actually worked to the advantage of the evidently guilty by assaulting them too drastically. P. Scipio Aemilianus accused L. Cotta before the people. Although the latter's case was riddled with the gravest charges, it was adjourned seven times and finally at the eighth hearing he was acquitted, because

[14] 54: successfully defended by Cicero, but then convicted of electoral wrongdoing and went into exile (Cic. *Att.* 4.15.9 etc.).

197

homines verebantur ne praecipuae accusatoris amplitudini damnatio eius donata existimaretur. quos haec secum locutos crediderim: 'nolumus caput alterius petentem in iudicium triumphos et tropaea spoliaque et devictarum navium rostra deferre: terribilis sit ⟨h⟩is[10] adversus hostem, civis vero salutem tanto fragore gloriae subnixus ne insequatur.'

absol. 12   Tam vehementes iudices adversus excellentissimum accusatorem quam mites in longe inferioris fortunae reo. Calidius Bononiensis in cubiculo mariti noctu deprehensus, cum ob id causam adulterii diceret, inter maximos et gravissimos infamiae fluctus emersit, tamquam fragmentum naufragii leve admodum genus defensionis amplexus: adfirmavit enim se ob amorem pueri servi eo esse perductum. suspectus erat locus, suspectum tempus, suspecta matris familiae persona, suspecta etiam adulescentia ipsius, sed crimen libidinis confessio intemperantiae liberavit.

absol. 13   Remissioris hoc, illud aliquanto gravioris materiae exemplum. cum parricidii causam fratres C⟨l⟩oelii[11] dicerent, splendido Tarracinae loco nati, quorum pater T. C⟨l⟩oelius in cubiculo quiescens, filiis altero cubantibus lecto, erat interemptus, neque aut servus quisquam aut liber inveniretur ad quem suspicio caedis pertineret, hoc uno nomine absoluti sunt, quia iudicibus planum factum est illos aperto ostio inventos esse dormientes. somnus, innoxiae securitatis certissimus index, miseris opem tulit: iudicatum est enim Rerum Naturam non recipere ut occi-

[10] add. Gertz

[11] Cloelii ... Cloelius *Pighius* (*cf. SB*[4], *p. 14*): Caelii ... Coelius ALP

of a fear that a conviction might be thought to have been yielded to the exceptional prestige of his accuser.[15] I imagine people said to themselves: "We don't want somebody out for somebody else's blood bringing triumphs and trophies and spoils and beaks of vanquished ships into the courtroom. Let him be a terror with all this to an enemy of Rome, but not attack the life of a citizen in reliance on such a fanfare of glory."

As hostile as jurors were to a very eminent prosecutor, so merciful were they in the case of a defendant of far lesser degree. Calidius of Bononia was caught at night in a married man's bedroom and brought up on a charge of adultery. Struggling in the big rough breakers of ill fame, he emerged, clutching a pretty flimsy sort of defence like the fragment of a wreck; for he said he had been led there because of a passion for a boy slave. The place was suspicious, as was the time, as was the person of the wife, as too was his own early life, but the confession of incontinence cleared the charge of lust.[16]

That example was of lighter content, the following of considerably graver. The brothers Cloelii, born in a high station in Tarracina, were charged with parricide. Their father T. Cloelius had been killed when sleeping in his bedroom while his sons were lying in the other bed. Nobody either slave or free was found as a suspect to the murder. They were acquitted on one sole ground: it was made clear to the jury that when the door was opened they were found sleeping. Sleep, the surest sign of innocent security, came to the aid of the unfortunates. For the jury thought it

[15] *Ca.* 130: Cic. *Mur.* 58 etc.
[16] Not found elsewhere.

so patre supra vulnera et cruorem eius quietem capere potuerint.

damn. 1　　　Percurremus nunc eos quibus in causae dictione magis quae extra quaestionem erant nocuerunt quam sua innocentia opem tulit.

　　　L. Scipio post speciosissimum triumphum de rege Antiocho ductum, perinde ac pecuniam ab eo accepisset, damnatus est; non, puto, quod pretio corruptus fuerat ut illum totius Asiae dominum et iam Europae victrices manus inicientem ultra Taurum montem summoveret. sed <et>[12] alioqui vir sincerissimae vitae et ab hac suspicione procul remotus invidiae, quae tunc in duorum fratrum inclitis cognominibus habitabat, resistere non potuit.

damn. 2　　　Ac Scipioni quidem maximus fortunae fulgor, C. autem Deciano, spectatae integritatis viro, vox sua exitium attulit: nam cum P. Furium inquinatissimae vitae pro rostris accusaret, quia quadam in parte actionis de morte L. Saturnini queri ausus fuerat, nec reum damnavit et insuper ei poenas addictas pependit.

damn. 3　　　Sex. quoque Titium similis casus prostravit. erat innocens, erat agraria lege lata gratiosus apud populum: tamen, quod Saturnini imaginem domi habuerat, suffragiis eum tota contio oppressit.

damn. 4　　　Adiciatur his Claudia, quam insontem crimine quo accusabatur votum impium subvertit, quia cum a ludis domum rediens turba elideretur, optaverat ut frater

_____

[12] *add. Madvig*

[17] *Ca.* 85: Cic. *Rosc. Am.* 64.　　[18] 187: Livy 38.55.4–60 etc.
[19] 98: Cic. *Rab. perd.* 24.　　[20] 98: ibid.

not in nature that after killing their father they could take their rest upon his wounds and blood.[17]

CONDEMNED

We shall now run through persons who at their trials were more harmed by matters exterior to the case than helped by their innocence.

L. Scipio, after celebrating a splendid triumph over king Antiochus, was convicted as having taken a bribe from him, not, I think, because he had been corrupted by money to push the king back beyond Mount Taurus when he was lord of all Asia and already stretching victorious hands towards Europe; no, a man of otherwise irreproachable life and far removed from such a suspicion, he could not resist the envy which then resided in the famous surnames of the two brothers.[18]

Scipio was brought to destruction by the dazzling brilliance of success; C. Decianus, a man of recognized integrity, by his own words. Accusing from the rostra P. Furius, a person of the foulest character, at some point in his speech he ventured to complain about the death of L. Saturninus. On that account he failed to get a guilty verdict and on top of that paid an assigned penalty to Furius.[19]

A like cause laid Sex. Titius in the dust. He was innocent and popular as the author of an agrarian law. But because he had kept a portrait of Saturninus in his house, the whole assembly condemned him by their votes.[20]

Let Claudia be added to the above. Innocent of the charge brought against her, she was ruined by an impious prayer. When she was jostled by a crowd as she was returning home from the games, she had prayed that her brother,

suus, maritimarum virium nostrarum praecipua iactura, revivesceret, saepiusque consul factus infelici ductu nimis magnam urbis frequentiam minueret.

damn. 5   Possumus et ad illos brevi deverticulo transgredi quos leves ob causas damnationis incursus abripuit.

M. Mulvius Cn. Lollius L. Sextilius triumviri, quod ad incendium in Sacra Via ortum exstinguendum tardius venerant, a tribunis plebis die dicta apud populum damnati sunt.

damn. 6   Item P. Villius triumvir nocturnus a P. Aquillio tribuno plebis accusatus populi iudicio concidit, quia vigilias neglegentius circumierat.

damn. 7   Admodum severae notae et illud populi iudicium, cum M. Aemilium Porcinam a L. Cassio accusatum crimine nimis sublime exstructae villae in Alsiensi agro gravi multa adfecit.

damn. 8   Non supprimenda illius quoque damnatio qui pueruli sui nimio amore correptus, rogatus ab eo ruri ut omasum in cenam fieri iuberet, cum bubulae carnis in propinquo emendae nulla facultas esset, domito bove occiso desiderium eius explevit, eoque nomine publica quaestione adflictus est, innocens, nisi tam prisco saeculo natus esset.

amb. 1   Atque ut eos quoque referamus qui in discrimen capitis adducti neque damnati neque absoluti sunt, apud M. Popillium Laenatem praetorem quaedam, quod matrem fuste percussam interemerat, causam dixit. de qua neu-

---

21 246: Livy *Per.* 19 etc.; cf. VM 8.1.abs.4.   22 241 (?): see Broughton I.220.   23 211 (?): see Gundel, *RE* Villius 3.

24 125: cf. Vell. 2.10.1, Broughton I.510.

25 Pliny *N.H.* 8.180.

the principal disaster of our naval forces, might come to life again and be often elected Consul, so as to reduce the overpopulation of the city by his ill-starred leadership.[21]

We can also pass in a brief digression to persons swept away by the onslaught of a conviction for trivial reasons.

Because M. Mulvius, Cn. Lollius, and L. Sextilius, Triumvirs, had been slow in arriving to extinguish a fire that had broken out on the Sacred Way, they were brought to trial before the people by Tribunes of the Plebs and condemned.[22]

Likewise Nocturnal Triumvir P. Villius was accused by Tribune of the Plebs P. Aquillius and condemned by judgment of the people because he had been negligent in making his rounds of the watch.[23]

Of a very severe stamp was the judgment of the people when they imposed a heavy fine on M. Aemilius Porcina, who was prosecuted by L. Cassius on a charge of having built a villa to an improper height in the district of Alsium.[24]

Nor must I suppress the condemnation of a man who was swept away by excessive passion for a little boy of his. Asked by him in the country to order tripe for dinner, he satisfied the boy's craving by killing a domestic ox, since there was no means of buying beef in the neighbourhood. For that reason he was condemned by a public court—innocent if he had not been born in so ancient an epoch.[25]

"SCORCHED"

And to mention persons brought to trial on capital charges and neither acquitted nor convicted, a woman was tried before Praetor M. Popillius Laenas because she had beaten her mother to death with a stick. The verdict on her

tram in partem latae sententiae sunt, quia abunde constabat eandem veneno necatorum liberorum dolore commotam, quos avia filiae infensa sustulerat, parricidium ultam esse parricidio. quorum alterum ‹dignum›[13] ultione, alterum absolutione non dignum[14] iudicatum est.

amb. 2　　Eadem haesitatione P. quoque Dolabellae, proconsulari imperio Asiam obtinentis, animus fluctuatus est. mater familiae Zmyrnaea virum et filium interemit, cum ab iis optimae indolis iuvenem, quem ex priore viro enixa fuerat, occisum comperisset. quam rem Dolabella ad se delatam Athenas ad Areopagi cognitionem relegavit, quia ipse neque liberare duabus caedibus contaminatam neque punire tam[15] iusto dolore impulsam sustinebat. consideranter et mansuete populi Romani magistratus, sed Areopagitae quoque non minus sapienter, qui inspecta causa et accusatorem et ream post centum annos ad se reverti iusserunt, eodem adfectu moti quo Dolabella. sed ille transferendo quaestionem, hi differendo damnandi atque absolvendi inexplicabilem cogitationem[16] vitabant.[17]

2. DE PRIVATIS IUDICIIS INSIGNIBUS

praef.　　Publicis iudiciis adiciam privata, quorum magis aequitas quaestionum delectare quam immoderata turba offendere lectorem poterit.

1　　Claudius Centumalus, ab auguribus iussus altitudinem

---

[13] *add. Kempf*
[14] ultione ... dignum *intra cruces Briscoe*
[15] tam *Torr.*: eam AL
[16] cogitationem *SB*[3]: cuncta- AL
[17] vitabant *Guyet*: mut- AL

was neither one thing nor the other, because it was quite clear that she had done it out of grief for her children who had been poisoned, killed by their grandmother to spite her daughter; she had avenged one unnatural murder by another. The former slaying was judged deserving of vengeance, the latter not deserving of acquittal.[26]

The mind of P. Dolabella, governing Asia with proconsular authority, wavered in the same hesitation. A housewife in Smyrna killed her husband and son because she had found out that they had murdered her son by her former husband, a young man of excellent promise. When the case was brought to Dolabella, he referred it to Athens for cognizance in the Areopagus, because he did not himself feel able either to release a woman guilty of two murders nor to punish her when her motive was so just an indignation.[27] The Roman magistrate's action was well-considered and merciful, but that of the Areopagus was no less wise. After examining the case they directed both prosecutor and defendant to come back to them in a hundred years' time, influenced by the same feeling as Dolabella. But he by shifting the trial, they by delaying it avoided the baffling deliberation whether to convict or acquit.

2. OF REMARKABLE PRIVATE TRIALS

To public trials I shall add private ones. They will perhaps more please the reader by the equity of their conduct than annoy him by their excessive number.

Claudius Centumalus had been ordered by the Augurs

---

[26] 142 or earlier: not attested elsewhere.
[27] 68: Gell. 12.7, Amm. Marc. 29.2.19.

domus suae, quam in Caelio monte habebat, summittere, quia iis ex arce augurium capientibus officiebat, vendidit eam Calpurnio Lanario nec indicavit quod imperatum <a>[18] collegio augurum erat. a quibus Calpurnius demoliri domum coactus M. Catonem, incliti Catonis patrem, arbitrum cum Claudio adduxit <in>[19] formulam 'quidquid sibi dare facere oporteret ex fide bona.' Cato, ut est edoctus de industria Claudium praedictum sacerdotum suppressisse, continuo illum Calpurnio damnavit, summa quidem cum aequitate, quia bonae fidei venditorem nec commodorum spem augere nec incommodorum cognitionem obscurare oportet.

2   Notum suis temporibus iudicium commemoravi, sed ne quod relaturus quidem sum oblitteratum silentio. C. Visellius Varro, gravi morbo correptus, trecenta milia nummum ab Otacilia Laterensis, cum qua commercium libidinis habuerat, expensa ferri sibi passus est, eo consilio ut si decessisset, ab heredibus eam summam peteret, quam legati genus esse voluit, libidinosam liberalitatem debiti nomine colorando. evasit deinde ex illa tempestate adversus vota Otaciliae. quae offensa, quod spem praedae suae morte non maturasset, ex amica obsequenti subito destrictam feneratricem agere coepit, nummos petendo, quos ut fronte inverecunda ita inani stipulatione captaverat. de qua re C. Aquillius, vir magnae auctoritatis et scientia iuris civilis excellens, iudex adductus, adhibitis in consilium

---

[18] *add.* A *corr.*, G   [19] *add. Halm*

---

[1] Died before 91: Cic. *Off.* 3.66.

[2] I.e. (in this case) whatever Claudius was obligated to give Calpurnius.

to lower the height of his house on the Caelian hill because it was in their way as they took auguries from the citadel. He sold it to Calpurnius Lanarius without informing him of what the College of Augurs had commanded. Obliged by them to pull the house down, Calpurnius along with Claudius took the case to M. Porcius Cato, father of the famous Cato,[1] as arbiter under the legal formula "whatever he was obligated to give himself[2] or do in good faith." When Cato was told that Claudius had deliberately suppressed the directive of the priests, he immediately found against him in favour of Calpurnius, an eminently fair decision; for a seller in good faith should neither exaggerate prospective advantages nor conceal knowledge of disadvantages.

The judgment I have just recalled was well known in its day, nor is the one I am about to relate erased in silence. C. Visellius Varro, being seized with a grave illness, let Otacilia, wife of Laterensis, with whom he had had carnal commerce, record a loan to himself of three hundred thousand sesterces. His plan was that if he died she would claim that sum from his heirs. He wanted it to be a sort of legacy, colouring a gift deriving from lust with the name of debt. Then, contrary to Otacilia's prayers, he came out of the crisis. Annoyed that he had not speeded up the hope of her plunder by dying, from an obliging mistress she suddenly began to play the uncompromising creditor, claiming the money which she had tried to extract by a face of brass and an empty contract. C. Aquillius,[3] a highly respected personage eminent in knowledge of civil law, was appointed arbiter. He called in leading members of the community as

---

[3] Praetor in 66. The case is not recorded elsewhere.

principibus civitatis, prudentia et religione sua mulierem reppulit. quod si eadem formula Varro et damnari et adversariae[20] absolvi potuisset, eius quoque non dubito quin turpem et inconcessum ardorem[21] libenter castigaturus fuerit: nunc privatae actionis calumniam ipse compescuit, adulterii crimen publicae quaestioni vindicandum reliquit.

3   Multo animosius et ut militari spiritu dignum erat se in consimili genere iudicii C. Marius gessit: nam cum C. Titinius Minturnensis Fanniam uxorem, quam impudicam de industria duxerat, eo crimine repudiatam dote spoliare conaretur, sumptus inter eos iudex, in conspectu habita quaestione, seductum Titinium monuit ut incepto desisteret ac mulieri dotem redderet. quod cum saepius frustra fecisset, coactus ab eo sententiam pronuntiare, mulierem impudicitiae sestertio nummo, Titinium summa totius dotis damnavit, praefatus idcirco se hunc iudicandi modum secutum, cum liqueret sibi Titinium patrimonio Fanniae insidias struentem impudicae coniugium expetisse. Fannia autem haec est quae postea Marium hostem a senatu iudicatum caenoque paludis, qua extractus erat, oblitum et iam[22] in domum suam custodiendum Minturnis deductum, ope quantacumque potuit adiuvit, memor quod impudica iudicata esset suis moribus, quod dotem servasset illius religioni acceptum ferri debere.

4   Multus sermo eo etiam iudicio manavit in quo quidam

---

[20] -ri(a)e AL (*cf. Cic. Verr. 2.2.22 hominem Veneri absolvit*).
[21] ardorem *Gertz*: errorem AL   [22] et iam *Kempf*: etiam AL

---

4 In 88: Plut. *Mar.* 38; cf. VM 1.5.5.

his assessors and, guided by his skill and conscience, rebuffed the woman. If it had been possible for Varro to be
both condemned and (in respect of his female opponent)
acquitted under the same formula, I do not doubt that
Aquillius would gladly have chastised *his* shameful and
illicit ardour. As it was, he quashed the chicanery of the
private suit, leaving the charge of adultery to be pursued in
a public court.

In a similar sort of trial C. Marius comported himself
with much more vigour, as befitted his military spirit. C.
Titinius of Minturnae had divorced his wife Fannia, of
whose unchastity he was aware when he married her, on
that ground and was trying to strip her of her dowry.
Marius was taken as arbiter between them and the hearing
was held in public. Drawing Titinius aside, Marius warned
him to give up his attempt and return the dowry to the
woman. After he had done this several times to no effect
and Titinius forced him to pronounce a decision, he ruled
that the woman was guilty of unchastity and should pay
one sesterce and that Titinius should pay the full amount of
the dowry, prefacing that he had followed this mode of
judgment because it was clear to him that Titinius had
sought the hand of a loose woman with designs on Fannia's
property. This is the Fannia who later[4] did everything in
her power to help Marius when the senate adjudged him a
public enemy and, smeared with the mud of the swamp
from which he had been dragged, he was brought to her
house in Minturnae for custody. She bore in mind that the
judgment of unchastity was attributable to her own character, her retention of her dowry to Marius' judicial conscience.

Much talk too flowed from a trial in which a man was

furti damnatus est, qui equo, cuius usus illi Ariciam com-
modatus fuerat, ulteriore eius municipii clivo vectus esset.
quid aliud hoc loci quam verecundiam illius saeculi laude-
mus in quo tam minuti a pudore excessus puniebantur?

3. QUAE MULIERES APUD
MAGISTRATUS PRO SE AUT PRO
ALIIS CAUSAS EGERUNT

praef.　　Ne de iis quidem feminis tacendum est quas condicio
naturae et verecundia stolae[23] ut in foro et iudiciis tacerent
cohibere non valuit.

1　　Maesia Sentinas rea causam suam, L. Titio praetore
iudicium cogente, maximo populi concursu egit, modosque[24] omnes ac numeros defensionis non solum diligenter
sed etiam fortiter exsecuta, et prima actione et paene
cunctis sententiis liberata est. quam, quia sub specie feminae virilem animum gerebat, Androgynen appellabant.

2　　Carfania[25] vero, Licinii Buccionis[26] senatoris uxor,
prompta ad lites contrahendas, pro se semper apud praetorem verba fecit, non quod advocatis deficiebatur, sed
quod impudentia abundabat. itaque inusitatis foro latrati-
bus adsidue tribunalia exercendo muliebris calumniae notissimum exemplum evasit, adeo ut pro crimine improbis
feminarum moribus Carfaniae nomen obiciatur. proro-
gavit autem spiritum suum ad C. Caesarem iterum ⟨P.⟩[27]

[23] -dia stolae *Per.*: -diae stola AL
[24] modosque *Halm*: mortuus- L: motus- G: partes- A *corr.*
[25] Carfania *Ulpianus*: Cafra- *Schulze*: C. Afra- AL (*item infra*)
[26] Bucconis P
[27] *add. Pighius*

found guilty of theft who had ridden a horse, the use of which he had been loaned to go to Aricia, up a hill beyond that town. What should we do at this point but praise the scrupulousness of a period in which such minute departures from honourable conduct were penalized?[5]

3. WOMEN WHO PLEADED BEFORE MAGISTRATES FOR THEMSELVES OR FOR OTHERS

Nor should I be silent about those women whose natural condition and the modesty of the matron's robe could not make them keep silent in the Forum and the courts of law.

Maesia of Sentinum pleaded her own case as defendant with Praetor L. Titius as president of the court and a great concourse of people, going through all the forms and stages of a defence not only thoroughly but boldly. She was acquitted at the first hearing and by an almost unanimous vote. Because she bore a man's spirit under the form of a woman, they called her Androgyne.[1]

Carfania, wife of the senator Licinius Buccio, was ever ready for a lawsuit and always spoke on her own behalf before the Praetor, not because she could not find advocates but because she had impudence to spare. So by constantly plaguing the tribunals with barkings to which the Forum was unaccustomed she became a notorious example of female litigiousness, so much so that women of shameless habit are taunted with the name Carfania by way of re-

[5] Not found elsewhere. [1] Not found elsewhere.

Servilium consules: tale enim monstrum magis quo tempore exstinctum quam quo sit ortum memoriae tradendum est.

3   Hortensia vero, Q. Hortensii filia, cum ordo matronarum gravi tributo a triumviris esset oneratus ⟨nec⟩[28] quisquam virorum patrocinium iis accommodare auderet, causam feminarum apud triumviros et constanter et feliciter egit: repraesentata enim patris facundia impetravit ut maior pars imperatae pecuniae iis remitteretur. revixit tum muliebri stirpe Q. Hortensius verbisque filiae aspiravit; cuius si virilis sexus posteri vi⟨a⟩m[29] sequi voluissent, Hortensianae eloquentiae tanta hereditas una feminae actione abscissa non esset.

4. DE QUAESTIONIBUS

praef.   Atque ut omnes iudiciorum numeros exsequamur, quaestiones quibus aut creditum non est aut temere habita fides est, referamus.

1   M. Agrii argentarii servus Alexander A. Fannii servum occidisse insimulatus est, eoque nomine tortus a domino admisisse id facinus constantissime adseveravit. itaque Fannio deditus supplicio est adfectus. parvulo deinde tempore interiecto, ille cuius de nece creditum erat domum rediit.

2   Contra P. Atinii servus [Alexander],[30] cum in suspicio-

[28] *add. A corr.,* G
[29] *add. Novák*   [30] *del. SB*[3]

---

[2] 48; cf. Ulp. *Dig.* 3.1.1.5.
[3] 42: Quint. *Inst.* 1.1.6, App. *B.C.* 4.32–34.

proach. She prolonged her life to the Consulship of C. Caesar (second time) and P. Servilius:[2] in the case of such a monster the date of extinction rather than of origin is to be recorded.

Hortensia, daughter of Q. Hortensius, pleaded the cause of women before the Triumvirs resolutely and successfully when the order of matrons had been burdened by them with a heavy tax and none of the other sex ventured to lend them his advocacy. Reviving her father's eloquence, she won the remission of the greater part of the impost.[3] Q. Hortensius then lived again in his female progeny and inspired his daughter's words. If his male descendants had chosen to follow her example, the great heritage of Hortensian eloquence would not have been cut short with a single speech by a woman.

4. OF INTERROGATIONS

To cover all aspects of trials, let us relate interrogations which were not believed or to which credence was given inadvisedly.

A slave of the banker M. Agrius called Alexander was accused of killing a slave of A. Fannius and tortured by his master on that account. He steadfastly asserted that he had committed the crime. So he was handed over to Fannius and executed. A little time passed and the man believed to have been murdered returned home.[1]

Contrarywise, a slave of P. Atinius came under suspi-

---

[1] Not found elsewhere. The facts are evidently garbled. A man might confess under torture to a crime he had not committed, but not *constantissime;* see SB[3].

VALERIUS MAXIMUS

nem C. Flavii equitis Romani occisi venisset, sexies tortus pernegavit ei se culpae adfinem fuisse, sed perinde atque confessus ⟨esset⟩[31] et a iudicibus damnatus et a L. Calpurnio triumviro in crucem actus est.

3 Item Fulvio Flacco causam dicente, Philippus, servus eius, in quo tota quaestio nitebatur, octies tortus nullum omnino verbum quo dominus perstringeretur emisit; et tamen reus damnatus est, cum certius argumentum innocentiae unus octies tortus exhiberet quam octo semel torti praebuissent.

5. DE TESTIBUS

praef. Sequitur ut ad testes pertinentia exempla commemorem.

1 Cn. et Q. Serviliis Caepionibus, iisdem parentibus natis et per omnes honorum gradus ad summam amplitudinem provectis, item fratribus Metellis Quinto et Lucio, consularibus et censoriis, altero etiam triumphali, in Q. Pompeium A. f. repetundarum reum acerrime dicentibus testimonium non abrogata fides absoluto Pompeio, sed ne potentia inimicum oppressisse viderentur occursum est.

2 M. etiam Aemilius Scaurus, princeps senatus, C. Memmium repetundarum reum destricto testimonio insecutus

[31] esset et *SB*: et A*L*: esset *Kempf*

2 Not found elsewhere.
3 This cannot be Cn. Fulvius Flaccus, defeated by Hannibal in 212 and condemned in 211 on that account: a slave would not have been the key witness in that trial. The case will have concerned a private offence, perhaps sexual, running parallel with that of M.

cion of the murder of C. Flavius, a Roman knight. Tortured six times, he continued to deny any part in that crime, but as though he had confessed he was convicted by a jury and crucified by the Triumvir L. Calpurnius.[2]

Likewise when Fulvius Flaccus was on trial, his slave Philippus, on whose evidence the whole case depended, was tortured eight times and uttered no word prejudicial to his master. Nevertheless the defendant was found guilty, although one man tortured eight times provided a more reliable proof of innocence than eight men tortured once would have furnished.[3]

5. OF WITNESSES

I next proceed to examples pertaining to witnesses.

Cn. and Q. Servilius Caepio, born of the same parents and advanced to the highest eminence by progress through all stages of official rank, likewise the brothers Metelli, Quintus and Lucius, ex-Consuls and ex-Censors, one of them a triumphator, spoke very strongly in evidence against Q. Pompeius, son of Aulus, accused of extortion. Pompeius was acquitted, not because they were disbelieved but to counter the impression that they had crushed an enemy by their influence.[1]

M. Aemilius Scaurus too, Leader of the Senate, attacked C. Memmius, on trial for extortion, with damning

Antonius (VM 6.8.1). Very probably the accused was Ser. Fulvius, who was defended in 121 by C. Scribonius Curio in a celebrated speech (Cic. *Inv.* 1.80, *Brut.* 122). Fulvii Flacci seem to have survived into the middle of the first century (see commentary on Cic. *Att.* 4.3.3).   [1] *Ca.* 138: cf. Cic. *Font.* 23.

est, item C. Flavium eadem lege accusatum testis pro-
scidit: iam C. Norbanum maiestatis crimine publicae
quaestioni subiectum ex professo opprimere conatus est.
nec tamen aut auctoritate, qua plurimum pollebat, aut
religione, de qua nemo dubitabat, quemquam eorum
adfligere potuit.

3   L. quoque Crassus, tantus apud iudices quantus apud
patres conscriptos Aemilius Scaurus—namque eorum suffragia robustissimis et felicissimis eloquentiae stipendiis
regebat, eratque sic fori ut ille curiae princeps—, cum
vehementissimum testimonii fulmen in M. Marcellum
reum iniecisset, impetu gravis, exitu vanus apparuit.

4   Age, Q. Metellus Pius L. <et>[32] M. Luculli Q. Hortensius M.[33] Lepidus C. Cornelii maiestatis rei quam non one-
rarunt tantummodo testes salutem, sed etiam, negantes
illo incolumi stare rem publicam posse, depoposcerunt!
quae decora civitatis, pudet referre, umbone iudiciali
repulsa sunt!

5   Quid? M. Cicero forensi militia summos honores am-
plissimumque dignitatis locum adeptus, nonne in ipsis eloquentiae suae castris testis abiectus est, dum P. Clodium
Romae apud se fuisse iurat,[34] illo sacrilegum flagitium uno
argumento absentiae tuente? si quidem iudices Clodium

[32] *add.* P   [33] M'. *Sigonius, edd.*
[34] iurat *Kellerbauer*: iuravit AL

2 The first two trials were *ca.* 102, the third in 94; cf. Cic.
Font. 24 (Memmius and Flavius), 26 (Flavius), *De orat.* 2.203 etc.
(Norbanus).

3 Cic. *Font.* 24. Crassus died in 91.

testimony; and likewise as a witness cut C. Flavius, accused under the same statute, to pieces; and by his own profession set out to crush C. Norbanus, who was brought to a public court on a charge of lèse-majesté.[2] And yet neither by his authority, which was of the most powerful, nor by his scrupulous honesty, which nobody doubted, did he succeed in bringing any of them down.

L. Crassus too was as great a man in the courts as was Aemilius Scaurus in the senate, for he ruled their votes with his stout and successful campaigns of eloquence and was leader of the Forum as Scaurus was of the House; but when he launched a very violent thunderbolt of testimony against the defendant M. Marcellus, he turned out to be heavy in the onslaught but flimsy in the outcome.[3]

And again: Q. Metellus Pius, L. and M. Lucullus, Q. Hortensius, and M.[4] Lepidus not only as witnesses sought the downfall of C. Cornelius, charged with lèse-majesté, but demanded him, asserting that the commonwealth could not survive if he remained a member of it. What ornaments of the community (I am ashamed to relate it) were rebuffed by the judicial shield![5]

And again: campaigning in the courts M. Cicero won the highest offices and a most eminent status, but was he not rejected as a witness in the very camp of his eloquence, when he swore that P. Clodius had been in his (Cicero's) house in Rome and Clodius' denial of a sacrilegious offence rested solely on his alibi? The jury preferred to clear

[4] Should be Mam. (Mamercus), Consul in 77, not M'. (Manius), Consul in 66, as shown by G. V. Sumner (*Journ. Rom. Stud.* 54 (1964).41–48).

[5] 65: Ascon. 60 and 79 Clark.

incesti crimine quam Ciceronem infamia periurii liberare
maluerunt.

6   Tot elevatis testibus, unum cuius nova ratione iudicium
ingressa auctoritas confirmata est referam. P. Servilius,
consularis censorius triumphalis, qui maiorum suorum ti-
tulis Isaurici cognomen adiecit, cum forum praeteriens
testes in reum dari vidisset, loco testis constitit ac summam inter patronorum pariter et accusatorum admirationem sic orsus est: 'hunc ego, iudices, qui causam dicit,
cuias sit aut quam vitam egerit quamque merito vel iniuria
accusetur ignoro: illud tantum scio, cum occurrisset mihi
Laurentina via iter facienti admodum angusto loco, equo
descendere noluisse. quod an aliquid ad religionem ves-
tram pertineat ipsi aestimabitis: ego id supprimendum non
putavi.' iudices reum, vix auditis[35] ceteris testibus, damna-
runt: valuit enim apud eos cum amplitudo viri tum gravis
neglectae dignitatis eius indignatio, eumque qui venerari
principes nesciret in quodlibet facinus procursurum crediderunt.

6. QUI QUAE IN ALIIS VINDICARANT
IPSI COMMISERUNT

praef.   Ne illos quidem latere patiamur, qui quae in aliis vindi-
carant ipsi commiserunt.

1   C. Licinius, cognomine Hoplomachus, a praetore pos-
tulavit ut patri suo bonis tamquam ea dissipanti interdice-

---

[35] auditis P: addi- AL

---

[6] 61: Cic. *Att.* 1.16.10, Plut. *Cic.* 29, Schol. Bob. 85 Stangl.
[7] Reported only here.

Clodius of the charge of impurity rather than Cicero of the ill-repute of perjury.[6]

After so many witnesses made light of, I shall tell of one whose authority entered the court in a novel fashion and was confirmed. P. Servilius, ex-Consul and ex-Censor, triumphator, who added the surname of Isauricus to the titles of his ancestors, as he passed by the Forum saw witnesses giving evidence against a defendant. He took the stand as a witness and to the great surprise of the advocates, both prosecuting and defending, spoke as follows: "Gentlemen of the jury, I don't know where this man on trial comes from or what life he has led or how rightly or wrongly he stands accused: I know only this much, that when he met me as I was travelling on the Laurentine Way in a pretty narrow passage, he refused to get off his horse. Whether that concerns you as a jury, you will judge. I thought I ought not to keep it back." The jury found the defendant guilty almost without hearing the other witnesses. They were impressed by Servilius' eminence and his grave indignation at the neglect of his dignity and believed that someone who did not know how to respect our leading men would rush into any villainy.[7]

6. OF THOSE WHO THEMSELVES COMMITTED ACTIONS WHICH THEY HAD PUNISHED IN OTHERS

Nor let us suffer those who themselves committed actions which they had punished in others to lie concealed.

C. Licinius, surnamed Hoplomachus, asked the Praetor to restrain his father from handling his property on the

retur, et quidem quod petierat impetravit; sed ipse, parvo post tempore mortuo sene, amplam ab eo relictam pecuniam festinanter consumpsit. a<t> vicissitudine<m> poenae effugit[36] quoniam hereditatem absumere quam heredem maluit tollere.

2   C. autem Marius, cum magnum et salutarem rei publicae civem in L. Saturnino opprimendo egisset, a quo in modum vexilli pilleum servituti ad arma capienda ostentatum erat, L. Sulla cum exercitu in urbem irrumpente ad auxilium servorum pilleo sublato confugit. itaque, dum facinus quod punierat imitatur, alterum Marium, a quo adfligeretur, invenit.

3   C. vero Licinius Stolo, cuius beneficio plebi petendi consulatus potestas facta est, cum lege sanxisset ne quis amplius quingenta agri iugera possideret, ipse mille comparavit, <dis>simulandique[37] criminis gratia dimidiam partem filio emancipavit. quam ob causam a M. Popillio Laenate accusatus, primus sua lege cecidit, ac docuit nihil aliud praecipi debere nisi quod prius quisque sibi imperav<er>it.[38]

4   Q. autem Varius, propter obscurum ius civitatis Hybrida cognominatus, tribunus plebis legem adversus intercessionem collegarum perrogavit, quae iubebat quaeri quorum dolo malo socii ad arma ire coacti essent, magna cum clade rei publicae: sociale enim prius, deinde civile

---

[36] at -nem ... effugit *Foertsch*: a -ne ... fuit AL (afuit *Halm, edd.*)   [37] *add.* P   [38] *add. Pighius*

---

[1] Reported only here, aside from Münzer's very tentative identification with Crassus Dives of VM 6.9.12 (*RE* XIII.295.47,

plea that he was wasting it and the application was granted. But when the old man died a little later, he himself hurriedly made away with the ample sum his father had left. He escaped punishment in his turn because he preferred to squander his heritage rather than pick up an heir.[1]

C. Marius acted like a great citizen and public benefactor in crushing L. Saturninus, who had summoned the slaves to arms by showing them a cap of liberty in lieu of a standard. But when L. Sulla and his army were breaking into the city he raised a cap of liberty to call in the help of the slaves.[2] So imitating the misdeed he had punished, he found another Marius to bring him down.

C. Licinius Stolo, thanks to whom plebians were given the right to stand for the Consulship, had put through a law providing that no one should occupy more than five hundred *iugera* of land. He himself acquired a thousand, and to disguise the offence transferred half of it to his son. On that account he was prosecuted by M. Popillius Laenas and became the first to go down under his own law; a lesson that nothing should be prescribed to others which the prescriber has not previously imposed upon himself.[3]

Q. Varius, surnamed Hybrida because of doubts about his citizen status, carried through as Tribune of the Plebs against the veto of his colleagues a law ordering an investigation into persons through whom by malice aforethought the allies had been made to take up arms. That was a great public calamity, because it stirred up first a social[4] war and

---

371.3–18). To "pick up" (*tollere*) a son was to acknowledge paternity.   [2] 88: cf. Plut. *Mar.* 35 etc.

[3] Livy 7.16.9 etc. (Broughton I.114).

[4] I.e. between allies (*socii*).

bellum excitavit. sed dum ante pestiferum tribunum plebis quam certum civem agit, sua lex eum domesticis
laqueis constrictum absumpsit.

7. DE STUDIO ET INDUSTRIA

praef.　　Quid cesso vires Industriae commemorare, cuius alacri
spiritu militiae stipendia roborantur, forensis gloria accen-
ditur, fido sinu cuncta studia recepta nutriuntur, quidquid
animo, quidquid manu, quidquid lingua admirabile est, ad
cumulum laudis perducitur? qua, cum[39] sit perfectissima
virtus, duramento sui confirmatur.

1　　Cato sextum et octogesimum annum agens, dum in re
publica tuenda iuvenili animo perstat, ab inimicis capitali
crimine accusatus causam suam egit, neque aut memoriam eius quisquam tardiorem aut firmitatem lateris ulla ex
parte quassatam aut os haesitatione impeditum animadvertit, quia omnia ista in suo statu aequali ac perpetua
industria continebat. quin etiam in ipso diutissime actae
vitae fine disertissimi oratoris Galbae defensioni accusationem[40] suam pro Hispania opposuit. idem Graecis
litteris erudiri concupivit—quam sero inde aestimemus
quod etiam Latinas paene iam senex didicit—, cumque
eloquentia magnam gloriam partam haberet, id egit ut
iuris civilis quoque esset peritissimus.

[39] qua, cum *SB*[1]: quae cum AL; Br
[40] defensioni accusationem *Gertz*: -tioni -sionem AL

[5] 90/89 (Broughton II.26f.).
[1] 149: Plut. *Cat. mai.* 15.4.
[2] See VM 8.1.abs.2.

then a civil one. But as he played the role of a pernicious Tribune of the Plebs before that of a well-established citizen, his own law carried him off, caught in a noose of his own tightening.[5]

7. ON STUDY AND DILIGENCE

Why do I delay to record the power of Diligence? By her active spirit military service is fortified, civilian glory fired, all studies are received in her faithful bosom and nourished, whatever is admirable in mind, hand, or tongue is brought to the acme of excellence. By diligence virtue even at its most perfect is confirmed through a hardening of itself.

In his eighty-sixth year Cato took part in public affairs with the spirit of a young man. Prosecuted by his enemies on a capital charge, he pleaded his own case, nor did anyone notice that his memory was slower or the strength of his lungs in any degree enfeebled or his mouth impeded by hesitation.[1] For by steady and perpetual diligence he used to keep all these things in going order. Even at the very end of his extremely long life he countered the defence of Galba, a very eloquent orator, with his accusation on behalf of Spain.[2] He also formed a wish to be instructed in Greek literature,[3] at how late in the day we may judge from the fact that he was almost an old man when he learned Latin literature. And although he had won great fame in eloquence, he made himself a past master of civil law as well.

[3] Cic. *Sen.* 26. A difficult statement to evaluate, still more that which follows.

2   Cuius mirifica proles, propior aetati nostrae Cato, ita doctrinae cupiditate flagravit ut ne in curia quidem, dum senatus cogitur, temperaret sibi quo minus Graecos libros lectitaret. qua quidem industria ostendit aliis tempora deesse, alios superesse temporibus.

3   Terentius autem Varro, humanae vitae exemplo et[41] spatio ⟨nominandus⟩[42], non annis, quibus saeculi tempus aequavit, quam stilo vivacior fuit: in eodem enim lectulo et spiritus eius et egregiorum operum cursus exstinctus est.

4   Consimilis perseverantiae Livius Drusus, qui ⟨et⟩[43] aetatis viribus et acie oculorum defectus ius civile populo benignissime interpretatus est, utilissimaque discere id cupientibus monumenta composuit: nam ut senem illum Natura, caecum Fortuna facere potuit, ita neutra interpellare valuit ne non animo et videret et vigeret.

5   Publilius vero senator et Lupus Pontius eques Romanus, suis temporibus celebres causarum actores, luminibus capti eadem industria forensia stipendia exsecuti sunt. itaque frequentius etiam audiebantur, concurrentibus aliis quia ingenio eorum delectabantur, aliis quia constantiam admirabantur: namque alii ⟨qui tali⟩[44] ⟨in⟩commodo[45] perculsi secessum petunt, duplicant tenebras fortuitis voluntaria⟨s⟩[46] adicientes.

[41] exemplo et *intra cruces Briscoe*   [42] *add.* A *corr.*
[43] *add.* A *corr.*   [44] namque alii ⟨qui tali⟩ *Kempf*: namque alii* AL   [45] *add.* L *corr.*   [46] *add. Coler*

---

[4] Cic. *Fin.* 3.7, Plut. *Cat. min.* 19.1.
[5] The text has been questioned. Is there a play on two senses of *tempora,* time and circumstances?

His marvellous progeny, a Cato nearer to our own time, was so aflame with desire for learning that even in the senate house, while the members were assembling, he did not refrain from reading Greek books.[4] By such diligence he showed that some lack time, whereas others are superior to times.[5]

Terentius Varro, to be celebrated for the example he gave of human life and for his length of it, was no more longeval in his years, with which he equalled the duration of a century, than in his pen. For his breath and the series of his excellent works ended in the same bed.

Livius Drusus was similarly persevering. Failing both in the strength of youth and in his eyesight, he quite ungrudgingly interpreted civil law for the public and composed works of the greatest use to those wishful to learn it. Nature could make an old man of him, Fortune a blind man, but neither the one nor the other could interrupt his mind's sight and activity.[6]

When the senator Publilius and the Roman knight Lupus Pontius, well-known pleaders in their day,[7] went blind, they carried on their forensic activities with the same diligence. And so they drew even larger audiences as people gathered, some because they took pleasure in their oratorical gift, others because they admired their resolution. For others, who seek retirement when so afflicted, double their darkness, adding voluntary to fortuitous.

[6] His praenomen, Gaius, being the same as his father's, indicates that he was older than his brother Marcus, Tribune in 122, who was born *ca.* 154 (Münzer, *RE* Livius 15).

[7] Neither otherwise known.

6   Iam P. Crassus, cum in Asiam ad Aristonicum regem debellandum consul venisset, tanta cura Graecae linguae notitiam animo comprehendit ut eam in quinque divisam genera per omnes partes ac numeros penitus cognosceret. quae res maximum ei sociorum amorem conciliavit, qua quis eorum lingua apud tribunal illius postulaverat, eadem decreta reddenti.

7   Ne Roscius quidem subtrahatur, scaenicae industriae notissimum exemplum, qui nullum umquam spectante populo gestum, nisi quem domi meditatus fuerat, promere[47] ausus est. quapropter non ludicra ars Roscium sed Roscius ludicram artem commendavit, nec vulgi tantum favorem verum etiam principum familiaritates amplexus est. haec sunt attenti et anxii et numquam cessantis studii praemia, propter quae tantorum virorum laudibus non impudenter se persona histrionis inserit.

ext. 1   Graeca quoque industria, quoniam nostrae multum profuit, quem meretur fructum Latina lingua recipiat.

Demosthenes, cuius commemorato nomine maximae eloquentiae consummatio audientis animo oboritur, cum inter initia iuventae artis, quam adfectabat, primam litteram dicere non posset, oris sui vitium tanto studio expugnavit ut ea a nullo expressius referretur. deinde propter nimiam exilitatem acerbam auditu vocem suam exercitatione continua ad maturum et gratum auribus sonum perduxit. lateris etiam firmitate defectus, quas corporis

---

[47] promere *Schulze*: ponere AL

[8] 131: Quint. *Inst.* 11.2.50.
[9] *Persona,* worn by actors on the stage.

When P. Crassus came to Asia to put down king Aristonicus,[8] he was so careful to master the Greek language that divided as it was into five branches he learned each of them thoroughly in all its parts and aspects. That won him great affection among the allies. In whatever dialect one of them applied at his tribunal, he gave his ruling in the same.

We must not leave out Roscius, a very celebrated example of theatrical diligence. He never ventured to produce a gesture before a public audience which he had not practised at home. Therefore the art of acting did not commend Roscius, Roscius commended the art of acting, and he not only encompassed the favour of the crowd but friendship with leading men as well. Such are the rewards of attentive, anxious, unremitting study, and that is why the mask[9] of a player without presumption makes a place for itself among the eulogies of such great men.

EXTERNAL

Let Greek diligence too, since it has done so much for our own, receive its deserved reward in the Latin tongue.

When the name of Demosthenes is spoken, the consummation of eloquence at its greatest leaps to the hearer's mind. Yet in earliest youth he could not pronounce the first letter[10] of his chosen art.[11] But he broke down his speech defect with such determination that nobody pronounced that letter more distinctly. Next, by constant practice he brought his voice, which was too reedy and so disagreeable in the hearing, to a well-developed timbre, pleasant to the ears. His lungs too lacked strength, but he borrowed from

10 R (rho).
11 Rhetoric.

habitus vires negaverat, a labore mutuatus est: multos enim versus uno impetu spiritus complectebatur, eosque adversa loca celeri gradu scandens pronuntiabat, ac vadosis litoribus insistens declamationes fluctuum fragoribus obluctantibus edebat, ut ad fremitus concitatarum contionum patientia duratis auribus uteretur. fertur quoque ori insertis calculis multum ac diu loqui solitus, quo vacuum promptius esset et solutius. proeliatus est cum Rerum Natura et quidem victor abiit, malignitatem eius pertinacissimo animi robore superando. itaque alterum Demosthenen mater, alterum Industria enixa est.

ext. 2   Atque ut ad vetustiorem Industriae actum transgrediar, Pythagoras perfectissimae[48] opus sapientiae a iuventa ⟨scientiae⟩[49] pariter et omnis honestatis percipiendae cupiditate ingressus[50]—nihil enim quod ad ultimum sui perventurum est finem non et mature et celeriter incipit—, Aegyptum petiit, ubi litteris gentis eius adsuefactus, praeteriti aevi sacerdotum commentarios scrutatus, innumerabilium saeculorum observationes cognovit. inde ad Persas profectus, magorum exactissimae prudentiae se formandum tradidit, a quibus siderum motus cursusque stellarum et uniuscuiusque vim proprietatem effectum benignissime demonstratum docili animo sorpsit. Cretam deinde et Lacedaemona navigavit, quarum legibus ac moribus inspectis ad Olympicum certamen descendit, cumque multiplicis scientiae maximam inter totius Graeciae admirationem specimen exhibuisset, quo cognomine cen-

---

[48] -imae *SB*: -imum AL
[49] *add. SB*[3]
[50] a iuventa ... ingressus* *intra cruces Briscoe*

toil the power that his bodily constitution had denied him. He used to include many lines of verse in one emission of breath and recite them climbing uphill at a smart pace. Standing in shoals, he would give out declamations against the roaring of the waves to harden his ears and enable him to endure the clamour of excited assemblies. He is also said to have been in the habit of putting pebbles in his mouth and speaking much and long to make it readier and looser when empty. He did battle with the Nature of Things and won, overcoming her malignity with the pertinacious strength of his spirit.[12] And so his mother gave birth to one Demosthenes, Diligence to another.

To pass to a more ancient performance of diligence: Pythagoras, who from his youth embarked upon the work of most perfect wisdom with the desire of acquiring knowledge and all that is good (for everything destined to arrive at its ultimate goal also begins early and rapidly), repaired to Egypt. There familiarizing himself with the writings of that people and scrutinizing the memoranda left by priests of ages gone by, he learned the observations of countless cycles. From Egypt he went to Persia and gave himself over to the finished wisdom of the magi for them to mould. His docile mind absorbed what they ungrudgingly displayed to him: the motions of the stars, the courses of the planets, the force, individuality, and effect of each one. Then he sailed to Crete and Lacedaemon, and after inspecting their laws and manners came to the Olympic competition. There he displayed a specimen of his multifarious knowledge amid the enthusiastic admiration of all Greece. Asked under what title he was registered, he pro-

[12] Cic. *De orat.* 1.260f. etc.

seretur interrogatus, non se sapientem—iam enim illud septem excellentes viri occupaverant—sed amatorem sapientiae, id est Graece philosophon, edidit. in Italiae etiam partem, quae tunc maior Graecia appellabatur, perrexit, in qua plurimis et opulentissimis urbibus effectus studiorum suorum approbavit. cuius ardentem rogum plenis venerationis oculis Metapontus aspexit oppidum, Pythagorae quam suorum cinerum nobilius clariusque monumentum.

ext. 3   Platon autem, patriam Athenas, praeceptorem Socratem sortitus, et locum et hominem doctrinae fertilissimum, ingenii quoque divina instructus abundantia, cum omnium iam mortalium sapientissimus haberetur, eo quidem usque ut si ipse Iuppiter caelo descendisset, nec elegantiore nec beatiore facundia usurus videretur, Aegyptum peragravit, dum a sacerdotibus eius gentis geometriae multiplices numeros ⟨et⟩[51] caelestium observationum rationem percipit. quoque tempore a studiosis iuvenibus certatim Athenae Platonem doctorem quaerentibus petebantur, ipse Nili fluminis inexplicabiles ripas vastissimosque campos, ⟨et⟩ effusam Mariam[52] et flexuosos fossarum ambitus Agyptiorum senum discipulus lustrabat. quo minus miror in Italiam transgressum ut ab Archyta Tarenti, a Timaeo et Arione et Echecrate Locris, Pythagorae praecepta et instituta acciperet: tanta enim vis, tanta copia litterarum undique colligenda erat ut invicem

---

[51] *add.* P   [52] et effusam Mariam *Kempf, duce Gertz*: eff-barbariam* (-iem A) AL

---

[13] Cic. *Fin.* 5.87 etc.

[14] Perhaps an obscure way of saying that the ruins preserved the memory of Pythagoras rather than of the town they once were.

fessed himself, not a wise man (for that had been pre-empted by the surpassing Seven), but a lover of wisdom, that is, in Greek, a philosopher. He also proceeded to that part of Italy which was then called Greater Greece, in which he commended the results of his studies to many flourishing cities.[13] The town of Metapontus beheld his burning pyre with eyes full of reverence, a more famous and renowned memorial of Pythagoras' ashes than of its own.[14]

Plato was allotted Athens as his country and Socrates as his teacher, both the place and the man most fertile in learning. He was also furnished with a divine plenitude of intellect, being reputed the wisest of all mortals to date, so much so that if Jupiter himself came down from heaven he would not, so it was thought, speak with an eloquence more choice and copious. He travelled through Egypt, where he acquired the multifarious calculations of geometry and the system of celestial observations from the priests of that nation. While studious young men were going to Athens to vie with one another in seeking Plato as their teacher, Plato himself was traversing the labyrinthine banks of the river Nile, vast plains, the sprawl of Maria, the winding courses of dykes, as a pupil of aged Egyptians. I am the less surprised that he passed on to Italy to receive the precepts and doctrine of Pythagoras from Archytas at Tarentum and from Timaeus and Arion and Echecrates at Locri. For he had to collect such a mass and abundance of

Metapontus (usually Metapontum), on the south coast of Italy, became the home of the Pythagorean community. It practically disappeared from history when its population was evacuated by Hannibal in 207 (Livy 25.11). Read *monumentum ⟨futurum⟩*?

per totum terrarum orbem dispergi et dilatari posset. altero etiam et octogesimo anno decedens sub capite Sophro-
nis mimos habuisse fertur. sic ne extrema quidem eius hora
agitatione studii vacua fuit.

ext. 4   At Democritus, cum divitiis censeri posset, quae tantae
fuerunt ut pater eius Xerxis exercitui epulum dare ex facili
potuerit, quo magis vacuo animo studiis litterarum esset
operatus, parva admodum summa retenta patrimonium
suum patriae donavit. Athenis autem compluribus annis
moratus, omnia temporum momenta ad percipiendam et
exercendam doctrinam conferens, ignotus illi urbi vixit,
quod ipse quodam volumine testatur. stupet mens admiratione tantae industriae et iam transit alio.

ext. 5   Carneades, laboriosus et diuturnus sapientiae miles, si
quidem nonaginta expletis annis idem illi vivendi ac philo-
sophandi finis fuit, ita se mirificum doctrinae operibus
addixerat ut cum cibi capiendi causa recubuisset, cogitationibus inhaerens manum ad mensam porrigere obli-
visceretur. sed ei[53] Melissa, quam uxoris loco habebat,
temperato [inter][54] studia non interpellandi et inediae suc-
currendi officio dexteram suam[55] necessariis usibus apta-
bat. ergo animo tantummodo vita fruebatur, corpore vero
quasi alieno et supervacuo circumdatus erat. idem cum
Chrysippo disputaturus elleboro se ante purgabat, ad ex-

---

[53] ei *Per.*: eum AL   [54] *del. Madvig*   [55] dexteram suam
A: -ra -sua LG   eum ... -ra sua *intra cruces Briscoe*

---

[15] Diog. Laert. 3.6.18 etc.
[16] Cic. *Fin.* 5.87, Aelian *Var. hist.* 4.20 etc. Xerxes comes to
Abdera, Democritus' home town, in Herod. 8.120.

learning from all quarters that it might in turn be dispersed and spread through the entire globe. As he lay dying in his eighty-first year, he is said to have had the mimes of Sophron under his head.[15] Thus even his last hour was not void of studious activity.

Democritus might have been valued for his riches, which were so great that his father was easily able to give a feast to Xerxes' army. But so that he should apply himself to literary studies with a mind more disengaged, he gave his wealth to his country, reserving quite a small sum. Passing a number of years in Athens, devoting every moment of his time to the gathering and use of learning, he lived unknown to that city, as he himself attests in a certain book.[16] The mind boggles in admiration of such diligence and now passes elsewhere.

Carneades was a hard-working and long-serving soldier of wisdom. After he had completed ninety years, the end of his living and his philosophizing was the same. So marvellously had he devoted himself to the operations of learning that when he had lain down to take a meal, wrapped in thought he would forget to stretch out his hand to the table. But Melissa,[17] whom he had in lieu of a wife, adjusted her duty so as on the one hand not to interrupt his studies and on the other to minister to his fasting, adapting her own hand to the necessary uses. So Carneades enjoyed life only with his mind, enveloped by a quasi-alien and superfluous body. The same, when about to hold a debate with Chrysippus, used to purge himself with hellebore[18] with a

[17] Nowhere else mentioned by name, but see von Fritz, *RE* Melissa 5.

[18] Gell. 17.15.1f., Mart. Cap. 327 etc.

promendum ingenium suum attentius et illius refellendum acrius. quas potiones Industria solidae laudis cupidis appetendas effecit!

ext. 6   Quali porro studio Anaxagoran flagrasse credimus? qui cum e diutina peregrinatione patriam repetisset, possessionesque desertas vidisset, 'non essem' inquit 'ego salvus, nisi istae perissent.' vocem petitae sapientiae compotem! nam si praediorum potius quam ingenii culturae vacasset, dominus rei familiaris intra penates mansisset, non tantus Anaxagoras ad eos redisset.

ext. 7   Archimedis quoque fructuosam industriam fuisse dicerem, nisi eadem illi et dedisset vitam et abstulisset: captis enim Syracusis Marcellus ⟨etsi⟩[56] machinationibus eius multum ac diu victoriam suam inhibitam senserat, eximia tamen hominis prudentia delectatus ut capiti illius parceretur edixit, paene tantum gloriae in Archimede servato quantum in oppressis Syracusis reponens. at is, dum animo et oculis in terra defixis formas describit, militi, qui praedandi gratia ⟨in⟩[57] domum irruperat strictoque super caput gladio quisnam esset interrogabat, propter nimiam cupiditatem investigandi quod requirebat nomen suum indicare non potuit, sed protecto[58] manibus pulvere 'noli' inquit, 'obsecro, istum disturbare,' ac perinde quasi neglegens imperii victoris obtruncatus sanguine suo artis suae liniamenta confudit. quo accidit ut propter idem studium modo donaretur vita, modo spoliaretur.

---

[56] add. Gertz   [57] add. Kempf
[58] protecto ⊊: protracto AL: proiecto P

[19] Cf. Plato Hipp. mai. 283a etc.
[20] 212: Livy 25.31.9f. etc.

view to bringing forward his own intellectual resources with more concentration and rebutting those of Chrysippus with greater vigour. What draughts did Diligence make attractive to men anxious for true glory!

With what enthusiasm moreover do we suppose Anaxagoras burned! Returning to his country after a long absence abroad and seeing that his holdings had been deserted, he said, "I should not be alive if these had not perished."[19] A saying possessed of the wisdom he sought. For if he had spent his time cultivating his estates rather than his mind, he would have stayed among his household gods master of his property and would not have come back to them the great Anaxagoras.

I should say that Archimedes' diligence also bore fruit if it had not both given him life and taken it away. At the capture of Syracuse Marcellus had been aware that his victory had been held up much and long by Archimedes' machines. However, pleased with the man's exceptional skill, he gave out that his life was to be spared, putting almost as much glory in saving Archimedes as in crushing Syracuse. But as Archimedes was drawing diagrams with mind and eyes fixed on the ground, a soldier who had broken into the house in quest of loot with sword drawn over his head asked him who he was. Too much absorbed in tracking down his objective, Archimedes could not give his name but said, protecting the dust with his hands, "I beg you, don't disturb this," and was slaughtered as neglectful of the victor's command; with his blood he confused the lines of his art. So it fell out that he was first granted his life and then stripped of it by reason of the same pursuit.[20]

ext. 8 Socraten etiam constat aetate provectum fidibus trac-
tandis operam dare coepisse, satius iudicantem eius artis
usum sero quam numquam percipere. et quantula Socrati
accessio illa futura scientia erat! sed pervicax hominis industria tantis doctrinae suae divitiis etiam musicae rationis
vilissimum elementum accedere voluit. ergo dum ad dis-
cendum semper se pauperem credit,[59] ad docendum fecit
locupletissimum.

ext. 9 Atque ut longae et felicis industriae quasi in unum
acervum exempla redigamus, Isocrates nobilissimum li-
brum qui Παναθηναϊκός inscribitur quartum et nonagesimum annum agens, ita ut ipse significat, composuit, opus
ardentis spiritus plenum. ex quo apparet senescentibus
membris eruditorum intus animos industriae beneficio
florem iuventae retinere. neque hoc stilo terminos vitae
suae clausit: namque admirationis eius fructum quinquen-
nio percepit.

ext. 10 Citerioris aetatis metas sed non parvi tamen spatii
Chrysippi vivacitas flexit: nam octogesimo anno coeptum
undequadragesimum Λογικῶν exactissimae subtilitatis
volumen reliquit. cuius studium in tradendis ingenii sui
monumentis tantum operae laborisque sustinuit ut ad ea
quae scripsit penitus cognoscenda longa vita sit opus.

ext. 11 Te quoque, Cleanthe, tam laboriose haurientem et tam
pertinaciter tradentem sapientiam numen ipsius Industriae suspexit, cum adulescentem quaestu extrahendae
aquae nocturno tempore inopiam tuam sustentantem,

---

[59] credit *Kempf*: -didit AL

---

[21] Plato *Euthyd.* 272c, Cic. *Sen.* 26.
[22] 342: Isocr. *Panath.* 3, Cic. *Sen.* 13.

Socrates too is believed to have begun to learn to play the lyre when well on in years, thinking it better to acquire proficiency in that art late than never. And how slight an addition would that knowledge have been to Socrates! But the man's persevering diligence wished the trivial rudiments of musical science to accrue to his vast wealth of erudition. So always believing himself a poor man as to learning, he made himself a very rich one as to teaching.[21]

To bring our examples of long and fruitful diligence as it were into a single heap, Isocrates composed his famous book entitled "Panathenaicus" in his ninety-fourth year[22] as he tells us himself, a work full of fiery spirit. Hence it is evident that while the limbs of learned men grow old, their minds within thanks to diligence retain the bloom of youth. Nor did he close the boundaries of his life with the pen that wrote this book, for he enjoyed the admiration it excited for five years.

Chrysippus' longevity rounded the turning post of a shorter existence, but still one of no small span. For he left a thirty-ninth volume of "Logical Problems," of the nicest subtlety, begun in his eightieth year.[23] His zeal in handing down the monuments of his intellect was equal to so much effort and labour that it takes a long life to master his writings thoroughly.

You too, Cleanthes, so laboriously taking in wisdom and so perseveringly handing it on, did the divine power of Diligence herself admire. She saw you as a young man sustaining your poverty at night by drawing water for money,

[23] According to better authority he died at 73, between 208 and 204 (von Arnim, *RE* Chrysippos 14).

diurno Chrysippi praeceptis percipiendis vacantem , eundemque ad undecentesimum annum attenta cura erudientem auditores tuos videret: duplici enim labore unius saeculi spatium occupasti, incertum reddendo discipulusne an praeceptor esses laudabilior.

ext. 12 Sophocles quoque gloriosum cum Rerum Natura certamen habuit, tam benigne mirifica illi opera sua exhibendo quam illa operibus eius tempora liberaliter sumministrando: prope enim centesimum annum attigit, sub ipsum transitum ad mortem Oedipode ἐπὶ Κολωνῷ scripto, qua sola fabula omnium eiusdem studii poetarum praeripere gloriam potuit. idque ignotum esse posteris filius Sophoclis Iophon noluit, sepulcro patris quae rettuli insculpendo.

ext. 13 Simonides vero poeta octogesimo anno et docuisse se carmina et in eorum certamen descendisse ipse gloriatur. nec fuit iniquum illum voluptatem ex ingenio suo diu percipere, cum eam omni aevo fruendam traditurus esset.

ext. 14 Nam Solon quanta industria flagraverit et versibus complexus est, quibus significat se cotidie aliquid addiscentem senescere, et supremo vitae die confirmavit, quod, adsidentibus amicis et quadam de re sermonem inter se conferentibus, fatis iam pressum caput erexit, interrogatusque quapropter id fecisset, respondit 'ut cum istud, quidquid est, de quo disputatis percepero, moriar.' migrasset profecto ex hominibus inertia, si eo animo vitam ingrederentur quo eam Solon egressus est.

---

24 Sen. *Ep.* 44.3, Lucian *Macrob.* 19 etc. "Chrysippus" seems to be the author's error for Zeno (von Arnim, *RE* XI.558.68–559.34). Chrysippus succeeded Cleanthes as head of Stoa.
25 Cic. *Sen.* 22 etc.   26 In 477/6: Simon. fr. 147 Diehl.

leaving time to study the teachings of Chrysippus by day, and instructing your pupils with the closest care until your ninety-ninth year.[24] For you occupied the space of one century in a double labour, making it doubtful whether you deserved more praise as pupil or as teacher.

Sophocles too had a glorious contest with the Nature of Things, producing his marvellous works for her as unstintingly as she generously provided the time to compose them. For he almost attained his century, writing "Oedipus at Colonus" just at the point of passing from life to death; a play by which in itself he was able to preempt the glory of all poets in the same genre. Sophocles' son Iophon did not wish posterity to be ignorant of this, engraving what I have related on his father's tomb.[25]

The poet Simonides himself boasts that in his eightieth year he taught his poems and personally attended the competitions.[26] Nor was it unfair that he should long take pleasure in his genius since he was to hand it on for the enjoyment of all time.

With what diligence Solon was inspired, he put into the verses in which he tells us that he grew old learning something every day,[27] and he confirmed it on the last day of his life. His friends who were sitting by his side were talking about some matter among themselves, when he raised a head already weighed down by the fates. Asked why he did so he replied: "So that as soon as I find out what you are discussing, whatever it is, I may die."[28] Surely sluggishness would have departed from men if they had entered life in the same spirit as Solon left it.

---

[27] Solon fr. 22 Diehl, Plato *Laches* 189a etc.
[28] Not found elsewhere.

ext. 15 Quam porro industrius Themistocles, qui maximarum rerum cura districtus omnium tamen civium suorum nomina memoria comprehendit, per summamque iniquitatem patria pulsus et ad Xerxem, quem paulo ante devicerat, confugere coactus, prius quam in conspectum[60] eius veniret, Persico sermone se adsuefecit, ut labore parta commendatione regiis auribus familiarem et adsuetum sonum vocis adhiberet.

ext. 16 Cuius utriusque industriae laudem duo reges partiti sunt, Cyrus omnium militum suorum nomina, Mithridates duarum et viginti gentium, quae sub regno eius erant, linguas ediscendo, ille ut sine monitore exercitum salutaret, hic ut eos quibus imperabat sine interprete alloqui posset.

8. DE OTIO

praef. Otium, quod industriae et studio maxime contrarium videtur, praecipue subnecti debet, non quo evanescit virtus sed quo recreatur: alterum enim etiam inertibus vitandum, alterum strenuis quoque interdum appetendum est, illis ne perpetuam[61] vitam enervem[62] exigant, his ut tempestiva laboris intermissione ad laborandum fiant vegetiores.

1 Par verae amicitae clarissimum Scipio et Laelius, cum

---

[60] conspectum ⊊: -tu AL
[61] perpetuam *Watt*[3]: propri(a)e* AL
[62] enervem A *corr.*: inermem* AL

---

[29] Cic. *Sen.* 21.
[30] Thuc. 1.138.1 etc. Cf. VM 5.3.ext.3e.

How diligent moreover was Themistocles! Preoccupied as he was with attention to matters of the greatest importance, he nonetheless embraced in his memory the names of all his fellow citizens.[29] Driven by a gross injustice from his country, he was forced to go for refuge to Xerxes, whom he had just recently defeated. Before coming into his presence, he acquainted himself with the Persian language in order that, winning recommendation by labour, he might bring to the royal ears a familiar, accustomed sound of voice.[30]

The praise due to his diligence in both respects two kings have divided between them. Cyrus learned the names of all his soldiers, Mithridates the languages of the twenty-two nations that were under his sovereignty, the former so that he could greet his army without a prompter, the latter so that he could speak to his subjects without an interpreter.[31]

8. OF LEISURE

Since leisure appears to be diametrically opposed to diligence and study, it has the best claim to be subjoined to them, not leisure by which efficiency loses strength but by which it is revived. For the former is to be avoided even by the lazy, the latter is sometimes to be sought even by the energetic, so that as to the first they do not lead a life of perpetual inactivity, and as to the second that by timely intermission of work they may come the brisker to its resumption.

That illustrious pair of true friends, Scipio and Laelius,

[31] Xen. *Cyr.* 5.3.46–51, Pliny *N.H.* 7.88 etc.

amoris vinculo tum etiam omnium virtutum inter se iunctum societate, ut actuosae vitae iter aequali gradu exsequebantur ita animi quoque remissioni communiter acquiescebant: constat namque eos Caietae et Laurenti vagos litoribus conchulas et umbilicos lectitasse, idque se P. Crassus ex socero suo Scaevola, qui gener Laelii fuit, audisse saepenumero praedicavit.

2   Scaevola autem, quietis et[63] remissionis eorum certissimus testis, optime pila lusisse traditur, quia videlicet ad hoc deverticulum animum suum forensibus ministeriis fatigatum transferre solebat. alveo quoque et calculis interdum vacasse dicitur, cum bene ac diu iura civium, caerimonias deorum ordinasset; ut enim in rebus seriis Scaevolam ita in [scaelus][64] lusibus hominem agebat, quem Rerum Natura continui laboris patientem esse non sinit.

ext. 1   Idque vidit cui nulla pars sapientiae obscura fuit, Socrates, ideoque non erubuit tunc cum interposita harundine cruribus suis cum parvulis filiolis ludens ab Alcibiade risus[65] est.

ext. 2   Homerus quoque, ingenii caelestis vates, non aliud sensit vehementissimis Achillis manibus canoras fides aptando, ut earum militare robur leni pacis studio relaxaret.

[63] quietis et *Gertz*: quiestis A (?): -et(a)e LG
[64] *del.* Vahlen
[65] visus P

joined one to another by the bond of affection and also by partnership in all virtues, just as they followed the path of active life with equal tread, so did they find relief together in mental relaxations. For it is agreed that they used to pick up shells and pebbles wandering on the beaches of Caieta and Laurentum, and P. Crassus often declared that he had learned this from his father-in-law Scaevola, who was Laelius' son-in-law.[1]

Scaevola, who was the most reliable witness to their repose and relaxation, is reported to have been an excellent ball player; no doubt because he used to divert his mind to this avocation when wearied by forensic work. He is said also to have sometimes spent time with gaming board and pieces, after ordering long and well the rights of citizens and the rituals of the gods. In serious matters he behaved as Scaevola, in play as a human being, whom the Nature of Things does not permit to endure unbroken labour.[2]

EXTERNAL

Socrates, to whom no part of wisdom was dark, saw this. And so he was not embarrassed when he was laughed at by Alcibiades as he played with his little children with a reed between his legs.[3]

Homer too, poet of celestial genius, felt no differently when he put the tuneful lyre into Achilles' violent hands to relax their soldierly strength in a mild pursuit of peace.[4]

---

[1] Cic. *De orat.* 2.22; cf. Hor. *Sat.* 2.1.71–74. P should be L.
[2] Ibid. 1.217, Quint. *Inst.* 11.2.38.
[3] Aelian *Var. hist.* 12.15.
[4] Hom. *Il.* 9.186.

9. QUANTA VIS SIT ELOQUENTIAE

praef.   Potentiam vero eloquentiae, etsi plurimum valere
⟨iam⟩[66] animadvertimus, tamen sub propriis exemplis,
quo scilicet vires eius testatiores fiant, recognosci convenit.

1   Regibus exactis, plebs dissidens a patribus iuxta ripam
fluminis Anienis in colle qui Sacer appellatur armata consedit, eratque non solum deformis sed etiam miserrimus
rei publicae status, a capite eius cetera parte corporis pestifera seditione divisa. ac ni Valerii subvenisset eloquentia,
spes tanti imperii in ipso paene ortu suo corruisset: is
namque populum nova et insolita libertate temere gaudentem oratione ad meliora et saniora consilia revocatum
senatui subiecit, id est urbem urbi iunxit. verbis ergo
facundis ira consternatio arma cesserunt.

2   Quae etiam Marianos Cinnanosque mucrones civilis
profundendi sanguinis cupiditate furentes inhibuerunt:
missi enim a saevissimis ducibus milites ad M. Antonium
obtruncandum, sermone eius obstupefacti destrictos iam
et vibrantes gladios cruore vacuos vaginis reddiderunt.
quibus digressis P. Annius—is enim solus in aditu expers
Antonianae eloquentiae steterat—crudele imperium truculento ministerio peregit. quam disertum igitur eum
fuisse putemus quem ne hostium quidem quisquam occidere sustinuit, qui modo vocem eius ad aures suas voluit
admittere?

[66] *add. Gertz*

---

1 494: Cicero (*Brut.* 54) gives the role to Publicola, but from
Livy (2.32.8) onwards it goes to Menenius Agrippa, except here.

9. HOW GREAT IS THE FORCE
OF ELOQUENCE

Although we have already seen that the power of eloquence is mighty, it may properly be reviewed in examples of its own so that its strength may be the better attested.

After the expulsion of the kings the plebians quarrelled with the patricians and settled in arms on the hill which is called "Sacred" by the bank of the river Anio. The state of the commonwealth was not only sorry but quite wretched, with the head divided from the rest of the body by internecine strife. And if Valerius' eloquence had not come to the rescue, the hope of so great an empire would have collapsed almost at birth. For by a speech he brought the people, which was rashly exulting in its new, unaccustomed freedom, back to better and saner counsels and subjected it to the senate; that is, he joined Rome to Rome. So by eloquent words anger, confusion, and arms subsided.[1]

Such words also checked the Marian and Cinnan blades, mad with the lust of shedding the blood of countrymen. Soldiers sent by the ruthless leaders to slaughter M. Antonius, struck with amazement by his speech, returned their swords already drawn and flashing unbloodied to their scabbards. After they left, P. Annius (for he alone standing at the entrance had been outside the range of Antonius' eloquence) carried out the cruel order in savage obedience.[2] How eloquent are we to think him whom none even of his enemies could bear to kill, none that is who was willing to let the orator's voice enter his ears?

So too in Paris, an apparent case of correction by the epitomist.

[2] Plut. *Mar.* 44, App. *B.C.* 1.72, Vell. 2.22.3.

3   Divus quoque Iulius, quam caelestis numinis tam etiam
humani ingenii perfectissimum columen, vim facundiae
proprie expressit dicendo in accusatione Cn. Dolabellae,
quem reum egit, extorqueri sibi causam optimam L.[67]
Cottae patrocinio, si quidem maxima tunc ‹eloquentia de
vi›[68] eloquentiae questa est. cuius facta mentione, quoniam domesticum nullum maius adiecerim exemplum,
peregrinandum est.

ext. 1   Pisistratus dicendo tantum valuisse traditus est ut ei
Athenienses regium imperium oratione capti permitte-
rent, cum praesertim e contraria parte amantissimus
patriae Solo niteretur. sed alterius salubriores erant contiones,[69] alterius disertiores. quo evenit ut alioqui prudentissima civitas libertati servitutem praeferret.

ext. 2   Pericles autem, felicissimis naturae incrementis sub
Anaxagora praeceptore summo studio perpolitis instructus, liberis Athenarum cervicibus iugum servitutis impo-
suit: egit enim illam urbem et versavit arbitrio suo,
cumque adversus voluntatem populi loqueretur, iucunda
nihilo minus et popularis eius vox erat. itaque veteris
comoediae maledica lingua, quamvis potentiam viri per-
stringere cupiebat, tamen in labris omni[70] melle dulciorem
leporem fatebatur habitare, inque animis eorum qui illum
audierant quasi aculeos quosdam relinqui praedicabat.
fertur quidam, cum admodum senex primae contioni Peri-
clis adulescentuli interesset, idemque iuvenis Pisistratum

[67] L. AL: C. *Pighius*
[68] *add.* Kempf*
[69] contiones A *corr.*, L *corr.*: content- AL
[70] omni *SB*[1]: hominis AL

The divine Julius too, the most perfect pinnacle of celestial deity and of human genius, aptly expressed the force of eloquence when he said in his speech against Cn. Dolabella, whom he was prosecuting, that his excellent case was being wrenched away from him by L. Cotta's advocacy.[3] For on that occasion eloquence at its greatest complained of the power of eloquence. Having mentioned him, since I could add no greater domestic example, I must go abroad.

EXTERNAL

Pisistratus is said to have been so forceful an orator that the Athenians allowed him royal power, captivated by speech, even though Solon, who loved his country so well, exerted himself on the other side. But the harangues of the latter were more wholesome, those of the former more eloquent. So it fell out that an otherwise very sensible community preferred slavery to freedom.

Pericles, equipped as he was with abundant natural advantages zealously polished under his teacher Anaxagoras, placed a yoke of slavery on the free necks of the Athenians. For he drove and turned that city just as he pleased, and when he spoke against the people's wishes, his voice was none the less welcome and popular. So the railing tongue of Old Comedy, though eager to take shots at the great man's power, yet confessed that charm sweeter than any honey dwelt on his lips and declared that it was as though stings were left in the minds of those who heard him.[4] It is said that a very old man who in his youth had heard Pisistratus in his decrepitude making a speech was also present when young Pericles made his first speech in

---

[3] 77: cf. Cic. *Brut.* 317 etc., but Caesar's complaint is found only here. Cotta's praenomen was Gaius.   [4] Cic. *Brut.* 59 etc.

decrepitum iam contionantem audisset, non temperasse
sibi quominus exclamaret cavere illum civem oportere,
quod Pisistrati orationi simillima eius esset oratio. nec
hominem aut aestimatio eloquii aut morum augurium
fefellit. quid enim inter Pisistratum et Periclen interfuit,
nisi quod ille armatus, hic sine armis tyrannidem gessit?

ext. 3   Quantum eloquentia valuisse Hegesian Cyrenaicum
philosophum arbitramur? qui sic mala vitae repraesenta-
bat ut eorum miseranda imagine audientium pectoribus
inserta multis voluntariae mortis oppetendae cupiditatem
ingeneraret: ideoque a rege Ptolomaeo ulterius hac de re
disserere prohibitus est.

10. QUANTUM MOMENTUM SIT
IN PRONUNTIATIONE ET
APTO MOTU CORPORIS

praef.   Eloquentiae autem ornamenta in pronuntiatione apta
et convenienti motu corporis consistunt. quibus cum se
instruxit, tribus modis homines adgreditur, animos eorum
ipsa invadendo, horum alteri aures, alteri oculos permul-
cendos tradendo.

1   Sed ut propositi fides in personis illustribus exhibeatur,
C. Gracchus, eloquentiae quam consilii[71] felicioris adulescens, quoniam flagrantissimo ingenio, cum optime rem
publicam tueri posset, perturbare impie maluit, quotiens

---

[71] consilii *Damsté*: propositi AL

---

5 Not found elsewhere.

public; and he could not restrain himself from crying out, "Beware of that citizen. He speaks just like Pisistratus used to speak."[5] Nor was he mistaken either in his judgment of the oratory or in his prediction of character. For what difference was there between Pisistratus and Pericles except that the one exercised his tyranny armed, the other without arms?

What power do we imagine was in the eloquence of the Cyrenaic philosopher Hegesias? He made the evils of life so vivid that when their pitiful image was thrust into the hearts of his hearers he generated in many the desire for suicide. And on that account he was forbidden by king Ptolemy to discourse any further on the subject.[6]

10. HOW MUCH IMPORTANCE LIES IN ELOCUTION AND APT BODILY MOVEMENT

The ornaments of Eloquence lie in appropriate elocution and suitable bodily movement. When she has equipped herself with these, she attacks men in three ways: by herself invading their minds and by handing their ears over to the one and their eyes to the other to be charmed.

But to verify my statement in illustrious personages, C. Gracchus, a young man happier in his eloquence than in his aims (for with his shining talent he could have been a splendid defender of the commonwealth but preferred to be an impious revolutionary), whenever he spoke before

[6] *Ca.* 290: Cic. *Tusc.* 1.83, Diog. Laert. 2.86 (who calls him "the prompter of suicide").

apud populum contionatus est, servum post se musicae artis peritum habuit, qui occulte eburnea fistula pronuntiationis eius modos formabat, aut nimis remissos excitando aut plus iusto concitatos revocando, quia ipsum calor atque impetus actionis attentum huiusce temperamenti aestimatorem esse non patiebatur.

2   Q. autem Hortensius, plurimum in corporis decoro motu repositum credens, paene plus studii in eo[72] ⟨e⟩laborando[73] quam in ipsa eloquentia adfectanda impendit. itaque nescires utrum cupidius ad audiendum eum an ad spectandum concurreretur: sic verbis oratoris aspectus et rursus aspectui verba serviebant. constat Aesopum Rosciumque ludicrae artis peritissimos illo causas agente in corona frequenter adstitisse, ut foro petitos gestus in scaenam referrent.

3   Nam M. Cicero quantum in utraque re de qua loquimur momenti sit oratione quam pro Gallio habuit significavit, M. Calidio accusatori exprobrando quod, praeparatum sibi a reo venenum testibus chirographis quaestionibus probaturum adfirmans, remisso vultu et languida voce et soluto genere orationis usus esset, pariterque et oratoris vitium detexit et causae periclitantis argumentum adiecit totum hunc locum ita claudendo: 'tu istud, M. Calidi, nisi fingeres, sic ageres?'

[72] eo P: eodem AL
[73] *add. Pighius*

the public, had a slave skilled in the art of music stationed behind him. With an ivory pipe the man secretly shaped Gracchus' elocution. When the rhythm was too relaxed, he would heighten it, when over-agitated, he would tone it down; for the heat and impetus of his discourse did not let the speaker be himself an attentive judge of this balance.[1]

Q. Hortensius believed that a great deal depended on graceful bodily movement and devoted almost more effort to its elaboration than to striving after eloquence itself. So it was a question whether people flocked more eagerly to hear him or to watch him. So well did his appearance set off the orator's words and the words in turn his appearance. It is well established that Aesopus and Roscius, two most skilful actors, often stood in the audience when he was conducting a case in order to bring back to the stage the gestures they had sought in the Forum.[2]

M. Cicero showed the importance of the two factors of which I speak in the speech he delivered in defence of Gallius. He taunted the prosecutor M. Calidius in that, while asserting his intention to prove by witnesses, writings, and interrogations that the defendant had prepared to poison him, he spoke with a relaxed countenance, languid voice, and a slack oratorical style. At one and the same time Cicero exposed a fault in the speaker and added an argument to the case of the accused, wrapping up the whole topic thus: "If you were not making up this story of yours, M. Calidius, is this the way you would plead?"[3]

---

[1] Cic. *De orat.* 3.225 etc.

[2] Quint. *Inst.* 11.3.8f., Gell. 1.5.2 (neither mention the actors); cf. Cic. *Att.* 6.1.8 fin.

[3] 64: Cic. *Brut.* 277f.

ext. 1 Consentaneum huic Demosthenis iudicium. cuidam,[74]
cum interrogaretur quidnam esset in dicendo efficacissimum, respondit 'ή ύπόκρισις.' iterum deinde et tertio
interpellatus idem dixit, paene totum se illi debere confitendo. recte itaque Aeschines, cum propter iudicialem
ignominiam relictis Athenis Rhodum petisset, atque ibi
rogatu civitatis suam prius in Ctesiphontem, deinde Demosthenis pro eodem orationem clarissima et suavissima
voce recitasset, admirantibus cunctis utriusque voluminis
eloquentiam sed aliquanto magis Demosthenis, 'quid si'
inquit 'ipsum audissetis?' tantus orator et modo tam in-
festus adversarius sic inimici vim ardoremque dicendi
suspexit ut se scriptorum eius parum idoneum lectorem
esse praedicaret, expertus acerrimum vigorem oculorum,
terribile vultus pondus, accommodatum singulis verbis
sonum vocis, efficacissimos corporis motus. ergo etsi operi
illius adici nihil potest, tamen in Demosthene magna pars
Demosthenis abest quod legitur potius quam auditur.

11. QUAM MAGNI EFFECTUS
ARTIUM SINT

praef. Effectus etiam artium recognosci potest[75] aliquid adferre voluptatis, protinusque et quam utiliter excogitatae
sint patebit et memoratu dignae res lucido in loco repo-
nentur et labor in iis edendis suo fructu non carebit.

[74] cuidam G: qu- AL: qui ⊆   [75] potest *Per.*: posse AL
recog- ... adferre *intra cruces Briscoe*

---

[4] Cic. *De Orat.* 3.213 etc.

In line with the above is the judgment of Demosthenes. When somebody asked him what factor in oratory counted for most, he answered: "The acting"; challenged a second and a third time, he said the same, confessing that he owed almost all he was to that. So Aeschines was right. After his judicial humiliation he left Athens and went to Rhodes, where, at the request of the community he recited first his own speech against Ctesiphon, then that of Demosthenes on behalf of the same in very loud and melodious tones. Everyone admired the eloquence of both works, but that of Demosthenes somewhat the more of the two. "What if you had heard himself?" said Aeschines.[4] So great an orator and recently so bitter an adversary, he had so high an esteem for his enemy's oratorical force and ardour as to declare himself ill qualified to read his writings aloud. He had experienced the piercing force of the eyes, the formidable gravity of the countenance, the timbre of the voice accommodated to the several words, the arresting movements of the body. So although nothing can be added to his work, yet a great part of Demosthenes is absent in Demosthenes because he is read, not heard.

11. HOW GREAT ARE THE EFFECTS OF THE ARTS

Recognition of the effects of the arts can bring pleasure, and it will at once appear how usefully they have been devised, things worthy of remembrance will be placed in full light, and the labour which went into their production will not lack its reward.

1   Sulpicii Gali[76] maximum in omni genere litterarum recipiendo studium plurimum rei publicae profuit: nam cum L. Paulli bellum adversum regem Persen gerentis legatus esset, ac serena nocte subito luna defecisset, eoque velut diro quodam monstro perterritus exercitus noster manus cum hoste conserendi fiduciam amisisset, de caeli ratione et siderum natura peritissime disputando alacrem eum in aciem misit. itaque inclitae illi Paullianae victoriae liberales artes Gali[77] aditum dederunt, quia nisi ille metum nostrorum militum vicisset, imperator vincere hostes non potuisset.

2   Spurinnae quoque in coniectandis[78] deorum monitis efficacior scientia apparuit quam urbs Romana voluit. praedixerat C. Caesari ut proximos triginta dies quasi fatales caveret, quorum ultimus erat idus Martiae. eo cum forte mane uterque in domum Calvini Domitii ad officium convenissent, Caesar Spurinnae 'ecquid scis idus iam Martias venisse?' at[79] is 'ecquid scis illas nondum praeterisse?' abiecerat alter timorem tamquam exacto tempore suspecto, alter ne extremam quidem eius partem periculo vacuam esse arbitratus est. utinam haruspicem potius augurium quam patriae parentem securitas fefellisset.

ext. 1   Sed ut alienigena scrutemur, cum obscurato repente sole inusitatis perfusae tenebris Athenae sollicitudine an-

---

[76] Gali *Briscoe*: Galli AL   [77] Gali L *corr.*: Galli A *corr.*, G: Gall L   [78] coniectandis *Halm*: consectantis AL
[79] at P: et AL

---

[1] 168: Livy 44.37.5–8 etc.

The ardent zeal of Sulpicius Galus in absorbing every sort of literary work was of the greatest benefit to the commonwealth. When he was Legate to L. Paullus, who was campaigning against king Perses, on a clear night the moon suddenly went into eclipse. Our army was terrified as by a dire prodigy and no longer had confidence to join battle with the enemy. But by discoursing expertly on the celestial system and the nature of the stars Galus sent them eager into the fray. So the liberal arts of Galus gave access to that famous Paullian victory; for if he had not overcome our soldiers' fear, the general would not have been able to overcome the enemy.[1]

Spurinna's science in divining the warnings of the gods proved more efficacious than the Roman city would have desired. He had foretold to C. Caesar that he should beware of the next thirty days as fateful, the last of which was the ides of March. Early that day they both came to call at the house of Calvinus Domitius. Caesar said to Spurinna, "Do you know that the ides of March are already come?" He answered, "Do you know that they are not yet gone?"[2] Caesar had put fear aside as though the danger period had expired, whereas Spurinna thought that even its ultimate portion was not free of peril. Would that the soothsayer had been mistaken in his augury rather than the father of his country in his security!

EXTERNAL

But to scrutinize alien-born examples, when Athens was in dire anxiety, enveloped in unaccustomed darkness because of a sudden eclipse of the sun, believing that her

---

[2] 44: Plut. *Caes.* 63, Suet. *Iul.* 81.2.

gerentur, interitum sibi caelesti denuntiatione portendi credentes, Pericles processit in medium, et quae a praeceptore suo Anaxagora pertinentia ad solis et lunae cursum acceperat disseruit, nec ulterius trepidare cives suos vano metu passus est.

ext. 2   Quantum porro dignitatis a rege Alexandro tributum arti existimamus, qui se et pingi ab uno Apelle et fingi a Lysippo tantummodo voluit?

ext. 3   Tenet visentes Athenis Vulcanus Alcamenis manibus fabricatus: praeter cetera enim perfectissimae artis in eo procurrentia[80] indicia etiam illud mirantur, quod stat dissimulatae claudicationis sub veste leviter vestigium repraesentans, ut non exprobratum tamquam vitium ita tamquam certam propriamque dei notam decore significans.

ext. 4   Cuius coniugem Praxiteles in marmore quasi spirantem in templo Cnidiorum collocavit, propter pulchritudinem operis a libidinoso cuiusdam complexu parum tutam. quo excusabilior est error equi, qui visa pictura equae hinnitum edere coactus est, et canum latratus aspectu picti canis incitatus, taurusque ad amorem et concubitum aeneae vaccae Syracusis nimiae similitudinis irritamento compulsus: quid enim vacua rationis animalia arte decepta miremur, cum hominis sacrilegam cupiditatem muti lapidis liniamentis excitatam videamus?

---

[80] proc- *Gertz*: praec-* AL

---

3 430: Quint. *Inst.* 1.10.47, Plut. *Per.* 35.   4 "None of the Greek sources asserts the exclusion of other artists by royal edict. This looks like a pleasant but legendary touch in the Latin tradition and not the whole of it either. Cic. *Fam.* 5.12.7 only has *potissimum*" (C. O. Brink on Hor. *Ep.* 2.1.239).

destruction was portended by the celestial warning, Pericles came forward and discoursed on what he had learned from his teacher Anaxagoras pertaining to the courses of the sun and moon. Nor did he let his countrymen tremble any longer in their baseless fear.[3]

Moreover, how great do we suppose was the respect paid by king Alexander to the dignity of art, who would have himself painted only by Apelles and sculpted only by Lysippus?[4]

Vulcan, fabricated by the hands of Alcamenes, engrosses visitors in Athens. Besides other outstanding manifestations of artistic perfection in that statue, they are struck with how in its stance it offers a gentle hint of lameness disguised under the drapery, not reproaching as a blemish but all the same decorously indicating it as a definite and peculiar characteristic of the god.[5]

Praxiteles set up Vulcan's consort breathing as it were in marble in the temple at Cnidos. The beauty of the work is such that it was hardly safe from a libidinous embrace,[6] so providing some excuse for the mistake of a stallion which on seeing the picture of a mare could not help neighing, or of the dogs which the sight of a dog in a painting caused to bark, or of the bull in Syracuse that was driven to erotic intercourse with a bronze cow[7] by the stimulus of too close a likeness. For why should we be surprised that animals void of reason should be deceived by art, when we see a human being's sacrilegious lust excited by the outlines of voiceless stone?

[5] Cic. *Nat. deor.* 1.83.
[6] Pliny *N.H.* 36.20f. etc.
[7] Livy 41.13.2.

QUAEDAM NULLA ARTE EFFICI POSSE

ext. 5   Ceterum Natura, quem ad modum saepenumero ae-
mulam virium suarum Artem esse patitur ita aliquando
irritam fesso labore dimittit. quod summi artificis Euphra-
noris manus senserunt: nam cum Athenis duodecim deos
pingeret, Neptuni imaginem quam poterat excellentissi-
mis maiestatis coloribus complexus est, perinde ac Iovis
aliquanto augustiorem repraesentaturus. sed omni impetu
cogitationis in superiore opere absumpto, posteriores eius
conatus adsurgere quo tendebant nequiverunt.

ext. 6   Quid? ille alter aeque nobilis pictor, luctuosum immo-
latae Iphigeniae sacrificium referens, cum Calchantem
tristem, maestum Ulixen, [clamantem Aiacem][81] lamen-
tantem Menelaum circa aram statuisset, caput Agamem-
nonis involvendo nonne summi maeroris acerbitatem arte
non posse exprimi confessus est? itaque pictura eius haru-
spicis et amici et fratris lacrimis madet, patris fletum spec-
tantis adfectu aestimandum reliquit.

ext. 7   Atque ut eiusdem studii adiciam exemplum, praecipuae artis pictor equum ab exercitatione venientem modo
non vivum labore industriae suae comprehenderat. cuius
naribus spumas adicere cupiens, tantus artifex in tam par-
vula materia multum ac diu frustra terebatur. indignatione
deinde accensus spongeam omnibus imbutam coloribus
forte iuxta se positam apprehendit, et veluti corrupturus
opus suum tabulae illisit. quam Fortuna ad ipsas equi na-
res directam desiderium pictoris coegit explere. itaque

[81] *del. Kempf*

8 Not found elsewhere.
9 Cic. *Orat.* 74 etc.

THAT SOME THINGS CANNOT BE
EFFECTED BY ANY ART

Even as Nature often allows Art to emulate her powers, so sometimes she lets her go frustrated with labour in vain, as the hands of the great artist Euphranor discovered. When he was painting the twelve gods in Athens, he endowed the image of Neptune with the most striking colours of majesty he could muster, as though intending to exhibit Jupiter in guise yet more august. But he had exhausted all the force of his imagination in the earlier work and his later attempts could not rise to their objective.[8]

Consider too that other no less famous painter who portrayed the grievous sacrifice of immolated Iphigenia, placing a sad Calchas, a mournful Ulysses, and a lamenting Menelaus around the altar. Did he not confess by veiling Agamemnon's head that the bitterness of deepest grief cannot be expressed in art? So his painting is wet with the tears of the soothsayer and the friend and the brother, but left the father's weeping to be judged by the emotion of the spectator.[9]

And to add an example from the same field of endeavour,[10] a painter of outstanding quality presented in his industrious toil a horse, almost alive, returning from exercise. Wishing to add foam to the horse's nostrils, great artist that he was, he laboured much and long in vain upon so petty a subject. Then in a fit of anger he seized a sponge impregnated with all colours which happened to be beside him and dashed it against the panel as though to destroy his work. Fortune directed it right at the horse's nostrils

[10] Pliny *N.H.* 35.104, Plut. *Moral.* 99B.

quod ars adumbrare non valuit, casus imitatus est.

12. SUAE QUEMQUE ARTIS OPTIMUM ET AUCTOREM ESSE ET DISPUTATOREM

praef.   Suae autem artis unumquemque et auctorem et dispu-
tatorem optimum esse ne dubitemus, paucis exemplis ad-
moneamur.

1   Q. Scaevola, legum clarissimus et certissimus vates,
quotienscumque de iure praediatorio consulebatur, ad
Furium et Cascellium, quia huic scientiae dediti erant,
consultores reiciebat. quo quidem facto moderationem
magis suam commendabat quam auctoritatem minuebat,
ab iis id negotium aptius explicari posse confitendo qui co-
tidiano usu eius callebant. sapientissimi igitur artis suae
professores sunt a quibus et propria studia verecunde et
aliena candide[82] aestimantur.

ext. 1   Platonis quoque eruditissimum pectus haec cogitatio
attigit, qui conductores sacrae arae ⟨de⟩[83] modo et forma
eius secum sermonem conferre conatos ad Eucliden geo-
metren ire iussit, scientiae eius cedens, immo professioni.

ext. 2   Gloriantur Athenae armamentario suo, nec sine causa:
est enim illud opus et impensa et elegantia visendum.
cuius architectum Philonem ita facunde rationem institu-

---

[82] candide *Cornelissen*: callide AL
[83] *add.* GP

---

[1] Cic. *Balb.* 45. On N. (?) Furius see his entry in SB
Onomasticon to Cicero's Treatises.

and made it fulfil the artist's desire. So what art could not depict, chance imitated.

12. THAT EACH MAN IS BOTH THE BEST EXECUTANT AND THE BEST EXPONENT OF HIS ART

So that we do not doubt that each man is both the best executant of his art and its best exponent, let us be admonished by a few examples.

Q. Scaevola was a very famous and reliable prophet of the laws, but whenever he was consulted on real estate law he would refer his clients to Furius and Cascellius as specialists in that area.[1] By so doing he did not so much diminish his authority as let them approve his restraint, confessing that the business in question could better be explained by those expert in it by daily practice. So the wisest professors of their art are those who judge their own pursuits modestly and those of others candidly.

EXTERNAL

This reflection also touched the most learned bosom of Plato. He told persons who had contracted to build a sacred altar and wished to discuss its measurements and shape with him that they should go to Euclid the geometer. He yielded to Euclid's knowledge, or rather to his profession.[2]

Athens glories in her arsenal, with good reason, for that work is worth a visit for its costliness and elegance. We are told that its architect, Philo, gave so eloquent an account of

---

[2] Plut. *Moral.* 579B–C.

tionis suae in theatro reddidisse constat ut disertissimus populus non minorem laudem eloquentiae eius quam arti tribueret.

ext. 3   Mirifice et ille artifex, qui in opere suo moneri se a sutore de crepida et ansulis passus, de crure etiam disputare incipientem supra plantam ascendere vetuit.

13. DE SENECTUTE

praef.   Senectus quoque ad ultimum sui finem provecta in hoc eodem opere inter exempla industriae in aliquot claris viris conspecta est. separatum tamen et proprium titulum habeat, ne cui deorum immortalium praecipua indulgentia adfuit, nostra ⟨h⟩on⟨or⟩ata[84] mentio defuisse existimetur, et simul spei diuturnioris vitae quasi adminicula quaedam dentur, quibus insistens alacriorem se respectu vetustae felicitatis facere possit, tranquillitatemque saeculi nostri, qua nulla umquam beatior fuit, subinde fiducia confirmet, salutaris principis incolumitatem ad longissimos humanae condicionis terminos prorogando.

1   M. Valerius Corvinus centesimum annum complevit. cuius inter primum et sextum consulatum quadraginta et sex anni intercesserunt, suffecitque integris viribus corporis non solum speciosissimis publicis ministeriis, sed etiam exactissimae agrorum suorum culturae, et civis et patris familiae optabile exemplum.

---

[84] honorata *Halm*: onata AL: orn- A *corr.*, G

---

[3] *Ca.* 330: Cic. *De orat.* 1.62 etc.
[4] Pliny *N.H.* 35.85.

his dispositions in the theatre, that the people, lettered as they were, praised his oratorical no less than his artistic skill.[3]

Admirably spoken too by the artist who let himself be advised in his work by a cobbler concerning sandals and loops, but told him to go no higher than the sole when he started to talk about the shin.[4]

13. OF OLD AGE

Old age too carried to its furthest term has been viewed in this same work among examples of diligence in a number of famous men. But let it have its own separate heading, lest any recipient of the immortal gods' exceptional indulgence be thought to have lacked honourable mention by us. At the same time let certain supports as it were be given to the hope of a long life, leaning on which a man may make himself more cheerful by contemplation of ancient felicity. And let confidence ever and anon confirm the tranquillity of our epoch, than which there never was a happier, by prolonging the safety of our leader and saviour to the longest limits allowed to the human condition.

M. Valerius Corvinus completed his hundredth year. Between his first and sixth Consulships forty-six years elapsed,[1] and with his bodily powers unimpaired he was equal not only to the most distinguished public employments but also to the most thorough cultivation of his land: an enviable example of both citizen and paterfamilias.

[1] See Broughton I.170 n.2. "Corvinus" should have been "Corvus," but the eminent Valerius Corvinus who revived the cognomen in that form was the author's contemporary; cf. VM 8.15.5.

2   Cuius vitae spatium aequavit Metellus, quartoque anno post consularia imperia senex admodum pontifex maximus creatus tutelam caerimoniarum per duo et viginti annos neque ore in votis nuncupandis haesitante neque in sacrificiis faciendis tremula manu gessit.

3   Q. autem Fabius Maximus duobus et sexaginta annis auguratus sacerdotium sustinuit, robusta iam aetate id adeptus. quae utraque tempora si in unum conferantur, facile saeculi modum expleverint.

4   Iam de M. Perperna[85] quid loquar? qui omnibus quos in senatum consul vocaverat superstes fuit, septemque tantummodo quos censor, collega L. Philippi, legerat e patribus conscriptis reliquos vidit, toto ordine amplissimo diuturnior.

5   Appii vero aevum clade metirer, quia infinitum numerum annorum orbatus luminibus exegit, nisi quattuor filios, quinque filias, plurimas clientelas, rem denique publicam hoc casu gravatus fortissime rexisset. quin etiam fessus iam vivendo lectica se in curiam deferri iussit, ut cum Pyrrho deformem pacem fieri prohiberet. hunc caecum aliquis nominet, a quo patria quod honestum erat per se parum cernens coacta est pervidere?

6   Muliebris etiam vitae spatium non minus longum in compluribus apparuit, quarum aliquas strictim rettulisse me satis erit: nam et Livia Rutilii septimum et nonagesimum, et Terentia Ciceronis tertium et centesimum, et

85 Perperna P: -enna AL

---

2 Cic. *Sen.* 30, Pliny *N.H.* 7.157.
3 Livy 30.26.7, Pliny *N.H.* 7.157.

Metellus equalled Corvinus' life span and in the fourth year following his consular power when quite an old man was made Chief Pontiff. For twenty-two years he took care of public rituals with a voice that never faltered in the taking of vows and a hand that never quavered in the performance of sacrifices.[2]

Q. Fabius Maximus supported his priestly office of Augur for sixty-two years, having acquired it when already of mature age. If the two periods be added together, they would easily complete the measure of a century.[3]

What shall I now say of M. Perperna, who outlived all those whom as Consul he had summoned to the senate and who saw only seven survivors out of the Conscript Fathers whom he had appointed as Censor, colleague of L. Philippus?[4] He lived longer than the entire honourable order.

I should measure Appius' life by his calamity, in that he spent an infinite number of years deprived of his eyesight, but for the fact that weighed down by this misfortune he stoutly governed four sons, five daughters, a large number of clients, and finally the commonwealth. What is more, already weary of living, he had himself carried to the senate house in a litter in order to prevent the conclusion of a discreditable peace with Pyrrhus. Call him blind if you will, by whom his country, which ill perceived what was honourable by herself, was forced to see it plain.[5]

A female life span no less long has appeared in a number of cases. It will be enough for me to mention a few briefly. Livia wife of Rutilius completed her ninety-seventh year, Terentia wife of Cicero her hundred and

---

[4] In 86: Pliny *N.H.* 7.157.
[5] 280: Cic. *Sen.* 16 etc.

Clodia Ofilii, quindecim filiis ante amissis, quintum decimum et centesimum explevit annum.

ext. 1   Iungam his duos reges, quorum diuturnitas populo Romano fuit utilissima. Siciliae rector Hiero ad nonagesimum annum pervenit. Masinissa Numidiae rex hunc modum excessit, regni spatium sexaginta annis emensus, vel ante omnes homines robore senectae admirabilis. constat eum, quem ad modum Cicero refert libro quem de senectute scripsit, nullo umquam imbri, nullo frigore ut caput suum veste tegeret adduci potuisse. eundem ferunt aliquot horis in eodem vestigio perstare solitum, non ante moto pede quam consimili labore iuvenes fatigasset, ac si quid agi a sedente oporteret, toto die saepenumero nullam in partem converso corpore in solio durasse. ille vero etiam exercitus equo insidens noctem diei plerumque iungendo duxit, nihilque omnino ex his operibus quae adulescens sustinere adsueverat, quo mollius senectutem ageret, omisit. veneris etiam usu ita semper viguit ut post sextum et octogesimum annum filium generaret, cui Methymno nomen fuit. terram quoque, quam vastam et desertam acceperat, perpetuo culturae studio frugiferam reliquit.

ext. 2   Gorgias etiam Leontinus, Isocratis et complurium magni ingenii virorum praeceptor, sua sententia felicissimus: nam cum centesimum et septimum ageret annum, interrogatus quapropter tam diu vellet in vita remanere, 'quia nihil' inquit 'habeo quod senectutem meam accusem.' quid isto tractu aetatis aut longius aut beatius? iam alterum saeculum ingressus neque in hoc querellam ullam

---

6 Pliny *N.H.* 7.158.   7 Livy 24.4.4, Lucian *Macrob.* 10.
8 Cic. *Sen.* 34.

third, Clodia wife of Ofilius her hundred and fifteenth after losing fifteen children.[6]

To these I will join two kings whose longevity was much
to the advantage of the Roman people. The ruler of Sicily,
Hiero, reached his ninetieth year.[7] Masinissa, king of Numidia, exceeded this measure, ruling as king for the space
of sixty years, remarkable above all men for the vigour of
his old age. We are told, as Cicero relates in the book he
wrote on old age, that he could never be induced by any
rain or cold to cover his head with a cloth. They also say
that he would stand for some hours in one spot, not moving
a foot until he had worn out his juniors in the like exercise;
and if something had to be done seated, he often held out
on his throne the whole day, turning his body neither right
nor left. He also led armies on horseback, frequently join-
ing night to day, and not a single one of those tasks which
he had been accustomed to discharge as a young man did
he omit to ease his old age. His sexual activity too was always vigorous, so that he fathered a son after his eighty-
sixth year, whose name was Methymnus. The land moreover, which was waste and desert when he took it over, he
left productive by dint of constant care for its cultivation.[8]

Gorgias of Leontini also, teacher of Isocrates and a
number of other highly gifted men, was in his own opinion
most fortunate. When he was in his hundred and seventh
year, he was asked why he wanted to remain in life so long.
"Because," he replied, "I have nothing to say against my
old age." What could be longer and happier than his
stretch of life? He had already begun a second century and

invenit neque in illo reliquit.

ext. 3   Biennio minor Xenophilus Chalcidensis Pythagoricus, sed felicitate non inferior, si quidem, ut ait Aristoxenus musicus, omnis humani incommodi expers in summo perfectissimae doctrinae splendore exstinctus est.

ext. 4   Arganthonius autem Gaditanus tam diu regnavit quam diu etiam ad satietatem vixisse abunde foret: octoginta enim annis patriam suam rexit, cum ad imperium quadraginta annos natus accessisset. cuius rei certi sunt auctores. Asinius etiam Pollio, non minima pars Romani stili, in tertio historiarum suarum libro centum illum et triginta annos explesse commemorat, et ipse nervosae vivacitatis haud parvum exemplum.

ext. 5   Huius regis consummationem annorum minus admirabilem faciunt Aethiopes, quos Herodotus scribit centesimum et vicesimum annum transgredi, et Indi, de quibus Ctesias idem tradit, et Epimenides Cnosius, quem Theopompus dicit septem et quinquaginta et centum annos vixisse.

ext. 6   Hellanicus vero ait quosdam ex gente Epiorum, quae pars Aetoliae ⟨est⟩,[86] ducenos explere annos, eique subscribit Damastes, hoc amplius adfirmans, Litorium quendam ex iis maximarum virium staturaeque praecipuae trecentesimum annum cumulasse.

ext. 7   Alexander vero, in eo volumine quod de Illyrico tractu composuit, adfirmat Dandonem quendam ad quingentesi-

[86] *add.* A *corr.*

9 Ibid. 13 etc.
10 Pliny *N.H.* 7.168, Lucian *Macrob.* 18.
11 Cic. *Sen.* 69 etc. Pollio died aged 79.

found no complaint in it nor left any in its predecessor.[9]

Xenophilus of Chalcis, the Pythagorean, was two years younger but in good fortune not inferior; for as Aristoxenus the musician says, he died in the full brilliance of the most consummate learning, without any experience of human adversity.[10]

Arganthonius of Gades reigned for so long a period that to have lived that long would be more than enough to produce satiety. For he ruled his country for eighty years, having ascended the throne at the age of forty. For that fact there are reliable authorities. And Asinius Pollio, not the least part of Roman literature, relates in the third book of his histories that he completed a hundred and thirty years. Pollio himself was no mean example of vigorous longevity.[11]

That king's consummation of years is made the less remarkable by the Ethiopians, of whom Herodotus[12] writes that they go beyond the hundred and twentieth year, and the Indians, of whom Ctesias reports the same, and Epimenides of Cnossus, who according to Theopompus lived a hundred and fifty-seven years.

Hellanicus says that certain of the nation of the Epii, which is a part of Aetolia, live two hundred years and Damastes supports him, further affirming that one of them, Litorius, a man of great strength and extraordinary stature, made up his three hundredth year.[13]

Alexander in the book he composed on the Illyrian region affirms that a certain Dando advanced to his five

[12] 3.23.
[13] Pliny *N.H.* 7.154.

mum usque annum nulla ex parte senescentem proces-
sisse. sed multo liberalius Xenophon, cuius περίπλους
legitur: insulae enim Latmiorum regem octingentis vitae
annis donavit. ac ne pater eius parum benigne acceptus
videretur, ei quoque sescentos adsignavit annos.

14. DE CUPIDITATE GLORIAE

praef.   Gloria vero aut unde oriatur aut cuius sit habitus aut
qua ratione debeat comparari, et an melius a virtute velut
non necessaria neglegatur viderint ii quorum in contem-
plandis eius modi rebus cura teritur, quibusque quae prudenter animadverterunt facunde contigit eloqui. ego in
hoc opere factis auctores et auctoribus facta sua reddere
contentus, quanta cupiditas eius esse soleat propriis exemplis demonstrare conabor.

1   Superior Africanus Ennii poetae effigiem in monumentis Corneliae gentis collocari voluit, quod ingenio eius
opera sua illustrata iudicaret, non quidem ignarus quam
diu Romanum imperium floreret, et Africa Italiae pedibus
esset subiecta, totiusque terrarum orbis summum columen arx Capitolina possideret, eorum exstingui memoriam non posse, si tamen litterarum quoque illis lumen
accessisset, magni aestimans, vir Homerico quam rudi
atque impolito praeconio dignior.

2   Similiter honoratus animus erga poetam Accium D.
Bruti, suis temporibus clari ducis, exstitit, cuius familiari
cultu et prompta laudatione delectatus versibus templorum aditus, quae ex manubiis consecraverat, adornavit.

---

14 Pliny *N.H.* 7.155.
1 Cic. *Arch.* 22 etc.   2 Ibid. 27.

hundredth year without any sign of old age. But Xenophon, whose "Circumnavigation" is read, is much more
generous, giving the king of Latmos island eight hundred
years of life. And so that his father should not seem hardly
done by, he assigned him too six hundred years.[14]

14. OF APPETITE FOR GLORY

Whence comes glory? What is it like? How should it be
gained? Is it better neglected by virtue as unnecessary? I
leave these questions to those who take pains in contem-
plating such matters and who have the faculty to express
eloquently what they have wisely observed. In this work I
am content to give to deeds their doers and to doers their
deeds, and shall attempt to show by appropriate examples
how strong the appetite for it is wont to be.

The elder Africanus wanted the portrait of the poet
Ennius placed among the monuments of the Cornelian
clan because he judged that by Ennius' genius his own performances had been illuminated. He was not ignorant that
as long as Roman empire flourished and Africa lay subject
at Italy's feet and the citadel of the Capitol possessed the
topmost pinnacle of the globe their memory could not be
extinguished, but he thought it of great moment that the
light of letters too should accrue to them. A man worthy to
be celebrated by Homer rather than in rude, unpolished
strains.[1]

D. Brutus, a famous general in his own time, showed a
similar disposition to honour the poet Accius. Pleased with
his familiar attentions and ready encomiums, he decorated
the approaches to the temples which he had consecrated
out of his spoils with Accius' verses.[2]

3   Ne Pompeius quidem Magnus ab hoc adfectu gloriae
aversus, qui Theophanen Mitylenaeum scriptorem rerum
suarum in contione militum civitate donavit, beneficium
per se amplum accurata etiam et testata oratione prosecutus. quo effectum est ut ne quis dubitaret quin referret
potius gratiam quam incoharet.

4   L. autem Sulla, etsi ad neminem scriptorem animum
direxit, tamen Iugurthae a Boccho rege ad Marium per-
ducti totam sibi laudem ⟨tam⟩[87] cupide adseruit ut anulo
quo signatorio utebatur insculptam illam traditionem haberet. et quantus⟨quantus⟩[88] postea, ne minimum quidem
gloriae vestigium contempsit.

5   Atque ut imperatoribus militis gloriosum spiritum subnectam, Scipionem, dona militaria iis qui strenuam operam ediderant dividentem, T. Labienus ut forti equiti
aureas armillas tribueret admonuit, eoque se negante id
factu⟨ru⟩m,[89] ne castrensis honos in eo qui paulo ante ser-
visset violaretur, ipse ex praeda Gallica aurum equiti largitus est. nec tacite id Scipio tulit: namque equiti 'habebis'
inquit 'donum viri divitis.' quod ubi ille accepit, proiecto
ante pedes Labieni auro vultum demisit. idem, ut audiit
Scipionem dicentem 'imperator te argenteis armillis do-
nat,' alacer gaudio abiit. nulla est ergo tanta humilitas quae
dulcedine gloriae non tangatur.

6   Illa vero etiam a claris viris interdum ex humillimis rebus petita est: nam quid sibi voluit C. Fabius, nobilissimus

---

[87] *add.* A *corr.*   [88] *add. Per.*
[89] *add.* A *corr.*, L *corr.*, G

---

3 62: ibid. 24.
4 Pliny *N.H.* 37.9 etc.

Pompeius Magnus too was not averse from this hankering after glory. He bestowed citizenship on Theophanes of Mitylene, the chronicler of his exploits, in a military assembly and followed up the gift, ample in itself, with a detailed and well publicized speech. As a result no one doubted that Pompey was repaying a favour rather than initiating one.[3]

L. Sulla did not pay attention to any writer. However, he claimed for himself the whole credit for king Bocchus' bringing Jugurtha to Marius, so eagerly that he kept the surrender engraved on a ring which he used as a signet.[4] And however great he subsequently became, he never despised the slightest trace of glory.

To subjoin to the generals the glory-loving spirit of a soldier: when Scipio was distributing military awards among those who had distinguished themselves, T. Labienus told him that he should give golden bracelets to a brave trooper. When Scipio refused on the ground that a military honour should not be degraded in the person of a man who had recently been a slave, Labienus gave the trooper gold from the Gallic booty. Scipio did not take that in silence. He said to the trooper, "You will have the gift of a rich man." Hearing that, the man flung the gold at Labienus' feet and hung his head. But when he heard Scipio say "Your commander presents you with silver bracelets," he went cheerfully away, rejoicing.[5] So there is no rank too humble to be affected by the sweetness of glory.

Glory has sometimes been sought even by men of note from the lowliest materials. For what was C. Fabius about,

[5] 46: not found elsewhere.

civis, qui cum in aede Salutis, quam C. Iunius Bubulcus
dedicaverat, parietes pinxisset, nomen iis suum inscripsit?
id enim demum ornamenti familiae consulatibus et sacer-
dotiis et triumphis celeberrimae deerat. ceterum sordido
studio deditum ingenium qualemcumque illum laborem
suum silentio oblitterari noluit, videlicet Phidiae secutus
exemplum, qui clipeo Minervae effigiem suam inclusit,
qua convulsa tota operis colligatio solveretur.

ext. 1   Sed melius aliquanto, si aliena imitatione capiebatur,
Themistoclis ardorem esset aemulatus, quem ferunt, stimulis virtutum[90] agitatum et ob id noctes inquietas exigentem, quaerentibus quid ita eo tempore in publico versaretur respondisse 'quia me tropaea Miltiadis de somno
excitant.' Marathon nimirum animum eius ad Artemisium
et Salamina, navalis gloriae fertilia nomina, illustranda
tacitis facibus incitabat. idem theatrum petens cum interrogaretur cuius vox auditu illi futura esset gratissima, dixit
'eius a quo artes[91] meae optime canentur.' dulcedinem
gloriae, paene adieci gloriosam!

ext. 2   Nam Alexandri pectus insatiabile laudis, qui Anaxarcho
comiti suo ex auctoritate Democriti praeceptoris innume-
rabiles mundos esse referenti 'heu me' inquit 'miserum,
quod ne uno quidem adhuc sum potitus!' angusta homini
possessio ‹avido›[92] gloriae fuit quae deorum omnium domicilio sufficit.

[90] virtutis P   [91] artes A: artis L: virtutes P (*cf. Cic.* virtus)
[92] *add.* SB*

[6] 304: Cic. *Tusc.* 1.4 etc.   [7] Cic. *De orat.* 2.73 etc.
[8] Plut. *Them.* 3.   [9] Cic. *Arch.* 20.

a citizen of the highest nobility, when he painted the walls in the temple of Welfare which C. Junius Bubulcus had dedicated and inscribed his name thereon?[6] *That* was the only distinction lacking in a family abounding in Consulates and priesthoods and triumphs! However, his mind devoted to a base pursuit did not wish that labour of his, whatever its nature, to be shrouded in silence. No doubt he was following the example of Phidias, who put his own likeness into Minerva's shield so that if it were dislodged the whole interconnection of the work would be dissolved.[7]

EXTERNAL

But if he was taken with the fancy to imitate foreigners, he had better have emulated Themistocles' enthusiasm. They say of him that he was agitated by the pricks of great achievements and so spent restless nights. To those who enquired why he went about in public at that time he replied: "Because Miltiades' trophies rouse me from my sleep." Doubtless Marathon urged his soul with silent goads to make Artemisium and Salamis illustrious, names fertile in naval glory.[8] The same Themistocles was asked on his way to the theatre whose voice he would most like to hear and answered, "Whosoever will best sing my skills."[9] Ah sweetness of glory—I had almost added "vainglorious"!

Alexander's appetite for fame was insatiable. He said to his companion Anaxarchus, who was retailing on the authority of his teacher Democritus the existence of innumerable worlds: "Alas for me, I have not yet made myself master of one!" A holding that suffices for the domicile of all the gods was not large enough for one glory-hungry man.[10]

[10] Plut. *Moral.* 466D, Aelian *Var. hist.* 4.29.

ext. 3   Regis et iuvenis flagrantissimae cupiditati similem Aristotelis in capessenda laude sitim subnectam: is namque Theodecti discipulo oratoriae artis libros quos ⟨pro suis⟩[93] ederet donaverat, molesteque postea ferens titulum eorum sic alii cessisse, proprio volumine quibusdam rebus insistens, plenius[94] sibi de his in Theodectis libris dictum esse adiecit. nisi me tantae et tam late patentis scientiae verecundia teneret, dicerem dignum philosophum cuius stabiliendi mores altioris animi philosopho traderentur.

    Ceterum gloria ne ab iis quidem qui contemptum eius introducere conantur neglegitur, quoniam quidem ⟨iis⟩[95] ipsis voluminibus nomina sua diligenter adiciunt, ut quod professione elevant usurpatione memoriae adsequantur. sed qualiscumque horum dissimulatio proposito illorum longe tolerabilior qui, dum aeternam memoriam adsequerentur, etiam sceleribus innotescere non dubitarunt.

ext. 4   Quorum e numero nescio an in primis Pausanias debeat referri: nam cum Hermoclen percontatus esset quonam modo subito clarus posset evadere atque is respondisset, si aliquem illustrem virum occidisset, futurum ut gloria eius ad ipsum redundaret, continuo Philippum interemit, et quidem quod petierat adsecutus est: tam enim se parricidio quam Philippus virtute notum posteris reddidit.

ext. 5   Illa vero gloriae cupiditas sacrilega: inventus est enim qui Dianae Ephesiae templum incendere vellet, ut opere

---

[93] *add.* P   [94] plenius *SB*[3]: plan- AL   [95] *add. SB*[3]

---

[11] This stricture is based on a misunderstanding. Aristotle wrote a compendium of Theodectes' treatise: see Solmsen *RE* VA.1729f.

To the voracious craving of a king and a young man I shall append Aristotle's similar thirsty grasping at credit. He had given his books on the art of oratory to his pupil Theodectes to publish as his own. Later he was irked that their title should have thus passed to another and so in a volume of his own, dwelling on certain matters, he added that he had spoken of them more fully in Theodectes' books. If I were not held back by my respect for knowledge so great and wide-ranging, I should say that here was a philosopher whose character should have been handed over to a higher-minded philosopher to be stabilized.[11]

Glory is not neglected even by such as attempt to inculcate contempt for it, since they are careful to add their names to those very volumes, in order to attain by use of remembrance what they belittle in their professions. But whatever may be thought of their dissimulation, it is far more tolerable than the design of those who in their desire to be remembered forever did not scruple to gain notoriety even by crimes.

Of their number perhaps Pausanias should be given first mention. For when he asked Hermocles how he could suddenly become famous and was told in reply that if he killed an illustrious man that man's glory would redound to himself, he went and slew Philip, and indeed he achieved his purpose. For he made himself as well known to posterity by the murder as Philip by his achievements.[12]

Here is appetite for glory involving sacrilege. A man was found to plan the burning of the temple of Ephesian

[12] 336: other sources ascribe a different motive, e.g. Justin 9.6f.

pulcherrimo consumpto nomen eius per totum terrarum orbem disiceretur; quem quidem mentis furorem eculeo impositus detexit. ac bene consuluerant Ephesii decreto memoriam taeterrimi hominis abolendo, nisi Theopompi magnae facundiae ingenium historiis eum suis comprehendisset.

15. QUAE CUIQUE MAGNIFICA CONTIGERUNT

praef.   Candidis autem animis voluptatem praebuerint in conspicuo posita quae cuique magnifica merito contigerunt, quia aeque praemiorum virtutis atque operum contemplatio iucunda[96] est, ipsa Natura nobis alacritatem sumministrante, cum honorem industrie appeti et exsolvi grate videmus. verum etsi mens hoc loco protinus ad Augustam domum, beneficentissimum et honoratissimum templum, omni impetu fertur, melius cohibebitur, quoniam cui ascensus in caelum patet, quamvis maxima, debito tamen minora sunt quae in terris tribuuntur.

1   Superiori Africano consulatus citerior legitimo tempore datus est, quod fieri oportere exercitus senatum litteris admonuit. ita nescias utrum illi plus decoris patrum conscriptorum auctoritas an militum consilium adiecerit: toga enim Scipionem ducem adversus Poenos creavit, arma poposcerunt. cui quae in vita praecipua adsignata

---

[96] iucunda *Badius*: iudicanda AL   aeque ... iud- *intra cruces Briscoe*

---

[13] 356: most writers who mention the matter do in fact sup-

Diana so that through the destruction of this most beautiful building his name might be spread through the whole world. This madness he unveiled when put upon the rack. The Ephesians had wisely abolished the memory of the villain by decree, but Theopompus' eloquent genius included him in his history.[13]

15. OF DISTINCTION FALLING TO INDIVIDUALS

Distinctions fallen deservedly to individuals would give pleasure to candid minds when placed conspicuously in view, because contemplation of the rewards of virtue and of its works is equally pleasing; for Nature herself gives us good cheer when we see honour strenuously sought and gratefully paid. But although the mind at this point is carried by its every impulse straight to the house of Augustus, a temple most beneficent and most honoured, it will better be held in check, since to him for whom ascent to heaven lies open earthly tributes, no matter how great, are still below his desert.

The Consulate was given to the elder Africanus before the legal time; the army admonished the senate by letter that this ought to be done. So it is hard to say whether the authority of the Conscript Fathers or the counsel of the soldiers did him more honour; the gown made Scipio commander against the Carthaginians, but arms demanded him.[1] The distinctions accorded to him in life would take

press the arsonist's name. Strabo gives it as Herostratus (Plaumann, *RE* VIII.1145).   [1] 148: cf. Livy *Per.* 50, App. *Lib.* 112 (who give the credit to the people, not the army).

sint et longum est referre, quia multa, et non necessarium, quia maiore ex parte iam relata sunt. itaque quod hodieque eximium capit adiciam. imaginem in cella Iovis Optimi Maximi positam habet, quae, quotienscumque funus aliquod Corneliae gentis celebrandum est, inde petitur, unique illi instar atrii Capitolium est.

2   Tam hercule quam curia superiori Catoni,[97] cuius effigies ad illius[98] generis officia expromitur. gratum ordinem, qui utilissimum rei publicae senatorem tantum non semper secum habitare voluit, omnibus numeris virtutis divitem magisque suo merito quam Fortunae beneficio magnum, cuius prius consilio quam Scipionis imperio deleta Carthago est!

3   Rarum specimen honoris ‹in›[99] Scipione quoque Nasica oboritur: eius namque manibus et penatibus nondum quaestori‹i›[100] senatus Pythii Apollinis monitu Pessinunte accersitam deam excipi voluit, quia eodem oraculo praeceptum erat ut haec ministeria Matri deum a sanctissimo viro praestarentur. explica totos fastos, constitue omnes currus triumphales, nihil tamen morum principatu speciosius reperies.

4   Tradunt subinde nobis ornamenta sua Scipiones commemoranda: Aemilianum enim populus ex candidato aedilitatis consulem fecit. eundem, cum quaestoriis comitiis suffragator Q. Fabii Maximi, fratris filii, in campum de-

---

[97] superiori Catoni *Pighius*: -ris -nis AL   [98] cuius effigies ad illius *SB, ducibus Gertz et Kempf*: eff- ill- ad cuius* AL
[99] *add.* A *corr.*
[100] *add. Briscoe*

---

[2] Cf. Auct. vir. ill. 47.9.   [3] "Carthago delenda est."

long to mention, because they are many, nor is it necessary, because the greater part has been mentioned already. So I will add an extraordinary one which he still receives to this day. He has his statue placed in the sanctuary of Jupiter Best and Greatest, and whenever a funeral is to be celebrated in the Cornelian clan, the statue is sought there, and to it alone the Capitol is like an entrance hall.

So to be sure is the senate house to the elder Cato, whose effigy is brought out for offices of this nature.[2] Grateful indeed was the senatorial order, which desired that a senator so useful to the commonwealth all but dwell always with itself, one rich in every kind of virtue and great more by his merit than by benefit of Fortune, by whose counsel[3] Carthage was earlier destroyed than by Scipio's generalship.

A rare example of an honour comes before us also in the case of Scipio Nasica. For when he had not yet been Quaestor the senate decided that the goddess summoned from Pessinus at the admonition of Pythian Apollo should be received by his hands and his household gods, because the same oracle had prescribed that these services should be rendered to the Mother of the Gods by the most blameless of men.[4] Roll out all the Fasti, place before you all the triumphal chariots, you will find nothing more splendid than primacy in morals.

The Scipios keep handing us their distinctions to be commemorated. The people made Aemilianus a Consul from being a candidate for the Aedileship.[5] When he went down to the Campus at the quaestorian elections to support his nephew Q. Fabius Maximus, they brought him

4 204: Livy 29.14.2f. etc.   5 See Broughton I.462.

scendisset, consulem iterum reduxit. eidem senatus bis
sine sorte provinciam, prius Africam, deinde Hispaniam
dedit, atque haec neque civi ambitioso ‹neque gratioso›[101]
senatori, quemadmodum non solum vitae eius severissi-
mus cursus sed etiam mors clandestinis illata insidiis de-
claravit.

5   M. quoque Valerium duabus rebus insignibus di pariter
atque cives speciosum reddiderunt, illi cum quodam Gallo
comminus pugnanti corvum propugnatorem subicientes,
hi tertium et vicesimum annum ingresso consulatum largi-
ti. quorum alterum decus vetustae originis, optimi nominis[102] gens, Corvini amplexa cognomen, usurpat, alterum
summo subiungit[103] ornamento, tam celeritate quam prin-
cipio consulatus gloriando.

6   Ac ne Q. quidem Scaevolae, quem L. Crassus in consulatu collegam habuit, gloria parum illustris, qui Asiam tam
sancte et tam fortiter obtinuit ut senatus deinceps in eam
provinciam ituris magistratibus exemplum atque formam
officii Scaevolam decreto suo proponeret.

7   Inhaerent uni[104] voci posterioris Africani septem C.
Marii consulatus ac duo amplissimi triumphi: ad rogum
enim usque gaudio exsultavit quod cum apud Numantiam
sub eo duce equestria stipendia mereret, et forte inter

---

[101] add.* Halm, duce Kempf   [102] nominis Per.: ho- A corr.
[103] subiungit Per.: -tur AL   [104] uni Kempf: illi AL

6 134: see Broughton I.491 n.1.

7 In 148 and 134 (Broughton I.462 and 490).

8 The argument seems to be that Scipio's murder proved his
unpopularity.   9 349: Livy 7.26.3–5 (Broughton I.129).

10 349: Livy 7.26.12 (Broughton I.129).

back as Consul for the second time.[6] The senate twice gave him a province without drawing lots, first Africa, then Spain,[7] and all this they did not do for a citizen eager to please or a popular senator, as was made plain not only by the austere course of his life but also by a death brought upon him by secret plots.[8]

The gods and his countrymen each conferred distinction on M. Valerius too in two notable ways, the first by sending a crow to fight for him in his hand-to-hand combat with a Gaul,[9] the second by bestowing the Consulship as he entered his twenty-third year.[10] The first honour is enjoyed by his clan, one of ancient origin and excellent reputation, which embraced the surname Corvinus;[11] the other it attaches to its highest ornament, glorying in the swiftness of the Consulate no less than in the fact that it was a beginning.[12]

Nor is the glory of Q. Scaevola, whom L. Crassus had as his colleague in the Consulship, lacking in lustre. He governed Asia[13] so incorruptably and so strongly that the senate in its decree proposed Scaevola as an example and model of administration for magistrates going out to that province thenceforward.

The seven Consulships and two splendid triumphs of C. Marius lie embedded in a single remark of the younger Africanus. For until the day of his death Marius delighted to recall that when he was serving in the cavalry under

[11] Cf. VM 8.13.1.

[12] The Consulship was additionally distinguished because it came early and because it was the first of six.

[13] In 97 or 94 (see Broughton III.145f.): Cic. *Att.* 5.17.5 etc. (Broughton II.7).

cenam quidam Scipionem interrogasset, si quid illi accidisset, quemnam res publica aeque magnum habitura esset imperatorem, respiciens se supra ipsum cubantem 'vel hunc' dixerit. quo augurio perfectissima virtus maximam orientem virtutem videritne certius an efficacius accenderit perpendi vix potest: illa nimirum cena militaris speciosissimas tota in urbe Mario futuras cenas ominata est: postquam enim Cimbros ab eo deletos initio noctis nuntius pervenit, nemo fuit qui non illi tamquam dis immortalibus apud sacra mensae suae libaverit.

8   Iam quae in Cn. Pompeium et ampla et nova congesta sunt, hinc adsensione favoris, illinc fremitu invidiae litterarum monumentis obstrepunt.[105] eques Romanus pro consule in Hispaniam adversus Sertorium pari imperio cum Pio Metello, principe civitatis, missus est. nondum ullum honorem ‹curulem›[106] auspicatus bis triumphavit. initia magistratuum a summo imperio cepit. tertium consulatum decreto senatus solus gessit. de Mithridate et Tigrane, de multis praeterea regibus plurimisque civitatibus et gentibus et praedonibus unum duxit triumphum.

9   Q. etiam Catulum populus Romanus voce sua tantum non ad sidera usque evexit: nam cum ab eo pro rostris interrogaretur, si ‹in›[107] uno Pompeio Magno omnia reponere perseverasset, absumpto illo subiti casus incursu in quo spem esset habiturus, summo consensu acclamavit 'in

---

[105] obstrepunt *Madvig*: -ntur AL
[106] *add.* P
[107] in uno A *corr.*: uno AL; vivo G

---

[14] 134/3: Plut. *Mar.* 3.

Scipio at Numantia, somebody asked the latter at dinner what equally great general the commonwealth would have if anything happened to himself. Scipio looked at Marius, who was in the place above him, and said, "Perhaps our friend here."[14] Whether in that augury consummate excellence more surely perceived excellence of the highest order in the making or more effectively ignited it can hardly be assessed. But surely that military dinner was an omen for future dinners most glorious to Marius throughout Rome. For after news came at nightfall of his destruction of the Cimbri, nobody but in the ritual of the table poured a libation to him as to the immortal gods.

The ample and novel distinctions heaped on Cn. Pompeius assault our ears in literary memorials with choruses of approving support on the one hand and of clamorous envy on the other. A Roman knight, he was despatched as Proconsul to Spain against Sertorius with authority equal to Pius Metellus, Rome's leading citizen. Not yet having entered upon any curule office, he triumphed twice. He took the first steps in magistracy from supreme command. He held his third Consulship alone by decree of the senate. He celebrated victory over Mithridates and Tigranes, many other kings, and a multitude of communities and nations and pirates in a single triumph.[15]

Q. Catulus too was almost borne to the stars by the voice of the Roman people. For when he asked them from the rostra the question: if they persisted in staking everything on Pompeius Magnus, in whom would they have hope should he be taken away by some sudden stroke of chance, the people cried out with the greatest unanimity,

15 See Miltner's account in *RE* XXI.2063ff.

te.' vim ho<no>rati[108] iudicii admirabilem, si quidem
Magnum Pompeium cum omnibus ornamentis quae rettuli duarum syllabarum spatio inclusum Catulo aequavit!

10   Potest et M. Catonis ex Cypro cum regia pecunia rever-
tentis appulsus ad ripam Tiberis[109] memorabilis videri, cui
nave egredienti consules et ceteri magistratus et universus
senatus populusque Romanus officii gratia praesto fuit,
non quod magnum pondus auri et argenti sed quod M. Catonem classis illa incolumem advexerat laetatus.

11   Sed nescio an praecipuum L. Marci<us>[110] inusitati decoris exemplum, quem equitem Romanum duo exercitus,
P. et Cn. Scipionum interitu victoriaque Hannibalis lacera-
ti, ducem legerunt, quo tempore salus eorum in ultimas
angustias deducta nullum ambitioni locum relinquebat.

12   Merito virorum commemorationi Sulpicia Ser. Pater-
culi filia, Q. Fulvii Flacci uxor, adicitur. quae, cum senatus
libris Sibyllinis per decemviros inspectis censuisset ut Veneris Verticordiae simulacrum consecraretur, quo facilius
virginum mulierumque mens a libidine ad pudicitiam con-
verteretur, et ex omnibus matronis centum, ex centum autem decem sorte ductae de sanctissima femina iudicium
facerent, cunctis castitate praelata est.

---

[108] *add.* A *corr.,* G
[109] Tiberis ⅁: urbis AL
[110] *add. Gertz*

"In you."[16] Admirable force of honorific judgment! In two syllables they equalled Magnus Pompeius to Catulus, along with all the ornaments I have related.

And M. Cato's putting in at the city's waterside as he returned from Cyprus with the royal treasure may seem worth remembrance. As he left the ship, the Consuls and other magistrates and the entire senate and the Roman people were on hand to greet him, rejoicing that the fleet brought, not a great mass of gold and silver, but M. Cato safe and sound.[17]

But perhaps L. Marcius' example of unprecedented honour takes first place. A Roman knight, two armies lacerated by the deaths of P. and Cn. Scipio and Hannibal's victory,[18] chose him as their commander at a point when their survival hung upon a thread and there was no room for popularity-mongering.[19]

To the commemoration of men Sulpicia, daughter of Ser. Paterculus and wife of Q. Fulvius Flaccus, deserves to be added. After the Sibylline books had been inspected by the Board of Ten, the Senate ordained that an image of Venus Vertcordia be consecrated, the more easily to turn the minds of virgins and married women from lust to chastity; and that from all the matrons one hundred and from the one hundred ten drawn by lot should make a judgment, who was the most blameless of the sex. Sulpicia was placed above them all for purity.[20]

[16] 67: Cic. *Leg. Man.* 59 etc.
[17] 56: Vell. 2.45.5, Plut. *Cat. min.* 39.
[18] Actually Hasdrubal's (Valerius' error?).
[19] 212: Livy 25.37.5f. Cf. VM 1.6.2, 2.7.15.
[20] *Ca.* 220: Pliny *N.H.* 7.120; cf. Ov. *Fast.* 4.157–60.

ext. 1 Ceterum quia sine ulla deminutione Romanae maiestatis extera quoque insignia respici possunt, ad ea transgrediemur. Pythagorae tanta veneratio ab auditoribus tributa est ut quae ab eo acceperant in disputatione deducere nefas existimarent. quin etiam interpellati ad reddendam causam hoc solum respondebant, ipsum dixisse. magnus honos, sed schola tenus: illa urbium suffragiis tributa. enixo Crotoniatae studio ab eo petierunt ut senatum ipsorum, qui mille hominum numero constabat, consiliis suis uti pateretur, opulentissimaque civitas ⟨Metapontini⟩[111] iam praesentem[112] venerati post mortem domum Cereris sacrarium fecerunt, quoadque[113] illa urbs viguit, et dea in hominis memoria et homo in deae religione cultus est.

ext. 2 Gorgiae vero Leontino studiis litterarum aetatis suae cunctos praestanti, adeo ut primus in conventu poscere qua de re quisque audire vellet ausus sit, universa Graecia in templo Delphici Apollinis statuam solido ex auro posuit, cum ceterorum ad id tempus auratas collocasset.

ext. 3 Eadem gens summo consensu ad Amphiaraum decorandum incubuit, locum quo humatus est in formam condicionemque templi redigendo atque inde oracula capi instituendo. cuius cineres idem honoris possident quod Pythicae cortinae, quod aheno Dodonae, quod Hammonis fonti datur.

---

[111] add. Gertz, duce Madvig
[112] iam praesentem Gertz: tam frequen- * AL
[113] quoadque Kempf: quaque* AL

---

[21] Cic. Nat. deor. 1.10 etc.
[22] Cic. De orat. 1.103 etc.

EXTERNAL

But since foreign notabilities can be taken into account without derogation to the majesty of Rome, we shall pass thereto. Such reverence was accorded Pythagoras by his auditors that they held it a sin to make what they heard from him a subject of debate. They even, when challenged to give a reason, would answer only this, that *he* had said it. A great honour, but extending no further than the school;[21] the following was paid by the votes of cities. The people of Croton pressingly requested him to allow their senate, numbering a thousand men, to avail itself of his advice; and the very thriving community of Metapontus, which had venerated him in his lifetime, made his house a shrine of Ceres after his death. As long as the city flourished, the goddess was worshipped in the remembrance of the man and the man in the religious observance of the goddess.

Gorgias of Leontini was ahead of all his contemporaries in literary studies. So much so, that he was the first to venture to ask in a gathering on what subject each one would like to hear him.[22] The whole of Greece set up his statue of solid gold in the temple of Delphic Apollo, although up to that time it had placed gilded statues of other men.[23]

The same nation laid itself out with the greatest unanimity to honour Amphiaraus, converting his burial place into the form and function of a temple and instituting the taking of oracles therefrom.[24] His ashes have the same honour as is given to the Pythian tripod, the cauldron at Dodona, and the fountain of Hammon.

---

[23] Ibid. 3.129 etc.
[24] Cic. *Div.* 1.88 etc.

ext. 4　　　Berenices quoque non vulgaris honos, cui soli omnium feminarum gymnico spectaculo interesse permissum est, cum ad Olympia filium Euclea certamen ingressu‹rum›[114] adduxisset, Olympionice patre genita, fratribus eandem palmam adsecutis latera eius cingentibus.

[114] *add.* P

No ordinary honour was paid to Berenice too, the only woman allowed to be present at a gymnastic spectacle. That was when she brought her son Eucles to the Olympics to enter the competition.[25] She was the daughter of an Olympic champion, and she came flanked by her brothers who had won the same palm.

[25] 396 (?), cf. *RE* Eukles 14: Pliny *N.H.* 7.133, Aelian *Var. hist.* 10.1, Pausan. 6.7.2 etc.

LIBER NONUS

1. DE LUXURIA ET LIBIDINE

praef.   Blandum etiam malum Luxuria, quam accusare aliquanto facilius est quam vitare, operi nostro inseratur, non
quidem ut ullum honorem recipiat, sed ut se ipsam recog-
noscens ad paenitentiam impelli possit. iungatur illi Libido, quoniam ex iisdem vitiorum principiis oritur, neque
aut a reprehensione aut ab emendatione separentur, gemi-
no mentis errore conexae.

1   C. Sergius Orata pensilia balnea primus facere instituit.
quae impensa ⟨a⟩[1] levibus initiis coepta ad suspensa[2]
caldae aquae tantum non aequora penetravit. idem, videlicet ne gulam Neptuni arbitrio subiectam haberet, pe-
culiaria sibi maria excogitavit, aestuariis intercipiendo
fluctus, pisciumque diversos greges separatim molibus in-
cludendo, ut nulla tam saeva tempestas inciderit qua
non Oratae mensae varietate ferculorum abundarent.
aedificiis etiam spatiosis et excelsis deserta ad id tempus
ora Lucrini lacus pressit, quo recentiore usu conchyliorum
frueretur: ubi ⟨dum⟩[3] se publicae aquae cupidius immer-
git, cum Considio publicano iudicium nanctus est. in quo
L. Crassus, adversus illum causam agens, errare amicum

---

[1] *add. Novák*   [2] suspensa ϛ: -ae AL   [3] *add.* ϛ

BOOK IX

1. OF LUXURY AND LUST

Let Luxury, that cozening evil, which is somewhat more easily denounced than avoided, be introduced into our work, not to receive any honour but so that recognizing herself she may perhaps be impelled to repentance. Let Lust be joined to her, since she arises from the same vicious origins, and let them not be separated either by way of blame or by way of amendment, connected as they are by a twin psychic error.

C. Sergius Orata was the first to make hanging baths. This expense, starting from small beginnings, went nearly so far as suspended seas of hot water. The same, unwilling it would seem to have his appetite subject to the control of Neptune, devised private seas for himself, intercepting the waves by means of inlets and enclosing different shoals of fish with separate dams, so that no weather could be so rough but that Orata's tables abounded in a variety of dishes. He also covered the mouth of the Lucrine lake, hitherto deserted, with spacious, lofty buildings, so as to enjoy the shellfish fresher. Plunging too greedily into public water, he got himself a lawsuit with the contractor Considius, in which L. Crassus, who was appearing against the latter, said that his friend Considius was mistaken in

suum Considium dixit, quod putaret Oratam remotum a lacu cariturum ostreis: namque ea, si inde petere non licuisset, in tegulis reperturum.

2   Huic nimirum magis Aesopus tragoedus in adoptionem dare filium suum quam bonorum suorum heredem relinquere debuit, non solum perditae sed etiam furiosae luxuriae iuvenem. quem constat cantu commendabiles aviculas immanibus emptas pretiis pro ficedulis ponere, acetoque liquatos magnae summae uniones potionibus aspergere solitum, amplissimum patrimonium tamquam amaram aliquam sarcinam quam celerrime abicere cupientem. quorum alterius senis, alterius adulescentis sectam secuti longius manus porrexerunt: neque enim ullum vitium finitur ibi ubi oritur. inde ab oceani litoribus attracti pisces, inde infusae culinis arcae censusque[4] edendi ac bibendi voluptas reperta.

3   Urbi autem nostrae secundi Punici belli finis et Philippus, Macedoniae rex, devictus licentioris vitae fiduciam dedit. quo tempore matronae Brutorum domum ausae sunt obsidere, qui abrogationi legis Oppiae intercedere parati erant, quam feminae tolli cupiebant, quia iis nec veste varii coloris uti nec auri plus semunciam habere nec iuncto vehiculo propius urbem mille passus nisi sacrificii gratia vehi permittebat. et quidem obtinuerunt ut ius per continuos viginti annos servatum aboleretur: non enim

---

[4] censusque *Kempf*: censibusque AL

---

[1] *Ca.* 95 (?), see Münzer, *RE* Sergius 33. Considius will have bought rights in the oyster fisheries from the state.

[2] Cf. Hor. *Sat.* 2.3.239–42 etc. According to Pliny *N.H.* 9.122,

thinking that Orata would have no oysters if he were away from the lake, for if he could not get them from there he would find them among his rooftiles.[1]

The tragic actor Aesopus would surely have done better to have given his son in adoption to Orata rather than leaving him heir to his estate, a young man not merely desperate but frenzied in his extravagance. He is said to have been in the habit of buying little birds in demand for their song at enormous prices and serving them up as beccaficos and of dissolving pearls of great value in vinegar and sprinkling them over drinks, eager to throw away his large patrimony with all possible speed as though it were a galling load.[2] Following the lead of these two, the old man and the young, people stretched their hands out further. For no vice ends where it begins. So came fish hauled from the shores of Ocean, so money chests poured into kitchens, and so was discovered the pleasure of eating and drinking a fortune.

For our city the end of the Second Punic War and the defeat of king Philip of Macedonia gave confidence for a more untrammeled way of life. At that period the matrons dared to lay siege to the house of the Bruti, who were prepared to veto the repeal of the Oppian law. Women wanted this law annulled because it forbade them to wear multicoloured dresses or to own more than half an ounce of gold or to ride in a yoked vehicle within a mile of the city except for the purpose of sacrifice. And they did in fact succeed in getting abolished a statute that had been observed for twenty years.[3] For the men of that epoch did not foresee to

his procedure with pearls had been anticipated by Cleopatra during her stay in Rome in 46–44.   [3] 195: Livy 34.1–8.3 etc.

providerunt saeculi illius viri ad quem cumulum[5] tenderet insoliti cultus[6] pertinax studium aut quo se usque effusura esset legum victrix audacia. quod si animi muliebres apparatus intueri potuissent quibus cotidie aliquid novitatis sumptuosius adiectum est, in ipso introitu ruenti luxuriae obstitissent.

Sed quid ego de feminis ulterius loquor, quas et imbecillitas mentis et graviorum operum negata adfectatio omne studium ad curiosiorem sui cultum hortatur conferre, cum temporum superiorum et nominis et animi excellentis[7] viros in hoc priscae continentiae ignotum deverticulum prolapsos videam, idque iurgio ipsorum pateat?

4   Cn. Domitius L. Crasso collegae suo altercatione orta obiecit quod columnas Hymettias in porticu domus haberet. quem continuo Crassus quanti ipse domum suam aestimaret interrogavit, atque ut respondit 'sexagies sestertio,' 'qu⟨ant⟩o[8] ergo eam' inquit 'minoris fore existimas si decem arbusculas inde succidero?' 'ipso tricies sestertio' Domitius. tunc Crassus: 'uter igitur luxuriosior est, egone, qui decem columnas centum milibus nummum emi, an tu, qui decem arbuscularum umbram tricies sestertii summa compensas?' sermonem oblitum Pyrrhi, immemorem Hannibalis, iamque transmarinorum stipendiorum abundantia oscitantem! et quanto tamen insequentium saeculorum aedificiis et nemoribus angustiorem †quam†[9] introduxerunt! atqui[10] incohatam a se lautitiam posteris relinquere quam a maioribus acceptam continentiam retinere maluerunt.

---

[5] cumulum *Wensky*: cultum AL   [6] cultus *Eberhard*: coetus AL   [7] excellentis *Halm*: -tes AL   [8] *add.* ⛌
[9] quam *intra cruces Briscoe*   [10] atqui *Kapp*: -ue AL

what a pitch the insistent urge for unaccustomed finery was leading or how far audacity victorious over the laws would spread. If their minds could have envisaged those feminine displays to which some more expensive novelty has been added every day, they would have blocked the career of extravagance at the very outset.

But why do I speak further of women, who are encouraged by their mental infirmity and the denial of opportunity for serious work to put all their efforts into the refining of their personal adornment, when I see men of earlier times, outstanding both in name and spirit, sliding into this deviation unknown to ancient frugality, and when this is evident from a quarrel between themselves?

Cn. Domitius reproached his colleague L. Crassus with having columns of Hymettian marble in the portico of his house. Crassus immediately asked him how much he considered his own house to be worth. "Six million sesterces," was the reply. "Well then," said Crassus, "how much less do you think it will be worth if I cut down ten of your trees?" "Just three million," said Domitius. "So which of us is the more extravagant, I, that bought ten columns for a hundred thousand or you who balance the shade of ten trees with three million sesterces?"[4] A conversation oblivious of Pyrrhus, forgetful of Hannibal, already yawning at the abundance of transmarine taxes! And yet how much more restrained than the buildings and groves of subsequent epochs * * * which they introduced! But they preferred to leave to posterity the sumptuousness they initiated rather than the continence they had received from their forebears.

[4] 92: Pliny *N.H.* 36.7. Crassus and Domitius were Censors.

5   Quid enim sibi voluit princeps suorum temporum Metellus Pius, tunc cum in Hispania adventus suos ab hospitibus aris et ture excipi patiebatur? cum Attalicis aulaeis contectos parietes laeto animo intuebatur? cum immanibus epulis apparatissimos interponi ludos sinebat? cum palmata veste convivia celebrabat, demissasque lacunaribus aureas coronas velut caelesti capite recipiebat? et ubi ista? non in Graecia neque in Asia, quarum luxuria Severitas ipsa corrumpi poterat, sed in horrida et bellicosa provincia, cum praesertim acerrimus hostis Sertorius Romanorum exercituum oculos Lusitanis telis praestringeret: adeo illi patris sui Numidica castra exciderant. patet igitur quam celeri transitu luxuria adfluxerit: nam cuius adulescentia priscos mores vidit, senectus novos orsa est.

6   Consimilis mutatio in domo Curionum exstitit, si quidem forum nostrum et patris gravissimum supercilium et filii sescenties sestertium aeris alieni aspexit, contractum famosa iniuria nobilium iuvenum. itaque eodem tempore et in iisdem penatibus diversa saecula habitarunt, frugalissimum alterum, alterum nequissimum.

7   P. autem Clodii iudicium quanta luxuria et libidine abundavit! in quo, ut evidenter incesti crimine nocens reus absolveretur, noctes matronarum et adulescentium nobilium magna summa emptae mercedis loco iudicibus erogatae sunt. quo in flagitio tam taetro tamque multiplici nescias primum quem detestere, qui istud corruptelae genus excogitavit, an qui pudicitiam suam sequestrem periurii fieri passi sunt, an qui religionem stupro permutarunt.

---

5 88–82: Sall. *Hist.* 2.70 Maurenbrecher; Plut. *Sert.* 13, 22, *Pomp.* 18.   6 Cf. Cic. *Phil.* 2.45f.
7 61: Cic. *Att.* 1.16.5 etc.

For what was Metellus Pius about, the leading man of his time, when in Spain he allowed his comings to be greeted by his hosts with altars and incense? When he gazed happily at walls draped in curtains of cloth of gold? When he permitted elaborate games to be interposed between enormous feasts? When he attended dinners in palm-embroidered garments and received golden garlands let down from the ceilings on his head as though it were divine?[5] And where all this? Not in Greece or Asia, whose luxury could corrupt Austerity herself, but in a rough, warlike province, and that when a relentless enemy, Sertorius, was dazzling the eyes of Roman armies with Lusitanian spears. So completely had his father's Numidian warfare faded from his mind. Thus it is evident with how swift a passage luxury flowed in; his youth saw the old morals, his old age began the new.

A similar revolution appeared in the house of the Curios. Our Forum saw the father's solemn frown and the son's sixty millions of debt, contracted by infamous outrage upon noble youths. Thus at the same time and in the same residence diverse epochs dwelt, one most frugal, the other most profligate.[6]

With what extravagance and lust did the trial of P. Clodius abound! In it, to the end that a defendant manifestly guilty of the charge of impurity might be acquitted, nights of married women and young noblemen were bought for a great sum and paid out as bribes to members of the jury.[7] In this abominable and manifold outrage it is hard to know which to execrate first, him who devised this form of corruption, those who allowed their chastity to become a bribery agent for perjury, or those who bartered their oath for illicit sex.

8   Aeque flagitiosum illud convivium, quod Gemellus, tribunicius viator, ingenui sanguinis sed officii intra servilem habitum deformis, Metello Scipioni consuli ac tribunis plebis magno cum rubore civitatis comparavit: lupanari enim domi suae instituto, Muciam[11] et Fulviam,[12] cum a patre tum a viro utramque inclitam,[13] et nobilem puerum Saturninum in eo prostituit. probrosae patientiae corpora, ludibrio temulentae libidini futura! epulas consuli[14] et tribunis non celebrandas sed vindicandas!

9   Verum praecipue Catilinae libido scelesta: nam vesano amore Aureliae Orestillae correptus, cum unum impedimentum videret quominus nuptiis inter se iungerentur filium suum, quem et solum et aetate iam puberem habebat, veneno sustulit, protinusque ex rogo eius maritalem facem accendit ac novae maritae orbitatem suam loco muneris erogavit. eodem deinde animo civem gerens quo patrem egerat, filii pariter manibus et nefarie attemptatae patriae poenas dedit.

---

11 Muciam ς: Muniam AL
12 Fulviam ς: Fluviam A: Flaviam LG, A corr.
13 inclitam ς: victoriam* AL
14 consuli Kempf: -ibus AL

---

8 52: Mucia was the daughter of Scaevola Augur and had been married to Pompey. Fulvia's father was a nobody (Cic. *Phil.* 3.16), and modern belief in his nobility is a mistake (SB, *Onomasticon to Cicero's Speeches*, 51), but she had a string of notorious husbands: Clodius, Curio, and Mark Antony; on her grandfather, the crazy Tuditanus, see VM 7.8.1. This is more than can be said about "Munia" and "Flavia" of the manuscripts.

Equally outrageous was the banquet which Gemellus, a tribunician messenger free by birth but by employment base below servile condition, prepared for Consul Metellus Scipio and the Tribunes of the Plebs to the signal shame of the community. He set up a brothel in his house and in it as prostitutes Mucia and Fulvia,[8] both famous through their fathers and husbands, and a boy of noble birth, Saturninus.[9] Bodies infamously patient, destined to be playthings for drunken lust! Feast for a Consul and Tribunes not to attend but to punish!

But especially criminal was the lust of Catiline. Seized with an infatuation for Aurelia Orestilla, he saw his son, an only child already past puberty, as the only obstacle to their union in marriage. He removed the lad by poison, kindling the nuptial torch from his pyre and offering his own childlessness as a gift to his new bride.[10] Then playing citizen in the same spirit as he had played father, he paid penalty equally to the shades of his son and to the country he had wickedly assailed.

[9] Sentius, not Appuleius; see SB[4], p. 10; fog, however, lingers, witness Briscoe's index: "Cn. (?Appuleius) Saturninus." The Sentii were not noble as yet (neither for that matter were the Appuleii), but the boy was grandson of C. Sentius, Praetor in 94 (or possibly his brother): see Cic. (Caelius) *Fam.* 8.14.2 with commentary. More important perhaps, the Sentii became very prominent under Augustus (with whom they had a minor family connection) and his successors, especially the redoubtable Cn. Saturninus, Consul in 19 B.C. One could not expect Valerius to be overcareful on such a point (cf. VM 6.4.2). The proscribed Sentius Saturninus Vetulo of VM 7.3.9 may have been Gnaeus' father and the "noble boy" his younger brother.

[10] Cic. *Catil.* 1.14, Sall. *Cat.* 15.2f., App. *B.C.* 2.2.

ext. 1   At Campana luxuria perquam utilis nostrae civitati fuit: invictum enim armis Hannibalem illecebris suis complexa vincendum Romano militi tradidit. illa vigilantissimum ducem, illa exercitum acerrimum dapibus largis, abundanti vino, unguentorum fragrantia, veneris usu lasciviore ad somnum et delicias evocavit. ac tum demum fracta et contusa Punica feritas est, cum Seplasia ei <et>[15] Albana castra esse coeperunt. quid iis ergo vitiis foedius, quid etiam damnosius, quibus virtus atteritur, victoriae relanguescunt, sopita gloria in infamiam convertitur, animique pariter et corporis vires expugnantur, adeo ut nescias ab hostibusne an[16] ab illis capi perniciosius habendum sit?

ext. 2   Quae etiam Volsiniensium urbem gravibus et erubescendis cladibus implicaverunt. erat opulenta, erat moribus et legibus ordinata, Etruriae caput habebatur: sed postquam luxuria prolapsa est, in profundum iniuriarum et turpitudinis decidit, ut servorum se insolentissimae dominationi subiceret. qui primum[17] admodum pauci senatorium ordinem intrare ausi, mox universam rem publicam occupaverunt, testamenta ad arbitrium suum scribi iubebant, convivia coetusque ingenuorum fieri vetabant, filias dominorum in matrimonium ducebant. postremo lege sanxerunt ut stupra sua in viduis pariter atque nuptis impunita essent, ac ne qua virgo ingenuo nuberet cuius castitatem non ante ex numero ipsorum aliquis delibasset.

15 *add.* A *corr.*   16 -busne an A *corr.*, G: -bus nec AL
17 primum ς: -mi AL

Campanian luxury was highly advantageous to our community, for embracing Hannibal, undefeated in arms, in its seductions, it handed him over for defeat to the soldiers of Rome. It lured a very vigilant general and a very brave army with lavish feasts, abundant wine, the fragrance of unguents, and unrestrained sexual indulgence into sleep and enjoyment. Punic savagery was broken and battered at last when Seplasia and Albana became its camps.[11] So what can be fouler, what more ruinous than those vices, by which manliness is worn away, victories grow languid, glory falls asleep and turns into disgrace, the forces alike of mind and body are destroyed? So much so that it is a question whether capture by enemies or by these should be accounted the more pernicious.

They involved the city of Volsinii too in grievous and shameful calamities. It was rich, well organized in manners and laws, regarded as the capital of Etruria. But after it degenerated with luxury, it fell into an abyss of outrage and turpitude ending in subjection to the insolent rule of slaves. At first quite a small number of these dared to enter the senatorial order, presently they took over the entire commonwealth, had wills written at their pleasure, forbade the freeborn to meet for dinner or otherwise, took their masters' daughters to wife. Finally they made it law that their rapes of widows and wives alike should go unpunished and that no virgin should marry a free man who had not first been deflowered by one of their number.[12]

[11] 216–15: Livy 23.18.10–16 etc.

[12] These happenings can be placed in the first half of the third century (Radke, *RE* IX A 843–44): Flor. 1.16 etc.

ext. 3   Age, Xerxes opum regiarum ostentatione eximia eo usque luxuria gaudens ut edicto praemium ei proponeret qui novum voluptatis genus repperisset, quanta, dum deliciis nimi<i>s[18] capitur, amplissimi imperii ruina evasit!

ext. 4   Antiochus quoque, Syriae rex, nihilo continentioris exempli. cuius caecam et amentem luxuriam exercitus imitatus magna ex parte aureos clavos crepidis subiectos habuit, argenteaque vasa ad usum culinae comparavit, et tabernacula textilibus sigillis adornata statuit, avaro potius hosti praeda optabilis quam ulla ad vincendum strenuo mora.

ext. 5   Nam Ptolomaeus rex accessio vitiorum suorum vixit, ideoque Physcon appellatus est. cuius nequitia quid nequius? sororem natu maiorem communi fratri nuptam sibi nubere coegit. postea deinde filia eius per vim stuprata ipsam dimisit, ut vacuum locum nuptiis puellae faceret.

ext. 6   Consentaneus igitur regibus suis gentis Aegyptiae populus, qui ductu Archelai adversus A. Gabinium moenibus urbis egressus, cum castra vallo atque fossa cingere iuberetur, universus succlamavit ut id opus publica pecunia faciendum locaretur. quapropter deliciis tam enerves animi spiritum exercitus nostri sustinere non potuerunt.

ext. 7   Sed tamen effeminatior multitudo Cypriorum, qui reginas suas mulierum corporibus velut gradibus constructis, quo mollius vestigia pedum ponerent, currus

18 *add.* A *corr.*

---

13 Cic. *Tusc.* 5.20. The story is also told of Darius Codomannus and Persian kings generally.

Then Xerxes. In the extravagant ostentation of royal wealth he so revelled in luxury that he published an edict offering a reward to anyone who discovered a new sort of pleasure. A prisoner to excessive enjoyment, what ruin he brought upon his vast empire![13]

Antiochus too, king of Syria, set an example no whit more continent. His army in imitation of his blind, frantic luxury in great part had gold hobnails under their sandals, acquired silver kitchen utensils, and set up tents decorated with tapestries—welcome plunder for a greedy enemy rather than any obstacle to victory for a brisk one.[14]

King Ptolemy lived as an adjunct to his vices, hence he was called Physcon. What could be more profligate than his profligacy? He forced his elder sister, who was married to their common brother, to marry him. Later, after raping her daughter, he divorced her to make room to marry the girl.[15]

The Egyptian people was of a piece with its kings. Under the leadership of Archelaus they came out of their city walls to fight A. Gabinius, but when ordered to surround their camp with a rampart and ditch, they cried out in a body that the work should be contracted out at public expense. So minds thus enervated by pleasure could not hold up against the spirit of our army.[16]

More effeminate, however, was the multitude of the Cypriots, who calmly tolerated that their queens should mount chariots on the bodies of women piled up like steps,

---

[14] 131, of Antiochus VII Sidetes: Justin 38.10.

[15] 142: Livy *Per.* 59, Justin 38.8. Φύσκων = pot-belly.

[16] 55: see Broughton II.218.

conscendere aequo animo sustinebant: viris enim, si modo viri erant, vita carere quam tam delicato imperio obtemperare satius fuit.

2. DE CRUDELITATE

praef.

Haec societas vitiorum lascivi vultus et novae cupiditati inhaerentium oculorum ac delicato cultu adfluentis perque varios illecebrarum motus volitantis animi: Crudelitatis vero horridus habitus, truculenta species, violenti spiritus, vox terribilis, omnia minis et cruentis imperiis referta. cui silentium donare crementum est adicere: ⟨et⟩enim[19] quem modum sibi ipsa statuet, si ne suggillationis quidem frenis fuerit revocata? ad summam, cum penes illam sit timeri, penes nos sit odisse.

1

L. Sulla, quem neque laudare neque vituperare quisquam satis digne potest, quia, dum quaerit victorias, Scipionem [se][20] populo Romano, dum exercet, Hannibalem repraesentavit—egregie namque auctoritate nobilitatis defensa crudeliter totam urbem atque omnes Italiae partes civilis sanguinis fluminibus inundavit—quattuor legiones contrariae partis fidem suam secutas in publica villa nequiquam fallacis dexterae misericordiam implorantes obtruncari iussit. quarum lamentabiles quiritatus trepidae civitatis aures receperunt, lacerata ferro corpora Tiberis impatiens tanti oneris cruentatis aquis vehere est coactus. quinque milia Praenestinorum, spe salutis per P. Cethegum data, extra moenia municipii evocata, cum abiectis

[19] add. ⟨ [20] del. Madvig

[17] Athen. 256d.

so that they should place their footsteps more softly.[17] As for the men, if men they were, it would have been better for them to lose life rather than obey so luxurious a regime.

2. OF CRUELTY

This partnership of vices has a lewd countenance and eyes fixed on novel desire and a mind overflowing with dainty living and wallowing in various motions of enticement. Cruelty on the other hand has a rough make-up, a fierce appearance, violent breathings, a voice of terror, everything filled with threats and bloody commands. To grant her silence is to add increase. For what limit will she set herself if she be not recalled even by the bridle of rebuke? In sum, if it is her prerogative to be feared, let it be ours to hate.

No one can either praise or blame L. Sulla as he deserved. In seeking his victories he presented a Scipio to the Roman people, in using them a Hannibal. For after laudably defending the authority of the nobility he cruelly swamped all Rome and every part of Italy with rivers of civil blood. He ordered four legions on the opposing side, which had taken his word, to be cut down in the Villa Publica on the Campus Martius as they vainly implored the mercy of his perfidious right hand. The ears of the trembling community took in their lamentable cries and Tiber, impatient of so great a burden, was forced to carry their sword-torn bodies with his bloodstained waters. Five thousand men of Praeneste were lured outside the walls of their township by hope of quarter given through P. Cethegus. When they had thrown away their arms and

armis humi corpora prostravissent, interficienda protinusque per agros dispergenda curavit. quattuor milia et
septingentos dirae proscriptionis edicto iugulatos in tabulas publicas rettulit, videlicet ne memoria tam praeclarae
rei dilueretur. nec contentus in eos saevire qui armis a se
dissenserant, etiam quieti animi cives propter pecuniae
magnitudinem per nomenclatorem conquisitos proscriptorum numero adiecit. adversus mulieres quoque gladios
destrinxit, quasi parum caedibus virorum satiatus. id quoque inexplebilis feritatis indicium est: abscisa miserorum
capita modo non vultum ac spiritum retinentia in conspectum suum adferri voluit, ut oculis illa, quia ore nefas erat,
manderet. quam porro crudeliter se in M. Mario praetore
gessit! quem per ora vulgi ad sepulcrum Lutatiae gentis
pertractum non prius vita privavit quam oculos infelicis[21]
erueret et singulas corporis partes confringeret. vix mihi
veri similia narrare videor: at ille etiam M. Plaetorium,
quod ad eius supplicium exanimis ceciderat, continuo ibi
mactavit, novus punitor misericordiae, apud quem iniquo
animo scelus intueri scelus admittere fuit. sed mortuorum
umbris saltem pepercit? minime: nam C. Marii, cuius, etsi
postea hostis, quaestor tamen aliquando fuerat, erutos cineres in Anienis[22] alveum sparsit. en quibus actis felicitatis
nomen adserendum putavit!

2   Cuius tamen crudelitatis C. Marius invidiam levat:

---

[21] infelicis A *corr.*: -ces AL
[22] Anienis ⛌: amnis AL: amnis Anienis *coni. Briscoe*

---

1 82. Sulla's cruelties are extensively reported (Broughton
II.69), except in the case of Plaetorius, the details of which are
found only here.

prostrated their bodies on the ground, Sulla had them killed and forthwith scattered over the countryside. Four thousand seven hundred were slaughtered by an edict of dire proscription; he entered them in public records, presumably to make sure that the memory of so splendid a feat should not be washed away. Not content with savaging those who had fought against him, he added even peace-loving citizens to the number of the proscribed on account of their wealth, searching them out through a nomenclator. He drew swords even against women, as though the slaughter of men was not enough for him. Another sign of insatiable savagery: he had the severed heads of the victims, still all but retaining expression and breath, brought into his presence, so that he could chew them with his eyes, since it was forbidden to do it with his mouth. How cruelly, moreover, he behaved in the case of Praetor M. Marius! He had him dragged before the eyes of the populace to the tomb of the Lutatian clan and did not take his life away before he gouged out the wretched man's eyes and broke his body limb by limb. I feel I am narrating the barely believable: he actually slew M. Plaetorius on the spot because he had fainted away at Marius' execution, a novel chastiser of pity, with whom to look upon a crime reluctantly was to commit one. But at least he spared the shades of the dead? Far from it. He dug up the ashes of C. Marius, whose Quaestor he had once been though afterwards his enemy, and scattered them over the channel of the Anio. Such were the acts by which he thought it proper to claim the name of "Fortunate."[1]

However, the hatred we feel for his cruelty is mitigated

nam et ille nimia cupiditate persequendi inimicos iram
suam nefarie destrinxit, C. Caesaris consularis et censorii
nobilissimum corpus ignobili saevitia trucidando, et quidem apud seditiosissimi et abiectissimi hominis bustum: id
enim malorum miserrimae tunc rei publicae deerat, ut
Vario Caesar piaculo caderet. paene tanti victoriae eius
non fuerunt, quarum oblitus plus criminis domi quam laudis in militia meruit. idem caput M. Antonii abscisum laetis manibus inter epulas per summam animi ac verborum
insolentiam aliquamdiu tenuit, clarissimique et civis et
oratoris sanguine contaminari mensae sacra passus
<est>,[23] atque etiam P. Annium, qui id attulerat, in sinum
suum recentis caedis vestigiis aspersum recepit.

3   Damasippus nihil laudis habuit quod corrumperet,
itaque memoria eius licentiore accusatione perstringitur.
cuius iussu principum civitatis capita hostiarum capitibus
permixta sunt, Carbonisque Arvinae truncum corpus pati-
bulo adfixum gestatum est. adeo aut flagitiosissimi hominis

---

[23] add. Per.

---

[2] The Consul and Censor was L. Caesar (cos. 90, cens. 89), not
his younger brother Gaius (aed. cur. 90), but the latter is likely to
be intended, as particularly obnoxious to Marians: his clash with
Sulpicius Rufus in 88 in Asconius' view (25.7 Clark) was the cause
of the civil war. Varius was condemned under his own law and
went into exile; according to H. Gundel (*RE* VIII A 388.18) he
died in exile. But on Valerius' showing here he must have been
brought back to Rome (presumably by Sulla in 88) and executed
there, which seems in line with Cicero's statement (*Nat. deor.*
3.81) that he was put to death in a most painful manner. Nobody
but Valerius, however, says anything about Caesar's slaughter at

by C. Marius. For he too wreaked his wrath wickedly in his overeagerness to pursue his enemies, butchering with ignoble ferocity the noble body of C. Caesar, ex-Consul and ex-Censor, and that at the tomb of a thoroughly base and seditious individual. For only this calamity was then wanting to the hapless commonwealth, that Caesar should fall as an expiatory offering to Varius. Marius' victories almost cost too dear. Forgetful of them, he deserved more blame at home than praise in the field. He also held the severed head of M. Antonius for some time between his exultant hands at dinner, in gross insolence of mind and words, and allowed the rites of the table to be polluted with the blood of an illustrious citizen and orator. And he even took to his bosom P. Annius, who had brought it, bespattered as he was with the marks of recent slaughter.[2]

Damasippus had no glory to spoil, so his memory is scored with more outspoken indictment. By his orders the heads of leaders of the community were mingled with the heads of sacrificial victims and the mutilated body of Carbo Arvina was borne around fastened to a gibbet.[3] So

the tomb. Florus in a corrupt passage (2.9.14), followed by Augustine *Civ. Dei* 3.27, seems to say that the Caesars were killed in their homes. Their severed heads were displayed on the rostra (Cic. *De orat.* 3.10; cf. *Tusc.* 5.55, Livy *Per.* 80). The parallel with Marius Gratidianus' torture and death at the tomb of Catulus, mentioned in the preceding section, can hardly be coincidence if Valerius' story is true; rather a deliberate tit-for-tat. Even after E. Badian's discussion in "Quaestiones Variae," *Historia* 18 (1969).447–91 (see 463–65), which makes some good points but overlooks Valerius, the matter remains problematic. On Antonius: *Flor.* 2.9.14 etc. Cf. VM 8.9.2.

[3] 82: App. *B.C.* 1.88 etc.

praetura multum aut rei publicae maiestas nihil potuit.

4　　Munatius etiam Flaccus, Pompeiani nominis acrior quam probabilior defensor, cum ab imperatore Caesare in Hispania inclusus moenibus Ateguensium obsideretur, efferatam crudelitatem suam truculentissimo genere vesaniae exercuit: omnes enim eius oppidi cives quos studiosiores Caesaris senserat iugulatos muris praecipitavit. feminas quoque, citatis nominibus virorum qui in contrariis castris erant, ut caedes coniugum suarum cernerent, maternis⟨que⟩[24] gremiis superpositos liberos trucidavit. infantes alios in conspectu parentum humo infligi, alios superiactatos pilis excipi iussit. quae auditu etiam intolerabilia Romano iussu Lusitanis manibus administrata sunt, cuius gentis praesidio Flaccus vallatus divinis opibus vecordi pertinacia resistebat.

ext. 1　　Transgrediemur nunc ad illa quibus, ut par dolor, ita nullus nostrae civitatis rubor inest. Carthaginienses Atilium Regulum palpebris resectis machinae, in qua undique praeacuti stimuli eminebant, inclusum vigilantia pariter et continuo tractu doloris necaverunt, tormenti genus indignum[25] passo, auctoribus dignissimum. eadem usi crudelitate milites nostros [quos][26] maritimo certamine in suam potestatem redactos navibus substraverunt, ut earum carinis ac pondere elisi inusitata ratione mortis barba-

---

[24] *add.* A *corr.*
[25] indignum A *corr.*, G: addig- AL: haud dig- A *in marg.*
[26] quos* *om.* ⅽ: aliquos *Watt*[4]

powerful was the Praetorship of a miscreant or so power-
less the majesty of the commonwealth.

Munatius Flaccus too, a more zealous than respectable
defender of the Pompeian name, vented his savage cruelty
in a most brutal form of madness when general Caesar
shut him inside the town of the Ateguenses in Spain. For
he butchered all the citizens of that place whom he had
thought were favouring Caesar and flung them from the
walls. He also slaughtered women, proclaiming the names
of their husbands who were in the opposing camp, so that
these should see the murder of their wives, likewise children in their mothers' lap. He ordered infants to be dashed
on the ground in sight of their parents, others to be im-
paled on javelins.[4] These atrocities, intolerable even in the
hearing, were carried out on Roman order by Lusitanian
hands. Guarded by a force of that nation, Flaccus resisted
divine power with frantic obstinacy.

EXTERNAL

We shall now pass to actions equally painful but containing nothing to shame our community. The Carthaginians cut off Atilius Regulus' eyelids, shut him in a machine
in which sharp points stood out from all angles, and killed
him from lack of sleep and extension of pain, a torture un-
deserved by the sufferer but richly deserved by its authors.[5] With the same cruelty they strewed our men who
had fallen into their hands in a naval engagement under
ships to be crushed by the weight of the keels, satiating
their barbarous savagery by the extraordinary manner of

---

[4] 45: to very different effect *Bell. Hisp.* 19.4, Front. *Strat.*
3.14.1, Dio 43.33.4–34. Perhaps some confusion.

[5] Cf. VM 1.1.14.

ram feritatem satiarent, taetro facinore pollutis classibus ipsum mare violaturi.

ext. 2   Eorum dux Hannibal, cuius maiore ex parte virtus saevitia constabat, in flumine ⟨Ver⟩gello[27] corporibus Romanis ponte facto exercitum transduxit, ut aeque terrestrium scelestum Carthaginiensium copiarum ingressum[28] Terra quam maritimarum Neptunus experiretur. idem captivos nostros oneribus et itinere fessos [iam] prima[29] pedum parte succisa relinquebat. quos vero in castra perduxerat, paria fere fratrum et propinquorum iungens ferro decernere cogebat, neque ante sanguine explebatur quam ad unum victorem omnes redegisset. iusto ergo illum [odia][30] verum tamen tardo supplicio senatus, Prusiae regis factum supplicem, ad voluntariam mortem compulit.

ext. 3   Tam hercule quam Mithridatem regem, qui una epistula octoginta milia civium Romanorum in Asia per urbes negotiandi gratia dispersa interemit, tantaeque provinciae hospitales deos iniusto sed non inulto cruore respersit, quoniam cum maximo cruciatu veneno repugnantem spiritum suum tandem succumbere coegit simulque piacula crucibus illis dedit, quibus [illos][31] amicos suos auctore Gauro spadone, libidinosus obsequio, scelestus imperio adfecerat.

ext. 4   Zisemis, Diogyridis filii, Thraciae regis, etsi minus ad-

---

[27] *add. Parrhasius ex Flor.*: Gello* LG: Gallo A
[28] ingressum *Madvig*: eg- * AL
[29] prima *SB*: iam p- AL: iam P: ima *Gertz*
[30] *del. Gertz*: credo *Watt*1
[31] *del. Kempf*: fidos *Watt*4

---

6 Varro, *Vit. pop. Rom.* Riposati, fr. 98.

their death. With fleets polluted by the foul deed they would violate the very sea.[6]

Their leader Hannibal, whose prowess mainly consisted in ferocity, made a bridge over the river Vergellus with Roman bodies and led his army across it, so that Earth suffered an advance of Carthaginian land forces as criminal as that which Neptune had of their sea forces. He further used to cut off the forepart of our prisoners' feet when they were weary with marching under loads and so left them. Those he brought into camp he would make fight in pairs, mostly pitting brothers and kin against each other, and did not get his fill of blood before he had reduced them all to one victor.[7] So the senate's hatred of him was just but their vengeance was slow when as a suppliant of king Prusias they forced him to commit suicide.[8]

So too to be sure with king Mithridates. With one letter he killed eighty thousand Roman citizens, businessmen dispersed among the cities of Asia, and bespattered that great province's gods of hospitality with blood unlawful but not unavenged.[9] For in great pain he finally forced his reluctant breath to yield to poison[10] and at the same time expiated those crosses with which he had afflicted friends of his at the instance of the eunuch Gaurus:[11] lustful in compliance, criminal in command.

The cruelty of Zisemis,[12] son of Diogyris, king of

----

[7] Cf. Pliny *N.H.* 8.18, Flor. 1.22.18: "Wretched inventions which furnish their own refutation" (Mommsen).

[8] 183: Livy 39.51 etc.   [9] 88: App. *Mithr.* 22f. etc.

[10] 63: see Geyer, *RE* XV.2197.   [11] Not mentioned elsewhere.   [12] Zibelmios in Diodor. 34/35.12. The time is after mid-second century (*RE* Zibelmios).

mirabilem crudelitatem gentis ipsius feritas, narrandam tamen rabies saevitiae facit, cui neque vivos homines medios secare neque parentes liberorum vesci ⟨cogere⟩[32] corporibus nefas fuit.

ext. 5   Iterum Ptolomaeus Physcon emergit, paulo ante libidinosae amentiae taeterrimum exemplum, idem inter praecipua crudelitatis indicia referendus: quid enim hoc facto truculentius? filium suum nomine Memphiten, quem ex Cleopatra, eadem sorore et uxore, sustulerat, liberalis formae, optimae spei puerum, in conspectu suo occidi iussit, protinusque caput eius et manus[33] et pedes praecisos in cista chlamyde opertos pro munere natalicio matri misit, perinde quasi ipse cladis quam illi inferebat expers, ac non infelicior, quod in communi orbitate Cleopatram miserabilem cunctis, se invisum reddiderat. adeo caeco furore summa quaeque effervescit crudelitas, cum munimentum ex se ipsa repperit: nam cum animadverteret quanto sui odio patria teneretur, timori remedium scelere petivit, quoque tutius plebe trucidata regnaret, frequens iuventute gymnasium armis et igni circumdedit, omnesque qui in eo erant partim ferro, partim flamma necavit.

ext. 6   Ochus autem, qui postea Dareus appellatus est, sanctissimo Persis iure iurando obstrictus ne quem ex coniuratione quae septem magos cum eo oppresserat aut veneno aut ferro aut ulla vi aut inopia alimentorum necaret, cru-

---

[32] *add. Madvig, duce Kempf*
[33] et manus *hic* SB: *post* praecisos AL

Thrace, is less surprising in view of the savagery of the nation itself, but his rabid ferocity makes it worthy of narration. He did not balk at cutting living men in half and forcing parents to feed upon their children's bodies.

Once more Ptolemy Physcon crops up, recently[13] a foul example of lustful madness, but also to be mentioned among the prime revelations of cruelty. For what could be more brutal than this act of his? He had his acknowledged son by Cleopatra, both his sister and his wife, a handsome boy of the fairest promise, Memphites by name, put to death before his eyes and then sent his severed head and hands and feet covered with a mantle in a box as a birthday gift to his mother[14]—as though he himself had no share in the calamity that he was inflicting upon her, as though he was not the more unhappy of the two in that in their common bereavement he had made Cleopatra an object of compassion to all, himself an object of hate. Such is the blind madness in which the ultimate in cruelty boils over, finding its bulwark in itself. For since he perceived how much his country hated him, he sought a remedy for fear in crime, and so that he might reign more safely after massacring the populace he surrounded a gymnasium full of young men with arms and fire and killed all who were inside partly by steel, partly by the flames.

Ochus, who was afterwards called Darius, had bound himself by an oath most sacred to the Persians not to kill any one of his accomplices in the suppression of the seven magi either by poison or steel or any violence or lack of

---

13 VM 9.1.ext.5.
14 129: cf. Diodor. 34/35.14, Justin 38.8.

deliorem mortis rationem excogitavit, qua onerosos[34] sibi non perrupto vinculo religionis tolleret: saeptum enim altis parietibus locum cinere complevit, superpositoque tigno prominente benigne cibo et potione exceptos in eo collocabat, e quo somno sopiti in illam insidiosam congeriem decidebant.

ext. 7   Apertior et taetrior alterius Ochi cognomine Artaxerxis crudelitas, qui Atossam[35] sororem atque eandem socrum vivam capite defodit, et patruum cum centum amplius filiis ac nepotibus vacua area destitutum iaculis confixit, nulla iniuria lacessitus, sed quod in iis maximam apud Persas probitatis et fortitudinis laudem consistere videbat.

ext. 8   Consimili genere aemulationis instincta, civitas Atheniensium indigno gloriae suae decreto Aeginensium iuventuti pollices abscidit, ut classe potens populus in certamen maritimarum virium secum descendere nequiret. non agnosco Athenas timori remedium a crudelitate mutuantes.

ext. 9   Saevus etiam ille aenei tauri inventor, quo inclusi subditis ignibus longo et abdito cruciatu mugitus resonantem spiritum edere cogebantur, ne eiulatus eorum humano sono vocis expressi Phalaridis tyranni misericordiam

---

[34] onerosos *Pighius*: hos ustos* LG: hostustos A; *Br*
[35] Atossam *Rumpf*: otiosam AL

---

[15] Errors compounded: "Ochus, afterwards called Darius" (i.e. Darius II, reigned 424/3–405) is confused with Darius I, son of Hydaspes. The number seven seems to reflect the latter and his six co-conspirators who overthrew the magi (cf. VM 3.2.ext.2, 7.3.ext.2).

food.[15] He therefore devised a more cruel method of death whereby he might remove those burdensome to himself without violating the religious constraint. He filled a space fenced in by high walls with ashes and placed above them a protruding beam on which he put his victims after plying them with food and drink. From it they fell in their sleep on to the treacherous heap.[16]

More open and abominable was the cruelty of the other Ochus, surnamed Artaxerxes,[17] who buried his sister (also his mother-in-law) Atossa alive head downward and killed with darts his uncle along with more than a hundred sons and grandsons, left at his mercy in an empty space; not provoked by any injury but because he saw that they had a great name among the Persians for uprightness and bravery.

Prompted by a similar sort of jealousy the Athenian community by a decree unworthy of its glory cut off the thumbs of the young men of Aegina, so that her people, which had a powerful navy, should not be able to come to a contest of maritime strength with themselves.[18] I do not recognize an Athens that would borrow a remedy for fear from cruelty.

Savage too was that inventor of the bronze bull in which men were shut and fires lit underneath, so that they were forced by long and hidden torture to give out breath producing a sound like lowing, lest their howls extorted in the sound of the human voice should implore the pity of the

16 Ov. *Ibis* 315f. The ashes were presumably hot.

17 Reigned 358–38: cf. Justin 10.3.1, Curt. 10.5.23.

18 (?): Cic. *Off.* 3.46 (see Dyke), Plut. *Lys.* 9, Aelian *Var. hist.* 2.9. It is nowhere stated that the decree was put into effect.

implorare possent. quam quia calamitosis deesse voluit,
taeterrimum artis suae opus primus inclusus merito auspicatus est.

ext. 10   Ac ne Etrusci quidem parum feroces in poena excogi-
tanda, qui vivorum corpora cadaveribus adversa adversis
alligata atque constricta, ita ut singulae membrorum partes singulis essent accommodatae, tabescere simul patie-
bantur, amari vitae pariter ac mortis tortores.

ext. 11   Sicut illi barbari, quos ferunt mactatarum pecudum in-
testinis et visceribus egestis homines inserere, ita ut capitibus tantummodo emineant, quoque diutius poenae
sufficiant, cibo et potione infelicem spiritum prorogare,
donec intus putrefacti laniatui sint animalibus quae tabidis
in corporibus nasci solent.

Queramur nunc cum Rerum Natura quod nos multis et
asperis adversae valetudinis incommodis obnoxios esse
voluerit, habitumque caelestis roboris humanae condicio-
ni denegatum moleste feramus, cum tot cruciatus sibimet
ipsa mortalitas impulsu crudelitatis excogitaverit.

3. DE IRA AUT ODIO

praef.   Ira quoque aut odium in pectoribus humanis magnos
fluctus excitant, procursu celerior illa, nocendi cupidine
hoc pertinacius, uterque consternationis plenus adfectus
ac numquam sine tormento sui violentus, quia dolorem,
cum inferre vult, patitur, amara sollicitudine ne non
contingat ultio anxius. sed proprietatis eorum certissimae

---

19 *Ca.* 560: Pind. *Pyth.* 1.95f., Callim. *Aetia* fr. 46 etc. The inventor's name was Perilaus (Perillus in Latin sources).

20 Cic. *Hort.* fr. 95, Mueller, Virg. *Aen.* 8.485–88.

tyrant Phalaris. That pity he did not wish the unfortunates to have, so he was the first to be shut in, deservedly inaugurating the horrible product of his skill.[19]

Nor did the Etruscans lack ferocity in devising punishment. They bound and clamped the bodies of the living to corpses, face to face, fitting the several parts of their limbs each to each, and let them rot together, harsh tormentors of life and death alike.[20]

Just like those barbarians who are said to sew men into slaughtered cattle after removing the bowels and inner organs so that only their heads emerge; and in order that they may the longer withstand the punishment, they extend their miserable lives with food and drink until they rot inside and are left for tearing by the creatures that come to birth in putrifying bodies.[21]

Let us now take issue with the Nature of Things because she has wished us exposed to the many harsh ordeals of ill health and grumble that a sturdy celestial constitution has been denied to our human state, when mortality has itself devised so many tortures for mortality under the impulse of cruelty.

3. OF ANGER OR HATRED

Anger too and hatred raise mighty waves in human hearts. The former is swifter in the outbreak, the latter more persistent in desire to harm. Either emotion is full of confusion and never fails in its violence to torment itself, because it suffers hurt when it would fain inflict it, uneasy in painful anxiety lest it fail of vengeance. But there are

[21] Not found elsewhere.

sunt imagines, quas <di>[36] ipsi in claris personis aut dicto aliquo aut facto vehementiore conspici voluerunt.

1   Cum adversus Hasdrubalem Livius Salinator bellum gesturus urbe egrederetur, monente Fabio Maximo ne ante descenderet in aciem quam hostium vires animumque cognosset, primam occasionem pugnandi non omissurum se respondit, interrogatusque ab eodem quid ita tam festinanter manum conserere vellet, 'ut quam celerrime' inquit 'aut gloriam ex hostibus victis aut ex civibus prostratis gaudium capiam.' ira tunc et[37] virtus sermonem eius inter se diviserunt, illa iniustae damnationis memor, haec triumphi gloriae intenta. sed nescio an eiusdem fuerit hoc dicere et sic vincere.

2   Ardentis spiritus virum et bellicis operibus adsuetum huc iracundiae stimuli egerunt. C. autem Figulum mansuetissimum, pacato iuris civilis studio[38] celeberrimum, prudentiae moderationisque immemorem reddiderunt: consulatus enim repulsae dolore accensus, eo quidem magis quod illum bis patri suo datum meminerat, cum ad eum postero comitiorum die multi consulendi causa venissent, omnes dimisit, praefatus [omnes][39] 'consulere scitis, consulem facere nescitis?' dictum graviter et merito, sed tamen aliquanto melius non dictum: nam quis populo Romano irasci sapienter potest?

3   Itaque ne illi quidem probandi, quamvis factum eorum nobilitatis splendore protectum sit, qui, quod Cn. Flavius

---

[36] dii A *corr.*: *om.* AL   [37] et Ꮸ: aut* AL
[38] studio *Gertz*: iudicio AL
[39] *secl. SB*: an vos P: an nos Ꮸ

---

[1] 207: Livy 27.40.8f. Cf. VM 2.9.6b.

sure images of their peculiar nature which the gods themselves have wished to be visible in famous personages through some passionate speech or act.

When Livius Salinator was leaving Rome to wage war against Hasdrubal, Fabius Maximus warned him not to go into battle before he had acquainted himself with the enemy's power and morale. Livius replied that he would not let slip the first opportunity to fight. When Fabius asked him why he was in such a hurry to engage, he answered: "So that I get either glory from the defeated enemy or joy from countrymen laid low as quickly as possible." Anger and valour divided his words between them, one remembering an unjust condemnation, the other intent on the glory of a triumph. But I do not know whether this to speak and thus to conquer belonged to the same individual.[1]

So far did the goads of wrath drive a man of ardent spirit, familiar with warfare. But C. Figulus was of the mildest temper, very well known from his peaceable pursuit of civil law, and they made him forget good sense and moderation. He was bitterly hurt by his rejection for the Consulship, all the more because he remembered that his father had been given the office twice.[2] The day after the election when many came to consult him he dismissed them all with the words, "You know how to consult me, don't you know how to make me Consul?" A weighty saying and deserved, and yet rather better not said. For who can wisely be angry with the Roman people?

So the following too are not to be approved of, though what they did was defended by the lustre of nobility: those who in dudgeon because Cn. Flavius, a man of the lowest

[2] For 162 and 156. The son is found only here.

humillimae quondam sortis praeturam adeptus erat offensi, anulos aureos sibimet ipsis et phaleras equis suis detractas abiecerunt, doloris impotentiam tantum non luctu professo testati.

4   Talis irae motus aut singulorum aut paucorum adversus populum universum: multitudinis erga principes ac duces eius modi: Manlio Torquato amplissimam et gloriosissimam ex Latinis et Campanis victoriam in urbem referenti, cum seniores omnes laetitia ovantes occurrerent, iuniorum nemo obviam processit, quod filium adulescentem fortissime adversus imperium suum proeliatum securi percusserat. miserti sunt aequalis nimis aspere puniti: nec factum eorum defendo, sed irae vim indico, quae unius civitatis et aetates et adfectus dividere valuit.

5   Eademque tantum potuit ut universum populi Romani equitatum a Fabio consule ad hostium copias persequendas missum, cum et tuto et facile eas liceret delere, legis agrariae ab eo impeditae memores, immobilem retineret. illa vero etiam Appio duci, cuius pater, dum pro senatus amplitudine nititur, commoda plebis acerrime impugnaverat, infensum exercitum faciendo voluntaria fuga terga hosti, ne triumphum imperatori quaereret, dare coegit, quotiens victoriae victrix! congratulationem eius in Torquato spernendam, in Fabio pulcherrimam partem omittendam, in Appio totam fugae postponendam reddidit.

---

3 304: Livy 9.46.12, Pliny *N.H.* 33.18.   4 Cf. VM 2.7.6.

5 481: Livy 2.43.5–10. The correction *peditatum* (infantry) in inferior manuscripts flatters the author, who misunderstood Livy because pursuit is usually the cavalry's job. He failed to realize that the cavalry will have been the Consul's political allies.

antecedents, had attained the Praetorship, stripped their gold rings from their fingers and the trappings from their horses and threw them away, advertising their lack of self-control by almost open mourning.[3]

Such was the stirring of anger against the whole people on the part of one individual or a few; of the multitude against leaders and commanders, thus: Manlius Torquatus brought back to the city a great and glorious victory over the Latins and Campanians. All the older folk met him in high rejoicing, but none of the younger ones came out to his passing because he had beheaded his son, a young man who had fought most bravely in combat against his orders. They pitied their coeval, too harshly punished. Nor am I defending their action, but I am showing the force of anger that could split the generations and emotions of one community.[4]

The same sentiment had the power to keep the entire cavalry[5] of the Roman people motionless when despatched by Consul Fabius in pursuit of an enemy force, although they could safely and easily have destroyed it, because they remembered that he had blocked an agrarian law. Anger too made an army hostile to its commander Appius, whose father in championing the prestige of the senate had energetically assailed the interests of the plebs. Not wishing to earn a triumph for their general, they turned their backs in voluntary flight.[6] How often has anger been victorious over victory! It made congratulation worthless in the case of Torquatus, caused omission of its fairest part in that of Fabius, and in that of Appius let it be totally sacrificed to rout.

[6] 471: Livy 2.59.2f. (Broughton I.30).

6   Age, quam violenter se in pectore universi populi Romani gessit eo[dem][40] tempore quo suffragiis eius dedicatio aedis Mercurii M. Plaetorio[41] primi pili centurioni data est praeteritis consulibus, Appio quod obstitisset quominus aere alieno suo succurreretur, Servilio, quod susceptam causam suam languido patrocinio protexisset. negas[42] efficacem esse iram, cuius hortatu miles summo imperio praelatus est?

7   Quae quidem non proculcavit tantum imperia, sed etiam gessit impotenter: nam Q. Metellus, cum utramque Hispaniam consul prius, deinde pro consule paene ⟨to⟩tam[43] subegisset, postquam cognovit Q. Pompeium consulem inimicum suum successorem sibi mitti, omnes qui modo militiam suam voluerunt finiri dimisit, commeatus petentibus neque causis excussis neque constituto tempore dedit, horrea custodibus remotis opportuna rapinae praebuit, arcus sagittasque Cretensium frangi atque in amnem abici iussit, elephantis cibaria dari vetuit. quibus factis ut ⟨laedendi⟩[44] cupiditati suae indulsit ita magnifice gestarum rerum gloriam corrupit, meritumque honorem triumphi hostium quam irae fortior victor amisit.

8   Quid? Sulla, dum huic vitio obtemperat, nonne multo alieno sanguine profuso ad ultimum et suum erogavit? Puteolis enim ardens indignatione, quod Granius princeps eius coloniae pecuniam a decurionibus ad refectionem Capitolii promissam cunctantius daret, animi concitatione

---

[40] eo *Kempf*: eodem AL
[41] Pletorio AL: Laet- *Per. ex Liv.*
[42] negas A *corr.*: -at AL: -a *Per.*
[43] *add.* G *corr.*
[44] *add.* SB[3] (*cf. Apul. Apol. 6, VM 9.3 praef.*).

See now how violently anger acted in the bosom of the entire Roman people when by their votes they gave the dedication of the temple of Mercury to Chief Centurion M. Plaetorius[7] over the heads of the Consuls: Appius because he had opposed relieving their debt, Servilius because after taking up their cause he had proved a half-hearted advocate in its defence.[8] Can you deny the efficacy of anger at whose urging a soldier was preferred over the supreme command?

Anger not only trod command under foot but exercised it unconscionably. Q. Metellus had subjugated almost all of both Spains first as Consul, then as Proconsul. When he learned that Consul Q. Pompeius, his enemy, was being sent to succeed him, he discharged all soldiers who wanted their service terminated, granted leave of absence to all who applied for it without examining reasons or fixing times, removed the guards of the storehouses making them an easy target for looters, ordered the bows and arrows of the Cretans to be broken and thrown into the river, and forbade their rations to be given the elephants. By these actions he indulged his spite but spoiled the glory of his splendid campaigns and lost the honour of a triumph, a braver victor over the enemy than over anger.[9]

Again: obeying this vice, did not Sulla shed other people's blood in plenty and finally pay out his own? For at Puteoli, in a fit of irritation because Granius, the leading man in that colony, was rather slow in giving money promised by the decurions for the reconstruction of the Capitol,

7 M. Laetorius in Livy, 2.27.6.
8 495: Livy 2.27.1–6.
9 141: not found elsewhere.

nimia atque immoderato vocis impetu convulso pectore,
spiritum cruore ac minis mixtum evomuit, nec senio iam
prolapsus, utpote sexagesimum ingrediens annum, sed ali-
ta miseriis rei publicae impotentia furens. igitur in dubio
est Sullane prior an iracundia Sullae sit exstincta.

ext.
praef.

Neque ab ignotis exempla petere iuvat et maximis viris
exprobrare vitia sua verecundiae est. ceterum cum propositi fides excellentissima quaeque complecti moneat,
voluntas operi cedat, dum praeclara libenter probandi[45]
necessaria narranti[46] conscientia non desit.

ext. 1

Alexandrum iracundia sua propemodum caelo deri-
puit: nam quid obstitit quominus illuc adsurgeret nisi
Lysimachus leoni obiectus et Clitus hasta traiectus et
Callisthenes mori iussus, quibus[47] tres maximas victorias
totidem amicorum iniustis caedibus victas[48] reddidit?

ext. 2

Quam vehemens deinde adversus populum Romanum
Hamilcaris odium! quattuor enim puerilis aetatis filios
intuens, eiusdem numeri catulos leoninos in perniciem
imperii nostri alere se praedicabat. digna nutrimenta quae
in exitium patriae suae, ut evenit, ‹se›[49] converterent![50]

ext. 3

E quibus Hannibal mature adeo patria vestigia subsecutus est ut, eo exercitum in Hispaniam traiecturo et ob id

---

[45] probandi A *corr.*: -da AL   [46] narranti *Madvig*: -ndi AL
(*cf. SB3*)   [47] quibus *SB3*: quia AL
[48] victas *SB1 et SB3*: -tor (edidit) AL
[49] *add. coni.* Briscoe
[50] converterent A *corr.*: -runt* AL: -rentur ⊊

---

[10] 78: Plut. *Sull.* 37 etc.
[11] Discredited by Curt. 8.1.14–17; cf. Justin 15.3 etc.

his breast convulsed with excessive agitation of mind and immoderate shouting, he vomited his life-breath mingled with blood and threats. He did not collapse from old age (he was entering his sixtieth year) but from an ungovernable temper fostered in the miseries of the commonwealth. So it is a question whether Sulla or Sulla's irascibility was extinguished first.[10]

One does not want to seek examples from unknowns and is reluctant to reproach great men with their vices. But since fidelity to my undertaking bids me embrace what stands out most conspicuously, let inclination yield to performance, provided that the narrator of what is necessary does not forget his ready approval of what is admirable.

Alexander's irascibility almost snatched him from heaven. For what stood in the way of his ascending thither except for Lysimachus exposed to a lion[11] and Clitus transfixed by a spear and Callisthenes ordered to die? Thereby he turned three great victories into defeats with an equal number of unjustified slayings of his friends.[12]

How passionate was Hamilcar's hate of the Roman people! Looking at his four sons in their boyhood he used to declare that he was rearing so many lion cubs to the ruin of our empire.[13] Nurture worthy to turn to the destruction of his own country, as it did.

One of them, Hannibal, followed at an early age in his father's footsteps so closely that when Hamilcar was about to transport an army into Spain and was offering sacrifice

[12] The victories are Granicus, Issus, and Arbela; but Lysimachus was not killed by Alexander.

[13] Not found elsewhere.

sacrificante, novem annorum altaria tenens iuraret se, cum primum per aetatem potuisset, acerrimum hostem populi Romani futurum ⟨et⟩[51] pertinacissimis precibus instantis belli commilitium exprimeret. idem significare cupiens quanto inter se odio Carthago et Roma dissiderent, inflicto in terram pede suscitatoque pulvere, tunc inter eas finem fore belli dixit, cum alterutra urbs[52] in habitum pulveris esset redacta.

ext. 4   In puerili pectore tantum vis odii potuit, sed in muliebri quoque aeque multum valuit: namque Samiramis, Assyriorum regina, cum ei circa cultum capitis sui occupatae nuntiatum esset Babylona defecisse, altera parte crinium adhuc soluta protinus ad eam expugnandam cucurrit, nec prius decorem capillorum in ordinem quam[53] urbem in potestatem suam redegit. quocirca statua eius Babylone posita est, illo habitu quo ad ultionem exigendam celeritate praecipiti tetendit.

4. DE AVARITIA

praef.   Protrahatur etiam Avaritia, latentium indagatrix lucrorum, manifestae praedae avidissima vorago, neque habendi fructu felix et cupiditate quaerendi miserrima.

1   Cum admodum locupleti L. Minucio Basilo falsum testamentum quidam in Graecia subiecisset, eiusdemque confirmandi gratia potentissimos civitatis nostrae viros, M. Crassum et Q. Hortensium, quibus Minucius ignotus fuerat, tabulis heredes inseruisset, quamquam evidens

---

[51] *add. Halm*
[52] urbs P: pars LG: *om.* ⌐
[53] quam *Gertz*: quantam A: quam tantam A *corr.*, LG

on that account, the nine-year-old boy swore with his hands upon the altar that as soon as he was old enough he would be a deadly enemy to the Roman people,[14] and by persistent entreaties extorted permission to serve in the impending war. The same, wishing to signify the mutual hatred in the quarrel between Rome and Carthage, stamped his foot upon the ground, raising dust: the war between the cities, he said, would end only when one or the other had been reduced to that substance.

Such was the force of hate in a boy's heart, but in a woman's too it was no less potent. Samiramis, queen of Assyria, was busy doing her hair when news came that Babylon had revolted. Leaving one half of it loose, she immediately ran to storm the city and did not restore her coiffure to a seemly order before she brought it back into her power. For that reason her statue was set up in Babylon showing her as she moved in precipitate haste to take her vengeance.[15]

4. OF AVARICE

Let Avarice too be dragged forth, tracker-down of hidden gains, greedy sucker-in of visible plunder, never happy in the enjoyment of possession and most miserable in the craving of acquisition.

L. Minucius Basilus was a very rich man. A certain person in Greece produced a forged will and for confirmation of the same put in as heirs two very powerful persons in our community, M. Crassus and Q. Hortensius, who did not know Minucius. The fraud was apparent, but in their

[14] 237: Livy 21.1.4 etc.   [15] Not found elsewhere.

fraus erat, tamen uterque pecuniae cupidus facinoris alieni munus non repudiavit. quantam culpam quam leviter rettuli! lumina curiae, ornamenta fori, quod scelus vindicare debebant, inhonesti lucri captura invitati auctoritatibus suis texerunt.

2 Verum aliquanto maiores vires in Q. Cassio exhibuit, qui in Hispania Silium et Calpurnium, occidendi sui gratia cum pugionibus deprehensos, quinquagies sestertium ab illo, ab hoc sexagies pactus dimisit. en quem[54] dubites, si alterum tantum daretur, iugulum quoque suum aequo animo illis fuisse praebiturum!

3 Ceterum avaritia ante omnes L. Septimuleii praecordia possedit; qui cum C. Gracchi familiaris fuisset, caput eius abscidere et per urbem pilo fixum ferre sustinuit, quia Opimius consul auro id se repensurum edixerat. sunt qui tradant liquato plumbo eum cavatam partem capitis, quo ponderosius esset, explesse. fuerit ille seditiosus, bono perierit exemplo, clientis tamen scelesta fames in has usque iacentis iniurias esurire non debuit.

ext. 1 Odium merita Septimuleii avaritia, Ptolomaei autem, regis Cypriorum, risu prosequenda: nam cum anxiis sordibus magnas opes corripuisset, propterque eas periturum se videret et ideo omni pecunia imposita navibus in altum processisset, ut classe perforata suo arbitrio periret et hostes praeda carerent, non sustinuit mergere aurum et ar-

---

[54] en quem *Kempf*: at q-* LG (*silet* A): an ⌐

1 *Ca.* 67: Cic. *Off.* 3.73.
2 48: *Bell. Alex.* 55.4f., with Q. Sestius instead of Silius.
3 121: Cic. *De orat.* 2.269; Plut. *C. Gracch.* 17.

greed for money neither of the two repudiated the gift of another's misdeed. What guilt, how lightly here reported! Luminaries of the senate house, ornaments of the Forum, lured by the getting of disgraceful gain they covered with their authority a crime that they ought to have punished.[1]

But avarice showed considerably greater power in the person of Q. Cassius. In Spain Silius and Calpurnius were caught with daggers intending to assassinate him. He released them, at the price of five million sesterces from the one and six million from the other.[2] Doubt if you can that, if as much again had been forthcoming, he would willingly have offered them his throat!

But above all others avarice possessed the heart of L. Septimuleius. He brought himself to cut off the head of C. Gracchus, whose close friend he had been, and carry it through the city on a javelin because Consul Opimius had publicly promised its weight in gold. Some say that to make the head heavier he hollowed out part and filled it with molten lead.[3] Granted that Gracchus was a revolutionary and that his death was a good example, yet the criminal hunger of the client should not have waxed so ravenous as to inflict these injuries upon him as he lay dead.

EXTERNAL

Septimuleius' avarice deserved hatred, that of Ptolemy, king of the Cypriots, was laughable. With anxious cheese-parings he had amassed great wealth and saw that on account of it he was likely to perish. He therefore placed all his money on ships and put out to sea, intending to scuttle his fleet and perish at his own will, depriving his enemies of their plunder. But he did not have the heart to sink the gold

gentum, sed futurum necis suae praemium domum
revexit. procul dubio hic non possedit divitias, sed a divitiis possessus est, titulo rex insulae, animo pecuniae miserabile mancipium.

5. DE SUPERBIA ET IMPOTENTIA

1   Atque ut superbia quoque et impotentia in conspicuo
ponatur, M. Fulvius Flaccus consul, M. Plautii Hypsaei
collega, cum perniciosissimas rei publicae leges introduce-
ret de civitate danda et de provocatione ad populum
eorum qui civitatem mutare noluissent, aegre compulsus
est ut in curiam veniret: deinde partim monenti, partim
oranti senatui ut incepto desisteret, responsum non dedit.
tyrannici spiritus consul haberetur, si adversus unum senatorem hoc modo se gessisset quo Flaccus in totius amplissimi ordinis contemnenda maiestate versatus est.

2   Quae a M. quoque Druso tribuno plebis per summam
contumeliam vexata est: parum enim habuit L. Philippum
consulem, quia interfari se contionantem ausus fuerat, ob-
torta gula, et quidem non per viatorem sed per clientem
suum, adeo violenter in carcerem praecipitem egisse ut
multus e naribus eius cruor profunderetur; verum etiam,
cum senatus ad eum misisset ut in curiam veniret, ʻquare
non potius' inquit ʻipse in Hostiliam curiam propinquam
rostris, id est ad me, venit?' piget adicere quod sequitur:
tribunus senatus imperium despexit, senatus tribuni verbis paruit.

---

4 57: cf. App. *B.C.* 2.23.
1 125: ibid. 1.21.
2 91: Flor. 2.5.8, Auct. vir. ill. 66.9.

and silver, and so brought home the future reward of his own death. No question, he did not possess riches but was possessed by them, in title the king of an island, in mind a miserable slave of pelf.[4]

5. OF ARROGANCE AND OUTRAGEOUSNESS

And to put arrogance too and outrageousness conspicuously in view, Consul M. Fulvius Flaccus, colleague of M. Plautius Hypsaeus, was introducing laws highly detrimental to the commonwealth about granting citizenship and about appeal to the people by persons unwilling to change their citizenship status. With difficulty he was compelled to come to the senate house, but then gave no answer to the senate as it partly warned and partly entreated him to give up his program. A Consul would be thought to have the spirit of a tyrant if he behaved to one senator in the manner adopted by Flaccus in contempt of the majesty of the whole most honourable order.[1]

That order was also harassed in the most insulting fashion by Tribune of the Plebs M. Drusus. He was not content with throttling Consul L. Philippus (using a client of his own, not an orderly) because he had dared to interrupt him as he was addressing a public meeting and driving him headlong to prison with such violence that a quantity of blood gushed from his nostrils.[2] He actually said when the senate sent him a message to come to their house, "Why don't *they* come to the Curia Hostilia close to the rostra, that is to say, to me?" It pains me to write what follows. The Tribune despised the command of the senate, the senate obeyed the words of the Tribune.

3   Cn. autem Pompeius quam insolenter! qui balneo
egressus ante pedes suos prostratum Hypsaeum ambitus
reum, et nobilem virum et sibi amicum, iacentem reliquit
contumeliosa voce proculcatum: nihil enim eum aliud
agere quam ut convivium suum moraretur respondit; et
huius dicti conscius securo animo cenare potuit. ille vero
etiam in foro non erubuit P. Scipionem, socerum suum,
legibus <ob>noxium[55] quas ipse tulerat, in maxima quidem
reorum illustrium ruina muneris loco a iudicibus depos-
cere, maritalis lecti blanditiis statum rei publicae temeran-
do.

4   Taetrum facto pariter ac dicto M. Antonii convivium:
nam cum ad eum triumvirum Caesetii Rufi senatoris caput allatum esset, aversantibus id ceteris propius ad-
moveri iussit ac diu diligenterque consideravit. cunctis
deinde exspectantibus quidnam esset dicturus, 'hunc ego'
inquit 'notum non habui.' superba de senatore, impotens
de occiso confessio.

ext. 1   Satis multa de nostris: aliena nunc adiciantur. Alexandri
regis virtus ac felicitas tribus insolentiae evidentissimis
gradibus exsultavit: fastidio enim Philippi Iovem Hammo-
nem patrem ascivit, taedio morum et cultus Macedonici
vestem et instituta Persica adsumpsit, spreto mortali habitu divinum aemulatus est, nec fuit ei pudori filium civem
hominem dissimulare.

[55] *add.* P

---

3 52: Plut. *Pomp.* 55.   4 52: App. *B.C.* 2.24, Dio 40.51.3,
53.2; cf. Tac. *Ann.* 3.28.1.   5 43: Apparently a garbled version
of the incident in App. *B.C.* 4.29.   6 Standard items.

How insolent, moreover, the conduct of Cn. Pompeius! Coming from his bath he left Hypsaeus, who was under prosecution for electoral malpractice, a nobleman and a friend, lying at his feet after trampling him with an insult. For he told him that he was doing nothing but hold up his (Pompey's) dinner; and with this speech on his mind he could dine without a qualm.[3] But even in the Forum he did not blush to ask the jury to acquit his father-in-law P. Scipio as a present to himself when Scipio was answerable to the laws that Pompey himself had carried, and that too when a great many illustrious defendants were coming to grief. The blandishments of the nuptial bed made him violate the stability of the commonwealth.[4]

Horrible was a dinner of Mark Antony's in act and word alike. The head of Caesetius Rufus, a senator, being brought to him as Triumvir, the rest of the company averted their eyes but Antony ordered it moved closer and contemplated it long and carefully. Then, as they all waited to hear what he would say, he remarked, "I didn't know this fellow." In speaking of a senator an arrogant admission, in speaking of one put to death an outrageous one.[5]

EXTERNAL

Enough of native examples, let external ones now be added. The prowess and good fortune of king Alexander ran riot in three conspicuous stages of insolence.[6] Despising Philip he adopted Jupiter Hammon as his father; wearying of Macedonian manners and attire he took up Persian dress and customs; scorning mortal state he imitated divine. He was not ashamed to falsify his identity as a son, a citizen, and a human being.

ext. 2   Iam Xerxes, cuius in nomine superbia et impotentia ha-
bitat, suo iure tam insolenter, quod Graeciae indicturus
bellum, adhibitis Asiae principibus, 'ne viderer' inquit
'meo tantummodo usus consilio, vos contraxi; ceterum
mementote parendum magis vobis esse quam suaden-
dum.' arroganter, etiam si victori repetere ei regiam
contigisset: tam deformiter victi nescias utrum insolentius
dictum an imp‹r›udentius.[56]

ext. 3   Hannibal[57] autem Cannensis pugnae successu elatus
nec admisit quemquam civium suorum [in][58] castris nec
responsum ulli nisi per interpretem dedit. Maharbalem
etiam, ante tabernaculum suum clara voce adfirmantem
prospexisse quonam modo paucis diebus Romae in Capitolio cenaret, aspernatus est. adeo felicitatis et moderatio-
nis dividuum contubernium est.

ext. 4   Insolentiae vero inter Carthaginiensem et Campanum
senatum quasi aemulatio fuit: ille enim separato a plebe
balneo lavabatur, hic diverso foro utebatur. quem morem
Capuae aliquamdiu retentum C. quoque Gracchi oratione
in Plautium scripta patet.

6. DE PERFIDIA

praef.   Occultum iam et insidiosum malum, perfidia, latebris
suis extrahatur. cuius efficacissimae vires sunt mentiri ac

---

[56] *add. Guyet*   [57] *hinc usque ad 13.2* merentur *deficit* L
[58] *del. Eberhard*

---

[7] 485: cf. Herod. 7.8.
[8] 216: Cato and Coelius ap. Gell. 10.24.6, Livy 22.5.1–4, Flor.

Xerxes now, in whose name dwells pride and outrageousness, was insolent as of right, in that when he was about to declare war on Greece, he summoned the leading men of Asia and said: "I have brought you together so I might not seem to have used only my own counsel. Remember, however, that your function is to obey rather than to advise."[7] An arrogant speech, even if he had had the luck to return to his palace victorious; in the mouth of one so disgracefully vanquished, whether more insolent or more unwise is hard to decide.

Elated by his victory at Cannae, Hannibal did not give admission to any of his countrymen in camp or reply to anyone except through an intermediary. Even when Maharbal announced in a loud voice in front of his tent that he had seen a way for him to dine on the Capitol in Rome in a few days time, he rebuffed him.[8] So hard is it for good fortune and moderation to share quarters.

There was a sort of competition in insolence between the senates of Carthage and Campania. The former used baths separated from the common folk, the latter a different forum. That this practice was retained in Capua for quite a long time is evident *inter alia* from C. Gracchus' speech against Plautius.[9]

6. OF TREACHERY

Let treachery, hidden and insidious evil, now be dragged from its lurking place. Its most effective strength

1.22.19 etc. Hannibal's arrogance seems to be Valerius' own contribution.

[9] C. Gracchus or. fr. 59 Malcovati.

fallere, fructus in aliquo admisso scelere consistit, tum certus cum credulitatem nefariis vinculis circumdedit, tantum incommodi humano generi adferens quantum salutis bona fides praestat. habeat igitur non minus reprehensionis quam illa laudis consequitur.

1   Romulo regnante Spurius Tarpeius arci praeerat. cuius filiam virginem aquam sacris petitum extra moenia egressam Tatius ut armatos Sabinos in arcem secum reciperet corrupit, mercedis nomine pactam quae in sinistris manibus gerebant: erant autem iis⁵⁹ armillae et anuli magno ex pondere auri. loco potitum agmen Sabinorum puellam praemium flagitantem armis obrutam necavit, perinde quasi promissum, quod ea quoque laevis gestaverant, solv⟨er⟩it.⁶⁰ absit reprehensio, quia impia proditio celeri poena vindicata est.

2   Ser. quoque Galba summae perfidiae: trium enim Lusitaniae civitatium convocato populo tamquam de commodis eius acturus, octo milia, in quibus flos iuventutis consistebat, electa et armis exuta partim trucidavit, partim vendidit. quo facinore maximam cladem barbarorum magnitudine criminis antecessit.

3   Cn. autem Domitium, summi generis et magni animi virum, nimia gloriae cupiditas perfidum exsistere coegit: iratus namque Bituito, regi Arvernorum, quod [tum]⁶¹ suam et Allobrogum gentem, se etiam tum in provincia morante, ad Q. Fabii successoris sui dexteram confugere

---

⁵⁹ ⟨in⟩ his (A) *Kempf*   ⁶⁰ *add.* Per.*   ⁶¹ *del.* Kempf*

---

1 Prop. 4.4 etc.
2 Cf. VM 8.1.absol.2.

is lying and deceit. Its reward consists in some committed crime and is sure when it has encompassed credulity with wicked bonds. It causes as much harm to the human race as good faith brings welfare. So let it have no less reprehension than good faith wins praise.

When Romulus was king, Spurius Tarpeius commanded the citadel. His young daughter, as she went outside the walls to fetch water for religious rites, was bribed by Tatius to let armed Sabines into the citadel along with herself. As her price she asked that which they wore on their left hands: they had golden bracelets and rings of great weight. When the column of Sabines had got possession of the place and the girl demanded her reward, they buried her under their shields and killed her, as though they had thus kept their promise; for they had carried shields too with their left hands.[1] Let them not be blamed, since impious betrayal was punished with swift retribution.

Ser. Galba too was treacherous in the extreme. He called together the people of three Lusitanian communities ostensibly to take action for their benefit. Then he selected eight thousand, comprising the flower of their young men, and stripped them of their weapons, after which he butchered some and sold the rest. By this misdeed he outdid the barbarians' great calamity by the magnitude of his crime.[2]

Cn. Domitius, a man of the highest lineage and of lofty spirit, was driven into treachery by his overeagerness for glory. He was angry with Bituitus, king of the Arverni, because the same had urged his own tribe and that of the Allobroges to resort to the right hand of his successor Q. Fabius while he himself was still in the province. Having

hortatus esset, per colloquii simulationem arcessitum hospitioque exceptum vinxit ac Romam nave deportandum curavit. cuius factum senatus neque probare potuit neque rescindere voluit, ne remissus in patriam Bituitus bellum renovaret. igitur eum Albam custodiae causa relegavit.

4   Viriathi etiam caedes duplicem perfidiae accusationem recipit,[62] in amicis quod eorum manibus interemptus est, in Q. Servilio Caepione consule quia is sceleris huius auctor impunitate promissa fuit, victoriamque non meruit sed emit.

ext. 1   Verum ut ipsum fontem perfidiae contemplemur, Carthaginienses Xanthippum Lacedaemonium, cuius optima opera primo Punico bello usi fuerant et quo iuvante Atilium Regulum ceperant, simulantes domum se revehere, in alto merserunt, quid tanto facinore petentes? an ne victoriae eorum socius superesset? exstat nihilo minus, et quidem cum opprobrio, quem sine ulla gloriae iactura inviolatum reliquissent.

ext. 2   Hannibal porro Nucerinos, hortatu suo cum binis vestimentis urbem inexpugnabilibus muris cinctam egressos, vapore et fumo balnearum strangulando, et Acerranorum senatum eadem ratione extra moenia evocatum in profunda[63] puteorum abiciendo, nonne bellum adversus popu-

---

[62] recipit *Kempf*: recepit A
[63] profunda *Eberhard*: -do A: -dum (puteum) P

---

3 121: accounts differ; cf. Klebs *RE* III.547f., Broughton I.520f.   4 139: Livy *Per.* 54 etc. (Broughton I.482).
5 Cf. H. Schaefer, *RE* IX A 1350. The story of the drowning seems to be a fiction.

summoned the king under the pretence of a parley and received him hospitably, he put him in bonds and had him deported by ship to Rome. The senate could not approve his action, neither did it wish to rescind it for fear that if Bituitus was sent back to his country he would start the war afresh. So it sent him to Alba for custody.[3]

The murder of Viriathus too is open to a double charge of treachery, one involving his friends, because he was killed by their hands, the other Consul Q. Servilius Caepio, in that he instigated the crime with a promise of immunity. He did not earn victory, he bought it.[4]

EXTERNAL

But to contemplate the very fountain of treachery: the Carthaginians drowned the Spartan Xanthippus in the sea while pretending to give him a passage home, whose excellent service they had used in the Second Punic War and with whose assistance they had captured Atilius Regulus.[5] What did they seek to gain by so great a misdeed? Was it that they did not want a partner in their victory to survive? None the less he is still here and to their reproach, whereas they might have left him unharmed without any loss of glory.

Hannibal urged the people of Nuceria to leave their city with its circuit of inexpugnable walls, each with two garments, and then suffocated them with the vapour and smoke of baths. By the same means he lured the senate of Acerrae outside their walls and threw them down deep wells.[6] Professing to make war against the Roman people

[6] 216: App. *Lib.* 63, Dio fr. 57.30. But Livy (23.15.3–6, 17.4–7) says nothing of the alleged treacheries, which belong with the atrocity stories in VM 9.2.ext.1f.

lum Romanum et Italiam professus adversus ipsam fidem
acrius gessit, mendaciis et fallacia quasi praeclaris artibus
gaudens? quo evenit ut alioqui insignem nominis sui memoriam relicturus, in dubio maiorne an peior vir haberi
deberet poneret.

7. DE VI ET SEDITIONE

1   Sed ut violentiae ⟨et⟩[64] seditionis tam togatae quam
etiam armatae facta referantur, L. Equitium, qui se Ti.
Gracchi filium simulabat tribunatumque adversus leges ⟨cum⟩[65] L. Saturnino petebat, a C. Mario quintum[66]
consulatum gerente in publicam custodiam ductum populus, claustris carceris convulsis, raptum umeris suis per
summam animorum alacritatem portavit.

2   Idemque Q. Metellum censorem, quod ab eo tamquam
Gracchi filio censum recipere nolebat, lapidibus prosternere conatus est, adfirmantem tres tantummodo filios Ti.
Graccho fuisse, e quibus unum in Sardinia stipendia me-
rentem, alterum infantem Praeneste, tertium post patris
mortem natum Romae decessisse, neque oportere clarissimae familiae ignotas sordes inseri, cum interim improvida concitatae multitudinis temeritas—pro impudentia[67] et
audacia!—adversus consulatum et censuram tetendit,
principesque suos omni petulantiae genere vexavit.

3   Vesana haec tantummodo, illa etiam cruenta seditio:
populus enim Nunnium, competitorem Saturnini, novem

64 et G: *om.* A
65 cum GP: *om.* A
66 sextum *Pighius, sc. auctorem corrigens*
67 impu- G: inpru- A

344

and Italy, did he not wage it more fiercely against good faith itself, revelling in lies and deceit as in fine arts? As a result he made it a question whether he should be considered more a great man or more a bad man, who otherwise would have left a glorious memory of his name.

7. OF VIOLENCE AND SEDITION

But to relate the deeds of violence and sedition in civil life and also under arms: L. Equitius, who was pretending to be Ti. Gracchus' son and illegally standing for the Tribunate along with L. Saturninus, was placed in public custody by C. Marius, then in his fifth Consulship. The people tore down the bars of the prison and snatched him away, carrying him on their shoulders in the highest of spirits.[1]

The same people tried to stone Censor Q. Metellus to the ground, because he refused to accept this man's census return as Gracchus' son.[2] He stated that Ti. Gracchus had only three sons, one of whom had died on military service in Sardinia, the second at Praeneste in infancy, the third, born after his father's death, in Rome. It was not right, he said, that unknowns of low origin should be thrust into a very illustrious family. But the blind temerity of the excited crowd (what impudence and audacity!) pressed on against Consulship and Censorship and harassed their leaders with every sort of offensive behaviour.

That sedition was only crazy, the following was bloody. Nine Tribunes had already been elected and one place re-

---

[1] 100: cf. Flor. 2.4.1 etc. He was elected.
[2] 102/1: Cic. *Sest.* 101. Cf. VM 3.8.6.

iam creatis tribunis unoque loco duobus candidatis restante, vi prius in aedes privatas compulit, extractum deinde interemit, ut caede integerrimi civis facultas a‹di›piscendae[68] potestatis taeterrimo homini[69] daretur.

4 Creditorum quoque consternatio adversus Sempronii Asellionis praetoris urbani caput intolerabili modo exarsit. quem, quia causam debitorum susceperat, concitati a L. Cassio tribuno plebis, pro aede Concordiae sacrificium facientem ab ipsis altaribus fugere extra forum coactum inque tabernula latitantem praetextatum discerpserunt.

mil.   Detestanda fori condicio, sed si castra respicias, aeque
Rom. 1 magna orietur indignatio. cum C. Mario lege Sulpicia provincia Asia, ut adversus Mithridatem bellum gereret, privato decreta esset, missum ab eo Gratidium legatum ad L. Sullam consulem accipiendarum legionum causa milites trucidarunt, procul dubio indignati quod a summo imperio ad eum qui nullo in honore versaretur transire cogerentur. sed quis ferat militem scita plebis exitio legati corrigentem?

mil.   Pro consule istud tam violenter exercitus, illud adver-
Rom. 2 sus consulem: Q. enim Pompeium, Sullae collegam, senatus iussu ad exercitum Cn. Pompeii, quem aliquamdiu invita civitate obtinebat, contendere ausum, ambitiosi

---

[68] adipisc- GP: apisc- A
[69] homini P: civi A: *del Kempf*

[3] 101: Livy *Per.* 69 etc.
[4] 89: Livy *Per.* 74; App. *B.C.* 1.54.
[5] 88: Oros. 5.19.4; cf. Plut. *Mar.* 35, *Sull.* 8.

mained for two candidates. The people first drove Nunnius, Saturninus' competitor, by violence into a private
house, then dragged him out and killed him so as to give a
detestable citizen the opportunity to gain power by the
murder of a perfectly blameless one.[3]

The dismay of creditors flared up against the life of
City Praetor Sempronius Asellio in a manner not to be
tolerated. Because he had taken up the cause of the debtors, persons stirred up by Tribune of the Plebs L. Cassius
forced him as he was sacrificing in front of the temple of
Concord to take flight from the very altar and out of the
Forum. Then, as he was hiding in a small shop, they tore
him limb from limb wearing his gown of office.[4]

ROMAN SOLDIERS

The state of the Forum is appalling, but if you look at
the camp, indignation equally great will spring up. When
Asia was decreed as his province to C. Marius, then a private citizen, by the Sulpician law in order for him to make
war against Mithridates, he sent his Legate Gratidius to
Consul L. Sulla to take over the legions. The soldiers killed
him.[5] No doubt they were indignant at being forced to
transfer from the highest command to one who held no
office; but who could tolerate a soldiery amending decrees
of the plebs by the destruction of a Legate?

The army perpetrated that deed of violence on behalf
of a Consul, but the following against a Consul. Q. Pompeius, Sulla's colleague, ventured to go by order of the senate to Cn. Pompeius' army, which he had for some time
been holding against the will of the community. Corrupted
by the enticements of their popularity-mongering general,
the soldiers attacked him as he was starting to perform a

ducis illecebris corrupti milites sacrificare incipientem adorti in modum hostiae mactarunt, tantumque scelus, curia castris cedere se confessa, inultum abiit.

mil.
Rom. 3

Ille quoque exercitus nefarie violentus qui C. Carbonem, fratrem Carbonis ter consulis, propter bella civilia dissolutam disciplinam militarem praefractius et rigidius astringere conatum privavit vita, satiusque duxit maximo scelere coinquinari quam pravos ac taetros mores mutare.

8. DE TEMERITATE

praef.

Temeritatis etiam subiti et[70] vehementes sunt impulsus, quorum ictibus hominum mentes concussae nec sua pericula dispicere nec aliena facta iusta aestimatione prosequi valent.

1

Quam enim temere se Africanus superior ex Hispania duabus quinqueremibus ad Syphacem traiecit, in unius Numidae infidis praecordiis suam pariter et patriae salutem depositurus! itaque exiguo momento maximae rei casus fluctuatus est, utrum interfector an captivus Scipionis Syphax fieret.

2

Nam C. Caesaris anceps conatus, etsi caelestium cura protectus est, non tamen [vix][71] sine horrore animi referri potest: si quidem impatiens legionum tardioris a Brundisio Apolloniam traiectus, per simulationem adversae valetudinis convivio egressus, maiestate sua servili veste occultata naviculam conscendit ⟨et⟩[72] e flumine Ao⟨o⟩[73] maris

[70] subiti et A *corr.*: et s- A
[71] *del.* * *coni Briscoe*
[72] *add.* ⌐
[73] Aoo *Gertz*: ac A

sacrifice and slew him like a sacrificial offering. And so great a crime went unpunished, the senate confessing that it yielded to the camp.[6]

Wickedly violent too was that army which took the life of C. Carbo, brother of Carbo three times Consul, who had tried somewhat abruptly and unbendingly to tighten military discipline, relaxed because of the civil wars. They thought it better to be sullied by a heinous crime than to change their depraved, vile ways.[7]

8. OF RASHNESS

Of rashness too the impulses are both sudden and violent. The minds of men shaken by their blows can neither discern their own dangers nor follow the acts of others in just estimation.

How rashly did the elder Africanus cross over from Spain with two quinqiremes to Syphax, to lay his own and his country's safety on the faithless breast of one Numidian! So for a brief moment the fate of a great matter hung in the balance: was Syphax to be Scipio's executioner or his prisoner?[1]

A hazardous attempt of C. Caesar, although he was protected by the care of the gods, can hardly be related without a shudder. Impatient at the tardy crossing of his legions from Brundisium to Apollonia, he left dinner pretending an indisposition, hid his majesty in a slave's dress, embarked on a small craft, and in stormy weather made his way from the river Aous to the mouth of the Adriatic and

---

[6] 88: Livy *Per.* 77, Vell. 2.20.1, App. *B.C.* 1.63.
[7] 80: Gran. Licin. 36.8.   [1] 206: Livy 28.17.10–18.12 etc.

Hadriatici saeva tempestate fauces petiit, protinusque in altum dirigi iusso navigio, multum ac diu contrariis iactatus fluctibus, tandem necessitati cessit.

3 Age, illa quam exsecrabilis militum temeritas! fecit enim ut A. Albinus, nobilitate moribus honorum omnium consummatione civis eximius, propter falsas et inanes suspiciones in castris ab exercitu lapidibus obrueretur, quodque accessionem indignationis non recipit, oranti atque obsecranti duci a militibus causae dicendae potestas negata est.

ext. 1 Itaque minus miror apud trucem et saevum animum Hannibalis defensionis locum innoxio gubernatori non fuisse, quem a Petelia classe Africam repetens freto appulsus, dum tam parvo spatio Italiam Siciliamque inter se divisas non credit, velut insidiosum cursus rectorem interemit, posteaque diligentius inspecta veritate tunc absolvit, cum eius innocentiae nihil ultra sepulcri honorem dari potuit. igitur angusti atque aestuosi maris alto e tumulo speculatrix statua quam ⟨in⟩ memoriam[74] Pelori tam Punicae temeritatis ultra citraque navigantium ⟨in⟩[75] oculis collocatum indicium est.

ext. 2 Iam Atheniensium civitas ad vesaniam usque temeraria, quae decem universos imperatores suos, et quidem a pulcherrima victoria venientes, capitali iudicio exceptos

---

[74] in memoriam *SB*: -riam AL: -riae ⟨
[75] *add. Kempf*

---

2 47: Lucan 5.497–677 etc.   3 89: Livy *Per.* 75 etc. Orosius (5.18.22) has a different assessment.   4 203: Strabo 10, Mela 2.116, Serv. *Aen.* 3.411. Strabo speaks of "the Carthaginians" instead of Hannibal (the entry in *RE* Peloros 3 is wild). Hannibal

then ordered the vessel to be steered into the open sea. But buffeted much and long by adverse waves, he finally bowed to necessity.[2]

And now how execrable the following rashness of soldiers! It caused A. Albinus, a citizen distinguished in birth, character, and the accumulation of all offices, to be overwhelmed with stones by his army in camp because of false, baseless suspicions; and, what admits of no increment of indignation, the general though begging and imploring was denied opportunity to plead his case by his soldiers.[3]

EXTERNAL

So I am the less surprised that the savage, pitiless heart of Hannibal gave a harmless steersman no chance to defend himself. Sailing in a fleet from Petelia to Africa, he put into the Strait. Not believing that Italy and Sicily were divided by so small a space, he accused the navigator of treachery and put him to death. Afterwards on more careful inspection of the truth he acquitted him, when his innocence could be granted nothing except the honour of burial. And so a statue looks from a high mound over the narrow, stormy sea, placed before the eyes of those sailing this way or that both in memory of Pelorus and as a token of Punic temerity.[4]

The Athenian community was rash to the point of madness when it received all ten of its generals,[5] coming as they did from a brilliant victory, with a capital trial and put them to death because they had been unable to consign

was sailing north through the Straits after rounding the toe of Italy on his way to Carthage. Mela, flouting geography, confuses this voyage with that of 195 when Hannibal fled from Carthage to Syria (cf. Livy 33.48.2f.).   [5] Cf. VM 1.1.ext.8.

351

necavit, quod militum corpora saevitia maris interpellante sepulturae mandare non potuissent, necessitatem puniens, cum honorare virtutem deberet.

9. DE ERRORE

praef.　　Temeritati proximus est error, quemadmodum ad laedendum par ita cui facilius quis ignoverit, quia non sua sponte sed vanis concitatus imaginibus culpae se implicat. qui quam late in pectoribus hominum vagetur si complecti coner, vitio de quo loquor sim obnoxius. paucos igitur eius lapsus referemus.

1　　C. Helvius Cinna tribunus plebis, ex funere C. Caesaris domum suam petens, populi manibus discerptus est pro Cornelio Cinna, in quem saevire se existimabat, iratus ei quod cum adfinis esset Caesaris, adversus eum nefarie raptum impiam pro rostris orationem habuisset, eoque errore propulsus est ut caput Helvii perinde atque Cornelii circa rogum Caesaris fixum iaculo ferret, officii sui, alieni erroris piaculum miserabile!

2　　Nam C. Cassium error a semet ipso poenas exigere coegit: inter illum enim pugnae quattuor exercituum apud Philippos varium ipsisque ducibus ignotum eventum missus ab eo Titinius centurio nocturno tempore, ut specularetur quonam in statu res M. Bruti essent, dum crebros excessus viae petit, quia tenebrarum obscuritas hostesne an commilitones occurrerent dinoscere non sinebat, tardius ad Cassium rediit. quem is exceptum ab hostibus omniaque in eorum potestatem recidisse existimans, finire

---

1 44: Plut. *Caes.* 68 etc.

the bodies of the soldiers to burial, the rough sea preventing. It punished necessity when it should have been rewarding merit.

9. OF ERROR

Error is next to rashness, equal in power to harm but more easily pardonable because it involves itself in guilt not voluntarily but stirred up by vain imaginings. If I were to try to embrace how widely it wanders in men's hearts, I should be chargeable with the fault of which I speak. So I shall relate a few of its lapses.

Tribune of the Plebs C. Helvius Cinna, as he was going home from the funeral of C. Caesar, was torn to pieces by the hands of the people in mistake for Cornelius Cinna, against whom they thought their fury was directed. They were angry with him because, though related to Caesar by marriage, he had made an impious speech against him from the rostra when he had been wickedly taken off. Driven by that error, the people carried Helvius' head on a javelin around Caesar's pyre, as though it was Cornelius'. A pitiable sacrifice to his own discharge of duty and the error of others.[1]

As for C. Cassius, error made him exact his own punishment. In the battle of the four armies at Philippi, of outcome various and unknown to the generals themselves, he sent Titinius, a Centurion, at night to find out how it was with M. Brutus. Titinius made frequent detours because the darkness did not allow him to tell friend from foe in his path, so he was rather slow in returning to Cassius; who for his part, thinking Titinius had been taken by the enemy and that everything had fallen into their hands, hastened

353

vitam properavit, cum et castra hostium invicem capta et
Bruti copiae magna ex parte incolumes essent. Titinii vero
non oblitteranda silentio virtus, qui oculis paulisper haesit
inopinato iacentis ducis spectaculo attonitus, deinde pro-
fusus in lacrimas 'etsi imprudens' inquit, 'imperator, causa
tibi mortis fui, tamen, ne id ipsum impunitum sit, accipe
me fati tui comitem,' superque exanime corpus eius iugulo
suo gladium capulo tenus demisit, ac permixto utriusque
sanguine duplex victima iacuit, pietatis haec, erroris illa.

3   Ceterum falsa opinatio nescio an praecipuam iniuriam
Lartis Tolumnii, Veientium regis, penatibus intulerit: nam
cum in tesserarum prospero iactu per iocum collusori
dixisset 'occide,' et forte Romanorum legati intervenis-
sent, satellites eius, errore vocis impulsi, interficiendo
legatos lusum ad imperium transtulerunt.

10. DE ULTIONE

praef.   Ultionis autem quemadmodum acres ita iusti aculei
sunt, qui lacessiti concitantur, acceptum dolorem ⟨do-
lore⟩[76] pensare cupientes: quos latius complecti non attinet.

1   Tribunus plebis M. Flavius ad populum de Tusculanis
rettulit, quod eorum consilio Veliterni Privernatesque rebellassent.[77] qui cum coniugibus ac liberis squalore obsiti

---

[76] *add. Kempf*   [77] rebellassent P: -aturos diceret A; Br

---

2 42: Plut. *Brut.* 43 etc.   3 Livy 4.17.1–6; cf. Cic. *Phil.*
9.4f., Pliny *N.H.* 34.23. The supposed mistake has not been satis-
factorily explained. According to this exculpatory version of what
happened, *occide,* which Livy calls ambiguous, referred to the

to end his life, although the enemy camp had been captured in turn and Brutus' forces were largely intact. But Titinius's noble conduct should not be effaced by silence. For a short while he stood gazing, amazed at the unexpected sight of his commander lying dead, then, bursting into tears, "General," he said, "though I caused your death unwittingly, even that must not go unpunished, so receive me as the companion of your fate," and above Cassius' lifeless body plunged his sword to the hilt in his own throat. There they lay in the mingled blood of both, two victims, one of loyalty, the other of error.[2]

Most remarkable perhaps was the injury which a mistaken opinion brought upon the household gods of Lars Tolumnius, king of Veii. After a lucky throw of the dice he said in jest to the other player, "Kill."[3] By chance Roman envoys arrived at that moment and his henchmen, mistaking his word, killed the same, changing a joke into an order.

10. OF REVENGE

Just are the pricks of revenge as they are sharp, when people are excited by provocation, desiring to balance pain received with pain. There is no need to cast our net very wide here.

Tribune of the Plebs M. Flavius brought the case of the Tusculans before the people, claiming that the men of Velitrae and Privernum had taken up arms again on their advice. The Tusculans came to Rome with their wives and

game. Did the henchmen hear *occĭde* (die, i.e. give up) as *occīde* (kill), despite the difference of accent and quantity? Or could *occide* be equivalent to "beat that," referring to the throw?

supplices Romam ⟨cum⟩[78] venissent, accidit ut reliquis tribubus salutarem sententiam secutis sola Pollia iudicaret oportere puberes[79] verberatos securi percuti, imbellem multitudinem sub corona venire. quam ob causam Papiria tribus, in qua plurimum postea Tusculani in civitatem recepti potuerunt, neminem umquam candidatum Polliae tribus fecit magistratum, ne ad eam ullus honor suffragiis ⟨suis⟩ perveniret, quae illis vitam ac libertatem, quantum in ipsa fuit, ademerat.

2   Illam vero ultionem et senatus et consensus omnium approbavit: cum enim Hadrianus cives Romanos, qui Uticae consistebant, sordido imperio vexasset idcircoque ab iis vivus esset exustus, nec quaestio ulla in urbe hac de re habita nec querella versata est.

ext. 1   Clarae ultionis utraque regina, et Tomyris, quae caput Cyri abscisum in utrem humano sanguine repletum demitti iussit, exprobrans illi insatiabilem cruoris sitim, simulque poenas occisi ab eo filii sui exigens, et Berenice, quae Laodices insidiis interceptum sibi filium graviter ferens armata currum conscendit, persecutaque satellitem regium, crudelis operis ministrum, nomine Caeneum, quem[80] hasta nequiquam petierat, saxo ictum prostravit, ac super eius corpus actis equis inter infesta contrariae partis agmina ad domum in qua interfecti pueri corpus occultari arbi-

---

[78] add. Halm: cum con- … Romam *intra cruces Briscoe*
[79] puberes *SB* (*coll. Liv.* 8.37.11): publice eos A
[80] quem ⌐: qm̄ (= quoniam) A

---

[1] 323: Livy 8.37.8–12.   [2] 83: Cic. *Verr.* 2.1.70, Livy *Per.* 86 etc.   [3] 529: Herod. 1.206–14 etc.

children, wearing mourning in supplication. The result was that all the tribes were for mercy except the Pollia, which ruled that the men of military age be flogged and beheaded and the multitude of noncombatants sold by auction. For that reason the tribe Papiria, in which the Tusculans later had great power after they had been received into the franchise, never voted for a candidate belonging to tribe Pollia, not wishing that any office should go by their votes to that tribe which, so far as in it lay, had taken away their lives and liberty.[1]

Both the senate and public opinion as a whole approved the following act of revenge. Hadrianus had harried Roman citizens living in Utica with his avarice as governor and on that account had been burned alive by them. No enquiry was made on the matter in Rome nor did anybody complain.[2]

EXTERNAL

Two queens are famous for their revenges. Tomyris ordered Cyrus' head to be cut off and let down into a bladder full of human gore, thus reproaching him with an insatiable thirst for blood and at the same time taking vengeance for her son whom he had killed.[3] Berenice was aggrieved that her son had been taken from her by the treachery of Laodice. Mounting a chariot with weapons, she pursued a royal attendant named Caeneus who had carried out the cruel work and having missed him with a spear brought him down flat with a stone, then drove her horses over his body and between the hostile ranks of the opposing party to reach the house in which she thought the corpse of the

[4] 246: Polyaen. 8.50; cf. Justin 27.1.

trabatur perrexit.

ext. 2   Iasonem Thessalum, Persarum regi bellum inferre parantem, an satis iusta ultio absumpserit ambiguae aestimationis est: Taxillo enim gymnasiarcho a quibusdam iuvenibus pulsatum se questo permisit ut aut tricenas ab iis drachmas exigeret aut denas plagas singulis imponeret. quo posteriore vindicta uso qui vapulaverant Iasonem interfecerunt, animi non corporis dolore poenae modum aestimantes. ceterum parvo irritamento ingenui pudoris maximae rei exspectatio subruta est, quoniam opinione Graeciae tantum in spe Iasonis quantum in effectu Alexandri reponitur.

11. DICTA IMPROBA AUT
FACTA SCELERATA

praef.   Nunc, quatenus vitae humanae cum bona tum etiam mala substitutis exemplorum imaginibus persequimur, dicta improba et facta scelerata referantur.

1   Unde autem potius quam a Tullia ordiar, quia tempore vetustissimum, conscientia[81] nefarium, voce monstri simile exemplum est? cum carpento veheretur et is qui iumenta agebat succussis frenis constitisset, repentinae morae causam requisivit, et ut comperit corpus patris Servii Tullii occisi ibi iacere, supra id duci vehiculum iussit, quo celerius in complexu interfectoris eius Tarquinii veniret. qua tam impia tamque probrosa festinatione non so-

81 *sic* A *corr.,* G; Br

murdered boy was hidden.[4]

It is a moot point whether the vengeance that carried off Jason of Thessaly as he was preparing for war against the king of Persia was sufficiently grounded. He had given permission to Taxillus, who was in charge of a gymnasium and complained that he had been beaten by some young fellows, either to make them pay three hundred drachmas apiece or to give each of them ten strokes. He chose the latter punishment. The recipients of the floggings, reckoning the extent of the punishment by pain of mind, not body, assassinated Jason.[5] A small wound to personal honour frustrated the expectation of a great event. For the opinion of Greece puts the hope of Jason on a par with the accomplishment of Alexander.

11. OUTRAGEOUS WORDS OR CRIMINAL DEEDS

Now, since we are going through both the good and bad of human life substituting likenesses in the form of examples, let outrageous words and criminal deeds be related.

Where to begin rather than with Tullia? For in time this is the most ancient example, in conscience nefarious, in word monstrous. She was travelling in a carriage when the driver shook his reins and stopped. Asking the reason for the sudden halt and being told that the body of her murdered father Servius Tullius was lying on the ground, she ordered the vehicle led over it so that she could come the faster to the embraces of his killer, Tarquinius. By that impious and scandalous haste she not only stained herself

[5] 370: cf. Xen. *Hellen.* 6.4.31f., Diodor. 15.60.5.

lum se aeterna infamia sed etiam ipsum vicum cognomine Sceleris commaculavit.

2   Non tam atrox C. Fimbriae est factum et dictum, sed si per se aestimetur, utrumque audacissimum. id egerat ut Scaevola in funere C. Marii iugularetur. quem postquam ex vulnere recreatum comperit, accusare apud populum instituit. interrogatus deinde quid de eo secus dicturus esset cui pro sanctitate morum satis digna laudatio reddi non posset, respondit obiecturum se illi quod parcius corpore telum recepisset. licentiam furoris aegrae rei publicae gemitu prosequendam!

3   L. vero Catilina in senatu, M. Cicerone incendium ab ipso excitatum dicente, 'sentio' inquit, 'et quidem illud, si aqua non potuero, ruina restinguam.' quem quid aliud existimemus quam conscientiae stimulis actum reum se[82] incohati parricidii peregisse?

4   Consternatum etiam Magii Chilonis amentia pectus, qui M. Marcello datum a Caesare spiritum sua manu eripuit, vetus ‹amicus›[83] et Pompeianae militiae comes, indignatus aliquos sibi amicorum ab eo praeferri: urbem enim a Mitylenis, quo se contulerat, repetentem in Atheniensium portu pugione confodit, protinusque ad irritamenta vesaniae suae trucidanda tetendit, amicitiae hostis, divini beneficii interceptor, publicae religionis, quod ad salutem clarissimi civis recuperandam attinuit, acerba labes.

---

[82] reum se *Per.*: a se A: reum ⊊   [83] *add.* A *corr.*

---

[1] Livy 1.48.6f. The street was called Sceleratus Vicus.

[2] 86: Cic. *Rosc. Am.* 33.   [3] 63: Cic. *Mur.* 51, Sall. *Cat.* 31.9, Flor. 2.12.7.   [4] 45: Cic. (Ser. Sulpicius) *Fam.* 4.12 etc.

with eternal infamy but the street itself with the name of crime.[1]

The deed and saying of C. Fimbria is less atrocious, but considered in themselves both are of the most audacious. He had intended that Scaevola should be murdered at C. Marius' funeral. Learning that he had recovered from his wound, Fimbria set about prosecuting him before the people. Then, asked what he was going to say against one whose blameless character could not be praised highly enough, he replied that he would charge him with receiving the weapon in his body too gingerly. Extravagance of madness, to be accompanied by the groans of the ailing commonwealth![2]

As M. Cicero was talking in the senate about the fire started by L. Catilina, "I feel it," said the latter, "and if I can't put it out with water, I'll do it with the falling house."[3] What are we to think but that driven by the goads of conscience he proved himself guilty of the parricide he had begun?

Magius Chilo's mind too was confused by madness. An old friend of M. Marcellus and his companion in the Pompeian service, with his own hand he snatched away the life Caesar had granted, out of resentment that some other friends were preferred by Marcellus to himself. As Marcellus was returning to Rome from Mitylene, where he had betaken himself, in the harbour of Athens, Magius stabbed him with a dagger and went straight on to slaughter the provocations of his lunacy: an enemy of friendship, an interceptor of the divine benefaction, a sad defilement of a sacred public obligation so far as concerned the restoration of a most illustrious citizen.[4]

361

5   Hanc crudelitatem, cui nihil adici posse videtur, C.
Toranius atrocitate parricidii superavit: namque trium-
virorum partes secutus, proscripti patris sui, praetorii et
ornati viri, latebras aetatem notasque corporis, quibus
agnosci posset, centurionibus edidit qui eum persecuti
sunt. senex, de filii magis vita et incrementis quam de reliquo spiritu suo sollicitus, an incolumis esset et an imperatoribus satis faceret interrogare eos coepit. e quibus unus
'ab illo' inquit 'quem tantopere diligis demonstratus nostro
ministerio, filii indicio, occideris,' protinusque pectus eius
gladio traiecit. collapsus itaque est infelix, auctore caedis
quam ipsa caede miserior.

6   Cuius fati acerbitatem L. Villius Annalis sortitus, cum
in campum ad quaestoria comitia filii descendens proscriptum se cognosset, ad clientem suum confugit. sed ne
fide eius tutus esse posset, scelere nefarii iuvenis effectum
est, si quidem per ipsa vestigia patris militibus ductis occidendum eum in conspectu suo obiecit, bis parricida, consilio prius, iterum spectaculo.

7   Ne Vettius quidem Salassus proscriptus parum amari
exitus. quem latentem uxor interficiendum, quid dicam,
tradidit an ipsa iugulavit? quanto enim levius est scelus cui
tantummodo manus abest?

---

[5] 43/42: cf. App. *B.C.* 4.18, Oros. 6.18.9. This victim was
C. Turranius, an ex-Praetor, confused in the sources with C.
Toranius, a former guardian of Octavian and colleague as Aedile
of his father. He too was proscribed but may have survived. See
Münzer, *RE* Toranius 4 and Turranius 4.

To this cruelty no addition seems possible, but C. Toranius outdid it in the ferocity of his parricide.[5] A partisan of the Triumvirs, he gave the Centurions who were in pursuit of his proscribed father, an ex-Praetor and a man of note, details of his hiding place, age, and bodily marks by which he could be recognized. The old man, who was more concerned about his son's life and advancement than about what was left of his own breath, started to ask them whether he was safe and in good standing with the generals. One of them replied: "Your son, whom you love so dearly, pointed you out. You die on his information," and forthwith ran him through the heart with his sword. So the unfortunate man collapsed, more unhappy in the author of his murder than in the murder itself.

L. Villius Annalis fell upon the same bitter fate. Coming down to the Campus to his son's quaestorian elections,[6] he learned that he himself had been proscribed and took refuge with a client. The latter's loyalty could not save him because of the crime of the wicked young man, who led the soldiers along his father's very tracks and put him in their way to be killed in his sight; twice a parricide, first by intent and again by eyewitness.

The end of the proscribed Vettius Salassus too was bitter enough. As he was in hiding, his wife—shall I say handed him over to be killed or slaughtered him herself?[7] Is a crime which lacks only the hand less a crime?

[6] 42: App. B.C. 4.18. Not aedilician, as Gundel, RE Villius 4. He was made Aedile as a reward for his treachery, but was killed on his way home from a party by the same soldiers who had killed his father (Appian).

[7] 43/2: App. B.C. 4.24.

ext. 1   Illud autem facinus, quia externum est, tranquilliore adfectu narrabitur. Scipione Africano patris et patrui memoriam gladiatorio munere Carthagine Nova celebrante, duo regis filii, nuper patre mortuo, in harenam processerunt, pollicitique sunt ibi se de regno proeliaturos, quo spectaculum illud illustrius pugna sua facerent. eos cum Scipio monuisset ut verbis quam ferro diiudicare mallent uter regnare deberet, ac iam maior natu consilio eius obtemperaret, minor corporis viribus fretus in amentia perstitit, initoque certamine pertinacior impietas Fortunae iudicio morte multata est.

ext. 2   Mithridates autem multo sceleratius, qui non cum fratre de paterno regno, sed cum ipso patre bellum de dominatione gessit. in quo qui aut homines ullos adiutores invenerit aut deos invocare ausus sit, parem admirationem[84] habet.

ext. 3   Quamquam quid hoc quasi inusitatum illis gentibus miremur, cum Sariaster adversus patrem suum Tigranen, Armeniae regem, ita cum amicis consenserit ut omnes <e d>exteris[85] manibus sanguinem mitterent atque eum invicem sorberent? vix ferrem pro salute parentis tam cruenta conspiratione foedus facientem.

ext. 4   Sed quid ego ista consector aut quid his immoror, cum

---

[84] parem admirationem *Halm*: prae -one * A
[85] *add. Halm*: dex- A *corr.*

---

[8] 206: Livy 28.21.5, Sil. Ital. 16.533–42, Zonaras 9.10.3. Zonaras makes them brothers and Silius twins, but according to Livy, they were cousins, their fathers having ruled in succession.
[9] There may be a textual error here. The person meant is

EXTERNAL

The misdeed that comes now will be narrated in a calmer frame of mind since it is external. Scipio Africanus was giving a gladiator show in New Carthage in memory of his father and uncle. Two king's sons whose father had recently died came into the arena and promised to do battle there for the throne in order to enhance the spectacle by their combat. Scipio urged them to settle which should be king with words rather than the sword, and the elder was inclined to obey his advice. But the younger, relying on his physical strength, persisted in his madness. The fight began, and by Fortune's decree the more pertinacious impiety was punished with death.[8]

Mithridates[9] was much more criminal. He did not war with a brother about a paternal throne but with his father himself about which should rule. How he found men to assist him therein or how he dared invoke the gods is equally matter for astonishment.

Yet why should we wonder at this as though it was something unfamiliar to those nations when Sariaster conspired with his friends against his father Tigranes, king of Armenia, all of them letting blood from their right hands and sucking it in turn?[10] I should find it hard to tolerate one making so sanguinary a pact in a conspiracy for his father's welfare.

But why do I upbraid these doings or dwell on them

Pharnaces, who in 63 rebelled against his father, the great Mithridates of Pontus (Livy *Per.* 102, Vell. 2.40.1 etc.).

[10] Cf. App. *Mithr.* 104. Which of the three sons of Tigranes I there mentioned is this one is questionable. Only Valerius reports the blood pact.

unius parricidii cogitatione cuncta scelera superata cernam? omni igitur impetu mentis, omnibus indignationis viribus ad id lacerandum pio magis quam valido adfectu rapior: quis enim amicitiae fide exstincta genus humanum cruentis in tenebris sepelire conatum profundo debitae exsecrationis satis efficacibus verbis adegerit? tu videlicet efferatae barbariae immanitate truculentior habenas Romani imperii, quas princeps parensque noster salutari dextera continet, capere potuisti? aut te compote furoris mundus in suo statu mansisset? urbem a Gallis captam, e trecentorum inclitae gentis virorum strage foedatum ⟨amnem Cremeram et⟩[86] Alliensem diem, et oppressos in Hispania Scipiones et Trasumennum lacum et Cannas, bellorumque civilium domestico sanguine manantes mucrones[87] amentibus propositis furoris tui repraesentare et vincere voluisti. sed vigilarunt oculi deorum, sidera suum vigorem obtinuerunt, arae pulvinaria templa praesenti numine vallata sunt, nihilque quod pro capite augusto[88] ac patria excubare debuit torporem sibi permisit, et in primis auctor ac tutela nostrae incolumitatis ne excellentissima merita sua totius orbis ruina collaberentur divino consilio providit. itaque stat pax, valent leges, sincerus privati ac publici officii tenor servatur. qui autem haec violatis amicitiae foederibus temptavit subvertere, omni cum stirpe sua populi Romani viribus obtritus etiam apud inferos, si tamen illuc receptus est, quae meretur supplicia pendit.

[86] *add. Gertz*
[87] mucrones *Kempf*: furoris* A
[88] augusto *Per.*: -ti G (*silet* A)

when I see all crimes surpassed by the thought of a single parricide?[11] So I am swept by an emotion more pious than potent, with all the energy of my mind, all the forces of indignation, to rend that deed. For who with words of due execration sufficiently effectual could drive into the abyss an attempt to bury the human race in bloody darkness, extinguishing the loyalty of friendship? Could you, more ferocious than the brutality of savage barbary, have taken the reins of Roman empire which our leader and father holds in his saving hand? Or if you had achieved your madness, would the world have stayed in place? Rome captured by the Gauls, the river Cremera disfigured by the slaughter of three hundred warriors of a famous clan, the day of the Allia, the Scipios destroyed in Spain, Trasimene lake, Cannae, the blades of the civil wars streaming with domestic blood: all these you wished to manifest and surpass by the crazy designs of your delirium. But the eyes of the gods were awake, the stars maintained their potency, the altars, sacred couches, temples were fenced with present deity, and nothing that was in duty bound to watch over that august life and our fatherland permitted itself torpor. And above all the author and guardian of our safety saw to it in his divine policy that his most excellent benefactions should not collapse amid the ruins of the whole world. So peace stands, the laws are valid, the course of private and public duty remains unimpaired. But he who essayed to subvert all this, violating the bonds of friendship, was trampled down along with all his race by the might of the Roman people, and in the underworld too, that is if it takes him in, he suffers the punishment he deserves.

11 See Introduction.

12. DE MORTIBUS NON VULGARIBUS

praef.   Humanae autem vitae condicionem praecipue primus et ultimus dies continet, quia plurimum interest quibus auspiciis incohetur et quo fine claudatur, ideoque eum demum felicem fuisse iudicamus cui et accipere lucem prospere et reddere placide contingit. medii temporis cursus, prout Fortuna gubernaculum rexit, modo aspero, modo tranquillo motu peragitur, spe semper minor, dum et cupide votis extenditur et fere sine ratione consumitur. nam [et]⁸⁹ si eo bene uti velis, etiam parvum amplissimum efficies, numerum annorum multitudine operum superando—alioquin quid attinet inerti mora gaudere, si magis exigis vitam quam approbas? sed ne longius evager, eorum mentionem faciam qui non vulgari genere mortis absumpti sunt.

1   Tullus Hostilius fulmine ictus cum tota domo conflagravit. singularem fati sortem, qua accidit ut columen urbis in ipsa urbe raptum ne supremo quidem funeris honore a civibus decorari posset, caelesti flamma in eam condicione<m> redactum ut eosdem penates et regiam et rogum et sepulcrum haberet!

2   Vix veri simile est in eripiendo spiritu idem gaudium potuisse quod fulmen, et tamen idem valuit. nuntiata enim clade quae ad lacum Trasumennum inciderat, altera, sospiti filio ad ipsam portam facta obvia, in complexu eius exspiravit, altera, cum falso mortis filii nuntio maesta domi

---

⁸⁹ *del. Per.*

---

¹ Livy 1.31.8 etc.

12. OF DEATHS OUT OF THE
ORDINARY

The condition of human life is chiefly determined by its first and last days, because it is of the greatest importance under what auspices it is begun and with what end it is terminated; and therefore we judge that he only has been fortunate whose lot it has been to receive the light propitiously and to yield it back quietly. The course of intervening time is accomplished with motion now rough, now tranquil, as Fortune guides the helm. It is always less than hoped for, as it is stretched out eagerly with prayers and generally consumed to no purpose; for if you choose to use it well, you will make even a small span fully ample, surpassing number of years by multitude of achievements. Otherwise what sense does it make to rejoice in idle delay, if you pass your life rather than prove its worth? But not to digress too far, I shall make mention of those who were carried off by a manner of death out of the ordinary.

Tullus Hostilius was struck by a thunderbolt and burnt up with his whole house.[1] A singular fatal lot, through which the city's crown, snatched away in the city itself, could not be glorified by the citizens with the final honour of a funeral and was reduced by celestial fire to a condition such that his household gods, his palace, his pyre, and his sepulchre were all one and the same.

It is scarcely plausible that joy had the same effect as a thunderbolt in snatching away life, and yet it was equally potent. When news came of the disaster that had befallen at Lake Trasimene, one mother who met her son, a survivor, at the gate died in his arms; another, as she was sitting at home in sadness at the false news of her son's death, at

sederet, ad primum conspectum redeuntis exanimata est.
genus casus inusitatum! quas dolor ⟨non⟩[90] exstinxerat,
laetitia consumpsit. sed minus miror, quod mulieres.

3   M'. Iuventius Thalna consul, collega Ti. Gracchi consulis iterum, cum in Corsica, quam nuper subegerat,
sacrificaret, receptis litteris decretas ei a senatu supplica-
tiones nuntiantibus, intento illas animo legens caligine
⟨ob⟩orta[91] ante foculum collapsus, mortuus humi iacuit.
quem quid aliud quam nimio gaudio enectum putemus?
en cui Numantia aut Carthago excidenda traderetur!

4   Maioris aliquanto spiritus dux Q. Catulus, Cimbrici
triumphi C. Mario particeps a senatu datus, sed exitus vio-
lentioris: namque ab hoc eodem Mario postea propter
civiles dissensiones mori iussus, recenti calce illito mul-
toque igni percalefacto cubiculo se inclusum peremit.
cuius tam dira necessitas maximus Marianae gloriae rubor
exstitit.

5   Qua tempestate rei publicae L. quoque Cornelius
Merula, consularis et flamen Dialis, ne ludibrio insolentis-
simis victoribus esset, in Iovis sacrario venis incisis contu-
meliosae mortis denuntiationem effugit, sacerdotisque sui
sanguine vetustissimi foci maduerunt.

6   Acer etiam et animosus vitae exitus Herennii Siculi,
quo C. Gracchus et haruspice et amico usus fuerat: nam
cum eo nomine in carcerem duceretur, in postem eius illi-

90 *add.* A *corr.*
91 *add.* P

---

2 217: Livy 22.7.12f. etc.
3 163: cf. Pliny *N.H.* 7.182.
4 87: Vell. 2.22.4 etc. (Münzer, *RE* XIII.2079.29).

the first sight of him as he returned fell lifeless.[2] A most unusual sort of happening! Whom grief had not extinguished, happiness consumed. But they were women, so I am the less surprised.

Consul M'. Juventius Thalna, colleague of Ti. Gracchus, Consul for the second time, was at sacrifice in Corsica, which he had recently conquered, when he received a letter informing him that the senate had decreed a Thanksgiving in his honour. As he read it with absorption, darkness overcame him; collapsing before the brazier, he lay dead on the ground. What are we to think but that he was killed by excessive joy?[3] A fine one he to be entrusted with the razing of Numantia or Carthage!

A general of considerably greater spirit was Q. Catulus, given to Marius by the senate to share the Cimbrian triumph, but his death was more violent. For later, ordered to die by this same Marius on account of civil strife, he had his bedroom, which had recently been coated with lime, heated with a great fire and shut himself inside.[4] His dire necessity was a crying shame to Marian glory.

In that stormy time of the commonwealth L. Cornelius Merula too, Consular and Flamen of Jupiter, not wishing to expose himself to the mockery of the insolent victors, severed his veins in Jupiter's sanctuary, thus escaping the injunction of a contumelious death. The ancient hearth was soaked in the blood of its priest.[5]

Fierce and courageous too was the departure of Herennius Siculus from life, who had been C. Gracchus' soothsayer and friend. As he was being led to prison on that account, he dashed his head against the doorpost and fell

[5] 87: Vell. 2.22.2 etc. (Broughton II.47).

so capite in ipso ignominiae aditu concidit ac spiritum posuit, uno gradu a publico supplicio manuque carnificis citerior.

7   Consimili impetu mortis C. Licinius Macer, vir praetorius, Calvi pater, repetundarum reus, dum sententiae diriberentur, in maenianum conscendit: si quidem, cum M. Ciceronem, qui id iudicium cogebat, praetextam ponentem vidisset, misit ad eum qui diceret se non damnatum sed reum perisse, nec sua bona hastae posse subici, ac protinus, sudario, quod forte in manu habebat, ore et faucibus suis coartatis, incluso spiritu poenam morte praecucurrit. qua cognita re Cicero de eo nihil pronuntiavit. igitur illustris ingenii orator et ab inopia rei familiaris et a crimine domesticae damnationis inusitato paterni fati genere vindicatus est.

8   Fortis huius mors, illorum perridicula: Cornelius enim Gallus praetorius et T. Hetereius eques Romanus inter usum puerilis veneris absumpti sunt. quamquam quorsum attinet eorum cavillari fata, quos non libido sua sed fragilitatis humanae ratio abstulit? fine namque vitae nostrae variis et occultis causis exposito, interdum quae[92] immerentia ⟨sunt⟩[93] supremi fati titulum occupant, cum magis in tempus mortis incidant quam ipsa mortem[94] accersant.

ext. 1   Sunt et externae mortes dignae adnotatu. qualis in primis Comae, quem ferunt maximi latronum ducis Cleonis

---

[92] quae *intra cruces Briscoe*   [93] *add.* ς
[94] ipsa mortem *Kempf*: in i- morte A

---

[6] 121: Vell. 2.7.2.   [7] While the jury deliberated.
[8] 66: but cf. Cic. *Att.* 1.4.2, Plut. *Cic.* 9.   [9] Pliny *N.H.* 7.184.

at the very entrance of ignominy, resigning his life, one step behind a public punishment and the hand of the executioner.[6]

In a similar hurry into death was C. Licinius Macer, an ex-Praetor, father of Calvus. He was on trial for extortion and climbed up to a balcony while the votes were being sorted. Seeing M. Cicero, who was president of the court, taking off his magistrate's gown,[7] he sent him a message to say that he had died, not as a man convicted, but as a defendant and his property could not be put to public auction. Then he covered his mouth and throat with a handkerchief that he happened to have in his hand and stopped his breathing, thus anticipating sentence by death. When Cicero learned of this, he pronounced no verdict.[8] So an orator of shining talent was saved from poverty and the reproach of a conviction in his family by his father's extraordinary mode of death.

Macer's death was brave, that of those I am about to mention quite ludicrous. Cornelius Gallus, an ex-Praetor, and T. Hetereius, a Roman knight, were carried off during sexual intercourse with boys.[9] And yet why mock their deaths? It was not their lust that took them off but the nature of human frailty. For the end of our life is subject to a variety of hidden causes, and sometimes innocent factors get the name for a demise when they coincide with the time of death rather than themselves bring it on.

EXTERNAL

There are external deaths too worth note, such as particularly that of Coma, who is said to have been brother to Cleon, the great brigand leader. He was brought to Consul

fratrem fuisse: is enim ad ‹ P. ›[95] Rupilium consulem Hennam, quam praedones tenuerant, in potestatem nostram redactam perductus, cum de viribus et conatibus fugitivorum interrogaretur, sumpto tempore ad se colligendum, caput operuit innixusque genibus compresso spiritu inter ipsas custodum manus inque conspectu summi imperii exoptata securitate acquievit. torqueant se miseri, quibus exstingui quam superesse utilius est, [in][96] trepido et anxio consilio quanam ratione vita exeant quaerentes: ferrum acuant, venena temperent, laqueos apprehendant, vastas altitudines circumspiciant, tamquam magno apparatu aut exquisita molitione opus sit ut corporis atque animi infirmo vinculo cohaerens societas dirimatur. nihil horum Coma, sed intra pectus inclusa anima finem sui repperit: enimvero non[97] nimio studio retinendum bonum, cuius caduca possessio tam levi adflatu violentiae concussa dilabi potuit.

ext. 2   Aeschyli vero poetae excessus quem ad modum non voluntarius sic propter novitatem casus referendus. in Sicilia moenibus urbis, in qua morabatur, egressus aprico in loco resedit. super quem aquila testudinem ferens elusa splendore capitis—erat enim capillis vacuum—perinde atque lapidi eam illisit, ut fractae carne vesceretur, eoque ictu origo et principium ‹per›fectioris[98] tragoediae exstinctum est.

ext. 3   Non vulgaris etiam Homeri mortis causa fertur, qui in ‹Io›[99] insula, quia quaestionem a piscatoribus positam sol-

---

[95] *add.* P   [96] in A: *om.* G
[97] non *Vorst*: in* G (*ras.* A)
[98] perf- *Watt*²: fortioris A: politioris *Kempf*
[99] *hic add. Kempf, post* insula *Vielhaber*

P. Rupilius in Henna, a bandit stronghold which we had captured. When asked about the strength and enterprises of the runaways, he took some time to collect himself, then covered his head, fell on his knees, and stopped his breath; so in the very hands of his guards and in the presence of highest command he found rest in the security for which he yearned.[10] Let those unfortunates for whom death is better than survival agonize, seeking in quavering anxiety to plan their way out of life; let them sharpen steel, compound poisons, catch at ropes, survey vast heights as though great preparation or ingenious contrivance were needed to dissolve the partnership between mind and body, linked by a fragile bond. Nothing of that sort for Coma; he found his end by shutting his breath inside his bosom. And indeed that blessing is not worth too much effort to retain, whose fragile possession could slip away at the shock of so slight a whiff of violence.

The poet Aeschylus' departure was not voluntary, but the novelty of the occurrence makes it worth mention. He was in Sicily. Leaving the walls of the town where he was staying, he sat down in a sunny spot. An eagle carrying a tortoise was above him. Deceived by the gleam of his hairless skull, it dashed the tortoise against it, as though it were a stone, in order to feed on the flesh of the broken animal.[11] By that blow the origin and beginning of more perfect tragedy was extinguished.

The cause of Homer's death too is said to have been out of the common run. He is believed to have died of chagrin on the island of Ios because he had been unable to resolve

[10] 132: cf. Diodor. 34/35.2.21.
[11] 456/5: Pliny *N.H.* 10.7 etc.

vere non potuisset, dolore absumptus creditur.

ext. 4   Sed atrocius aliquanto Euripides finitus est: ab Archelai enim regis cena in Macedonia domum hospitalem repetens, canum morsibus laniatus obiit: crudelitas fati tanto
ingenio non debita.

ext. 5   Sicut illi excessus illustrium poetarum et moribus et
operibus indignissimi.

Sophocles ultimae iam senectutis, cum in certamen
tragoediam demisisset, ancipiti sententiarum eventu diu
sollicitus, aliquando tamen una sententia victor causam
mortis gaudium habuit.

ext. 6   Philemonem autem vis risus immoderati abstulit. para-
tas ei ficus atque in conspectu positas asello consumente,
puerum ut illum abigeret inclamavit. qui cum iam comes-
tis omnibus supervenisset, 'quoniam' inquit 'tam tardus
fuisti, da nunc merum asello.' ac protinus urbanitatem dicti crebro anhelitu cachinnorum prosecutus, senile guttur
salebris spiritus gravavit.

ext. 7   At Pindarus, cum in gymnasio super gremium pueri,
quo unice delectabatur, capite posito quieti se dedisset,
non prius decessisse cognitus est quam gymnasiarcho clau-
dere iam eum locum volente nequiquam excitaretur. cui
quidem crediderim eadem benignitate deorum et tantum
poeticae facundiae et tam placidum vitae finem attribu-
tum.

ext. 8   Sicut Anacreonti quoque, quem usitatum humanae

---

12 [Herod.] *Vit. Hom.* 36, [Plut.] *Vit. Hom.* 1.4.
13 407/6. Gell. 15.20.9 etc.
14 *Ca.* 396: Pliny *N.H.* 7.180.

a question put to him by fishermen.[12]

But Euripides ended in a somewhat nastier fashion. In Macedonia, as he was returning from dinner with king Archelaus to the house where he was staying, he died torn by the bites of dogs. A cruelty of fate that such a genius did not deserve.[13]

So too the following deaths of famous poets were quite unworthy of their characters and works.

In extreme old age Sophocles put a tragedy in competition. For a long time he was kept in suspense with the issue of the voting in doubt, but finally he won by a single vote and his joy caused his death.[14]

The violence of immoderate laughter took off Philemon. A donkey was eating some figs that had been prepared for him and put where he could see them. He called for a slave to drive the animal off, but by the time he got there all the figs had been devoured. "Since you have been so slow," said Philemon, "now give the donkey wine." As he followed up the witticism with a rapid volley of guffaws, he overloaded his old man's windpipe with choking breaths.[15]

But Pindar had fallen asleep in the gymnasium with his head in the lap of a boy, his particular favorite, and it was only when the man in charge wanted to close the place and Pindar could not be aroused that they realised he was dead.[16] I could well believe that so much poetic eloquence and so peaceful an end[17] were bestowed upon him by the same divine favour.

So too with Anacreon, who was carried off after he had

---

[15] *Ca.* 364: Lucian *Macrob.* 25, Suda s.v. Φιλήμων.

[16] *Ca.* 435: Suda s.v. Πίνδαρος.

[17] "Quite unworthy of his character and works" (5)?

vitae modum supergressum passae uvae suco tenues et
exiles virium reliquias foventem unius grani pertinacior in
aridis faucibus mora[100] absumpsit.

ext. 9   Iungam illos quos et propositum et exitus pares fecit.
Milo Crotoniates, cum iter faciens quercum in agro cuneis
adactis fissam vidisset, fretus viribus accessit ad eam inser-
tisque manibus divellere conatus est. quas arbor excussis
cuneis in suam naturam revocata compressit, eumque cum
tot gymnicis palmis lacerandum feris praebuit.

ext. 10   Item Polydamas athleta tempestate speluncam subire
coactus, nimio et subito incursu aquae labefactata ea ac
ruente, ceteris comitibus fuga periculum egressis solus
restitit tamquam umeris suis totius ruinae molem susten-
taturus, sed pondere omni corpore humano potentiore
pressus imbris petitam latebram dementis fa<c>ti <auc-
tor>[101] sepulcrum habuit.

Possunt hi praebere documentum nimio robore membrorum vigorem mentis hebescere, quasi abnuente Natura utriusque boni largitionem, ne supra mortalem sit felici-
tatem eundem et valentissimum esse et sapientissimum.

13. DE CUPIDITATE VITAE

praef.   Verum quia excessus e vita et fortuitos et viriles, quosdam etiam temerarios oratione attigimus, subiciamus
nunc aestimationi enerves et effeminatos, ut ipsa compa-

---

[100] mora *Madvig*: umor A   [101] *add. Kellerbauer et SB*

[18] *Ca.* 490 (?) Pliny *N.H.* 7.44.
[19] Early fifth century (?): Ov. *Ibis* 609 etc.
[20] Fifth century, first half: Diodor. 9.14.2–15 etc.

passed the usual measure of human life by the moisture of a single seed sticking in his dry throat, as he pampered the thin and scanty remnants of his strength with the juice of dried grapes.[18]

I will add the following, whom intention and result make a pair. Milo of Croton was on the road when he saw an oak tree in a field that had been split by wedges driven into the wood. Relying on his strength, he went up to it and putting in his hands tried to pull it apart. The wedges were shaken out and the tree, recalled to its natural state, trapped his hands and made him and all his athletic victories a prey to wild beasts.[19]

Likewise the athlete Polydamas. A cave which he had entered for cover from a storm was shaken by a sudden violent influx of water and collapsed. All his companions escaped the danger by running away, only Polydamas remained, as though intending to prop up the whole falling structure with his shoulders. But a weight too great for any human frame crushed him, and in the commission of an act of folly his refuge from the rain became his sepulchre.[20]

These two can serve as a proof that mental vigour is dulled by excessive strength of limb, as though Nature refuses to lavish both gifts, lest for the same person to be both the strongest and the wisest of mankind might go beyond the limits of human felicity.

13. OF CRAVING FOR LIFE

But since I have touched in my discourse upon departures from life both fortuitous and courageous, some also temerarious, let me now submit for judgment others feeble and effeminate, so that it may become clear by the

ratione pateat quanto non solum fortior sed etiam sapientior mortis interdum quam vitae sit cupiditas.

1   M'. Aquillius, cum sibi gloriose ⟨exstingui⟩[102] posset, Mithridati maluit turpiter servire. quem non⟨ne⟩[103] aliquis merito dixerit Pontico supplicio quam Romano imperio digniorem, quoniam commisit ut privatum opprobrium publicus rubor exsisteret?

2   Cn. quoque Carbo magnae verecundiae est Latinis annalibus. tertio in consulatu suo iussu Pompeii in Sicilia ad supplicium ductus, petiit a militibus demisse et flebiliter ut sibi alvum levare prius quam exspiraret liceret, quo miserrimae lucis usu diutius frueretur, eo ⟨us⟩que[104] moram trahens donec caput eius sordido in loco sedentis abscideretur. ipsa verba tale flagitium narrantis secum luctantur, nec silentio amica, quia occultari non merentur, neque[105] relationi familiaria, quia dictu fastidienda sunt.

3   Quid? D. Brutus exiguum et infelix momentum vitae quanto dedecore emit! qui a Furio, quem ad eum occidendum Antonius miserat, comprehensus, non solum cervicem gladio subtraxit sed etiam constantius eam praebere admonitus ipsis his verbis iuravit: 'ita vivam, dabo.' o cunctationem fati aerumnosam! o iurandi stolidam fidem! sed hos tu furores, immoderata retinendi spiritus dulcedo, subicis sanae rationis modum expugnando, quae vitam diligere, mortem non timere praecipit.

[102] extingui P: exigui G: *om.* A
[103] nonne *Per.*: non A: *om.* G
[104] *add. Aldus*
[105] *rursus incipit* L

very comparison how much not only braver but wiser is sometimes the desire for death than for life.

M'. Aquillius could have died for himself gloriously; instead he preferred to be a slave to Mithridates shamefully. Might he not deservedly be said to be more worthy of Pontic execution than of Roman authority, since by his behaviour he caused a private reproach to become a public scandal?[1]

Cn. Carbo too is a great embarrassment to Latium's annals. In his third Consulship he was led to execution in Sicily by Pompey's orders. Abjectly and tearfully he begged the soldiers to let him relieve himself before he died, so that he might longer enjoy his miserable daylight, and he dragged out the delay until his head was cut off as he sat in the squalid place.[2] As I narrate such a disgrace my very words are at odds with themselves, not partial to silence because they do not deserve to be hidden nor easy with the narrative because they are revolting in the utterance.

Again: at what price of dishonour did D. Brutus buy a meagre and miserable moment of life! Arrested by Furius, whom Antony had sent to kill him, he not only pulled his neck away from the sword but when told to present it more steadily swore in these very words, "On my life, I'll give it."[3] What a wretched postponement of fate! What a stupid oath-backed guarantee! But the immoderate sweetness of continuing to breathe prompts such follies, driving out the measure of sane reason, which tells us to love life but not to fear death.

[1] 88: Broughton II.43. (Broughton II.66); cf. VM 5.3.5, 6.2.8.

[2] 82: Plut. *Pomp.* 10 etc.

[3] Cf. VM 4.7.6.

ext. 1   Eadem Xerxen regem pro totius Asiae armata iuventute, quod intra centum annos esset obitura, profundere
lacrimas coegisti. qui mihi specie alienam, re vera suam
condicionem deplorasse videtur, opum magnitudine quam
altiore animi sensu felicior: quis enim mediocriter pru-
dens mortalem se natum fleverit?

QUAM EXQUISITA CUSTODIA USI SINT QUIBUS
SUSPECTI DOMESTICI FUERUNT

ext. 2   Referam nunc eos quibus aliquos suspectos habentibus
exquisitior sui quaesita custodia est: nec a miserrimo, sed
ab eo qui inter paucos felicissimus fuisse creditur inci-
piam.

Masinissa rex parum fidei in pectoribus hominum reponens salutem suam custodia canum vallavit. quo tam
late patens imperium? quo tantum liberorum numerum?
quo denique tam arta benivolentia constricta‹m› Roma-
nam amicitiam,[106] si ad haec tuenda nihil canino latratu ac
morsu valentius duxit?

ext. 3   Hoc rege infelicior Alexander ‹Pheraeus›,[107] cuius
praecordia hinc amor, hinc metus torserunt: nam cum
infinito ardore coniugis Thebes teneretur, ad eam[108] ex
epulis in cubiculum veniens barbarum compunctum notis
Thraciis stricto gladio iubebat anteire, nec prius se
‹e›idem[109] lecto committebat quam a stipatoribus diligenter esset scrutatus. supplicium irato deorum numine com-

106 constrictam -nam (ς) -iam (ς) *Pighius*: -ta -na -ia AL
107 *add. SB*[1]
108 eam *Kempf*: eandem AL
109 *add. Gertz*

EXTERNAL

The same made king Xerxes shed tears for the armed manhood of all Asia, because within a hundred years it would pass away.[4] To me it seems that in appearance he lamented the lot of others, but in reality his own, more fortunate in the magnitude of his power than in any depth of understanding. For what man of tolerably good sense would weep that he was born mortal?

WHAT PARTICULAR CARE PERSONS SUSPECTING THEIR DOMESTICS TOOK FOR THEIR PROTECTION

I shall now mention those who, suspecting others, sought particular protection for themselves. And I shall not begin with a wretch but with a man who is believed to have had few equals in felicity.

King Masinissa, having little faith in the hearts of men, fenced his life with a guard of dogs.[5] What use so widespread an empire, what use so large a number of children, what use the friendship of Rome so tightly bonded with good will, if to protect these things he thought nothing more effectual than canine bark and bite?

More unhappy than this king was Alexander of Pherae, whose breast was tortured by love on the one hand and fear on the other. His passion for his wife Thebe knew no bounds, but when he came to her bedroom after dinner he had a barbarian tattooed with Thracian marks go in front with drawn sword, and did not entrust himself to the same bed until it had been carefully searched by his guards. A punishment contrived by the angry power of the gods, to

---

[4] 480: Herod. 7.46.2 etc.   [5] Not found elsewhere.

positum, neque libidini neque timori posse imperare. cuius timoris[110] eadem et causa et finis fuit: Alexandrum enim Thebe paelicatus ira mota interemit.

ext. 4   Age, Dionysius, Syracusanorum tyrannus, huiusce tormenti quam longa fabula! qui duodequadraginta annorum dominationem in hunc modum peregit. summotis amicis, in eorum locum ferocissimarum gentium homines et a familiis locupletium electos praevalidos servos, quibus latera sua committeret, substituit. tonsorum quoque metu tondere filias suas docuit. quarum ipsarum, postquam adultae aetati appropinquabant, manibus ferrum non ausus committere, instituit ut candentibus iuglandium nucum putaminibus barbam sibi et capillum adurerent. nec securiorem maritum egit quam patrem. duarum enim eodem tempore, Aristomaches Syracusanae et Locrensis Doridis, matrimoniis illigatus, neutrius umquam nisi excussae complexum petiit atque etiam cubicularem lectum perinde quasi castra lata fossa cinxit, in quem se ligneo ponte recipiebat, cum forem cubiculi, extrinsecus a custodibus opertam, interiorem claustro ipse diligenter obserasset.

14. DE SIMILITUDINE FORMAE

praef.   De similitudine autem oris et totius corporis altiore doctrina praediti subtilius disputant, eorumque alii in ea sunt opinione ut existiment illam origini et contextui sanguinis respondere, nec parvum argumentum ex ceteris animalibus trahunt, quae fere gignentibus similia nascun-

---

[110] timoris ⊊: tempore LG (*silet* A)

be unable to rule either lust or fear! The same woman was the cause of his fear and the end of it, for Thebe killed Alexander, angered by his relations with a concubine.[6]

And now for Dionysius, tyrant of Syracuse; what a long tale of this torture! He got through thirty-eight years of rule in the following fashion. He removed his friends and substituted in their place men of the most savage nations and slaves of great strength selected from the establishments of the wealthy; to these he trusted his flanks. Also in fear of barbers he taught his daughters to shave. Even to their hands, when they approached adult age, he did not dare to trust steel, but instead had them singe his beard and hair with hot walnut shells. And he showed no greater appearance of security as a husband than as a father. He had two women in wedlock at the same time, Aristomache of Syracuse and Doris of Locri. He never sought the embrace of either without having her searched and even surrounded the bedroom bed with a broad ditch like a camp. He would enter it by a wooden bridge when the door had been shut on the outside by the guards, while he himself had carefully bolted it on the inside.[7]

14. OF PHYSICAL LIKENESS

Concerning likeness of face and of the whole body persons possessed of deeper learning nicely dispute. Some of them hold the opinion that it corresponds to origin and connection of blood and derive an argument of no small weight from other living creatures, which are generally

---

[6] *Ca.* 359: Xen. *Hellen.* 6.4.35–37, Cic. *Off.* 2.25 etc.

[7] Cic. *Tusc.* 5.57–59 etc.

tur. alii negant hanc esse certam Naturae legem, sed species mortalium prout fortuita sors conceptionis obtulit attribui, atque ideo plerumque ex speciosis deformes et ex robustis invalidos partus edi. ⟨igi⟩tur,[111] quoniam ista quaestio in ambiguo versatur, pauca inter alienos conspectae similitudinis exempla referemus.

1   Magno Pompeio Vibius ingenuae stirpis et Publicius libertinus ita similes fuerunt ut permutato statu et Pompeius in illis et illi in Pompeio salutari possent. certe, quocumque aut Vibius aut Publicius accesserant, ora hominum in se obvertebant, unoquoque speciem amplissimi civis in personis mediocribus adnotante.

2   Quod quidem fortuitum ludibrium quasi hereditarium ad eum penetravit: nam pater quoque eius eo usque Menogenis coqui sui similis esse visus est ut vir et armis praepotens et ferox animo sordidum eius nomen repellere a se non valuerit.

3   Eximiae vero nobilitatis adulescens Cornelius Scipio, cum plurimis et clarissimis familiae suae cognominibus abundaret, in servilem Serapionis appellationem vulgi sermone impactus est, quod huiusce nominis victimarii ⟨per⟩quam[112] similis erat. neque illi aut morum probitas aut respectus tot imaginum quominus hac contumelia aspergeretur opitulatus est.

4   Generosissimus consulatus collegium Lentuli et Metelli fuit. qui ambo in scaena propter similitudinem histrio-

---

[111] edi. igitur *Kempf*: editur AL
[112] *add. Kellerbauer*: persim- P

---

[1] Pliny *N.H.* 7.53.
[2] Ibid. 54.

born similar to their parents. Others deny that this is a fixed law of Nature, maintaining that the aspects of mortals are assigned as the random chance of conception presents them and that for that reason ugly offspring are often produced from handsome parents and weak from sturdy. Therefore, since this question remains in doubt, I shall mention a few examples of striking resemblance between persons unconnected.

Vibius, of free descent, and Publicius, a freedman, bore such a resemblance to Pompeius Magnus that if they had exchanged conditions Pompey could have been greeted in their persons and they in Pompey's. Certainly, wherever Vibius or Publicius went, they drew people's eyes to themselves, as everybody noticed the appearance of the great man in these nobodies.[1]

This trick of chance came to Pompey as though by inheritance. For his father too was thought to resemble Menogenes, his cook, so closely that, powerful in arms and bold of spirit as he was, he could not keep the fellow's base name away from himself.[2]

A young man of outstandingly noble birth, Cornelius Scipio, with many illustrious family surnames to choose from, was thrust by common parlance into the servile appellation of Serapio because he looked very like a sacrificial assistant of that name. Neither the respectability of his character nor regard for so many ancestral masks saved him from this insulting aspersion.[3]

The combination of Lentulus and Metellus made a very aristocratic Consulship.[4] Both of them were almost specta-

---

[3] Ibid., Quint. *Inst.* 6.3.57.
[4] In 57.

num propemodum spectati sunt. sed alter ex quodam secundarum cognomen Spintheris traxit, alter, nisi Nepotis a
moribus accepisset, Pamphili tertiarum, cui simillimus
esse ferebatur, habuisset.

5   At M. Messalla consularis et censorius Menogenis, Cu-
rioque omnibus honoribus abundans Burbuleii; ille propter oris aspectum, hic propter parem corporis motum,
uterque scaenici nomen coactus est recipere.

Abunde sint haec de domesticis, quoniam et personis
sunt excellentia et non obscura notitia celebrantur.

ext. 1   Regi Antiocho unus ex aequalibus et ipse regiae stirpis
nomine Artemo perquam similis fuisse traditur. quem
Laodice, uxor Antiochi, interfecto viro, dissimulandi sceleris gratia in lectulo perinde quasi ipsum regem aegrum
collocavit, admissumque universum populum et sermone
eius et vultu consimili fefellit, credideruntque homines
ab Antiocho moriente Laodicen et natos eius sibi com-
mendari.

ext. 2   Hybreanta autem Mylasenum, copiosae atque concitatae facundiae oratorem, Cymaeorum servo strigmenta
gymnasii colligenti tantum non germanum fratrem totius
Asiae oculi adsignarunt: ita liniamentis oris et omnium
membrorum compares erant.

ext. 3   Ille vero, quem in Sicilia praetoris[113] admodum simi-

113 praetoris* G: -riis AL

5 Actually an inherited surname ("Waster").
6 Pliny *N.H.* 7.55.
7 Pliny *N.H.* 7.53. Cf. VM 9.10.ext.1.
8 First century; cf. Strabo 659.

cles on stage because of their likeness to actors. One got the surname of Spinther from a certain number two player, the other would have had that of Pamphilus, a number three, whom he was supposed to resemble very closely, if he had not received that of Nepos from his character.[5]

M. Messalla, ex-Consul and ex-Censor, and Curio, holder in abundance of all high offices, were each forced to receive the name of an actor, Menogenes and Barbuleius respectively, the first by reason of facial appearance, the second of like bodily movement.[6]

Let this choice of domestic examples be abundantly sufficient, they being outstanding in the personalities and of fairly common notoriety.

EXTERNAL

One of king Antiochus' coevals and himself a member of the royal house, by the name of Artemo, is said to have closely resembled the monarch. Antiochus' wife Laodice killed her husband and to conceal the crime put Artemo in bed as though he were the king himself fallen ill. Then she admitted all the people and deceived them by his likeness in speech and countenance, and folk believed Laodice and her children were being commended to them by the dying Antiochus.[7]

Hybreas of Mylasa was an orator of copious and lively eloquence.[8] The eyes of the whole of Asia all but put him down as brother german to a slave[9] of the Cymaeans who collected the scrapings of the gymnasium. So alike were they in the outlines of their faces and all their limbs.

A saucy fellow was he in Sicily who is agreed to have

[9] I.e. public slave.

lem fuisse constat, petulantis animi: pro consule enim dicente mirari se quapropter sui tam similis esset, cum pater suus in eam provinciam numquam accessisset, 'at meus' inquit 'Romam accessit': ioco namque lacessitam matris suae pudicitiam invicem suspicione in matrem eius regesta audacius quam virgis et securibus subiecto conveniebat ultus est.

15. DE IIS QUI INFIMO LOCO NATI MENDACIO SE CLARISSIMIS FAMILIIS INSERERE CONATI SUNT

praef.   Sed tolerabilis haec et uni tantummodo anceps temeritas. quod sequitur impudentiae genus nec ferendum ullo modo periculique cum privatim tum etiam publice late patentis.

1   Nam ut Equitium, Firmo Piceno monstrum veniens, relatum iam in huiusce libri superiore parte, praeteream, cuius in amplectendo Ti. Graccho patre evidens mendacium turbulento vulgi errore, amplissima tribunatus potestate vallatum est, Herophilus, equarius[114] medicus, C. Marium septiens consulem avum sibi vindicando ‹ita se›[115] extulit[116] ut et coloniae se veteranorum complures et municipia splendida collegiaque fere omnia patronum

---

[114] equarius A *corr.*, G: aequa- AL: ocula- P
[115] *add.* ς
[116] extulit *intra cruces Briscoe*

---

[10] *Praetor* is sometimes so used; cf. VM 6.3.5.

looked very like the governor of the province.[10] The Proconsul said he wondered why the man looked so like himself, seeing that his father had never gone to that province. "But mine went to Rome," was the reply. The chastity of his mother was impugned in jest and he avenged it by retorting the suspicion on to the governor's mother, more boldly than befitted one subject to the rods and axes.[11]

15. OF PERSONS BORN IN THE LOWEST STATION WHO TRIED BY FALSEHOOD TO THRUST THEMSELVES INTO ILLUSTRIOUS FAMILIES

But the above was tolerable temerity and dangerous only to a single individual. The type of impudence now to follow is altogether beyond bearing and fraught with extensive danger publicly as well as privately.

For to say nothing of Equitius, the monster from Firmum in Picenum, whom I mentioned in an earlier part of this book,[1] whose patent falsehood in embracing Ti. Gracchus as his father was defended by the unruly error of the common folk and the large power of the Tribunate, Herophilus, a horse doctor, claimed C. Marius, seven times Consul, as his grandfather and so puffed himself up that a number of colonies of veterans and distinguished municipalities and almost all the clubs adopted him as

[11] Macrobius (2.4.20) has virtually the same story about Augustus; Pliny *N.H.* 7.55, referring to (P. Lentulus) Sura (the Catilinarian conspirator), seems to be relevant.
[1] VM 3.2.18, 3.8.6, 9.7.1.

adoptarent. quin etiam cum C. Caesar, Cn. Pompeio adulescente in Hispania oppresso, populum in hortis suis admisisset, proximo intercolumnio paene pari studio frequentiae salutatus est. quod nisi divinae Caesaris vires huic erubescendae procellae obstitissent, simile vulnus res publica excepisset atque in Equitio acceperat. ceterum decreto eius extra Italiam relegatus, postquam ille caelo receptus est, in urbem rediit et consilium interficiendi senatus capere sustinuit. quo nomine iussu patrum necatus, in carcere seras prompti animi ad omne moliendum scelus poenas pependit.

2   Ne divi quidem Augusti etiam nunc terras regentis excellentissimum numen intemptatum ab hoc iniuriae genere. exstitit qui clarissimae ac sanctissimae sororis eius Octaviae utero se genitum fingere auderet, propter summam autem imbecillitatem corporis ‹iussu matris expositum, sed›[117] ab eo cui datus erat perinde atque ipsius filium retentum, subiecto in locum suum proprio filio, diceret, videlicet ut eodem tempore sanctissimi penates et veri sanguinis memoria spoliarentur et falsi sordida contagione inquinarentur. sed dum plenis impudentiae velis ad summum audaciae gradum fertur, imperio Augusti remo publicae triremis adfixus est.

3   Repertus est etiam qui se diceret esse Q. Sertorii

---

[117] *add. Kempf, duce Gertz*   propter ... retentum *intra cruces Briscoe*

---

2 Lit. "in the next intercolumnar space."
3 Cf. Cic. *Att.* 12.49.2 etc.
4 This and the following impostures are not reported else-

their patron. What is more, when C. Caesar, after crushing Cn. Pompeius the younger in Spain, admitted the public in his suburban estate, the pretender was greeted on the other side of the column[2] with almost equal enthusiasm by the throng. And if the divine might of Caesar had not opposed this shameful commotion, the commonwealth would have suffered a wound similar to that which it received in Equitius' case. Banished from Italy by his decree, after Caesar was received in heaven, he returned to Rome and actually made plans to murder the senate. On that account he was put to death in prison by order of the Fathers and paid a belated penalty for his readiness to engage in any crime.[3]

Not even the most excellent and holy power of the divine Augustus, when he still ruled the earth, was unattempted by this kind of outrage. There arose one who dared to make up a story that he was born from the womb of the most illustrious and blameless sister of the same, Octavia, and to say that because of his extreme bodily weakness he was exposed by his mother's order and kept by the person to whom he had been given as his own son and that person's real son put in his place.[4] Apparently he wanted that most sacred household at one and the same time despoiled of the memory of the true blood and defiled by the sordid contagion of the false. But as he was being borne to the highest pitch of audacity by full sails of impudence, on Augustus' command he was attached to the oar of a public trireme.[5]

One was also found to call himself the son of Q. Sertor-

where. Octavia's son C. Claudius Marcellus was probably born in 42. He died in 23.   [5] I.e. sent to the galleys.

393

filium; quem ut agnosceret uxor eius nulla vi compelli
potuit.

4   Quid? Trebellius Calcha quam adseveranter se Clodium tulit! et quidem dum de bonis eius contendit, in cen-
tumvirale iudicium adeo favorabilis descendit ut vix iustis
et aequis sententiis consternatio populi ullum relinqueret
locum. in illa tamen quaestione neque calumniae petitoris
neque violentiae plebis iudicantium religio cessit.

5   Multo fortius ille qui Cornelio Sulla rerum potiente in
domum Cn. Asinii Dionis irrupit, filiumque eius patris penatibus expulit, vociferando non illum sed se Dione esse
procreatum. verum postquam a Sullana violentia Caesa-
riana aequitas rem publicam[118] reduxit, gubernacula Romani imperii iustiore principe obtinente, in publica custodia spiritum posuit.

ext. 1   Eodem praeside rei publicae in consimili mendacio
muliebris temeritas Mediolani repressa est; si quidem cum
se pro Rubria quadam,[119] perinde ac falso credita esset in-
cendio perisse, nihil ad se pertinentibus bonis insereret,
neque ei aut tractus eius splendidi testes aut cohortis Au-
gustae favor deesset, propter inexpugnabilem Caesaris
constantiam irrita nefarii propositi abiit.

ext. 2   Idem barbarum quendam ob eximiam similitudinem
Cappadociae regnum adfectantem, tamquam Ariarathes

---

118 rem publicam *hic Kempf, ante* in A *corr.*
119 quadam *SB*[3]: quaedam AL

---

6 Clodius was killed in 52, leaving a son who died many years
later (cf. VM 3.5.3, Cic. *Att.* 14.13A,B, Dessau, *Inscr. Lat.* 882).
The imposter will have appeared after his death, claiming to be

ius, whose widow could not by any violence be compelled to recognize him.

Again: how insistently did Trebellius Calcha make himself out to be Clodius! And when he went to law for Clodius' property, he came to the Court of the Hundred in such public favour that the popular delusion scarce left room for just and equitable votes. But the conscience of the jury in that trial did not succumb to the false plea of the claimant or the violence of the populace.[6]

Much more forceful was the action of the person who under the rule of Cornelius Sulla broke into the house of Cn. Asinius Dio and expelled his son from his father's house, vociferating that he, not that son, was Dio's child. But after Caesarian equity brought the commonwealth back from Sullan violence and a juster leader held the rudder of Roman empire, he surrendered his life in public custody.

EXTERNAL

When the same was guardian of the commonwealth, feminine rashness in a similar falsehood was repressed in Mediolanum. She was thrusting herself into a property to which she had no right, claiming to be one Rubria, falsely believed to have died in a fire. But although she did not lack distinguished witnesses from that district and the favour of the august entourage, she left foiled of her wicked design by reason of Caesar's impregnable steadfastness.

A certain barbarian pretended to the throne of Cappadocia because of an extraordinary likeness, posing as

not Clodius himself (obviously absurd) but another son. Perhaps read *Clodi<i fili>um* or omit *eius*. But Valerius may have written carelessly.

esset, quem a M. Antonio interemptum luce clarius erat, quamquam paene totius orientis civitatium et gentium credula suffragatione fultum, caput imperio dementer imminens iusto impendere supplicio coegit.

Ariarathes, who, as was clear as daylight, had been executed by Antony. Backed though he was by the credulous support of the communities and nations of almost the entire East, the same Caesar compelled him to devote his head that in folly threatened the empire to a just punishment.

GLOSSARY

AEDILE: Third in rank of the regular Roman magistracies. In the later Republic four were elected annually, two Curule and two Plebeian. They were responsible for city administration and the holding of certain public Games.

AS: Copper coin. In 217 B.C. it was reduced in value, becoming 1/16 of a denarius or 1/4 of a sesterce.

ATELLANAE (FABULAE): Farcical comedies named from the town of Atella in Campania.

AUGURS: The priestly College of Augurs were official diviners interpreting signs, mostly from the flight and cries of wild birds or the behaviour of the Sacred Chickens, before major acts of public (and sometimes private) business.

AUSPICES: Divination, public or private, from birds or other signs. The taking of auspices by magistrates so empowered was obligatory as a preliminary to major public acts.

CAMPUS (MARTIUS), FIELD OF MARS: Plain adjoining the Tiber on which assemblies of the Centuries were held, often for elections.

CAPITE CENSI: Literally "assessed by head." Citizens registered as without property.

CENSOR: Two magistrates usually elected every five years for a tenure of eighteen months. They revised the roll

399

of citizens, with property assessments, and the rolls of knights and senators, removing those guilty of misconduct. They further supervised public contracts, including the leasing of revenues to the tax farmers, and issued decrees as guardians of public morals.

CENTURIES: (a) Assembly of *(comitia centuriata)*. Form of assembly in which voting took place by "Centuries," i.e. groups unequally composed so as to give preponderance to birth and wealth. It elected Consuls and Praetors, and voted on legislation proposed by them. (b) Military units, theoretically consisting of a hundred men.

CENTURION: See Legion.

CIVIC CROWN *(corona civica)*: Wreath of oak leaves awarded to a soldier for saving the life of a comrade.

COHORT: See Legion.

CONSCRIPT FATHERS: I.e. the senate.

CONSUL: Highest of the annual Roman magistrates. Two were elected, to take office the following January. In the event of a death while in office a Consul Suffect was elected in replacement.

COUCHES, SPREADING OF *(lectisternium)*: A banquet offered to gods, with couches spread for them to recline.

CURULE CHAIR *(sella curulis)*: Ivory chair, or rather stool, of state used by "curule magistrates," i.e. Consuls, Praetors, and Curule Aediles, also certain others.

DECURION: Member of a municipal governing body.

DENARIUS: Silver coin worth four sesterces.

DICTATOR: A supreme magistrate with quasi-regal powers appointed for six months to deal with emergencies under the early Republic; his second in command, called Master of the Horse, was appointed by himself. The

office was revived after long disuse to legitimize the autocratic regimes of Sulla and Julius Caesar.

DUUMVIR: One of a board of two. The Sibylline Books were originally in the charge of two such commissioners but the number was later increased to fifteen.

EQUESTRIAN ORDER: See Knights.

EXTORTION *(res repetundae)*: The term is customary but too narrow; it covers various kinds of financial malpractice by a governor of a province.

FASCES: A bundle of rods, usually with an axe, carried by a lictor in front of a magistrate as a symbol of authority.

FASTI *(consulares)*: Register of Consuls and other high magistrates kept in the public archives.

FETIAL: Member of a priestly college concerned with the maintenance of public faith, functioning in formal dealings with foreign communities, as in declarations of war or ratifications of treaties.

FIELD OF MARS: See Campus.

FLAMEN: Priest in charge of the cult of a particular deity. Those of Jupiter, Mars, and Quirinus were the most important.

FLORALES, FLORALIA: See Games.

FREEDMAN: A freed (manumitted) slave.

GABINE FASHION: A ritual mode of wearing the toga, for religious occasions such as sacrifice.

GAMES *(ludi)*: Gladiatorial and other shows, some recurring annually and supervised by magistrates, others put on by private initiative for a particular occasion. Among the former were those of Apollo, the Roman or Circus or Great Games, those of Flora, the Plebeian, the Megalesia (festival of Cybele, the Great Mother).

GEMONIAN STEPS: On the Capitoline, where the bodies

401

GLOSSARY

of executed criminals were exposed and finally hauled
down to the Tiber.

GOWN (*toga*): Formal civilian dress of a Roman citizen.
At sixteen or seventeen a boy was given his White (or
"Manly") Gown (*toga pura, toga virilis*) on coming of
age. Prior to that he wore a gown with a purple hem
(*toga praetexta*) also worn by magistrates.

HEXERIS: A kind of ship, perhaps with six rowers to each
bank of oars.

HUNDRED, COURT OF: A standing body of judges handling
civil cases.

IMPURITY (*incestus*): Sexual offence with religious con-
notation, especially involving a Vestal Virgin; also in-
cest.

IUGERUM: Land measure, about two-thirds of an acre.

KNIGHTS: Non-senators with property over a certain level,
recognized by the Censors as members of the equestrian order, possessing a "public horse." Sometimes
used more widely of any freeborn possessor of such
property.

LEADER OF THE SENATE (*princeps senatus*): Normally an
ex-Censor belonging to one of the leading patrician
clans. He was called upon to speak first in a debate. Sulla
abolished the title.

LEGATE: Specially applied to one commissioned by the
senate to assist a commander or provincial governor.
Also used for "envoy" in general and so translated where
appropriate.

LEGION: Roman army unit with a full complement of 6,000
men divided into ten cohorts. Each legion was officered
by six Military Tribunes. Each cohort had six Centurions, the highest in rank being called *primi pili* (Chief

Centurion). The ensign of a legion was an eagle, and each cohort had its standard.

LÈSE MAJESTÉ *(maiestas)*: The term covered acts "in derogation of the majesty of the Roman People," as of magistrates or governors exceeding their legitimate authority.

LICTOR: Official attendant on a magistrate. The numbers varied according to rank. The head (lit. "closest") lictor *(proximus lictor)* walked immediately ahead of the magistrate.

LUPERCALIA: Fertility festival on 15 February.

MAGUS: Member of a Persian priestly caste.

MANES: Spirits of the dead.

MASKS *(imagines)*: Wax death masks of ancestors with labels listing offices hung in the hall *(atrium)* of a Roman house along with the family tree.

MASTER OF THE HORSE: See Dictator.

MIME: Type of entertainment with dancing, music, and dialogue which became highly popular in the first century B.C. It was considered more sophisticated and risqué than the Atellane Farce, which it superseded.

MURMILLO: Category of gladiator wearing Gallic armour usually opposed to a *retiarius* with net and trident.

NOBILITY: Practically, a noble *(nobilis)* meant a direct descendant in the male line of a Consul. In the early Republic the community was divided into patricians and plebeians, the former holding a virtual monopoly of political power. But after the Consulship was opened to plebeians early in the fourth century many plebeian families became "noble."

NOMENCLATOR: A slave whose function it was to identify persons whom his master might encounter.

OVATION: A lesser form of triumph.

PALLADIUM: A statue of Pallas (Athena) supposed to have come from Troy, kept on the Capitol.

PONTIFF *(pontifex)*: Member of a priestly College in general charge of religious institutions (including the calendar), presided over by the Chief Pontiff *(pontifex maximus)*.

PRAETOR: Second in rank of the annually elected magistracies. The number rose in course of time from one to eight (Sulla) and twenty (Caesar). The City Praetor *(praetor urbanus)* and Foreign Praetor *(praetor peregrinus)* had judicial functions divided as the names imply. Others presided over standing criminal courts. After his year of office a Praetor in the later Republic normally went to govern a province as Propraetor or Proconsul. The term is also used as equivalent to "governor" (of a province).

PREFECT: Officer appointed by a magistrate (usually a provincial governor or army commander) for military or civil duties.

PROCONSUL *(pro consule)*: Acting Consul, one who exercised consular authority outside Rome by senatorial appointment. Similarly Propraetor *(pro praetore)*.

PROSCRIPTION *(proscriptio)*: A procedure employed by Sulla, then by the Triumvirs in 43. Lists of names were published, the persons thus proscribed being declared outlaws and their goods confiscated. Their killers were rewarded, their protectors punished.

QUAESTOR: The first stage in the regular course of offices, election carrying life membership of the senate. After Sulla twenty were elected annually. The two City Quaestors *(quaestores urbani)* had charge of the Trea-

sury and the Quaestors assigned to provincial governors (usually by lot) were largely concerned with finance.

QUINQUIREME: A large galley.

ROCK, TARPEIAN: A precipice on the Capitoline Hill from which criminals were thrown to their death.

ROSTRA: The speaker's platform in the place of assembly at the northwest corner of the Forum, so called from the beaks (*rostra*) of captured warships with which it was decorated.

SALII: A priestly College associated with Mars, with custody of twelve sacred shields, one of which was believed to have dropped from the sky. The name, from *salio*, jump, comes from their ritual dances.

SCRIBE (*scriba*): A corporation of civil servants working in the Treasury and otherwise. City magistrates and provincial governors might be assigned official secretaries from the body for their personal assistance.

SIBYLLINE BOOKS: A collection of sacred writings, prophetic or directive, supposed to derive from the Sibyl (wise woman) of Cumae or other ancient Sibyls. They were in the keeping of an elected board which ranked as one of the four principal priestly Colleges. See Duumvir.

SOOTHSAYER (haruspex): A diviner from entrails of sacrificial victims, also lightning and portents, according to a system borrowed from Etruria.

SPOLIA OPIMA: Spoils taken by a general from an enemy general whom he had killed in personal combat. They were offered to Jupiter Feretrius.

SUOLITAURILIA (*suouetaurilia*): Purificatory sacrifice of a boar, a ram, and a bull.

TALENT: A weight of silver, in Athens = 6,000 drachmas.

THANKSGIVING (*supplicatio*): A thanksgiving ceremony decreed by the senate in honour of a military success. It was generally regarded as a preliminary to a triumph.

TREASURY: The Roman state Treasury was in the temple of Saturn in the Forum, managed by scribes working under the City Quaestors.

TRIBE (*tribus*): A division, mainly by locality, of the Roman citizen body. The number rose over the centuries from three to thirty-five (four urban the rest rustic). Assemblies voting by tribes (*comitia tributa*) elected magistrates below Praetor and could pass legislation proposed by Tribunes.

TRIBUNE: (1) Of the plebs. A board of ten originally appointed to protect plebeians from patrician high-handedness. They had wide constitutional powers, the most important being that any one of them could veto any piece of public business, including laws and senatorial decrees. They could also initiate these. They took office on 10 December. (2) Military. See Legion.

TRIREME: A galley.

TRIUMPH: Victory parade by a general on his return to Rome. Permission had to be granted by the senate.

TRIUMVIR: Member of a board of three. One such were the *tresuiri capitales* in charge of city police. Called *tresuiri nocturni,* they were concerned with fire control.

VESTAL VIRGINS: Priestesses of Vesta, the hearth goddess, with residence in the Forum. They tended a perpetual sacred fire and were vowed to chastity.

VIRTUE: *Virtus* (manliness) has a wide range of meanings: courage (valour), energy and ability, moral excellence. Like other Roman abstractions it was personified as a divinity.

INDEX OF NAMES

References are to the Latin text by book, chapter, and paragraph. Parentheses set off references when the text contains merely an allusion rather than direct naming. A superscript letter r indicates that the order of words or names in the text is reversed.

Accaus, Vibius (prefect of a Paelignian cohort): III.2.20

Accius, (L.) (author of Latin tragedies): III.7.11. VIII.14.2

(Acerrae) (in Campania). Acerrani: IX.6.ext.2

Acestor *see* Alcestis

Achaia (Roman province of Greece): I.8.10. IV.3.2. VII.5.4

    Achaicum bellum: VII.5.4

Ἀχαιοί: III.7.ext.3

Achilles (Homeric hero): VIII.8.ext.2. *See also* Occius

Acilius (soldier of Caesar's tenth legion): III.2.22,23a

Acilius Aviola: I.8.12a

Acilius Glabrio, M'. (cos. suff. 154): II.5.1. His father (cos. 191): II.5.1

Acro (king of Caenina): III.2.3

Actium (in western Greece): I.7.7

Admetus (mythical king of Thessaly): IV.6.1

(Adrastus): I.7.ext.4

Adrianus *see* Fabius Adrianus

Aeas (= Aous, river in Epirus): I.5.ext.2

Aebutia (wife of L. Menenius Agrippa): VII.8.2

Aegates insulae (islands off western Sicily): I.3.2 (Nepot.). I.4.3 (Nepot.)

Aegeria *see* Egeria

Aegina (island off western Attica). Aeginenses: IX.2.ext.8

Aegyptus (Egypt): I.4.ext.1 (Paris). IV.1.15. V.1.1f. VI.4.3. VIII.7.ext.2,3.

    Aegyptii: I.4.ext.1 (Paris). Aegyptia, gens: IX.1.ext.6. -tia perfidia: V.1.10. -tii senes: VIII.7.ext.3

Aelia familia: IV.4.8. V.6.4.r (Aelia) gens: IV.4.9

Aelii (sixteen): IV.4.8

(Aelius) Lamia, L. (pr. 42 (?)): I.8.12b

(Aelius) Lamia, L. (cos. A.D. 3): I.8.11

(Aelius Paetus Catus, Sex.) *see* Aelius Tubero Catus

(Aelius Seianus, L.) (favourite of Emperor Tiberius): IX.11.ext.4

Aelius (Paetus or Tubero) (praetor): V.6.4

(Aelius) Tubero Catus, Q. (in mistake for Sex. (Aelius) Paetus Catus, cos. 198): IV.3.7

Aelius Tubero, Q. (son-in-law of L. Aemilius Paullus, II cos. 168): IV.4.9

Aelius Tubero, Q. (son of foregoing): VII.5.1

Aemilia, gens: III.1.1. VI 2.3^r

Aemilii *see* Aemilius Papus

Aemilia (chief Vestal Virgin): I.1.7

Aemilia, Tertia (daughter of L. Aemilius Paullus II, cos. 216, and wife of Scipio Africanus the elder): VI.7.1

(Aemilia), Tertia (daughter of L. Aemilius Paullus, II cos. 168): I.5.3

Aemilianus *see* Cornelius Scipio Aemilianus

Aemilius Lepidus (Livianus), Mam. (cos. 77): VII.7.6. VIII.5.4

Aemilius Lepidus, M. (II cos. 175, Pontifex Maximus, censor): III.1.1. IV.2.1. VI.6.1,3

(Aemilius) Lepidus, M. (cos. 78): II.8.7

Aemilius (Lepidus) Porcina, M. (cos. 137): VIII.1.damn.7

Aemilius Papus, Q. (II cos. 278): IV.4.3. IV.4.11 (Aemilii)

Aemilius Paullus, L. (II cos. 216, killed at Cannae): III.4.4. V.1.ext.6

Aemilius Paullus, L. (II cos. 168): I.5.3. I.8.1b. II.7.14. II.10.3. IV.3.8. IV.4.9. V.1.1d,8, 9. V.10.2. (VI.2.3). VII.5.1,3. VIII.11.1
 Paulliana victoria: VIII.11.1

Aemilius Paullus, L. (cos. 50): I.3.4 (Paris)

Aemilius Scaurus, M. (cos. 115, leader of the senate): III.2.18. III.7.8. IV.4.11. V.8.4,5. VI.5.5. (VIII.1.abs. 10). VIII.5.2,3

(Aemilius Scaurus) (son of the foregoing): 5.8.4

Aemilius Scaurus, M. (pr. 56, also son of the foregoing): II.4.6,7. III.6.7. VIII.1. abs.10

Aeneas (Trojan hero): I.8.7

Aequi (people of ancient Latium): V.2.2. Aequiculi: II.7.7

Aequimelium: VI.3.1c

Aeschines (Athenian orator): VIII.10.ext.1

Aeschylus (dramatist): IX.12.ext.2. Cf. VII.2.ext.7

Aesculapius (god of healing): I.1.19. I.1.ext.3. I.8.2

Aesopus (tragic actor):
VIII.10.2. IX.1.2
Aethiopes: VIII.13.ext.5
(Aetna) *(Etna).* Aetnaeus mons:
V.4.ext.5
Aetolia (region in northwest
Greece): VIII.13.ext.6
Aetoli, Aetolica: IV.3.7
Africa: I.1.2. I.5.5. I.8.ext.19.
II.7.2. II.10.4. III.2.13.
III.5.1a. III.6.1. III.7.1c,d,e.
IV.4.6. V.1.1d. V.2.ext.4.
V.6.ext.4. VI.9.6,14. VII.3.3.
VII.4.ext.1. VIII.14.1.
VIII.15.4. IX.8.ext.1
Africanus (cognomen): II.10.4.
(III.5.1a. III.7.1d). V.5.1.
VIII.1.damn.1. Africanus
uterque: V.3.2e. *See also*
Cornelius Scipio Africanus
Afronia (Afrania? Apronia?)
(daughter of Aebutia): VII.8.2
Agamemno(n) (leader of the
Greeks at Troy): IV.7.praef.
VIII.11.ext.6
Agathocles (tyrant of Syracuse):
VII.4.ext.1
Agesilaus (king of Sparta):
VII.2.ext.15
Aglaus (poor man of Psophis):
VII.1.2
Agrigentum (Agrigento, city of
southern Sicily): III.3.ext.2.
-ini IV.3.ext.2. -ina civitas:
IV.8.ext.2
Agrippa *see* Vipsanius Agrippa;
Menenius, Agrippa
Agrius, M. (banker): VIII.4.1

Ahala *see* Servilius Ahala
Ahenobarbus *see* Domitius
Ahenobarbus
[Aiax]: VIII.11.ext.6
Alba (Longa, in Latium): I.8.7.
V.1.1c. IX.6.3. Albani: II.2.9a.
VI.3.6. VII.4.1. -nus lacus:
I.6.3. -nus mons: III.6.5
Albana (street in Capua):
IX.1.ext.1
Albanius, L. (of Caere):
1.1.10
Albinus *see* Postumius Albinus
Alcaeus (of Lesbos, lyric poet,
7th-6th century): IV.1.ext.6
Alcamenes (5th-century sculp-
tor): VIII.11.ext.3
(Alcestis) (wife of Admetus):
IV.6.1
Alcestis (mistake for Acestor?
Athenian writer of tragedies):
III.7.ext.1b
Alcibiades (late 5th-century
Athenian statesman and gen-
eral): I.7.ext.9. III.1.ext.1.
VI.9.ext.4. (VII.2.ext.7).
VIII.8.ext.1
Alcyoneus (son of Antigonus
Gonatas): V.1.ext.4
Alexander (the Great): I.1.ext.5
(Paris, Nepot.). I.4.ext.1
(Paris). I.7.ext.2. I.8.ext.10.
III.3.ext.1,4. III.8.ext.6.
IV.3.ext.3b,4a. IV.7.ext.2a,b.
V.1.ext.1a. V.6.ext.5.
VI.4.ext.3,(4).
VII.2.ext.10,11a,13.
VII.3.ext.1,4. VIII.11.ext.2.

INDEX

VIII.14.ext.2. IX.3.ext.1.
IX.5.ext.1. IX.10.ext.2

Alexander (of Pherae, tyrant):
IX.13.ext.3

Alexander (Polyhistor, of
Miletus, historian and geog-
rapher, 1st century):
VIII.13.ext.7

Alexander (son of Pyrrhus):
V.1.ext.4

Alexander (slave of M. Agrius):
VIII.4.1

[Alexander] (slave): VIII.4.2

Alexandria: III.8.8. VI. 6.1
Alexandrinus pictor: V.1.1f.

(Allia) (river). Alliensis dies:
IX.11.ext.4

Allobroges (chief tribe of
Narbonese Gaul): IX.6.3

Allobrogicus see Fabius
Maximus Allobrogicus

Alpes: II.8.praef. III.7.ext.6.
V.5.3

(Alsium) (on the coast of
Etruria). Alsiensis ager:
VIII.1.damn.7

(Ambracia) (in western
Greece). Ambraciensis,
Timochares: VI.5.1d

Amphiaraus (legendary
prophet-king): VIII.15.ext.3

Amphinomus and Anapias
(brothers of Aetna): V.4.ext.4

Anacharsis (Scythian sage in the
time of Solon): VII.2.ext.14

Anacreon (6th-century lyric
poet): IX.12.ext.8

Anapias see Amphinomus

Anaxagoras (5th-century phi-

losopher): V.10.ext.3.
VII.2.ext.12. VIII.7.ext.6.
VIII.9.ext.2. VIII.11.ext.1

Anaxarchus (4th-century
philosopher, follower of
Democritus): III.3.ext.4.
VIII.14.ext.2

Anaximenes (4th-century
rhetor): VII.3.ext.4

Ancus see Marcius

(Andriscus) see Pseudophilippus

Androgyne see Maesia

Anio (river near Rome):
VIII.9.1. IX.2.1

Annalis see Villius Annalis

Anneius, M. (Roman knight of
Carseoli): VII.7.2

Anneius, M. (son of the foregoing): VII.7.2

Annius, L.: II.9.2

Annius (i.e. L. Annius of Setia,
cf. Livy 8.5): VI.4.1a

Annius, P. (killer of the orator
M. Antonius): VIII.9.2. IX.2.2

Antabagius (?) (Tiberius' guide
to Germany): V.5.3

Antigenidas (flautist): III.7.ext.2

Antigonus (Gonatas, king of
Macedonia): V.1.ext.4

Antiochia (chief city of Syria):
I.6.12.

Antiochus (I Soter, king of
Syria): V.7.ext.1

Antiochus (II Theos):
IX.14.ext.1

Antiochus (III, the Great):
II.5.1. II.10.2a. III.5.1a.
IV.1.ext.9. V.3.2c. VII.3.4b.
VIII.1.damn.1

Antiochensis pecunia:
III.7.1e

Antiochus (IV, Epiphanes):
VI.4.3

Antiochus (VII Sidetes):
IX.1.ext.4

Antipater (4th-century Macedonian general, later ruler):
I.7.ext.2

Antipater (of Sidon, 2nd-
century epigrammatist):
I.8.ext.16,(18)

(Antistius?) Reginus, L. (tr. pl.
103): IV.7.3

Antistius Vetus, Q.: VI.3.11

Antium (on the coast south of
Rome, Anzio): I.6.5. I.8.2.
Antiense templum (of
Aesculapius): I.8.2

Antius Restio: VI.8.7

Antonia (faithful wife and
widow of Drusus
Germanicus): IV.3.3

Antonius, C. (cos. 63, defeated
Catiline): II.4.6. II.8.7. IV.2.6

Antonius, M. (cos. 99, orator):
II.9.5. III.7.9. VI.8.1. VII.3.5.
VIII.9.2. IX.2.2
Antoniana eloquentia:
VIII.9.2

Antonius, M. (triumvir): I.1.19.
I.4.6 (Nepot.), 7 (Paris). I.5.7.
I.7.7. III.8.8. IV.7.4,6. V.1.11.
V.3.4. IX.5.4. IX.13.3.
IX.15.ext.2
Antonianum bellum:
III.8.8

Aous (river in Epirus): IX.8.2.
See also Aeas

Apelles (Alexander's preferred
painter): VIII.11.ext.2.
(VIII.12.ext.3)

Apollinares ludi: VI.2.9

Apollo: I.1.1a,18,ext.3,6
(Paris),9 (Paris, Nepot.). I.2.3
(Paris, Nepot.). I.6.10. I.8.10.
I.8.ext.8. III.4.ext.1.
Delphicus, Apollo: IV.1.ext.7.
V.6.8. V.6.ext.1. VIII.15.ext.2.
Pythius Apollo: I.1.ext.4.
V.3.ext.2.ʳ VII.1.2.ʳ VII.3.2.ʳ
VIII.15.3. See also Pythicus.
Λητοῦς υἱός: I.5.7

Apollonia (on the east coast of
the Adriatic): VI.6.5. IX.8.2.
Apolloniatae: I.5.ext.2

Appius see Claudius Caecus,
Claudius Crassus, Claudius
Pulcher

Appuleius, L. (tr. pl. 391):
V.3.2a

(Appuleius) Decianus, C. (tr. pl.
99): VIII.1.damn.2

(Appuleius) Saturninus, L. (tr.
pl. 103, 100): III.2.18. III.8.4.
VI.3.1c. VIII.1.damn.2,3.
VIII.6.2. IX.7.1,3

Apronius, Cn. (ex-aedile):
VI.6.5

Apulia (region of southeast Italy): VII.6.1a. Apula, regio:
IV.8.2

Aquillius, M'. (cos. 101):
IX.13.1

Aquillius, P. (tr. pl. 211?):
VIII.1.damn.6

Aquillius (Gallus), C. (pr. 66):
VIII.2.2

Aquilonia (in Samnium): VII.2.5

(Arcadia) (region of central Peloponnese). Arcades: I.7.ext.10 (duo). VII.1.2. Arcas, Evander: II.2.9a

Archelaus (Egyptian commander): IX.1.ext.6

Archelaus (king of Macedonia): IX.12.ext.4

Archilochus (7th-century poet): VI.3.ext.1

Archimedes (3rd-century mathematician and inventor): VIII.7.ext.7

Archytas (of Tarentum, Pythagorean, 5th-4th century): IV.1.ext.1,2. VIII.7.ext.3

Ardea (near Rome): IV.1.2

Areos pagos (variously spelt) (high court of Athens): II.6.4. V.3.ext.3g. VIII.1.ambust.2

Arganthonius (legendary king of Gades): VIII.13.ext.4

Arginus(s)ae (Aegean islands, scene of Athenian victory in 406): I.1.ext.8 (Paris). III.8.ext.3

(Argos) (city in western Peloponnese). Argiui: V.1.ext.4. Argiva laus: V.4.ext.5

Ariarathes (X, king of Cappadocia): IX.15.ext.2

Aricia (in Latium): VIII.2.4

(Ariminum) (on the Adriatic, Rimini). Ariminenses, Trochali: VII.7.4

Ariobarzanes (I and II, kings of Cappadocia): V.7.ext.2

Ario(n) (Pythagorean): VII.7.ext.3

Aristides (5th-century Athenian statesman): V.3.ext.3d,g. VI.5.ext.2

Aristippus (philosopher, 5th-4th century): IV.3.ext.4b

Aristogiton see Harmodius

Aristomache (wife of Dionysus I): IX.13.ext.4

Aristomenes (7th-century Messenian leader): I.8.ext.15,(18)

Aristonicus (late 2nd-century claimant king of Pergamus): III.2.12. III.4.5. VIII.7.6

Aristophanes (comic dramatist): VII.2.ext.7

Aristotle (philosopher): V.6.ext.5. VII.2.ext.11a,b. VIII.14.ext.3

Aristoxenus (4th-century philosopher and musicologist): VIII.13.ext.3

Armenia: V.1.9. IX.11.ext.3

Arpinum (in central Italy, Arpino): VI.9.14. -nas municipium: II.2.3

Arruns see Tarquinius

Arsia, silva (forest between Rome and Veii): I.8.5

Artaxerxes (II) see Dareus

Artaxerxes (III) Ochus (king of Persia): IX.2.ext.7

Artemisia (4th-century ruler of Caria): IV.6.ext.1

Artemisium (promontory in northern Euboea): V.3.ext.3g. VIII.14.ext.1

INDEX

Artemo ('double' of Antiochus II): IX.14.ext.1

Artorius (Caesar Octavian's doctor at Philippi): I.7.1,2

Arverni (tribe of central Gaul): IX.6.3

Arvina see (Papirius) Carbo Arvina

Ascanius (son of Aeneas): I.8.7

Asculum (in Picenum, Ascoli): VI.9.9

Asellio see Sempronius Asellio

Asellus see Claudius Asellus

Asia: I.7.ext.5. II.2.1,2. II.6.1,8. II.8.7. II.10.5. III.2.12. III.2.ext.3. III.5.1a. III.6.6. III.7.9. IV.1.13. IV.1.ext.9. IV.3.2. IV.6.3. IV.6.ext.3. IV.8.4. V.2.ext.3. V.3.2c. V.5.1. VI.9.7,15. VI.9.ext.2. VIII.1.damn.1. VIII.1.ambust.2. VIII.7.6. VIII.15.6. IX.1.5. IX.2.ext.3. IX.5.ext.2. IX.7.mil.Rom.1. IX.13.ext.1. IX.14.ext.2
  Asiaticae gazae: III.7.1e. -cae gentes: I.7.ext.5. -cum publicum: VI.9.7

Asiaticus (cognomen): V.5.1. VIII.1.damn.1. Cf. III.5.1a. See also Cornelius Scipio Asiaticus

Asina see Cornelius Scipio Asina

Asinius Dio, Cn.: IX.15.5

Asinius Pollio, (C.): VIII.13.ext.4

(Assyria). Assyrii: IX.3.ext.4

Astyages (king of the Medes): I.7.ext.5

(Ategua) (in southern Spain). Ateguenses: IX.2.4

Atellani (ludi) (farcical stage shows, named from Atella, town in Campania): II.4.4

Athenae: I.6.ext.1b. I.7.7. I.8.ext.2. II.1.10. II.6.(4,5,)6. II.10.ext.1,2. III.1.ext.1. III.7.ext.1a,7. III.8.ext.4. IV.3.6b. IV.3.ext.3a. IV.5.ext.2. V.3.ext.3a,d,g. V.6.ext.1,2. VI.4.ext.2. VI.9.ext.1. VII.3.ext.6. VIII.1.ambust.2. VIII.7.ext.3,4. VIII.9.ext.2. VIII.10.ext.1. VIII.11.ext.1,3,5. VIII.12.ext.2. IX.2.ext.8
  Athenienses: I.1.ext.7
  (Paris, Nepot.). I.2.ext.2
  (Paris). I.8.ext.15. II.6.3,4. III.1.ext.1. III.7.ext.7. III.8.ext.2,3. IV.1.ext.4. IV.3.ext.1. IV.5.ext.2. V.1.ext.2a. V.3.ext.3a,b,c,f. V.6.ext.1,2. V.10.ext.1, VI.3.ext.2. VI.5.ext.1,2. VI.9.ext.3. VII.2.ext.1d,7,13. VIII.9.ext.1. IX.2.ext.8. IX.8.ext.2. IX.11.4.
  Atheniensis, Cynegirus: III.2.22. -sis, lectulus: V.6.ext.5. -sis, Nausimenes: I.8.ext.3. -sis, populus: IV.1.ext.4. -sis, Theramenes: III.2.ext.6. See also Attica regio, Isocrates

Athesis (river of north Italy, modern Adige): V.8.4

Athos, mons: I.6.ext.1b

413

Atilius: IV.4.5

Atilius, C. (senator, killed by Gaul): III.2.7

Atilius, M. (custodian of sacred writings): I.1.13

Atilius Calatinus, (A.) (II cos. 254): II.8.2

Atilius Calatinus, A.: VIII.1.absol.9

Atilius Philiscus, P.: VI.1.6

Atilius Regulus, M. (II cos. 256): I.1.14. I.8.ext.19. (II.9.8). IV.4.6. IX.2.ext.1. IX.6.ext.1
    Atiliana, Virtus: IV.4.6

Atilius Regulus, M. (II cos. 217, son of the foregoing): II.9.8

Atilius Serranus, (A.?) (aed. cur. 194): II.4.3

Atinas, campus (in southwest Italy): I.7.5

Atinius, P.: VIII.4.2

Atossa (sister, wife, and victim of Artaxerxes III): IX.2.ext.7

Atratinus see Sempronius Atratinus

Attalica aulaea: IX.1.5

Attalus (I (?), king of Pergamus 241-197): I.8.ext.8. IV.8.4 (by mistake for Eumenes II). V.2.ext.3 (confused with Attalus III).

Attalus (III, king of Pergamus): V.2.ext.3

Attica regio: V.3.ext.3f. V.6.ext.1. -cum solum: I.8.10

Atticus see Pomponius Atticus

Attienus, Carbo: VI.1.13

Attius see Tullius, Attius

Attus see Naevius

Atys (son of Croesus): I.7.ext.4

Aufidianus see Pontius Aufidianus

Aufidius T. (governor of Asia ca. 66): VI.9.7

(Aufidius) Orestes, Cn. (cos. 71): VII.7.6,7

Augustus Caesar (I. praef.): I.1.19. I.4.7 (Paris, Nepot.). I.5.7. I.7.2,7. (IV.3.3. IV.7.7. V.5.3). VII.6.6. IX.15.ext.1. Divus Augustus: I.7.1. III.8.8. VII.7.3,4. VII.8.6. IX.15.2. See also Caesares
    Augusta cohors: IX.15.ext.1. -ta domus: II.8.7. VIII.15.praef. -ti penates: VI.1.praef. Caesariana aequitas: IX.15.5. -ni, milites: I.1.19

Aurelia Orestilla (wife of Catiline): IX.1.9

Aurelius Cotta, C. (II cos. 248): II.7.4

Aurelius (Cotta), L. (error for C.) (cos. 75): VIII.9.3

Aurelius Cotta, (L.) (cos. 144): VI.4.2b. VI.5.4. VIII.1.abs.11

(Aurelius Cotta, M.) (cos. 74): V.4.4

(Aurelius Cotta, M.) (son of the foregoing): V.4.4

Aurelius Pecuniola, P.: II.7.4

Aurelius Scaurus, C. (cos. 105?): II.3.2

Aventinus, mons (Aventine, one

of Rome's seven hills): I.8.3.
V.3.2f. VI.5.1c. VII.3.1
 Aventinensis Diana: VII.3.1
Aviola *see* Acilius Aviola

Babylon: IX.3.ext.4
Bacchanalia: I.3.1 (Paris,
Nepot.). VI.3.7
Badius (of Campania): V.1.3
Baebius Tamphilus (Cn.) (cos.
182): VII.2.6a
Baebius Tamphilus, (M.) (cos.
181): I.1.12. II.5.1
Bagrada (river near Utica):
I.8.ext.19
Balbus *see* Cornelius Balbus,
Octavius Balbus
Baria (in Spain): III.7.1b
Barrus (or Barrulus), T.: VII.8.8
Basilus *see* Minucius Basilus
Beneventum (in Samnium):
V.6.8
Berenice (wife of Antiochus II):
IX.10.ext.1
Berenice (daughter, sister, and
mother of Olympic victors):
VIII.15.ext.4
Bestia *see* Calpurnius Bestia
Bias (of Priene, one of the
Seven Wise Men): IV.1.ext.7.
VII.2.ext.3. VII.3.ext.3
Bibulus *see* Calpurnius Bibulus
Bithynia (kingdom in northwest
Asia Minor): I.8.ext.12.
III.7.ext.6. V.1.1e
Bito(n) *see* Cleobis
Bituitus (king of the Arverni):
IX.6.3

Blassius (of Salapia): III.8.ext.1
Blossius, C. (of Cumae, loyal
friend of C. Gracchus):
IV.7.1,2
Boarium, forum: I.6.5. II.4.7
Bocchus (king of Mauretania):
VIII.14.4
Boeotia (territory north of
Attica): I.8.ext.9
(Bononia) (Bologna).
Bononiensis, Calidius:
VIII.1.absol.12
(Bosporus, Cimmerian).
Bosporanus tractus: VII.6.6
Brennus (Gaulish chieftain):
I.1.ext.9 (Paris, Nepot.)
(Britannia). Britannica insula:
III.2.23b.
Brocchus *see* Furius Brocchus
Brundisium (Brindisi, port at
the heel of Italy): III.7.9.
V.1.1d. VI.6.5. IX.8.2
Bruttii (people at the toe of It-
aly): I.6.9. I.8.6
Bruttius, ager: V.1.ext.6
Brutus *see* Iunius Brutus
Bubulcus *see* Iunius Bubulcus
Brutus
Buccio *see* Licinius Buccio
Burbuleius (actor): IX.14.5
Busa (wealthy woman of
Apulia): IV.8.2

Caecilia, lex (repetundarum)
(error for Calpurnia or
Acilia?): VI.9.10
Caecilia Metelli: I.5.4
(Caecilii) Metelli, Q. et L.

(Macedonicus and Calvus): VIII.5.1

Caecilius, Q. (uncle of Pomponius Atticus): VII.8.5

(Caecilius) Cornutus, M. (pr. 43): V.2.10

(Caecilius) Metellus (unidentified; see Caecilia): I.5.4

(Caecilius) Metellus, (L.) (II cos. 247): I.1.2. I.4.5 (Paris, Nepot). VIII.13.2

(Caecilius) Metellus, Q. (actually L. or M.?) (quaest. 214): II.9.8 (M.). V.6.7

(Caecilius) Metellus, M.) (cos. 115): cf. IV.1.12, VII.1.1

(Caecilius) Metellus, Q. (cos. 206): VII.2.3. Cf. VII.1.1

(Caecilius Metellus Baliaricus, Q.) (cos. 123): Cf. IV.1.12, VII.1.1

(Caecilius) Metellus (Calvus), L. (cos. 142) see Caecilii Metelli

(Caecilius Metellus Caprarius, C.) (cos. 113): cf. IV.1.2, VII.1.1

(Caecilius) Metellus Celer, (Q.) (aed. cur. 88?): VI.1.8

(Caecilius) Metellus (Celer), Q. (cos. 60): VII.7.7

(Caecilius) Metellus (Creticus, Q.) (cos. 69): VII.6.ext.1

(Caecilius) Metellus (Diadematus), L. (cos. 117): II.9.9. Cf. IV.1.2. VII.1.1

Caecilius Metellus Macedonicus, Q. (cos. 143):
II.7.10. III.2.21. III.7.5. IV.1.12, V.1.5. VII.1.1. VII.4.5. VII.5.4. IX.3.7. *See also* Caecilii Metelli

(Caecilius) Metellus Nepos, (Q.) (cos. 57): VII.8.3. IX.14.4

(Caecilius) Metellus Numidicus, Q. (cos. 109): II.7.2. II.10.1,2a. III.8.4. IV.1.12,13. (V.2.7. IX.1.5). IX.7.2

(Caecilius) Metellus Pius, Q. (cos. 80): V.2.7. VIII.5.4. VIII.15.8. IX.1.5

(Caecilius) Metellus (Pius) Scipio (P. Cornelius Scipio Nasica) (consul 52): III.2.13. III.8.7. VIII.14.5. IX.1.8. IX.5.3 (P. Scipio).

Caelii (Cloelii) *see* Caelius, T.

Caelius (rather Cloelius), T. (of Tarracina): VIII.1. absol.13

Caelius mons (one of Rome's seven hills): VIII.2.1

Caelius Rufus, M. (pr. 48): IV.2.7. V.3.4

Caeneus: IX.10.ext.1

(Caenina) (in ancient Latium). Caeninenses: III.2.3

Caepio *see* Servilius Caepio

Caere (in Etruria): I.1.10. Caeretani: 11.10. Caerites aquae: I.6.5

Caesar *see* Augustus, Iulius, Tiberius Caesar

Caesares, diui: II.1.10. Cf. I.praef.

Caesetius (Roman knight, defies Caesar): V.7.2

(Caesetius Flavus, L.) (tr. pl. 44, son of the foregoing): V.7.2

Caesetius Rufus (senator): IX.5.4

Caesius, M. (scribe and successor to Vibellius in Rhegium): II.7.15f

Caesius (rather, Cassius) Scaeva, M. (centurion): III.2.23a

Caeso see Quinctius Cincinnatus, Tuccius

Caieta (port of Formiae, Gaeta): V.3.4. VIII.8.1. Caietanus, ager: I.4.6 (Nepot.). -na villa: I.4.6 (Paris)

(Calagurris) (in northern Spain). Calagurritani: VII.6.ext.3

Calatinus see Atilius Calatinus

Calchas (Homeric seer): VIII.11.ext.6

Cales (in north Campania): III.2.ext.1. III.8.1. Calenus ager: I.8.ext.18. -na custodia: III.8.1

Calidius (of Bononia): VIII.1.absol.12

Calidius, M. (pr. 57): VIII.10.3

Calidius, Q. (tr. pl. 98): V.2.7

Callanus (Indian sage): I.8.ext.10

Calliphana (of Velia, priestess of Ceres): I.1.1b

Callippus (of Syracuse, false friend of Dio): III.8.ext.5

Callisthenes (historian, put to death by Alexander): VII.2.ext.11a. IX.3.ext.1

Calpurnia (wife of Caesar): I.7.2

Calpurnius, L. (triumvir capitalis): VIII.4.2

(Calpurnius) Bestia, L. (cos. 111): I.8.11

(Calpurnius) Bibulus, M. (cos. 59): IV.1.15

Calpurnius Lanarius, (P.): VIII.2.1

(Calpurnius) Piso, C. (cos. 67): III.8.3. VII.7.5

(Calpurnius) Piso, Cn. (cos. 23): VI.2.4

(Calpurnius) Piso, L. (error for Cn.) (cos. 139): I.3.3 (Paris)

(Calpurnius) Piso (Caesoninus), L. (cos. 112): VIII.1.absol.6

Calpurnius Piso (Frugi), L. (cos. 133): II.7.9,10. IV.3.10

Calpurnius (Salvianus) (conspirator against Q. Cassius in Spain): IX.4.2

Calvinus see Domitius Calvinus

Calvus see Licinius Macer Calvus

Cambyses (king of Persia): VI.3.ext.3

(Cameria) (in Latium). Camerini: VI.5.1c

(Camerinum) (in Umbria). Camertes: V.2.8

Camillus see Furius Camillus

(Campania) (region south of Latium). Campani: II.3.3. III.8.1. V.I.3. V.1.ext.5. IX.3.4. Campanus, Annius: VI.4.1a.

-nus, Badius; V.1.3. -nus, T.
Vibellius Taurea: III.2.ext.1.
-na luxuria: II.4.6. IX.1.ext.1.
-na matrona: IV.4.praef. -nae
mulieres, duae: V.2.1b. -na
perfidia: II.3.3. III.2.ext.1.
-nus senatus: III.8.1.
IX.5.ext.4. [-na urbs: VII.6.2]
Caninius Gallus, (L.) (tr. pl. 56)
(or his son, cos. 37): IV.2.6
Cannae (in Apulia): I.1.16.
II.7.15c. III.4.4. III.7.ext.6.
V.1.ext.6. IX.11.ext.4
    Cannensis acies:
VII.4.ext.2. -sis clades: I.1.15.
III.7.10b. V.6.7. VI.4.1a.
VI.6.ext.2. VII.6.1b. -se
proelium: III.2.11. III.8.2.
IV.8.2. V.6.4. -sis pugna:
II.9.8. IV.5.2. VII.2.ext.16.
IX.5.ext.3
(Canusium) (in Apulia).
Canusina moenia: IV.8.2
Capena porta (gate of Rome):
III.7.10b
Capitolium (highest of the
seven Roman hills): I.1.11.
I.4.2 (Paris, Nepot.). II.1.2.
III.1.1. III.2.7. III.6.2.
III.7.1g. IV.2.3. IV.4.11.
V.4.4,6. V.6.8. V.10.1. VI.3.1a.
VI.9.9. VII.4.3. VII.5.4.
VIII.15.1. IX.3.8. IX.5.ext.3
    Capitolina, arx: VIII.14.1.
-num fastigium: VI.9.5. -na
pulvinaria: IV.1.6a. See also
Iuno, Iuppiter
Capitolinus see Scantinius
Capitolinus

Cappadocia (kingdom in Asia
Minor): V.7.ext.2. IX.15.ext.2
Capua (chief city of Campania):
II.3.3. II.8.4. III.2.20.
III.7.ext.6. III.8.1. V.1.1e.
V.2.1b. VI.4.1a. VII.6.2.
IX.5.ext.4
Carbo see Attienus, Carbo,
Papirius Carbo
Carfania: VIII.3.2
(Caria) (region of southwest
Asia Minor). Cares: I.5.ext.1.
Caria, gens: IV.6.ext.1
Carneades (2nd-century philos-
opher): VIII.7.ext.5
Carrhae (in Mesopotamia):
I.6.11
Carrinas, C. (cos. suff. 43):
VII.8.3
(Carseoli) (town of the Aequi).
Carseolanus, M. Anneius:
VII.7.2
Carthago (Kar-): I.1.14,18. I.3.2
(Nepot.). I.8.ext.19. II.7.1,12.
II.8.5. II.10.4. III.2.ext.8.
III.6.1. III.7.1g, 10a. III.8.2.
IV.3.1,13. IV.4.6. V.1.6.
V.3.2b,d. V.6.ext.4. VI.2.3.
VI.9.2. VI.9.ext.7. VII.2.3.
VII.2.ext.16. VII.3.3.
VII.3.ext.7. VII.4.ext.1.
VIII.15.2. IX.3.ext.3. IX.12.3
    Carthaginienses: I.1.14,16.
I.1.ext.3. I.7.ext.8. I.8.ext.14.
II.7.ext.1. II.9.8. II.10.4.
III.7.1a,10a. III.8.ext.1.
IV.1.6b. V.1.1a. V.1.2. V.2.5.
V.2.ext.4. V.3.ext.1. V.6.ext.4.
VI.6.3,4. VI.6.ext.2. VI.9.11.

VII.2.6c. VII.4.ext.1.
IX.2.ext.1,2. IX.6.ext.1. -ses
duo fratres: V.6.ext.4. -sis
senatus: IX.5.ext.4. *See also*
Poeni

Carthago Nova (modern
Cartagena): III.8.2. IV.3.1.
IX.11.ext.1

Carvilius (Maximus Ruga), Sp.
(II cos. 228): II.1.4

Carystus (in Euboea): I.8.10

Cascellius, A. (expert in real estate law): VIII.12.1

Cascellius, A. (jurist): VI.2.12

Casilinum (in Campania):
VII.6.2
    Casilinates: VII.6.2

Cassander (son of Antipater):
I.7.ext.2

Cassius (kills his son): V.8.2

Cassius, L. (tr. pl. 89): 9.7.4

Cassius (Longinus, C.) (cos.
171): II.4.2

Cassius (Longinus, C.) (pr. 44,
Caesar's assassin): I.4.7
(Nepot.). I.5.8. I.8.8. III.1.3.
IV.7.4. VI.8.4. IX.9.2

Cassius (Longinus), Q. (tr. pl.
49): IX.4.2

Cassius (Longinus Ravilla), L.
(cos. 127): III.7.9.
VIII.1.damn.7

Cassius Parmensis, (C.) (quaest,
43): I.7.7

Cassius Scaeva, M. *see*
Caesius

Cassius (Vecellinus), Sp. (III
cos. 486): V.8.2. VI.3.1b.
VI.3.2

Castor and Pollux: I.8.1a,b.
(I.8.ext.7.) V.5.3. *See also*
Tyndaridae

Castricius, M. (magistrate of
Placentia): VI.2.10

Catilina *see* Sergius Catilina

Cato *see* Porcius Cato

Catulus *see* Lutatius Catulus

Catus *see* Aelius Tubero Catus

Caucasus mons: III.3.ext.6

Caudinae furcae (Caudine
Forks, in Samnium):
V.1.ext.5. VII.2.ext.17[r]

Celer *see* Caecilius Metellus
Celer

Celtiberia (region of central
Spain): VII.4.5. Celtiber:
III.2.21. Celtiberi: II.6.11.
III.2.21. IV.3.1. VII.4.5. -rae
urbes: V.1.5. -ricum bellum:
III.2.21. V.1.5. -rica fides:
II.6.14

Censorinus *see* Marcius
(Rutilus) Censorinus

Centobriga (in Spain): V.1.5

Centumalus *see* Claudius
Centumalus

Cephallania (island in the
Ionian sea): I.8.ext.18

Cerco *see* Lutatius Cerco

Cerennius, P.: VI.1.13

Ceres: I.1.1b,c,15. I.1.ext.5
(Paris, Nepot.). V.8.2.
VIII.15.ext.1

Cethegus *see* Cornelius
Cethegus

(Chalcis) (in Euboea).
Chalcidensis, Xenophilus:

VIII.13.ext.3. Chalcidicum fretum: I.8.10

Chaldaei: I.3.3 (Paris, Nepot.)

Charondas (lawgiver of Thurii): VI.5.ext.4

Chilo see Magius Chilo

Chrysippus (3rd-century Stoic philosopher): VIII.7.ext.5,10,11. His Λογικά: VIII.7.ext.10

Cicereius, C. (pr. 173): III.5.1b. IV.5.3

Cicero see Tullius Cicero

Cilicia (region in southeast Asia Minor): III.8.ext.6

Cimbri (German tribe destroyed by Marius): II.6.11. IV.7.3. V.2.8. V.8.4. VI.9.14. VIII.15.7.
    Cimber: II.10.6. Cimbrica audacia: II.6.14. -ca calamitas: II.10.6. -ca spolia: VI.3.1c. -cus triumphus: III.6.6. IX.12.4

Cimo(n) (son of Miltiades): V.3.ext.3c,g. V.4.ext.2. VI.9.ext.3

Cincinnatus see Quinctius Cincinnatus

Cineas (minister of Pyrrhus): IV.3.6b

Cinginnia (in Lusitania): VI.4.ext.1

Cinna see Cornelius Cinna, Helvius Cinna

Cipus see Genucius Cipus

Circus Flaminius: I.7.4. IV.4.8. -cus Maximus: IV.4.8

Clastidium (in Transpadane Gaul): I.1.8

Claudii: VII.8.3. Claudia familia: IV.3.3. -dia gens: V.5.3

Claudia (sister of P. Claudius Pulcher, cos. 249): VIII.1.damn.4

Claudia (Vestal): V.4.6

Claudia, Quinta: I.8.11 (Paris, Nepot.)

Claudius, P.: VI.5.1c

Claudius Asellus: VI.3.8

Claudius (Caecus), Ap. (II cos. 296): I.1.17. VII.2.1. VIII.13.5

Claudius (Caudex), Ap. (cos. 264): II.4.7

Claudius Centumalus, (Ti.) VIII.2.1

Claudius (Clineas), M. (legate 236, handed over to the Corsi): VI.3.3a

Claudius (Crassus Inregillensis Sabinus), Ap. (the Decemvir): VI.1.2. IX.3.5

(Claudius) Drusus Germanicus, (Nero) (stepson of Augustus): IV.3.3. V.5.3

Claudius Marcellus, M. (V cos. 208): I.1.8,9. I.6.9. II.1.10. II.7.15c. II.8.5. III.2.5. III.8.ext.1. IV.1.7. V.1.4. V.1.ext.6. VI.1.7. VIII.7.ext.7

Claudius (Marcellus), M. (cos. 183): VI.6.3

(Claudius) Marcellus, M. (cos. 51): IX.11.4

(Claudius) Marcellus

(Aeserninus), M. (legate in 90): VIII.5.3

Claudius Nero, C. (cos. 207): II.9.6a. IV.1.9. IV.2.2. VII.2.6a. VII.4.4

Claudius Pulcher, Ap. (error for P.): VIII.1.absol.4

(Claudius Pulcher, Ap.) (cos. 143): (V.4.6)

(Claudius Pulcher), Ap. (consul 54): I.8.10

Claudius Pulcher, (C.) (cos. 177): VI.5.3

Claudius Pulcher, C. (cos. 92): II.4.6. VIII.1.absol.6

Claudius (Pulcher), P. (cos. 249): I.4.3,4 (Paris). VIII.1.absol.4. (VIII.1.damn.4)

(Claudius Sabinus Inregillensis), Ap. (cos. 495): IX.3.(5),6

Cleanthes (Stoic philosopher, 4th-3rd century): VIII.7.ext.11

Clearchus (military Spartan, 5th-4th century): II.7.ext.2

Cleobis and Bito(n) (of Argos): V.4.ext.4

Cleo(n) (brigand chief in Sicily): IX.12.ext.1

Cleopatra (sister and wife of Ptolemy Physcon): IX.2. ext.5

Cleopatra (VII, queen of Egypt): IV.1.15

Clitus (friend and victim of Alexander): IX.3.ext.1

Clodia (wife of Ofilius): VIII.13.6

Clodius Pulcher, P. (tr. pl. 58): III.5.3. IV.2.5. VIII.5.5. IX.1.7,(8). Cf. IX.15.4

(Clodius or Claudius) Pulcher, (P.) (son of the foregoing): III.5.3

Cloelia: III.2.2

Cloelius, T., and sons see Caelius, T.

Cloelius Siculus, P. (rex sacrorum (?)): I.1.4

Cluvia Faecula (Campanian prostitute): V.2.1b

(Cnidos) (in Caria). Cnidii: VIII.11.ext.4

(Cnosos) (in Crete). Cnosius, Epimenides: VIII.13.ext.5

Cocles see Horatius Cocles

Codrus (legendary king of Athens): V.6.ext.1

Coela Euboeae see Euboea

Coelius (Antipater, L.) (annalist): I.7.6

Coelius (Caldus), P.: IV.7.5

Colonius, M.: IV.2.6

Coma (brother of the brigand Cleo): IX.12.ext.1

Cominius (tr. pl. ca. 300): VI.1.11

Cominius (Auruncus), Postumus (II. cos. 493): IV.3.4

Concordia: I.8.ext.17. Her temple: IX.7.4

Considius (tax farmer): IX.1.1

Considius, Q.: IV.8.3

Consualia (festival of Consus, god of agriculture): II.4.4

Contrebia (Spanish town): II.7.10. VII.4.5

Corbio *see* Hortensius Corbio

Corinthus: III.4.2. VI.9.ext.6

Coriolanus *see* Marcius Coriolanus

Corioli (Volscian town): IV.3.4

Cornelia familia: V.2.ext.4. -ia gens: II.10.4. V.3.2f. V.10.2. VI.2.3. VIII.14.1. VIII.15.1

Cornelia (mother of the Gracchi): IV.2.3. IV.4.praef. IV.6.1. VI.7.1

Cornelia (mother of Q. Pompeius Rufus): IV.2.7

Cornelii: V.3.2f

Cornelius, C.: (chief centurion): VI.1.10

Cornelius, C. (tr. pl. 67): VIII.5.4

Cornelius Balbus, (L.) (cos. suff. 40): VII.8.7

Cornelius Cethegus, M. (flamen): I.1.4

Cornelius Cethegus, P. *see* Cornelius Lentulus, P.

(Cornelius) Cethegus (lieutenant of Sulla): IX.2.1

(Cornelius) Cinna, L. (IV cos. 84): I.6.10. II.8.7. IV.3.14b. V.6.4. VI.9.6
    Cinnanus exercitus: IV.7.5. -ni mucrones: VIII.9.2. -na proscriptio: V.3.3

Cornelius Cinna, (L.) (pr. 44): IX.9.1

Cornelius Cossus, (A.) (cos. 428): III.2.4

(Cornelius) Dolabella, Cn. (cos. 81): VIII.9.3

(Cornelius) Dolabella, P. (governor of Asia, 68?): VIII.1.ambust.2

Cornelius Gallus (ex-praetor): IX.12.8

(Cornelii) Lentuli, tres: IV.2.5

(Cornelius) Lentulus (Crus), L. (cos. 49): I.8.9. IV.2.5

(Cornelius) Lentulus Cruscellio, (L.) (pr. 44?): VI.7.3

Cornelius Lentulus, P. (really Cethegus, cos. 181): I.1.12. II.5.1

(Cornelius) Lentulus, P. (cos. suff. 162): V.3.2f

(Cornelius) Lentulus (Lupus), L. (cos. 156): VI.9.10

(Cornelius) Lentulus Marcellinus, Cn. (cos. 56): VI.2.6. *See also* (Cornelii) Lentuli, tres

(Cornelius Lentulus Niger, L.) (flamen Martialis) *see* (Cornelii) Lentuli, tres

(Cornelius) Lentulus Spinther, P. (cos. 57): II.4.6. VII.8.8. IX.14.4

(Cornelius Lentulus Sura, P.) (cos. 71): IX.14.ext.3

Cornelius Mammula, (A.) (governor of Sardinia 216): VII.6.1c

Cornelius Merula, L. (cos. suff. 87): IX.12.5

INDEX

Cornelius Rufinus (P.), (II cos. 277): II.9.4

(Cornelii) Scipiones: II.1.10. III.7.3. IV.4.11. VIII.15.4

(Cornelii) Scipiones, P. et Cn. (i.e. P. Scipio and Cn. Scipio Calvus): I.6.2. II.7.15a. III.7.1a. VI.6.ext.1. VIII.15.11. IX.11.ext.(1),4

(Cornelii) Scipiones (i.e. Africanus and Asiaticus): IV.1.8. (IX.11.ext.1)

(Cornelii) Scipiones (i.e. the two Africani): V.6.ext.4

(Cornelius) Scipio, Cn. (alleged son of Africanus maior): II.10.2a. III.5.1a,b. IV.5.3

Cornelius (Scipio), L. (cos. 259): V.1.2

(Cornelius Scipio, P.) (cos. 218): (V.4.2). See also Cornelii Scipiones

Cornelius Scipio, P. (really L.; quaest. 167): V.1.1e

(Cornelius) Scipio Africanus (maior), P. (II cos. 194): I.1.21. I.2.2 (Paris, Nepot.), II.7.12. II.8.5. II.10.2a,b. II.10.3. III.5.1a,b. III.6.1. III.7.1a,b,c,d,(e),f,g. (III.7.2). III.8.2. IV.1.6a,(b). IV.1.8. IV.2.3. IV.3.1,(2). IV.5.1,3. (IV.7.2. V.1.7: Africanus maior confused with minor). V.2.5. V.2.ext.4. V.3.2b, (c,d). V.4.2. V.5.1. V.6.7. (VI.2.3). VI.3.1d. VI.6.4. VI.7.1. VI.9.2. VI.9.ext.7. VII.2.2.

VII.3.3. (VIII.1.damn.1.) VIII.14.1. VIII.15.1. IX.2.1. IX.8.1. IX.11.ext.1. See also Cornelii Scipiones, Africani. Cf. II.4.3

Cornelius Scipio Aemilianus Africanus, P. (Africanus minor) (II cos. 134): II.4.3 (in error for Africanus maior). II.7.1,13. II.10.4. III.2.6a,b. III.2.ext.8. III.7.2. III.8.6. IV.1.10a,b,12. IV.3.13. (IV.7.7) V.1.6 (cf. 7). V.2.ext.4. V.3.2d. (V.10.2). VI.2.3. VI.4.2a,(b). VII.5.1. VII.6.ext.2. VIII.1.absol.11. VIII.8.1. VIII.15.1,2,4,7. See also Cornelii Scipiones

(Cornelius) Scipio Asiaticus (Asiagenus), L. (cos. 190): III.5.1a. III.6.2. III.7.1e. IV.1.8. IV.1.ext.9. (V.3.2c). V.5.1. VIII.1.damn.1,2

Cornelius Scipio Asina, Cn. (II cos. 254): VI.6.2. VI.9.11

(Cornelius) Scipio (Calvus), Cn. (cos. 222): IV.4.10. See also Cornelii Scipiones

(Cornelius Scipio) Hispalus, (Cn.) (cos. 176): VI.3.3b

Cornelius Scipio (Hispanus) Hispali filius, Cn. (pr. 139): I.3.3 (Paris, Nepot.). VI.3.3b.

(Cornelius) Scipio Nasica, P. (cos. 191): VIII.15.3. Cf. VII.5.2

(Cornelius) Scipio Nasica (Corculum), P. (II cos. 155): I.1.3. II.4.2. Cf. VII.5.2

423

Cornelius Scipio Nasica
Serapio, (P.) (cos. 138): I.4.2
(Paris, Nepot.). II.8.7.
III.2.17. III.7.3. V.3.2e.
IX.14.3. Cf. VII.5.2
(Cornelius) Scipio Nasica
Serapio, P. (cos. 111): I.8.11.
Cf. VII.5.2
(Cornelius Sulla), Faustus (son
of the following): III.1.3
(Cornelius) Sulla Felix, L.: I.2.3
(Paris, Nepot.). I.5.5. I.6.4.
II.8.7. II.10.6. III.1.2b.
III.6.3. III.8.5. V.2.9. V.3.5.
V.6.4. VI.4.4. VI.5.7. VI.9.6.
VII.5.5. VII.6.4. VIII.6.2.
VIII.14.4. IX.2.1. IX.3.8.
IX.7.mil.Rom.1,2. IX.15.5.
Cognomen Felix: VI.4.4.
VI.9.6. IX.2.1.
Sullana crudelitas: VI.8.2.
-na proscriptio: VII.3.6. -na
Victoria: VI.4.4. -na violentia:
IX.15.5
Cornutus see Caecilius
Cornutus
Corsica: I.1.3. IX.12.3. Corsi:
VI.3.3a
Corvinus (cognomen):
VIII.15.5. See also Valerius
(Maximus) Corvinus
Cosconius, C. (leg. 89?):
VIII.1.absol.8
Cotta see Aurelius Cotta
Cotys (king of Thrace):
III.7.ext.7
Crannon (in Thessaly): I.8.
ext.7
Crassus see Licinius Crassus

Cremera (river near Rome):
9.11.ext.4
Creta: I.8.ext.18. VIII.7.ext.2
Cretenses: I.2.ext.1 (Paris).
VII.6.ext.1. IX.3.7. Cretes:
VII.2. ext.18
Crispinus see Quinctius
Crispinus
Crispus see Manilius Crispus
Critias (leader of Athenian
Thirty Tyrants): III.2.ext.6
Croesus (king of Lydia):
I.7.ext.4. V.4.ext.6
Croton (in south Italy):
I.8.ext.18
Crotoniatae: VIII.15.ext.1.
Crotoniates, Milo: IX.12.ext.9
Cruscellio see Cornelius
Lentulus Cruscellio
Ctesias (historian, 5th-4th cen-
tury): VIII.13.ext.5
Ctesiphon: VIII.10.ext.1
Culleo see Terentius Culleo
(Cumae) (on the coast near Na-
ples). Cumanus, C. Blossius:
IV.7.1
Curetes (mythical dancers):
II.4.4
Curiatius, -tii: VI.3.6
Curiatius, C. (tr. pl. 138): III.7.3
Curiones see (Scribonii)
Curiones
Curius (Dentatus), M'. (III cos.
274): IV.3.5a,7. IV.4.11.
VI.3.4
Cursor see Papirius Cursor
Curtius, (M.): V.6.2
Cyclades (Aegean islands):
IV.3.2

INDEX

Cydnus (river in Cilicia): III.8.ext.6

(Cyme) (on the west coast of Asia Minor). Cymaei: IX.14.ext.2

Cynegirus (hero of Marathon): III.2.22

Cypros: I.5.6. IV.3.2. V.3.ext.3b. VIII.15.10
    Cyprii: III.3.ext.4. IX.1.ext.7. IX.4.ext.1. Cypriaca expeditio (of Cato): IV.3.2. -ca pecunia: IV.1.14

Cyrenae: V.6.ext.4
    Cyrenenses: V.6.ext.4. Cyrenaeus, Theodorus: VI.2.ext.3. Cyrenaicus philosophus (Hegesias): VIII.9.ext.3

Cyrus (king of Persia): I.7.ext.5. V.4.ext.6. VIII.7.ext.16. IX.10.ext.1

Damasippus *see* (Iunius Brutus) Damasippus

Damastes (5th-4th century writer): VIII.13.ext.6

Damo(n) (Pythagorean, friend of Phintias): IV.7.ext.1

Dando(n): (VIII.13.ext.7)

Daphnites (3rd-century (?) sophist): I.8.ext.8

Dareus (Darius) (I, king of Persia): III.2.ext.2 (error for Gobryas). V.2.ext.1. V.4.ext.5,6. VI.9.ext.5. VII.3.ext.2. IX.2.ext.6

Dareus (III): III.3.ext.1. III.8.ext.6. IV.3.ext.4a.

IV.7.ext.2a. V.1.ext.1a. VI.4.ext.3. His mother: IV.7.ext.2a

Dareus (error for Artaxerxes (II)): VI.3.ext.2

Dasius (of Salapia): III.8.ext.1

Decianus *see* (Appuleius) Decianus

Decii: V.6.6

Decius Mus, P. (cos. 340): I.7.3. V.6.5. *See also* Decii

Decius (Mus), P. (IV cos. 295, son of the foregoing): II.2.9b. (V.6.6)

Deiotarus (king of Galatia): I.4.ext.2

Delos (Aegean island): I.1.ext.b (Paris, Nepot.)

Delphi: I.1.ext.4 (Paris), 9 (Paris, Nepot.). I.2.3 (Paris, Nepot.). I.8.ext.8. VII.3.2
    Delphica cortina: I.8.10. -ca mensa: IV.1.ext.7. -cum oraculum: I.6.3. (I.8.ext.9). *See also* Apollo

Demades (4th-century Athenian politician): VII.2.ext.13

(Demaratus) (father of Tarquinius Priscus): III.4.2

Demochares (son of Demostratus): III.8.ext.4

Democritus (5th-century philosopher): VIII.7.ext.4. VIII.14.ext.2. His father: VIII.7.ext.4

Demosthenes (orator): III.4.ext.2. VII.3.ext.5. VIII.7.ext.1. VIII.10.ext.1

Demostratus: III.8.ext.4

INDEX

Dentatus *see* Siccius Dentatus

Dialis, flamen: IX.12.5

Diana (of the Aventine): VII.3.1. (of Ephesus): VIII.14.ext.5

Dinocrates (Alexander's architect): I.4.ext.1 (Paris)

Dio (of Syracuse): III.8.ext.5. IV.1.ext.3

Dio *see* Asinius Dio

Diogenes (Cynic): IV.3.ext.4a,b

Diogyris (father of Zisemis): IX.2.ext.4

Diomedon (one of the ten generals condemned to death by the Athenians): I.1.ext.8 (Paris; cf. Nepot.)

Dionysius (I, despot of Syracuse): I.1.ext.3. I.7.ext.6,7. IV.3.ext.4b? IV.7.ext.1? VI.2.ext.2. (VI.9.ext.6). IX.13.ext.4

Dionysius (II): (I.1.ext.3). IV.1.ext.3. IV.3.ext.4b? IV.7.ext.1? VI.9.ext.6

Diphilus (actor): VI.2.9

Dis, Dis pater: II.4.5. IV.7.4

Dives *see* Licinius Crassus Dives

Dodona (in Epirus, site of Zeus' oracle): VIII.15.ext.3

Dolabella *see* Cornelius Dolabella

Domitius (Ahenobarbus), Cn. (cos. 192): I.6.5

Domitius (Ahenobarbus), Cn. (cos. 122): II.9.9. IX.6.3

Domitius (Ahenobarbus), Cn. (cos. 96): VI.5.5. IX.1.4

Domitius Ahenobarbus, Cn. (proscribed): VI.2.8

Domitius (Ahenobarbus), L. (cos. 94): VI.3.5

Domitius, Calvinus, (Cn.). (II cos. 40): VIII.11.2

Doris (wife of Dionysius I): IX.13.ext.4

Dotata *see* Megullia

Drusus *see* Claudius Drusus, Livius Drusus

Drypetine (daughter of Mithridates VI): I.8.ext.13

Duilius, C. (cos. 260): III.6.4. VII.3.ext.7

Duronius, M. (tr. pl. by 97): II.9.5

Dyrrachium (on the Adriatic, Durazzo): I.6.12

Echecles: I.8.ext.4

Echecrates (Pythagorean): VIII.7.ext.3

Egeria (Numa's nymph): I.2.1 (Paris, Nepot.)

Egnatius Mecennius: VI.3.9

Egypt *see* Aegyptus

Elaea (in western Asia Minor): III.2.12

(Elea) (in Lucania, = Velia). Eleates, Zeno: III.3.ext.2

Ennius, (Q.) (poet): VIII.14.1

Epaminondas (4th-century Theban leader): III.2.ext.5. III.7.ext.5

(Ephesus) (on western coast of Asia Minor). Ephesii: VIII.14.ext.5. Ephesia, Diana: VIII.14.ext.5

Ephialtes: III.8.ext.4

Epicurus (philosopher): I.8.ext.17. IV.3.6b

(Epidamnus) (on the east coast of the Adriatic). Epidamnii: I.5.ext.2

Epidaurus (on the east coast of the Peloponnese, with temple of Aesculapius): I.1.ext.3. I.8.2

(Epidius) Marullus, (C.): V.7.2

Epii (people of Aetolia): VIII.13.ext.6

Epimenides (Cretan wonder-worker): VIII.13.ext.5

Epirus: IV.3.2. V.1.ext.4
     Epirota, Gorgias: I.8.ext.5.
     -rotica arma: IV.3.14a

Equitius, L. (false Gracchus): III.2.18. III.8.6. IX.7.1,(2). IX.15.1

Equi (crag): I.8.ext.8

Er (in Plato's *Republic*): I.8.ext.1

Erasistratus (3rd-century medical man): 5.7.ext.1

Eretum (Sabine village): II.4.5

(Erythrae) (in Ionia). Erythraeum litus: 6.1.ext.1

Etereius *see* Hetereius

Etpastus (Spanish tyrant): V.4.ext.3

Etruria: I.1.1b. II.4.4. III.4.2. IV.5.ext.1. IX.1.ext.2.
     Etrusci: I.8.5. III.2.1.
     III.3.1. V.5.2. IX.2.ext.10.
     Etrusca disciplina: I.1.1a. *See also* Tusci

Euboea, Coela, and Euboeae Coela: I.8.10

Eucles (Olympic victor): VIII.15.ext.4

Euclides (geometer): VIII.12.ext.1

Eumenes (II, king of Pergamus 197-159): II.2.1b. *See* Attalus (I)

Euphranor (4th-century painter): VIII.11.ext.5

Euporus (slave of C. Gracchus): VI.8.3

Euripides (dramatist): III.4.ext.2. III.7.ext.1a. IX.12.ext.4

Europa: VI.9.ext.2. VIII.1.damn.1

Evander (of Arcadia): II.2.9a

Fabia gens: I.1.11. III.5.2. IV.1.5. V.10.2. (IX.11.ext.4)

Fabii (Gurges and Pictor): IV.3.10

Fabius, Q. (i.e. Q. Fabius Maximus Eburnus?): II.7.3,(5)

Fabius, Q. (ex-aedile): VI.6.5

(Fabius) Adrianus (pr. 84): IX.10.2

Fabius (Ambustus, M.) (III cos. 354): II.7.8

Fabius Dorsuo, C.: I.1.11

Fabius Labeo, Q. (cos. 183): VII.3.4a,(b)

(Fabius Maximus, Q.) (cos. 213, son of Cunctator): II.2.4b. (IV.8.1). *See also* Fabius Maximus Gurges

Fabius Maximus, Q. (son of Allobrogicus): III.5.2

(Fabius Maximus Aemilianus, Q.) (cos. 145): VIII.15.4

Fabius Maximus Allobrogicus, Q. (cos. 121): III.5.2. VI.9.4. VII.5.1. VIII.15.4. IX.6.3

Fabius Maximus (Eburnus), Q. (cos. 116): II.7.3? VI.1.5. His son: VI.1.5

Fabius (Maximus) Gurges, Q. (III cos. 265): (II.2.4a),b (in error for Cunctator's son). IV.1.5. IV.3.9. V.7.1

Fabius Maximus Rullianus (V cos. 295): II.2.4a,b (in error for Cunctator), 9a,(b). II.7.8. III.2.9. V.7.1. VIII.1.absol.9

Fabius Maximus Servilianus, Q. (cos. 142): II.2.1a. II.7.11. (V.10.2). VI.1.5

Fabius Maximus (Verrucosus), Q. (Cunctator, V cos. 209): I.1.5. II.1.10 (Fabii). II.2.4b,5. III.8.2. IV.1.5. IV.8.1,2. V.2.3,4. VII.3.7. VII.3.ext.8. VIII.13.3. IX.3.1. Fabianae rei familiaris angustiae: IV.8.2

Fabius (Pictor), C. (cos. 269): VIII.14.6

Fabius Pictor, N. (cos. 266): IV.3.9. See also Fabius Maximus Gurges and Fabii

Fabius (Vibulanus), K. (III cos. 479): IX.3.5

Fabius (Vibulanus), M. (II cos. 480): V.5.2

Fabius (Vibulanus), Q. (II cos. 482): V.5.2

Fabricius Luscinus, C. (II cos. 278): I.8.6. II.1.10 (Fabricii). II.9.4. IV.3.6a,b,7. IV.4.3,10,11 (Fabricii). VI.5.1d

Facula see Cluvia Facula

Falerii (in Etruria): VI.5.1a Falisci: VI.5.1a,b

Fannia (of Minturnae): I.5.5. VIII.2.3

Fannius, A.: VIII.4.1

Fannius Saturninus (seducer): VI.1.3

(Faustulus (foster father of Romulus): II.2.9a)

Faustus see Cornelius Sulla, Faustus

Favonius, (M.) (pr. 49): II.10.8. VI.2.7

Febris (Fever): II.5.6

Felix see Cornelius Sulla Felix

Feretrius see Iuppiter

Fescenninus (triumvir capitalis): 6.1.10

Fidenae (near Rome): VII.4.1 Fidenates: III.2.4. VII.4.1

Fides (deity): VI.6.praef. VI.6.5. VI.6.ext.1. Fides publica: III.2.17

Figulus see Marcius Figulus

Fimbria see Flavius Fimbria

Firmum Picenum (Fermo): IX.15.1

Flaccus see Fulvius Flaccus, Munatius Flaccus, Valerius Flaccus

Flamininus *see* Quinctius
Flamininus

Flaminius, circus *see* Circus

Flaminius, C. (II cos. 217):
I.1.5. I.6.6,7. V.4.5

Flaminius, L. (error for C.)
(cos. 187): VI.6.3

Flavius (of Lucania): I.6.8

Flavius, C (Roman knight):
VIII.4.2

Flavius, Cn. (aed. cur. 304):
II.5.2. IX.3.3

Flavius, M. (tr. pl. 323): IX.10.1

Flavius, Q. (error for M.):
VIII.1.absol.7

Flavius Fimbria, C. (cos. 104):
VII.2.4 (false praenomen L.).
VIII.5.2

(Flavius) Fimbria, C. (leg.
87-85): IX.11.2

Florales, ludi: II.10.8

(Formiae) (on the coast of
Latium). Formianus, Helvius
Mancia: VI.2.8

Fortuna: I.8.9.11. III.2.12.
IV.5.3. IV.8.ext.2. VI.9.14.
Fortuna Equestris: I.1.20. -na
Muliebris: I.8.4. V.2.1a. -na
Praenestina: I.3.2 (Paris,
Nepot.)

Forum Boarium: I.6.5. II.4.7

Forum Romanum: (II.5.4).
V.6.2. VI.9.13. (IX.1.6)

(Fregellae) (ancient Volscian
town, destroyed in 125).
Fregellani: II.8.4

Fufetius, Mettius (Alban
leader): VII.4.1

Fulvia (wife of Clodius): IX.1.8
Fulviana stola: III.5.3

Fulvius, A. (senator) and son:
V.8.5

Fulvius Flaccus, Cn.: II.8.3

Fulvius (Flaccus, Cn.) (tr. mil.
180?): II.7.5

Fulvius Flaccus, M. (cos. 264):
II.4.7

Fulvius Flaccus (error for
Nobilior), M.: IV.2.1

Fulvius Flaccus, M. (cos. 125):
VI.3.1c. IX.5.1
Flacciana area: VI.3.1c

Fulvius Flaccus, Q. (IV cos.
209): II.3.3. II.8.4. III.2.ext.1.
III.8.1. V.2.1b. VIII.15.12

Fulvius Flaccus, Q. (cos. 179):
I.1.20. II.7.5. His sons:
I.1.20

Fulvius (Flaccus or Nobilior),
Q.: V.9.3

Fulvius Flaccus, (Ser.?):
VIII.4.3

Fulvius Nobilior, M. *see* Fulvius
Flaccus, M.

Furius, (N.?) (expert on real estate law): VIII.12.1

Furius (killer of D. Burtus):
IV.7.6. IX.13.3

Furius, P. (tr. pl. 99):
VIII.1.damn.2

Furius Bibaculus, L. (pr. before
219): I.1.9

Furius Brocchus, Cn.: VI.1.13

Furius Camillus, (M.) (dictator
367): I.5.2. I.8.3. II.1.10
(Camilli). II.9.1. IV.1.2,3.

V.3.2a. V.6.8. VI.5.1a.
VII.3.ext.9.
Furius Flaccus, M. (tr. pl. 270):
II.7.15f.
Furius Philus, L. (really P.) (cos.
233): II.9.8
Furius Philus, P. (really L.) (cos.
136): III.7.5

Gabii (ancient Latin town):
VII.4.2
    Gabinus ritus: I.1.11
Gabinius, A. (cos. 58): IV.2.4.
VIII.1.absol.3. IX.1.ext.6.
    Gabiniani milites: IV.1.15
(Gabinius) Sisenna, (A.)
    (adopted son of the forego-
    ing): VIII.1.absol.3
(Gades) (modern Cadiz),
    Gaditanus, Arganthonius:
    VIII.13.ext.4
Galba see Sulpicius Galba
Gallia (Cisalpina): I.1.3. I.6.5.
III.7.6. (Transalpina): II.6.8.
    Galliae: III.7.ext.6
        Gallus: III.2.7. VIII.15.5.
    Galli: I.1.10,11,ext.9. I.5.1.
    II.6.10,11. III.2.5,7. III.7.4.
    IV.1.2. V.6.8. VI.3.1a. VII.4.3.
    IX.11.ext.4. Gallicus ager:
    V.4.5. -ca peregrinatio:
    III.7.6. -ca praeda: VIII.14.5.
    -ca victoria: IV.1.2. VI.9.4
Gallius, C.: VI.1.13
Gallius, (Q.) (pr. 65): VIII.10.3
Gallograeci: VI.1.ext.2
Gallus (priest of Cybele):
    VII.7.6
Gallus see Caninius Gallus,

Cornelius Gallus, Oppius
    Gallus
Galus see Sulpicius Galus
Gaurus (eunuch of Mithridates
    VI): IX.2.ext.3
(Gela) (in southern Sicily).
    Gelenses: IV.8.ext.2
Gellius, L. (cos. 72): V.9.1
(Gellius Publicola, L.) (cos. 36):
    V.9.1
Gelo (tyrant of Syracuse):
    I.1.ext.3
Gelo (son of Hiero II):
    III.2.ext.9
Gemellus (tribunician messen-
    ger): IX.1.8
Geminus see Maecius, Geminus
Gemoniae scalae: VI.3.3a.
    VI.9.13
Gentius (Illyrian king): III.3.2
Genua (Genoa): I.6.7
Genucius (eunuch priest of
    Cybele): VII.7.6
Genucius Cipus: V.6.3
Germania: V.5.3
    Germanica tropaea:
    II.2.3
Germanicus see (Claudius)
    Drusus Germanicus
Geta see Licinius Geta
Gillias (rich man of
    Agrigentum): IV.8.ext.2
Glabrio see Acilius Glabrio
Glaucia see (Servilius) Glaucia
(Gobryas): III.2.ext.2. See also
    Dareus (I)
Gorgias (of Leontini, sophist):
    VIII.13.ext.2. VIII.15.ext.2
Gorgias (of Epirus): I.8.ext.5

Gracchus *see* Sempronius
    Gracchus
Graecia: I.1.ext.3. I.6.ext.1a.
    II.2.2,5. II.6.8. II.8.7.
    III.2.22. III.2.ext.5. IV.3.2.
    IV.6.ext.3. IV.7.4. IV.8.5.
    V.2.6. V.3.ext.3d,e,g. V.6.ext.3.
    VI.1.ext.1. VI.5.ext.2.
    VII.2.ext.10. VIII.7.ext.2.
    VIII.15.ext.2. IX.1.5. IX.4.1.
    IX.5.ext.2. IX.10.ext.2. maior
    Graecia: VIII.7.ext.2
        Graeci: II.2.2. III.1.ext.1.
    Graecae actiones: II.2.3. -ca
    doctrina: VI.4.ext.2. -ca
    femina: VI.1.ext.1. -ca indu-
    stria: VIII.7.ext.1. -ci, libri:
    1.1.12. VIII.7.2. -ca lingua:
    VIII.7.6. -cae litterae:
    VIII.7.1. -cus, mos: 1.1.1b.
    -ca pronuntiatio: VII.4.praef.
    -cus sermo: V.1.8. -cus versus:
    I.5.7. I.7.ext.2.ʳ Graece:
    VIII.7.ext.2. Graius sanguis:
    I.7.ext.7. VI.9.ext.2
Granius (magistrate of Puteoli):
    IX.3.8
Gratidius (legate): IX.7.mil.
    Rom.1
Gryllus (son of Xenophon):
    V.10.ext.2
Gurges *see* Fabius Maximus
    Gurges
Gyges (king of Lydia): VII.1.2
Gytheum (port in Laconia):
    VI.5.ext.2

Hadriaticum, mare: IX.8.2
Hamilcar (son of Gisgo,

Carthaginian general):
    I.7.ext.8
Hamilcar (Barca, father of
    Hannibal): VI.6.2. IX.3.
    ext.2
Hammon, Fountain of:
    VIII.15.ext.3. Iuppiter
    Hammon: IX.5.ext.1
Hannibal (son of Gisgo):
    VII.3.ext.7
Hannibal (Barca): I.6.6,9.
    I.7.ext.1. II.7.15e. II.9.8.
    III.2.11,20. III.7.1d,10b.
    III.7.ext.6. III.8.1,2.
    III.8.ext.1. IV.1.6b,7. IV.8.1.
    V.1.ext.5,6. V.2.4. V.3.ext.1.
    V.4.2. V.6.7. VI.6.ext.1,2.
    VII.2.3,6a,ext.16. VII.3.ext.8.
    VII.4.4. VII.4.ext.2. VII.6.2.
    VIII.15.11. IX.1.4. IX.1.ext.1.
    IX.2.1. IX.2.ext.2. IX.3.ext.3.
    IX.5.ext.3. IX.6.ext.2.
    IX.8.ext.1
Hanno (Carthaginian com-
    mander): V.1.2
Hanno ('the Great'): VI.6.2.
    VII.2.ext.16.
(Harma *see* Quadriga)
Harmodius and Aristogiton
    (Athenian tyrannicides):
    II.10.ext.1
Harmonia (daughter of 'king'
    Gelo of Syracuse): III.2.
    ext.9
Hasdrubal (son of Hanno,
    Carthaginian commander in
    First Punic War): I.1.14
Hasdrubal (son-in-law of
    Hamilcar Barca): III.3.ext.7

Hasdrubal (son of Gisgo): VI.9.ext.7. Cf. VIII.15.11

Hasdrubal (son of Hamilcar Barca): III.7.4. IV.1.9. VII.4.4. IX.3.1

Hasdrubal (Carthaginian commander spared by Scipio Aemilianus): III.2.ext.8

Haterius Rufus (Roman knight): I.7.8

Hegesias (Cyrenaic philosopher, 4th-3rd century): VIII.9.ext.3

Helena (of Troy, painted by Zeuxis): III.7.ext.3

Helenus (son of Pyrrhus): V.1.ext.4

(Helicon) (mountain of the Muses). Heliconii colles: I.6.ext.3

Hellanicus (5th-century historian): VIII.13.ext.6.

Helvius Cinna, C. (tr. pl. 44): IX.9.1

Helvius Mancia: VI.2.8

Henna (Enna, in central Sicily): I.1.1c. IX.12.ext.1

Hephaestio(n) (alter ego of Alexander): IV.7.ext.2a,b

Heptachordus see Valerius (Flaccus?) Heptachordus

Heraclides (of Syracuse, false friend of Dio): III.8.ext.5

Hercules: I.1.17. Herculis liberi (= Heraclidae): V.3.ext.3a

Herculis portus (in Liguria): I.6.7

Herennius see Pontius, Herennius

Herennius Siculus (friend and haruspex of C. Gracchus): IX.12.6

Hermocles (friend of Philip II's assassin Pausanias): VIII.14.ext.4

Herodotus (historian): VIII.13.ext.5

Herophilus (pretended son of the younger Marius): IX.15.1

(Herostratus) (arsonist of Diana's temple at Ephesus): VIII.14.ext.5

Hetereius, T. (Roman knight): IX.12.8

Hiero (II, king of Syracuse): IV.8.ext.1. VIII.13.ext.1

Hieronymus (successor to the foregoing): III.3.ext.5

(Himera) (on the north coast of Sicily). Himeraei: I.7.ext.6

Hippo: VI.1.ext.1

Hippoclides (Epicurean philosopher): I.8.ext.17,(18)

Hirtius, A. (cos. 43): V.2.10

Hispania: I.6.2,7. II.7.1,15a. II.8.5. II.10.4. III.2.6b,13,21. III.7.1a,b,5,10b. IV.3.1,2,11. IV.4.10. V.1.5. V.2.ext.4. V.4.ext.3. VI.3.3b. VI.4.2b. VI.4.ext.1. VI.6.ext.1. VII.4.5. VIII.1.absol.2. VIII.7.1. VIII.15.4.8. IX.1.5. IX.2.4. IX.3.7 (utraque). IX.3.ext.3. IX.4.2. IX.8.1. IX.11.ext.4. IX.15.1. Hispaniae: II.8.5. III.7.ext.6

Hispanus, exercitus: I.2.5 (Nepot.). -num sagulum: V.1.7

Homer: III.7.ext.3,4. VIII.8.ext.2. IX.12.ext.3
   Homericum, illud: I.5.7.
   -cum praeconium: VIII.14.1

Honos (temple and statue): I.1.8

Hoplomachus see Licinius Hoplomachus

Horatius, M.: VI.3.6. VIII.1.absol.1

Horatius Cocles: III.2.1. IV.7.2

Horatius Pulvillus, (M.) (cos. suff. 509): V.10.1

Hortalus see Hortensius Hortalus

Hortensia (daughter of the orator): VIII.3.3

Hortensius, L. (tr. pl. 422): 6.5.2

Hortensius Corbio, (Q.) (grandson or great-grandson of the following): III.5.4

Hortensius (Hortalus), Q. (cos. 69, orator): III.5.4. V.9.2. VIII.3.3. VIII.5.4. VIII.10.2. IX 4.1
   Hortensiana eloquentia: VIII.3.3

(Hortensius Hortalus, Q.) (son of the foregoing): V.9.2

Hostilia curia: IX.5.2

Hostilius, Tullus (third king of Rome): III.4.1,2. VII.4.1. VIII.1.absol.1. IX.12.1

Hostilius Mancinus, C. (cos. 137): I.6.7. II.7.1

Hybreas (of Mylasa, 1st-century orator): IX.14.ext.2

Hybrida (cognomen of Q. Varius): VIII.6.4

(Hymettus) (hill in Attica, famous for honey and marble). Hymettius, mons: I.6.ext.3. -tiae, columnae: I.1.4

Hypsaeus see Plautius Hypsaeus

Hypsicratea (wife of Mithridates): IV.6.ext.2

Ianiculum (Roman hill beyond Tiber): I.1.10,12

Iason (leader of the Argonauts): IV.6.ext.3

Iason (of Pherae): I.8.ext.6. IX.10.ext.2

Idaea Mater see Mater deum

Illyricum: I.1.20
   Illyricum, bellum: I.5.ext.2. -cus tractus: VIII.13.ext.7

(India). Indi: II.6.14. III.3.ext.6. VIII.13.ext.5. Indus, Callanus: I.8.ext.10. Indicus rogus: II.6.14. -cus triumphus: III.6.6

Indibilis (Spanish chieftain): IV.3.1

Intercatia (Spanish town): III.2.6b

Iones: II.6.1

Iopho(n) (son of Sophocles): VIII.7.ext.12

Ios (Aegean island): IX.12.ext.3

Iphigenia (daughter of Agamemnon): VIII.11.ext.6

Isauricus see Servilius (Vatia) Isauricus

Isis: I.3.4 (Paris). Isiacus: VII.3.8

INDEX

Isocrates (4th-century Athenian publicist): VIII.7.ext.9. VIII.13.ext.2

Isthmicum spectaculum (Isthmian games): IV.8.5

Italia: I.3.3 (Paris, Nepot.). I.6.9. I.7.ext.1,6. II.5.1. II.7.7,15c. II.8.praef. II.9.8. III.7.ext.6. III.8.1,5. IV.2.1. IV.3.5b. V.6.7. VI.2.3. VI.4.1a. VII.2.3. VII.3.ext.8. VII.4.4. VII.6.1a. VIII.7.ext.2,3. VIII.14.1. IX.2.1. IX.6.ext.2. IX.8.ext.1. IX.15.1
    Italicum bellum: V.4.ext.7. VI.3.3c. -cus sanguis: VI.2.1. -ca severitas: II.4.4

Iudaei: I.3.3 (Paris, Nepot.)

Iugurtha (Numidian king): II.7.2. VI.9.6,14. VII.5.2. VIII.14.4
    Iugurthinum bellum: II.7.2. -nus triumphus: III.6.6

Iulia gens: V.5.3

Iulia (mother of Sulpicia): VI.7.3

Iulia (daughter of Caesar and wife of Pompey): IV.6.4. (V.1.10)

Iulia (i.e. Livia Augusta): (IV.3.3. V.5.3). VI.1.praef.

Iulis (in Ceos): II.6.8

Iulius Caesar, C. (dictator): I.5.6. I.6.12. I.8.10. II.10.7. III.2.15. III.2.22,23b. III.8.7. IV.5.5,6. IV.6.4. V.1.10. V.7.2. VI.2.11. (VI.4.5). VI.9.15. (VII.6.6). VIII.3.2. VIII.11.2. IX.2.4. IX.8.2. IX.9.1.

IX.11.4. IX.15.1. Divus Iulius: I.6.13. I.7.2. I.8.8. III.2.19, 23a. VI.8.4. VII.6.5. VIII.9.3
    Caesariana aequitas: IX.15.5? -ni milites: III.2.13. *See also* Caesares

Iulius Caesar, L. (cos. 90): see the following and cf. IX.2.2

Iulius Caesar (Strabo Vopiscus), C. (aed. cur. 90): III.7.11. V.3.3. IX.2.2

(Iunii) Bruti (M. and P.) (tr. pl. 195): IX.1.3

(Iunius) Brutus, L. (first consul): IV.4.1. V.6.1. V.8.1. VII.3.2

(Iunius) Brutus, M. (tr. pl. 83): VI.2.8

(Iunius) Brutus, M. (Q. Servilius Caepio Brutus, Caesar's killer): I.4.7 (Paris, Nepot.). I.5.7. I.7.1. III.2.15. IV.6.5. IV.7.4. V.1.11. VI.4.5. VII.3.8. IX.9.2

(Iunius) Brutus (Albinus), D. (cos. desig. for 42): IV.7.6. IX.13.3
    Brutiana ultio: IV.7.6

(Iunius) Brutus (Callaicus), D. (cos. 138): VI.4.ext.1. VIII.14.2

(Iunius Brutus) Damasippus, (L.) (pr. 82): IX.2.3

(Iunius) Brutus Pera, (D.): II.4.7

Iunius Bubulcus (Brutus), C. (III cos. 311): II.9.2. VIII.14.6

(Iunii Perae), D. (cos. 266) and M.: II.4.7

Iunius Pera, M. (cos. 230): VII.6.1b

Iunius (Pullus), L. (cos. 249): I.4.4 (Paris)

Iunius Silanus (Manlianus), D. (pr. 141): V.8.3

Iuno: I.1.16. I.1.ext.2. II.1.2. V.4.ext.4. Capitolina: VI.1.praef. Lacinia (temple): I.1.20. I.8.ext.18. Moneta: I.8.3. VI.3.1a. regina: V.10.2

Iuppiter: I.2.ext.1 (Paris). I.6.12. I.7.4,5. I.7.ext.1,6. II.1.2. II.5.4. IV.2.3. V.5.3. VII.4.3,4. VIII.11.ext.5. IX.12.5. Capitolinus: I.2.2 (Paris, Nepot.). Feretrius: III.2.3-6a. Olympius: I.1.ext.3. III.7.ext.4. V.10.ext.1. Optimus Maximus: I.praef. I.1.16. III.7.1g. IV.1.6a. IV.7.1. V.10.1,2. VIII.15.1. Sabazius: I.3.3 (Paris). See also Dialis, flamen; Hammon

Iustuleius (Prefect of Pompey at Dyrracchium): III.2.23a

Iuturnae lacus: I.8.1b

(Iuventius?) Laterensis, (M.?) (pr. 51?): VIII.2.2

Iuventius Thalna, M'. (cos. 163): IX.12.3

J. See under I

Κατω βασίλεια: I.5.6
Κολωνός: VIII.7.ext.12
Κρονίων: III.7.ext.4

Labeo see Fabius Labeo

Labienus, T. (tr. pl. 63): VIII.14.5

Lacedaemon: I.6.ext.1b. III.2.ext.5. IV.1.ext.8. IV.6.ext.3. V.3.ext.2. VIII.7.ext.2. See also Sparta
Lacedaemonii: I.2.ext.3 (Paris). II.6.3. II.7.ext.2. III.2.ext.3. IV.5.ext.2. IV.6.ext.3. VI.3.ext.1. VI.4.ext.4. VI.5.ext.2. VII.2.ext.15. See also Spartani.
Lacedaemonia classis: III.8.ext.3. -ius, dux: I.1.14. -ius, Xanthippus: IX.6.ext.1

Lacinia see Iuno

Laelius, C. (cos. 190): V.5.1. VI.9.ext.7

Laelius, (D.) (tr. 54): VIII.1.absol.3

Laelius (Sapiens), C. (cos. 140): IV.7.1,7 (D. for C.). VIII.8.1

Laenas see Popillius Laenas

Laetorius, (P.) (friend of C. Gracchus): IV.7.2

Laetorius Mergus, M. (military tribune): VI.1.11

Laevinus see Valerius Laevinus

Lamia see Aelius Lamia

Lampsacus (on the Hellespont): VII.3.ext.4

Lanarius see Calpurnius Lanarius

Laodice (wife of Antiochus II): IX.10.ext.1. IX.14.ext.1

Laodice (wife of Mithridates): I.8.ext.13

Lares familiares: II.4.5

Larisa (in Thessaly): IV.5.5

Lars *see* Tolumnius, Lars

Laterensis *see* (Iuventius?) Laterensis

Latinius, T.: I.7.4

Latium: II.7.7. III.1.2a Latini: III.1.2a. III.2.20. VI.4.1a. IX.3.4. Latini annales: IX.13.2. -na appellatio: VII.4.praef. -num bellum: I.7.3. II.7.6. V.6.5. -ni libri: I.1.12. -na lingua: VIII.7.ext.1. -nae litterae: I.6.ext.praef. III.4.6. VIII.7.1. -ni transfugae: II.7.12. -nus tumultus: VI.9.1. -na via: I.8.4. -na vox: II.2.2. Latine: II.2.2

(Latmos) (Aegean island). Latmii: VIII.13.ext.7

Laurentum (in Latium): VIII.8.1. Laurentina via: VIII.5.6

Lavinium (in Latium): I.6.7. I.8.7

Leda (mother of Helen): III.7.ext.3

(Lemnos) (Aegean island). Lemnii: IV.6.ext.3

Lentulus *see* Cornelius Lentulus

Leonicus (loyal defender of Mithridates VI): V.2.ext.2

Leonidas (Spartan king): I.6.ext.1b. III.2.ext.3

(Leontini) (in Sicily). Leontinus, Gorgias: VIII.13.ext.2. VIII.15.ext.2

Lepidus *see* Aemilius Lepidus

Leptines (3rd-century astrologer): V.7.ext.1

Λητώ: I.5.7

Letum (mountain in Liguria): I.5.9

Leuctra (in Boeotia): III.2. ext.5

Liber pater: II.1.5b. III.6.6

Libertas: VI.3.1a

Libitina (goddess of funerals, hence undertaking business): V.2.10

Libo *see* Scribonius Libo

Licinia (murderess of her husband): VI.3.8

Licinius Buccio (senator): VIII.3.2

(Licinius) Crassus, L. (cos. 95): III.7.6. IV.5.4. VI.2.2. VI.5.6. VIII.5.3. VIII.8.1. VIII.15.6. IX.1.1,4

(Licinius) Crassus, M. ('triumvir'): I.6.11. VI.9.9. IX.4.1

(Licinius Crassus, P.) (son of the foregoing): I.6.11

Licinius (Crassus Dives), P. (cos. 205): I.1.6. VI.9.3

(Licinius) Crassus Dives, (P.) (pr. 57): VI.9.12 (confused with the foregoing), 13

(Licinius) Crassus (Dives Mucianus), P. (consul 131): II.2.1a. III.2.12. VIII.7.6. Crassiana strages: III.4.5

(Licinius) Geta, C. (cos. 116): II.9.9

Licinius Hoplomachus, C.: VIII.6.1

(Licinii) Luculli (L. and M.):
II.4.6. VIII.5.4

(Licinius) Lucullus, L. (cos.
151): II.10.4. III.2.6b.
V.2.ext.4

(Licinius) Lucullus, L. (cos. 74):
VII 8.5. *See also* Licinii
Luculli

(Licinius) Lucullus, M. (son of
the foregoing): IV.7.4

(Licinius) Lucullus, M. *see*
Terentius Varro Lucullus

Licinius Macer, C. (pr. 68?):
IX.12.7

(Licinius Macer) Calvus, (C.)
(son of the foregoing, orator
and poet): IX.12.7

Licinius Sacerdos, C. (Roman
knight): IV.1.10b

Licinius Stolo, C. (cos. 361?):
II.4.4. VIII.6.3

Liguria: I.5.9. III.7.ext.6
Ligures: II.7.15d. III.7.4

Lilybaeum (at the western end
of Sicily): I.8.ext.14

Liparae (islands off northeast
Sicily): VI.9.11
Liparitani: I.1.ext.4.
Liparitana, obsidio: II.7.4

(Liternum) (on the coast of
Latium). Liternina villa:
II.10.2b

Litorius (of the Epii):
VIII.13.ext.6

Livia (wife of Rutilius):
VIII.13.6

Livia Augusta *see* Iulia

Livius, T. (historian): I.8.
ext.19

Livius (Andronicus, L.) (poet):
II.4.4

Livius Drusus, (C.) (blind jurist): VIII.7.4

(Livius) Drusus, M. (tr. pl. 91):
III.1.2a. IX.5.2

Livius Salinator, (M.) (II cos.
207): II.9.6a,b. III.7.4. IV.1.9.
IV.2.2. VII.2.6a. VII.4.4.
IX.3.1

Livy *see* Livius, T.

Locri (in the toe of Italy):
I.1.20. I.1.ext.3. VIII.7.ext.3
Locrenses: I.1.ext.1.
I.2.ext.4 (Paris). VI.5.ext.3.
Locrensis Doris: IX.13.ext.4

Λογικά (of Chrysippus):
VIII.7.ext.10

Lollius, Cn. (triumvir
nocturnus): VIII.1.damn.5

(Lollius) Palicanus, M. (tr. pl.
71): III.8.3

Longus *see* (Sempronius)
Longus

Longus, vicus (street in Rome):
II.5.6

(Lucania) (region in south
Italy). Lucani I.6.8 (=
Lucania): I.8.6. V.1.ext.6.
VII.4.4. -nus eques: VII.3.7

Lucretia: VI.1.1

Lucretius, Q. (proscribed in
43): VI.7.2

Lucretius Tricipitinus, Sp. (cos.
suff. 509): IV.1.1

Lucretius (Vespillo) (aed. pl.
133): I.4.2 (Nepot.)

Lucrinus lacus (lagoon adjoining the gulf of Baiae): IX.1.1

Lucullus *see* Licinius Lucullus, Terentius Varro Lucullus
Lupercalia (fertility festival on 15 February): II.2.9a
Lupus *see* Pontius, Lupus
Luscinus *see* Fabricius Luscinus
Lusitania (approx. modern Portugal): I.2.5 (Paris). VI.4.ext.1. IX.6.2
    Lusitani: VII.3.6. VIII.1.absol.2. Lusitanae manus: IX.2.4. -na tela: IX.1.5
Lusius, C. (tr. mil., nephew of Marius): VI.1.12
Lutatia gens: IX.2.1
Lutatius (Catulus), C. (cos. 242): II.8.2. Cf. 1.3.2 (Paris, Nepot.)
(Lutatius) Catulus, Q. (cos. 102): V.8.4. VI.3.1c. IX.12.4
(Lutatius) Catulus, Q. (cos. 78): II.4.6. II.8.7. VI.9.5. VIII.15.9
Lutatius Cerco, (Q.) (cos. 241): I.3.2 (Paris, Nepot.). (confused with C. Catulus) VI.5.1b
Lutatius Pinthia, M. (Roman knight): VII.2.4
(Lycia) (region in southwest Asia Minor). Lycii: II.6.13,14
Lyco(n) (officer of Pyrrhus): V.1.ext.3b
Lycurgus (Spartan lawgiver): I.2.ext.3 (Paris). II.6.1. V.3.ext.2. VII.2.ext.15
Lydia (region in western Asia Minor): VII.1.2
    Lydi: II.4.4

Lysias (Athenian orator): VI.4.ext.2
Lysimachus (king of Thrace): VI.2.ext.3. IX.3.ext.1
Lysippus (Alexander's preferred sculptor): VIII.11.ext.2

(Macareus): VIII.11.ext.4
Macedonia: I.7.ext.2. I.8.ext.18. II.10.3. III.3.ext.1. IV.5.1. IV.8.5. V.1.ext.1a. V.8.3. VII.5.4. IX.1.3. IX.12.ext.4
    Macedo: VII.2.ext.11a.
    -dones: I.8.ext.9. III.8.ext.6. V.1.ext.4. V.6.ext.5. V.8.3. VII.2.ext.10. VII.3.ext.1.
    Macedo miles: V.1.ext.1a
    Macedonicum, bellum: I.8.1b. V.1.1d.ʳ -ici mores: VII.2.ext.11a. -icus, mores et cultus: IX.5.ext.1. -icae opes: IV.3.8. -ica (i.e. Philippensis) pugna: I.5.8. -ici triumphi: II.10.3. -ica, victoria: VI.2.3
Macedonicus *see* Caecilius Metellus Macedonicus
Macer *see* Licinius Macer
Maecia (tribe): II.9.6b
Maecius, Geminus (leader of the Tusculans): II.7.6
Maelius, Sp.: V.3.2g. VI.3.1c
Maenius, P.: VI.1.4
Maesia (called Androgyne): VIII.3.1.
Magius Chilo, (P.?): IX.11.4
Magnus *see* Pompeius Magnus
Mago (brother of Hannibal): VII.2.ext.16
Mago ('the Samnite'): I.6.8

Maharbal (lieutenant of Hannibal): IX.5.ext.3

Mallius (Maximus), Cn. (cos. 105): II.3.2

Mamercus *see* Aemilius Lepidus, Mam.

Mamilius, Octavius (leader of the Tusculans): I.8.1a

Mammula *see* Cornelius Mammula

Mancia *see* Helvius Mancia

Mancinus *see* Hostilius Mancinus

Mandane (daughter of Astyages): I.7.ext.5

Manes, di: I.7.3. Cf. V.6.ext.4

Manilius, M'. (cos. 149): V.2.ext.4

Manilius Crispus, (C.) (tr. pl. 66): VI.2.4

Manlius, L.: VI.6.3

Manlius (Capitolinus), M. (cos. 392): VI.3.1a

Manlius (Capitolinus Imperiosus), L. (dictator 363): V.4.3 (the cognomen Torquatus is erroneous). VI.9.1

Manlius Imperiosus Torquatus, (T.) (III cos. 340): I.7.3. II.7.6. III.2.6a. V.4.3. (VI.4.1a). VI.9.1. IX.3.4,5

(Manlius Torquatus) (son of the foregoing): II.7.6. VI.9.1

Manlius Torquatus (II cos. 224): VI.4.1a,b

Manlius Torquatus, T. (cos. 165): V.8.3

Manlius (Vulso), Cn. (cos. 189): VI.1.ext.2

Mantinea (in Arcadia): III.2.ext.5. V.10.ext.2

Marathon (in Attica): V.3.ext.3c,g. VIII.14.ext.1

Marcellinus *see* Cornelius Lentulus Marcellinus

Marcellus *see* Claudius Marcellus

Marcius, Ancus (fourth king of Rome): I.6.1 (in error for Tarquinius Priscus). IV.3.4

(Marcius) Censorinus, L. (cos. 149): (II.2.1a). VI.9.10

Marcius Coriolanus, Cn.: I.8.4. IV.3.4. V.2.1a. V.3.2b. V.4.1

(Marcius) Figulus, C. (II cos. 156): I.1.3. (IX.3.2)

(Marcius) Figulus, C. (son of the foregoing): IX.3.2

(Marcius) Philippus, L. (cos. 91): VI.2.2. VIII.13.4. IX.5.2

(Marcius) Philippus, Q. (II cos. 169): VI.3.7

Marcius Rex, Q. (cos. 118) and son: V.10.3

Marcius Rutilus Censorinus, (C.) (cos. 310): IV.1.3

Marcius (Septimus), L.: I.6.2. II.7.15a. VIII.15.11

Marius, C. (VII cos. 86): I.2.4 (Nepot.). I.5.5. I.7.5. II.2.3. II.3.1. II.8.7. II.10.6. III.1.2b. III.2.18. III.6.6. III.8.5. IV.3.14b. V.2.8,9. V.6.4. VI.1.12. VI.1.ext.3. VI.9.6,14. VII.6.4. VIII.2.3. VIII.6.2. VIII.14.4. VIII.15.7. IX.2.1.2. IX.7.1. IX.7.mil.Rom.1. IX.11.2. IX.12.4. IX.15.1.

Mariana, aedes Iouis: I.7.5.
-na gloria: IX.12.4. -na
monumenta: II.5.6. IV.4.8. -ni
mucrones: VIII.9.2
Marius, C. (cos. 82): VI.8.2.
VII.6.4
Marius, L. (tr. pl. 62): II.8.1
Marius, T. (of Urbinum):
VII.8.6.
Marius (Gratidianus), M. (II pr.
82?): IX.2.1
Mars: I.1.2. I.8.6. II.7.7.
III.7.ext.6. VI.5.1d. VII.2.2.
See also Areos pagos
Martius campus: II.4.5.
VI.9.14. VII.5.praef.
VIII.15.4. -ium certamen:
I.1.2. -ia, legio: III.2.19.
Martialis, flamen: I.1.2
Marullus *see* (Epidius) Marullus
Masinissa (king of Numidia):
I.1.ext.2. II.10.4. V.1.1d.
V.1.7. V.2.ext.4. VII.2.6c.
VIII.13.ext.1. IX.13.ext.2
Mas(s)o *see* Papirius Mas(s)o
(Massilia) (Marseilles).
Massilienses: II.6.7-10.
III.2.22
Mater deum: I.1.1c. I.8.11.
II.4.3. VIII.15.3. Mater,
Idaea: VII.5.2. Mater Magna:
VII.7.6
Mauritania: VII.2.6c
Mausolus (ruler of Caria):
IV.6.ext.1
Maximus *see* Fabius Maximus
Rullianus. Valerius Maximus:
(II.2.9b)
Maximus, circus *see* Circus

Mecennius *see* Egnatius
Mecennius
Medi (Medes): I.7.ext.5
Mediolanum (Milan):
IX.15.ext.1
Megara (on the Isthmus of Cor-
inth): I.7.ext.10. IV.1.ext.3
Megullia (Dotata): IV.4.10
Melissa (tends Carneades):
VIII.7.ext.5
Melita (Malta): I.1.ext.2
Memmia, lex: III.7.9
Memmius, C. (tr. pl. 111):
VIII.5.2
Memmius, C. (beats an adul-
terer): VI.1.13
Memmius, C. (tr. pl. 54):
VIII.1.absol.3
Memphites (son and victim of
Ptolemy Physcon): IX.2.ext.5
Menelaus (in painting):
VIII.11.ext.6
Menenius (Lanatus), Agrippa
(cos. 503): IV.4.2
Menenius Agrippa, L. (husband
of Aebutia): VII.8.2
Menogenes (Pompeius Strabo's
cook): IX.14.2
Menogenes (actor): IX.14.5
Mercurius: II.6.8. IX.3.6
Mergus *see* Laetorius Mergus
Merula *see* Cornelius Merula
Messalla *see* Valerius Messalla
Messana (Messina, in Sicily):
II.7.4
(Messene) (territory in south-
western Peloponnese).
Messenius, Aristomenes:
I.8.ext.15

Messius, (C.) (aed. cur. 55): II.10.8

Metapontus (on south coast of Italy): IV.1.ext.1. VIII.7.ext.2

Metaurus (river in Umbria): VII.4.4

Metellus *see* Caecilius Metellus

Methymnus (son of Masinissa): VIII.13.ext.1

Mettius *see* Fufetius, Mettius

Mevius (centurion): III.8.8

Midas (legendary king of Phrygia): I.6.ext.2,3. I.7.1

Miletus (on west coast of Asia Minor): I.1.ext.5 (Paris, Nepot.)
Milesii: IV.1.ext.7. Milesia Ceres: I.1.ext.5 (Paris). -sia regio: IV.1.ext.7

Milo (of Croton, athlete): IX.12.ext.9

Miltiades (victor of Marathon): V.3.ext.3c,g. VIII.14.ext.1

Minerva: I.1.ext.7 (Paris) (Phidias' statue): I.2.ext.2 and 4 (Paris). I.7.1. II.1.2. III.1.ext.1. V.3.ext.3g. (V.4.ext.2.) V.10.2. VIII.14.6

Minos (king of Cnosos): I.2.ext.1 (Paris). V.3.ext.3a

Minturnae (south of Formiae): I.5.5. II.10.6. VIII.2.3
Minturnenses: II.10.6. -nensis, C. Titinius: VIII.2.3

Minucius Basilus, L.: IX.4.1

Minucius (Esquilinus Augurinus), L. (cos. ?suff. 458): II.7.7. V.2.2

Minucius (Myrtilus), L.: VI.6.3

Minucius (Rufus, M.) (consul 221): III.8.2. V.2.4

Minyae: IV.6.ext.3

Misacenes (son of Masinissa): V.1.1d

Mithridates (VI, king of Pontus): I.8.ext.13, (18). III.7.8. IV.6.ext.2. V.1.9. V.2.ext.2. VI.9.6. VIII.7.ext.16. VIII.15.8. IX.2.ext.3. IX.7.mil.Rom.1. IX.11.ext.2. IX.13.1

Mitylenae (Mytil-) (in Lesbos): IX.11.4
Mitylenaei: VI.5.ext.1. Mitylenaeus, Pittacus: VI.5.ext.1. -naeus, Theophanes: VIII.14.3

Μοῖρα: I.5.7

Molo(n) (rhetor): II.2.3.

(Molossi) (people of Epirus). Molossus, Lyco(n): V.1.ext.3b

Moneta *see* Iuno

Mucia (wife of Pompey): IX.1.8

Mucius, P. (tr. pl. 486): VI.3.2

Mucius (Cordus Scaevola, C.): III.3.1

Mucius Scaevola, (P.) (cos. 133): III.2,17. Cf. 8.8.2. *See also* the following

(Mucius) Scaevola, Q. (Augur, cos. 117): III.8.5. IV.5.4. VIII.8.1. IV.1.11? VIII.12.1. (IX.1.8). Confused with the foregoing: 8.8.2

(Mucius) Scaevola, Q. (the Pontifex, cos. 95): IV.1.11? VIII.15.6. (IX.1.8). IX.11.2

Muliebris, Fortuna *see* Fortuna

INDEX

Mulvius, M. (triumvir nocturnus): VIII.1.damn.5

Mummius, L. (cos. 146): VI.4.2a. VII.5.4

Munatius Flaccus, L. (Pompeian commandant in Ategua): IX.2.4

Munatius Plancus, (L.) (cos. 42): VI.8.5

Munatius Rufus (friend of Cato the younger): IV.3.2

Munda (in Spain): VII.6.5

Mus see Decius Mus

Musae: I.6.ext.3. III.7.ext.2

Musca see Sempronius Musca

Mutina (Modena): IV.7.6

(Mycale) (on mainland opposite Samos). Mycalensis mons: VI.9.ext.5

Myco(n) (prisoner breast-fed by daughter): V.4.ext.1

(Mylasa) (in Caria). Mylasenus, Hybreas: IX.14.ext.2

Myrina (on the coast north of Smyrna): III.2.12

Mytilenae see Mitylenae

Naevius, Anus: VII.7.6

Naevius, M. (tr. pl. 184): III.7.1g

(Naevius) Surdinus: VII.7.6

Nasica see Cornelius Scipio Nasica

Nausimenes (Athenian): I.8.ext.3.

Nautius (Rutilus, C.) (II. cos. 458): V.2.2

Navius, Attus (augur): I.4.1 (Paris, Nepot.)

Navius, Q. (centurion): II.3.3

(Nealces) (third-century painter): VIII.11.ext.7

Neapolis (Naples): III.6.3 Neapolitani: VII.3.4a

Nearchus (tyrant): III.3.ext.3

Nepos see Caecilius Metellus Nepos

Neptunus: III.2.ext.3. VI.9.ext.5. VIII.11.ext.5. IX.1.1. IX.2.ext.2

Nero see Claudius Nero

Nervii (tribe inhabiting modern Belgium): III.2.19

Nicocreon (tyrant of Cyprus): III.3.ext.4

Nilus (river): VIII.7.ext.3

(Nola) (in Campania). Nolani: VII.3.4a. Nolanus, ager: I.6.4. -na moenia: I.6.9. -nus pedes: VII.3.7

(Nonius?) Sufenas see Sufenas

Norbanus, C. (cos. 83): VIII.5.2

(Nuceria) (in Campania). Nucerini: IX.6.ext.2

Numa see Pompilius, Numa

Numantia (Spanish town): II.7.1. IV.3.13. V.3.2d. VI.2.3. VIII.15.7. IX.12.3 Numantini: III.2.ext.7. VII.6.ext.2. Numantinus Rhoetogenes: III.2.ext.7. -na urbs: II.7.1. -na, victoria: VI.2.3

Numida see Plautius Numida

Numidia: II.6.17. V.1.1b. VII.2.6c. VIII.13.ext.1 Numida: III.2.11. V.1.7. IX.8.1. -dae: III.8.ext.1.

INDEX

Numidica castra: IX.1.5. -ci exercitus: V.2.ext.4. -ca tropaea: II.2.3

Numidicus see Caecilius Metellus Numidicus

Numitor, (Silvius) (king of Alba): II.2.9a

Nunnius, (A.) (competitor of Saturninus): IX.7.3

Occius, Q. (called Achilles): III.2.21

Oceanus: III.2.23b

Ochus see Artaxerxes (III). Darius I wrongly so called: IX.2.ext.6

Octavia (sister of Augustus): IX.15.2

Octavius see Mamilius

Octavius, Cn. (cos. 87): I.6.10. IV.7.5

Octavius, L. (adulterer): VI.1.13

Octavius Balbus (proscribed): V.7.3

Oebares (groom of Darius): VII.3.ext.2

Oedipus: V.3.ext.3g. ἐπὶ Κολωνῷ (of Sophocles): VIII.7.ext.12

Ofilius VIII.13.6

Ogulnius (Gallus), Q. (cos. 269): I.8.2. IV.3.9,10

Olbia (in Sardinia): V.1.2

Olympia (festival): VIII.15.ext.4 Olympicum certamen: VIII.7.ext.2. Olympionices: VIII.15.ext.4

Ὄλυμπος: III.7.ext.4

Olympus mons. (In Lydia):

I.7.ext.4. In Galatia: VI.1.ext.2

Opimius, L. (cos. 121): II.8.4,7. IX.4.3

Oppia see Vestia Oppia

Oppia, lex: IX.1.3

Oppius Gallus: VII.8.9

Orata see Sergius Orata

Orestes (son of Agamemnon): IV.7.praef.

Orestes see Aufidius Orestes

Orestilla (wife of M. Plautius): IV.6.3

Orestilla see Aurelia Orestilla

Orgiagon (Galatian petty king): VI.1.ext.2

Origines (historical work by elder Cato): VIII.1.absol.2

Orontes (actually Oroetes satrap of Darius I): VI.9.ext.5

Osci: II.4.4

Ostia: II.4.5. III.7.10a

Otacilia: VIII.2.2.

Otacilius (Crassus, T.) (pr. 217): VII.6.1c

Othryades (Spartan warrior): III.2.ext.4

Paciaeci (of Spain): V.4.ext.3

Padus (river Po): III.2.5

Paediculi (people of Apulia): VII.6.1a

(Paeligni) (people of central Italy). Paeligna cohors: III.2.20

Palatinus, mons: II.2.9a Palatium: II.1.6. II.5.6. VI.1.praef.

Palicanus see Lollius Palicanus

Palladium: I.4.5 (Paris, Nepot.)

INDEX

Pamphilus (actor): IX.14.4

(Pamphylia) (region on the south coast of Asia Minor). Pamphylius, Er: I.8.ext.1

Panapio see Urbinius Panapio

Παναθηναϊκός (of Isocrates): VIII.7.ext.9

Pansa see (Vibius) Pansa

Paphos (in Cyprus): I.5.6

Papia, lex: III.4.5

Papiria (tribe): IX.10.1

Papirius Carbo, C. (pr. 81?): IX.7.mil.Rom.3

(Papirius) Carbo, Cn. (error for C.) (consul 120): (3.7.6). VI.2.3. VI.5.6

(Papirius) Carbo, Cn. (error for C.) (pr. 61): V.4.4

(Papirius) Carbo, Cn. (III cos. 82): V.3.5. VI.2.8,10. VII.6.4. IX.7.mil.Rom.3. IX.13.2

(Papirius) Carbo Arvina, C. (pr. 85?, son of cos. 120): III.7.6. IX.2.3

Papirius Cursor, (L.) (V. cos. 313): II.7.8. III.2.9

Papirius Cursor, (L.) (II cos. 272): VII.2.5

Papirius Mas(s)o, (C.) (cos. 231): III.6.5. VI.5.1b(?)

Papus, see Aemilius Papus

(Parma) (in north Italy, Parma). Parmensis see Cassius Parmensis

Parmenio(n) (Macedonian general): III.8.ext.6. VI.4.ext.3

Parthi: I.6.11. VI.9.9. VII.6.6

Paterculus see Sulpicius Paterculus

Paullus see Aemilius Paullus

Pausanias (leading Spartan): II.6.1

Pausanias (assassin of Philip II): I.8.ext.9. VIII.14.ext.4

Pecuniola see Aurelius Pecuniola

Pedanius, T. (centurion): III.2.20

(Pelasgi). Pelasgica arma: IV.6.ext.3

Pelorus (helmsman): IX.8.ext.1

Pera see Iunius Pera, (Iunius) Brutus Pera

Pergamum (city in western Asia Minor): I.6.12. V.3.2e

Pericles (Athenian statesman): II.6.5. III.1.ext.1. IV.3.ext.1. V.10.ext.1. VII.2.ext.7. VIII.9.ext.2. VIII.11.ext.1

(Perillus) (creator of Phalaris' brazen bull): IX.2.ext.9

Pero (breast-feeds father in prison): V.4.ext.1

Perperna, M. (cos. 130): III.4.5

Perperna, M. (cos. 92): VIII.13.4

Perperna (Veiento), M. (pr. 82, killed by Pompey): VI.2.8

Persa (pet dog): I.5.3

Persae: I.1.ext.6 (Paris, Nepot.). I.7.ext.5. II.6.16. III.2.ext.2. III.7.ext.8. IV.7.ext.2a. V.1.ext.1a. V.3.ext.3c. V.4.ext.6. V.6.ext.3. VII.3.ext.2. VIII.7.ext.2. IX.2.ext.6,7. IX.10.ext.2
Persica dominatio: VI.3.ext.2. -ca salutatio:

444

VII.2.ext.11a. -cus sermo:
VIII.7.ext.15. -ca tropaea:
V.3.ext.3g. -ca, vestis et
instituta: IX.5.ext.1
Perse(u)s (last king of Macedo-
nia): I.5.3. I.8.1b. II.2.1b.
II.7.14. IV.3.8. IV.4.9.
V.1.1c,e. V.1.8. VI.2.3.
VIII.11.1
Pessinus (in Galatia): I.1.1c.
VIII.15.3
Petelia (town of the Bruttii):
VI.6.ext.2. IX.8.ext.1
Petelini: VI.6.ext.2
Petillii (Q. Petillius and Q.
Petillius Spurinus, tr. pl. 187):
III.7.1g
Petillius, L. (scriba): I.1.12
Petillius (Spurinus), Q. (cos.
176): I.1.12. I.5.9. II.7.15d.
See also Petillii
Petreius, (M.) (pr. 64?): II.4.6
Petronia (mother of C. Tettius):
VII.7.3
Petronius, L. (Roman knight):
IV.7.5,6
Petronius Sabinus (the
Sabine?): I.1.13
Phaenarete (mother of Socra-
tes): III.4.ext.1
Phalaris (tyrant of Agrigentum):
III.3.ext.2. IX.2.ext.9
Pharmacussa (Aegean island):
VI.9.15
(Pharnaces) (son of Mithridates
VI): cf. IX.11.ext.2
(Pharsalia). Pharsalica, acies:
I.5.6. IV.5.5. -cum certamen:
I.8.10

(Pherae) (in Thessaly).
Pheraeus Alexander:
IX.13.ext.3. -us Iason:
I.8.ext.6
Phidias (sculptor): I.1.ext.7
(Paris, Nepot.). III.7.ext.4.
VIII.14.6.
Philaeni (Carthaginian broth-
ers): V.6.ext.4
Philemo(n) (author of New
Comedy): IX.12.ext.6
Philippi (in Macedonia): IV.6.5.
IX.9.2
    Philippensis acies: I.5.7.
I.8.8.ͬ -se proelium: VI.8.4.
Philippii, campi: I.7.1.
V.1.11.ͬ Cf. Macedonica
pugna
Philippus (II, king of Macedo-
nia): I.8.ext.9,(10). VI.2.ext.1.
(VI.4.ext.4). VII.2.ext.10.
VIII.14.ext.4. IX.5.ext.1
Philippus (V, king of Macedo-
nia): II.9.3. IV.5.1. IV.8.5.
V.2.6. IX.1.3
Philippus (doctor): III.8.ext.6
Philippus (slave of Ser. (?)
Fulvius Flaccus): VIII.4.3
Philiscus see Atilius Philiscus
Philippus see Marcius Philippus
Philo(n) (architect of the Athe-
nian arsenal): VIII.12.ext.2
Philocrates (slave of C.
Gracchus): VI.8.3
Philus see Furius Philus
Phintias (Pythagorean):
IV.7.ext.1
Phocion (Athenian statesman):
III.8.ext.2. V.3.ext.3f,g

Phraates (IV, king of Parthia):
VII.6.6

Phrygia (region in central Asia
Minor): I.6.ext.2
Phrygiae sedes: VII.5.2

Phryne (courtesan):
IV.3.ext.3a,b

Phye: I.2.ext.2 (Paris)

Physcon see Ptolomaeus
(VIII)

Picenum (region south of
Ancona): I.6.5
Picena regio: V.3.4. -num,
Firmum (Fermo): IX.15.1

Pictor see Fabius Pictor

Pietas (temple of): II.5.1

Pindar (poet): IX.12.ext.7

Pindarus (freedman of C.
Cassius): VI.8.4

(Pinna) (in central Italy).
Pinnensis iuvenis: V.4.ext.7

Pinthia see Lutatius Pinthia

(Piraeus) (port of Athens):
IX.11.4

Pirithous (friend of Theseus):
IV.7.4

Pisistratus (Athenian despot):
I.2.ext.2 (Paris). V.1.ext.2a,b.
V.3.ext.3b. VIII.9.ext.1,2

Piso see Calpurnius Piso

Pittacus (despot of Mitylene):
IV.1.ext.6,7. VI.5.ext.1

Pius see Caecilius Metellus
Pius

Placentia (Piacenza): IV.7.5.
VI.2.10

Plaetoria (?) (preferred daughter of Aebutia): VII.8.2

Plaetorius, M. (chief centurion):
(IX.3.6)

Plaetorius, M. (killed by Sulla):
IX.2.1

Plancus see Munatius Plancus,
Plotius Plancus

Plato: I.6.ext.3. I.7.1. I.8.ext.1.
IV.1.ext.2a,(b),3. V.10.ext.2.
VII.2.ext.4. VIII.7.ext.3.
VIII.12.ext.1

Plautius (Hypsaeus?), M. (naval
commander): IV.6.3

Plautius Hypsaeus, M. (cos.
125): IX.5.1, ext.4

(Plautius) Hypsaeus, (P.) (aed.
cur. 58): IX.5.3

Plautius Numida, C. (senator):
IV.6.2

Plautius (Venno or Venox, C.)
(II cos. 341): VI.2.1

Pleminius, (Q.) (legate of elder
Africanus): I.1.21, ext.1

Plotius, C. (soldier): VI.1.12

Plotius, P.: VI.1.9

Plotius Plancus, C. (error for L.;
born C. Munatius Plancus):
VI.8.5

Poenus: III.2.11. -ni: I.1.14.
I.6.8,9. I.7.ext.8. II.7.12.
II.8.2. III.2.20. III.6.4.
III.7.1d,4,10b. III.8.2. IV.3.1.
V.1.6. V.1.ext.6. VI.6.2.
VI.9.11. VII.2.ext.16. VII.3.7.
VII.4.ext.1. VII.6.1a.
VIII.15.1. See also
Carthaginienses
Punica, acies: III.7.1a. -ca,
arma: II.7.15a. VII.4.ext.1.ʳ

-cus astus: V.1.ext.6. -ca bella:
V.2.6. -cum, bellum: V.3.2b.
-cum bellum, primum: I.3.2
(Paris, Nepot.). I.4.3 (Paris,
Nepot.). IV.4.6. V.1.2.
IX.6.ext.1. -cum bellum,
secundum: I.6.5. II.9.6a.
III.7.1c. IV.4.10. V.2.1b. V.6.8.
VI.9.3. VII.2.ext.16. VII.6.1a.
IX.1.3. -cum bellum, tertium:
I.1.14. II.2.1a. VII.2.ext.16.
-ca calliditas: VII.4.4. -ca
classis: II.8.2. -ci exercitus:
III.6.1. -cae feminae: II.6.15.
-ca feritas: VII.6.2. IX.1.ext.1.
-ca fortitudo: VII.4.ext.2. -cae
gazae: III.7.1e. -cum impe-
rium: II.7.13. V.6.ext.4. -cae
imiuriae: V.1.1a. -ca navis:
III.2.10. -cae opes: I.6.2.
-cum, praesidium: III.8.ext.1.
-cum sagulum et corona:
V.1.ext.6. -cus sanguis:
I.1.ext.2. -ca temeritas:
IX.8.ext.1. -ca tropaea: VI.9.2.
-cum vallum: III.2.20. -ca victoria: III.7.ext.6. -ca vincula:
VI.9.11. -ca, vis: VI.6.ext.1.
-cae vires: IV.2.2. Punicani,
lectuli: VII.5.1
Polemo(n) (4th-century Athenian philosopher): VI.9.ext.1
Pollia (tribe): II.9.6a. VI.3.4.
IX.10.1
Pollio see Asinius Pollio
Pollux see Castor
Polycrates (despot of Samos):
VI.9.ext.5

Polydamas (athlete, 5th-4th
century): IX.12.ext.10
Polystratus (Epicurean philoso-
pher): I.8.ext.17,(18)
Pompeius (envoy): III.3.2
Pompeius, Q. (cos. 141): III.7.5.
VIII.5.1. IX.3.7
Pompeius, Sex. (cos. A.D. 14,
Valerius' patron): II.6.8.
IV.7.ext.2b
Pompeius Magnus, Cn.: I.5.6.
I.6.12. I.8.9,10. I.8.ext.13.
II.4.6. III.2.13,23a. III.8.7.
IV.5.5. IV.6.4. IV.6.ext.2.
V.1.9,10. V.2.9. V.3.5. V.5.4.
V.7.ext.2. VI.2.4,5,6,(7),8,9,
11. VI.9.9. VII.6.ext.3.
VII.7.2. VIII.14.3.
VIII.15.8,9. (IX.1.8). IX.5.3.
IX.13.2. IX.14.1 Pompeiana
militia: IX.11.4. -num nomen:
IX.2.4
Pompeius (Magnus), Cn. (son
of the foregoing): IX.15.1
Pompeius Reginus: VII.8.4
Pompeius (Rufus), Q. (cos. 88):
III.5.2. IX.7.mil.Rom.2
Pompeius (Rufus), Q. (tr. pl.
52): IV.2.7
Pompeius (Strabo), Cn. (cos.
89): (V.2.9. VI.2.8). VI.9.9.
IX.7.mil.Rom.2. (IX.14.2)
Pompilius, Numa (second king
of Rome): I.1.12. I.2.1 (Paris,
Nepot.)
Pomponius, M. (tr. pl. 362):
V.4.3
Pomponius, (M.) (friend of C.

Gracchus): IV.7.2. Cf.
Pomponius Rufus
(Pomponius) Atticus, T. (Roman
knight): VII.8.5
Pomponius Rufus (author of
miscellany): IV.4.praef.
Pontius (adulterer): VI.1.13
Pontius, Herennius:
VII.2.ext.17
Pontius Aufidianus (Roman
knight): VI.1.3
Pontius, Lupus (Roman knight,
blind advocate): VIII.7.5
(Pontius) Telesinus (friend of
younger Marius): VI.8.2
Pontus (region in eastern Asia
Minor, bordering on Black
Sea): V.1.9
    Ponticus sinus: II.8.praef.
IV.6.ext.3. -cum supplicium:
IX.13.1
Popillius, M. (senator): VII.8.9
Popillius, P. (really Rutilius; tr.
pl. 169): VI.5.3
Popillius, P. (one of M. Anneius'
heirs): VII.7.2
Popillius Laenas, C. (II cos.
158): VI.4.3
Popillius Laenas, C. (Cicero's
killer): V.3.4
Popillius Laenas, M. (IV cos.
348): VIII.6.3
Popillius Laenas, M. (cos. 139):
I.3.3 (Paris). VIII.1.ambust.1
Popillius Laenas, P. (cos. 132):
IV.7.1
Poppaedius (Silo), Q. (Marsian):
III.1.2a

Porcia familia: III.2.16. -um
nomen: IV.1.14
Porcia (daughter of younger
Cato): III.2.15. IV.6.5.
(V.1.10)
Porcina: see Aemilius (Lepidus)
Porcina
Porcius Cato, M. (the Censor,
cos. 195): II.9.3. III.2.16.
III.4.6. III.7.7. IV.3.11.
IV.5.1. V.10.3. VIII.1.absol.2.
VIII.7.1. VIII.15.2
(Porcius Cato, M.) (grandson of
the Censor, cos. 118): cf.
V.10.3
Porcius Cato, M. (father of the
following): VIII.2.1
Porcius Cato, M. (the younger):
II.8.1. II.10.7,8. III.1.2a,b.
III.2.14. III.4.6. III.6.7.
IV.1.14. IV.3.2,12. IV.6.5.
V.1.10. VI.2.5. VII.5.6.
VIII.2.1. VIII.7.2. VIII.15.10
(Porcius Cato, M.) (son of the
foregoing): IV.3.12. (V.1.10)
(Porcius Cato Licinianus, M.)
(son of the Censor): cf.
III.2.16
Porsenna (king of the Etrus-
cans): III.2.2. III.3.1
Postumius, (C.) (Sulla's
haruspex): I.6.4
Postumius (Albinus, A.) (cos.
242, flamen Martialis): I.1.2
(Postumius) Albinus, A. (cos.
99): IX.8.3
Postumius Albinus, (L.) (cos.
154): VI.3.8

(Postumius) Albinus, Sp. (cos. 186): VI.3.7

(Postumius) Albinus, Sp. (cos. 110): II.7.2

(Postumius Albinus Caudinus, Sp.) (II cos. 321): V.1.ext.5

Postumius (Albinus Regillensis, M.) (censor 403): II.9.1

Postumius (Albus Regillensis), A. (dict. 498): I.8.1a

Postumius Tubertus, A. (dict. 431): II.7.6

Postumius (Tubertus, A.) (son of the foregoing): II.7.6

Potitii, -tium nomen: I.1.17

Praeneste (Palestrina): IX.7.2 Praenestini: VII.6.3. IX.2.1. Praenestina Fortuna: I.3.2 (Paris, Nepot.). -na obsidio: VI.8.2

Praxiteles (4th-century sculptor): VIII.11.ext.4

Priene (north of Miletus): VII.2.ext.3. VII.3.ext.3 Prienenses: I.5.ext.1

Privernum (in Latium): VI.2.1 Privernas: VI.2.2. -nates: VI.2.1. IX.10.1

Proserpina: I.1.21. I.1.ext.3. II.4.5

Protagoras (sophist, 5th-4th century): I.1.ext.7 (Paris, Nepot.)

(Protogenes) (late 5th-century painter): VIII.11.ext.7

Prusias (I, king of Bithynia): III.7.ext.6. IX.2.ext.2

Prusias (II): I.8.ext.12,(18). V.1.1e

Prusias (Monodus, son of the foregoing): I.8.ext.12,(18)

Pseudophilippus (Andriscus, Macedonian pretender): VII.5.4

(Psophis) (in Arcadia). Psophidius, Aglaus: VII.1.2

Ptolomaeus (II, Philadelphus): IV.3.9. VIII.9.ext.3 (or I, Lagus?)

Ptolomaeus (IV, Philopator): VI.6.1

Ptolomaeus (V, Epiphanes): VI.6.1

Ptolomaeus (VI, Philometor): V.1.1f (VI.6.1. IX.1.ext.5)

Ptolomaeus (VII, called Physcon): (V.1.1f). VI.4.3. IX.1.ext.5. IX.2.ext.5

Ptolomaeus (XIII): I.8.9

Ptolomaeus (king of Cyprus): (VIII.15.10). IX.4 ext.1

Ptolomais (in Syria): I.6.12

Publicia (poisoned her husband): VI.3.8

Publicius (old man married by Septicia): VII.7.4

Publicius (freedman): IX.14.1

Publicola see Valerius Publicola

Publilius (blind senator and advocate): VIII.7.5

Pudicitia: VI.1.praef.

Pulcher see Claudius Pulcher

Pulto (of Pinna): V.4.ext.7

Pulvillus see Horatius Pulvillus

Punicus see Poenus

Pupinia (land near Rome):
IV.4.4,6. IV.8.1

Puteoli (Pozzuoli, on the Bay of
Naples): VII.3.9. IX.3.8

Pylades (friend of Orestes):
IV.7.praef.

Pyresus (Celtiberian): III.2.21

Pyrrhus (king of Epirus):
I.1.ext.1. II.7.15b. III.7.10a.
IV.3.5b,6b,14a. V.1.ext.3a,4.
VI.5.1d. VIII.13.5. IX.1.4

Pythagoras (6th-century sage):
II.6.10. IV.1.ext.1.
VIII.7.ext.2,3. VIII.15.ext.1
    Pythagoricus, Xenophilus:
VIII.13.ext.3. -rica prudentia:
IV.7.ext.1

Pythica cortina: VIII.15.ext.3.
-ca vaticinatio: I.8.10. Pythius
Apollo see Apollo

Quadriga (= Ἅρμα, lake(?) in
Boeotia): I.8.ext.9

(Quinctius Cincinnatus), K.
(son of the following): IV.4.7

Quinctius Cincinnatus, L. (cos.
suff. 460): II.7.7. IV.1.4.
IV.4.7

Quinctius Crispinus, (T.) (cos.
208): V.1.3

(Quinctius) Flamininus, L. (cos.
192): II.9.3. V.5.1

Quinctius Flamininus, T. (cos.
198): II.9.3. IV.5.1. IV.8.5.
V.2.6

Quirinalis collis (one of the
seven hills of Rome): I.1.11

(Quirinus) (Romulus as god).
Quirinalis, flamen: I.1.10

Quirites II.9.5. III.7.1g.
III.7.3,8. V.10.2. VI.2.6.
VI.4.1b

Rauduscula (porta): V.6.3

(Reate) (Sabine town). Reatina
praefectura: I.8.1b. -na villa:
VI.8.6

Regillus, lacus: I.8.1a

Reginus see (Antistius) Reginus,
Pompeius Reginus

Regium (Reggio, at the toe of
Italy): II.7.15f

Regulus see Atilius Regulus

Remus: I.IV.praef. (Nepot.).
II.2.9a

Restio see Antius Restio

Rex see Marcius Rex

Rhamnus (in Attica): I.8.10

Rhenus (river Rhine): V.5.3

Rhodus (Rhodes): VIII.10.ext.1
    Rhodii: I.5.8. II.10.ext.1.
V.2.ext.2

Rhoetogenes (of Centobriga;
identical with the following?):
V.1.5

Rhoetogenes (of Numantia):
III.2.ext.7

Rome
    Romanus: I.8.10. III.2.11.
-ni: I.1.18. I.1.ext.4. 1.2.1
(Nepot.). I.3.3 (Nepot.).
I.6.3,6. I.8.2,5,6. II.4.4.
II.7.11,15e. II.10.2a.
III.2.1,7,11,20,21. III.7.10a.
III.8.ext.1. IV.3.1. IV.8.ext.1.
V.1.1d. V.1.3,7. V.1.ext.3b.
V.2.1b. V.4.1. VI.2.1. VI.4.1a.
VI.5.1a,b. VII.2.ext.16.

VII.3.6,7. VII.3.ext.7,9,10. VII.4.ext.2. VII.6.2. IX.9.3

Romana acies: V.6.5. -na, omnis aetas: IV.4.6. -nus, ager: V.4.1. -na amicitia: IV.7.4. IX.13.ext.2. -nus animus: VI.6.2. -na, arma: II.7.7. -na auspicia: I.3.2 (Nepot.)

Romana castra: I.8.ext.19. -nus, civis: III.4.5. IV.1.1. -ni, cives: II.7.15f. II.8.7. V.2.6. IX.2.ext.3. IX.10.2. -na civitas: V.4.3. V.6.6. -na clades: V.1.ext.5. -na concordia: IV.4.2. -na, corpora: IX.2.ext.2. -ni duces: V.1.ext.6

Romana eloquentia: II.2.3. V.3.4. V.9.2. -nus, eques: I.7.8. V.7.2. VI.1.3. VI.2.8. VII.2.4. VII.7.2. VIII.4.2. VIII.7.5. VIII.15.8,11. IX.12.8. -ni equites: II.9.8. V.8.4. -num exemplum: V.1.ext.1a. -na exempla: I.6.ext.praef. III.2.24. III.3.2. III.4.ext.1. III.8.ext.1. V.4.3. -nus exercitus: I.8.5. III.2.20. VII.4.1. -ni exercitus: I.7.1. II.3.1. IX.1.5

Romanae feminae: II.1.5b. -na fides: VI.6.2. -num, forum: V.6.2. VI.9.13. -na frugalitas: IV.3.5a. -na gens: II.4.2. V.1.1a

Romana historia: I.7.6. -na humanitas: V.1.1f. -nus imperator: III.2.12. V.4.ext.7. VI.6.4. -num imperium: I.6.6,11. II.7.praef. II.8.praef.

III.2.17. III.4.1^r,2. III.7.10b. III.8.2.^{r} IV.1.10a. V.1.8,10. V.2.1a. V.3.1. V.3.2d.^{r} V.5.3. VI.1.11. VI.4.1a.^{r} VII.4.2. VIII.14.1. IX.11.ext.4. IX.13.1. IX.15.5. -nus iussus: IX.2.4. -na iuventus: III.2.8. V.2.2. VII.6.1a

Romanae leges see -ni, mores et leges. -na, legio: VII.4.ext.2. -nae, legiones: VII.2.ext.17. -na liberalitas: IV.8.5. -na, libertas: V.8.1. VI.2.3

Romana maiestas: VIII.15.ext.1. -na mansuetudo: V.1.ext.6. -nus miles: II.7.2. IX.1.ext.1. -na militia: I.6.11. -ni mores: I.3.3 (Paris). -ni, mores et leges: II.5.3. -num nomen: I.5.1. V.1.ext.6. -ni oculi: III.2.23b

Romanae partes: I.8.1a. -ni, pedites: VII.3.3. -na, plebs: VI.2.3. -nus, populus: I.1.14. I.2.1 (Paris). I.5.2. I.6.3,6. I.8.1b. II.2.1b,2,8. II.6.7a. II.8.4. II.9.praef. III.2.ext.8. III.3.2. III.4.4. III.7.1a,8,10a. III.7.ext.6. IV.1.8,10a. V1.ext.9. IV.3.8,14a,b. IV.4.1,5. IV.8.2,4,5. V.1.1f,5,7,9. V.2.2,5. V.2.ext.3,4. V.3.2a,c. V.6.1,2. V.10.2. VI.1.1. VI.3.1b. V1.3.2. VI.5.1b,(c). VI.6.1. VII.2.1,3,6c. VII.3.4a,8. VII.3.ext.10.

VII.4.ext.2. VII.5.5. VII.8.5,9.
VIII.1.absol.2.
VIII.1.ambust.2.
VIII.13.ext.1. VIII.15.9,10.
IX.2.1. IX.3.2,5,6.
IX.3.ext.2,3. IX.6.ext.2.
IX.11.ext.4. -na prudentia:
VII.2.ext.1a. VII.4.4. -na
pudicitia: VI.1.1
　　Romanus sanguis: I.7.ext.1.
II.7.12. II.9.8. VI.1.9.
VI.6.ext.1. -nus, senatus
populusque (SPQR): I.1.14.
IV.8.5. VI.3.2. VIII.15.10. -na
severitas: VI.3.ext.1. -na
societas: VI.6.ext.2. -nus
stilus: VIII.13.ext.4
　　Romana templa: II.5.4. -ni
transfugae: II.7.12. -na,
triremis: I.8.2. -na urbs:
IV.7.ext.1. V.2.ext.4. V.3.2b.
VII.3.ext.8. VIII.11.2. -nae
vires: I.1.15. V.3.2a. -na
virtus: VIII.11.2.
Romulus I.4.praef. (Nepot.).
I.4.1 (Paris, Nepot.). I.8.11.
II.2.9a. II.4.4. II.8.praef.
III.2.praef.,3,4. IV.4.11.
(V.3.1a). V.8.1. (VI.5.1d).
IX.6.1
Roscius (Gallus), Q. (comic ac-
tor): VIII.7.7. VIII.10.2
Rubria (woman of
Mediolanum): IX.15.ext.1
Rufinus see Cornelius Rufinus
Rufus see Caelius, Caesetius,
Haterius, Minucius,
Munatius, Pomponius,
Sulpicius

Rullianus see Fabius Maximus
Rullianus
Rupilius, P. (cos. 132): II.7.3.
IV.7.1. VI.9.8. IX.12.ext.1
Rutilius: VI.5.3
Rutilius, P. see Popillius, P.
Rutilius (Rufus), P. (cos. 105):
II.3.2. II.10.5. VI.4.4. Cf.
VIII.13.6
Rutilus see Marcius Rutilus

Sabazius see Iuppiter
Sabelli (i.e. Sabini): III.4.5
Sabini: VII.3.1. IX.6.1. Sabinus,
ager: VII.3.1. -na regio:
II.4.5. -nae, virgines: II.4.4.
See also Petronius Sabinus
Sacer (collis): VIII.9.1
Sacerdos see Licinius Sacerdos
Saeculares (ludi): II.4.5
(Saguntum) (in Spain).
Saguntini: VI.6.ext.1
Salamis (-mina) (island off west-
ern Attica): V.3.ext.3b,g.
VIII.14.ext.1
Salapia (in Apulia): III.8.ext.1
Salassus see Vettius Salassus
(Salernum) (Salerno, on the
Bay of Naples). Salernitana
regio: VI.8.5
Salii: I.1.9. I.8.11
Salinator see Livius Salinator
Salus (Welfare, temple of):
VIII.14.6
Samiramis (queen of Assyria):
IX.3.ext.4
Samnium (region of central It-
aly): IV.3.6a. V.2.4
　　Samnites: I.6.4. II.2.4a.

II.7.8. III.2.9. IV.3.5a,6a,b.
V.1.ext.5. V.2.4. VI.1.9.
VII.2.ext.17
Samos (Aegean island):
  VI.9.ext.5
    Samii: I.5.ext.1. V.2.ext.1.
  VI.9.ext.5. Samia vasa:
  VII.5.1. Samius, Echecles:
  I.8.ext.4. -us, Syloso(n):
  V.2.ext.1
Sardanapallus (king of Assyria):
  IV.7.praef.
Sardes (capital of Lydia):
  V.4.ext.6
Sardinia: VII.6.1c. IX.7.2. Cf.
  I.6.5
Sariaster (son of Tigranes):
  IX.11.ext.3
Sarpedo(n) (Cato the younger's
  tutor): III.1.2b
Saturninus see (Appuleius)
  Saturninus, Fannius
  Saturninus, (Sentius)
  Saturninus
Satyriscus: I.7.ext.7
Scaeva see Caesius Scaeva
Scaevius, P. (soldier): III.2.23b
Scaevola see Mucius Scaevola
Scantinius Capitolinus, C. (tr.
  pl. (?) 226): VI.1.7
Scaurus see Aemilius Scaurus
(Sceleratus vicus) (in Rome):
  IX.11.1
Scipio see Caecilius Metellus
  Pius, Cornelius Scipio
Scopas (Thessalian magnate):
  I.8.ext.7
(Scribonii) Curiones (father and
  son): IX.1.6

(Scribonius) Curio, (C.) (cos.
  76): IX.14.5. See also the
  foregoing
(Scribonius Curio, C.) (tr. pl.
  50): see (Scribonii) Curiones
Scribonius (Libo), L. (aed. cur.
  194): II.4.3
(Scribonius) Libo, (L.) (tr. pl.
  149): VIII.1.absol.2
(Scribonius) Libo, L. (cos. 34):
  VI.2.8
Scyros (Aegean island):
  V.3.ext.3a
Scythia: VI.4.ext.2
    Scythae: V.4.ext.5
(Seianus) see Aelius Seianus
Seleucus (I, Nicator):
  II.10.ext.1. V.7.ext.1,2
Semiramis see Samiramis
Sempronia gens: III.8.6
Sempronia (wife of Scipio
  Aemilianus): III.8.6. (VI.2.3)
Sempronius Asellio, (A.) (pr.
  89): IX.7.4
Sempronius Atratinus, L. (actu-
  ally C.) (cos. 423): III.2.8.
  VI.5.2
(Sempronii) Gracchi (Ti. and
  C.): IV.4.praef. IV.7.2.
  VI.3.1d. VI.7.1
(Sempronius) Gracchus, C. (tr.
  pl. 123-22): I.7.6. II.8.7.
  III.8.6. IV.7.2. V.3.2f. VI.8.3.
  VIII.10.1. IX.4.3. IX.5.ext.4.
  IX.12.6. See also the preced-
  ing
Sempronius Gracchus, Ti. (II
  cos. 213): I.6.8,9. V.1.ext.6.
  V.6.8. VII.6.1a

(Sempronius) Gracchus, Ti. (II
cos. 163): I.1.3. III.7.7.
IV.1.8. IV.2.3. IV.6.1,2.
(IV.7.2). VI.3.1d. VI.5.3.
IX.12.3

(Sempronius) Gracchus, Ti. (tr.
pl. 133): I.4.2,3 (Paris,
Nepot.). I.7.6. II.8.7. III.2.17.
III.8.6. IV.7.1. V.3.2e. VI.2.3.
VII.2.6b. IX.7.1,2. IX.15.1.
See also Sempronii Gracchi
Gracchana seditio: VI.2.3.
-nus tumultus: I.1.1c

(Sempronius) Longus, Ti. (cos.
194): IV.5.1

(Sempronius) Longus, Ti.:
VII.8.1

Sempronius Musca: VI.1.13

Sempronius Sophus, P. (cos.
268): II.9.7. VI.3.12

(Sempronius) Tuditanus:
VII.8.1

Senones (tribe of Cisalpine
Gaul): VI.3.1a

(Sentinum) (in Umbria).
Sentinas, Maesia: VIII.3.1

(Sentius) Saturninus, (Cn.):
IX.1.8.

Sentius Saturninus Vetulo
(proscribed by triumvirs):
VII.3.9

Seplasia (street in Capua):
IX.1.ext.1

Septicia: VII.7.4

Septimuleius, L. (friend of C.
Gracchus): IX.4.3,ext.1

Serapio (sacrificial assistant):
IX.14.3

Serapis (Egyptian deity): I.3.4
(Paris)

(Sergius) Catilina, L.: II.8.7.
IV.8.3. V.8.5. IX.1.9. IX.11.3.
His son: 9.1.9

Sergius Orata, C. (builder and
epicure): IX.1.1,(2)

Sergius Silus, Cn.: VI.1.8

Serranus *see* Atilius Serranus

Sertorius, Q.: I.2.5 (Paris,
Nepot.). VII.3.6. VII.6.ext.3.
VIII.15.8. IX.1.5. IX.15.3
Sertorianus miles: V.5.4

Servilia lex: VIII.1.absol.8

Servilianus *see* Fabius Maximus
Servilianus

(Servilius) Ahala, (C.) (master
of horse 439): V.3.2g

Servilii Caepiones, Cn. (cos.
141) and Q. (cos. 140):
VIII.5.1

Servilius Caepio, Q. (cos. 140):
IX.6.4. *See also* the preceding

(Servilius) Caepio, Q. (cos.
106): IV.7.3. VI.9.13

Servilius (Nonianus?), M. (cos.
A.D. 3): I.8.11

(Servilius) Glaucia, (C.) (pr.
100, ally of Saturninus):
III.2.18

Servilius (Isauricus), P. (II cos.
41): VIII.3.2

Servilius (Priscus Structus, P.)
(cos. 495): IX.3.6

Servilius (Vatia) Isauricus, P.
(cos. 79): VIII.5.6

Severus *see* Varius Severus

Sextilius (betrayer of benefactor): V.3.3

Sextilius (triumvir nocturnus): VIII.1.damn.5

Sextilius, L. (one of M. Anneius' heirs): VII.7.2

Sibylla: I.5.ext.1
Sibyllini libri: I.1.1c. I.8.2. VIII.15.12

Sicca (in Numidia): II.6.15

Siccius Dentatus, L.: III.2.24

Sicilia: I.6.5. I.7.ext.6. II.7.3,9. II.8.2,5. II.9.7. III.6.1. III.7.1c. IV.1.7. IV.3.10. V.1.6. V.3.2f. VI.3.5. VI.6.2. VI.7.3. VI.9.8. VI.9.ext.6. VII.3.3,9. VII.4.ext.1. VII.6.1c. VIII.13.ext.1. IX.8.ext.1. IX.12.ext.2. IX.13.2. IX.14.ext.3.
Siculi: I.7.ext.8. IV.1.7. VI.9.8. Sicula arma: VII.4.ext.1

Siculus see Herennius Siculus

(Sidon) (in Phoenicia).
Sidonius, Antipater: I.8.ext.16

Sigeum (in the Troad): VI.5.ext.1

Silanus see Iunius Silanus

Silius, (Q.? or Sestius?) (conspirator against Q. Cassius): IX.4.2

Silus see Sergius Silus

Silvanus (woodland deity): I.8.5

Simonides (of Cos, poet, 6th-5th century): I.7.ext.3. I.8.ext.7,(18). VIII.7.ext.13

Sisenna see Gabinius Sisenna

Smyrna see Zmyrna

Socrates: I.1.ext.7 (Paris, Nepot.). III.4.ext.1. III.8.ext.2,3. VI.4.ext.2. VII.2.ext.1a-d. VIII.7.ext.3,8. VIII.8.ext.1
Socratica disciplina: V.10.ext.2

Sol (statue at Rhodes): I.5.8

Solo(n) (of Athens, one of the Seven Wise Men): IV.1.ext.7. V.3.ext.3b,g. VII.2.ext.2a,(b). VIII.7.ext.14. VIII.9.ext.1

Sophocles (dramatist): IV.3.ext.1,2. VIII.7.ext.12. IX.12.ext.5

Sophro(n) (writer of mimes, 5th-century): VIII.7.ext.3

Sophroniscus (father of Socrates): III.4.ext.1

Sophus see Sempronius Sophus

(Sora) (Volscian town). Sorani: VIII.1.absol.9

(Sparta)
Spartanus: III.2.ext.3. III.7.ext.8. VI.4.ext.5. Spartani: I.6.ext.1b. IV.1.ext.8. -na civitas: II.6.1,(2). III.2.ext.5.ᵣ IV.6.ext.3. -nae acies: II.7.ext.2. -na virtus: III.2.ext.5. See also Lacedaemon

Speusippus (Plato's nephrew): IV.1.ext.2a

Spinther (actor) see Cornelius Lentulus Spinther

INDEX

Spurinna (Etruscan youth):
IV.5.ext.1

Spurinna (haruspex): I.6.13.
VIII.11.2

(Stagira) (birthplace of Aristotle): V.6.ext.5

Stasippus (politician of Tegea):
IV.1.ext.5

Statilius, Statius (commander of
Bruttii and Lucani): I.8.6

Stolo see Licinius Stolo

(Strabo): I.8.ext.14

Stratonice (wife of Seleucus I):
V.7.ext.1

Sublicius, pons (Tiber bridge):
I.1.10. III.2.1. IV.7.2

(Sucro) (in Spain). Sucronensis,
Varius Severus: III.7.8

Suessa (Sezza, in Latium):
II.2.4b

Sufenas, (Nonius?): VII.7.2

Sulla see Cornelius Sulla

Sulpicia, lex: IX.7.mil. Rom.1

Sulpicia (wife of Q. Fulvius
Flaccus): VIII.15.12

Sulpicia (wife of Lentulus
Cruscellio): VI.7.3

Sulpicius, Q. (flamen): I.1.5

Sulpicius (Camerinus), Ser.
(cos. 461): I.6.5

Sulpicius Galba, Ser. (cos. 144):
VI.4.2b. VIII.1.absol.2.
VIII.7.1. IX.6.2

(Sulpicius) Galba, Ser. (pr. 54):
VI.2.11

Sulpicius Galus, C. (cos. 166):
VI.3.10. VIII.1.absol.2.
VIII.11.1

(Sulpicius) Paterculus, Ser. (father of virtuous Sulpicia):
VIII.15.12

Sulpicius Peticus, C. (V cos.
351): II.4.4

Sulpicius Rufus, (P.) (tr. pl. 88):
VI.5.7 See also Sulpicia, lex

Superbus see Tarquinius Superbus

Surdinus see Naevius Surdinus

Syloso(n) (ruler of Samos):
V.2.ext.1

Syphax (king of Numidia):
V.1.1b. VI.2.3. VI.9.ext.7.
IX.8.1

Syracusae: I.1.8. I.1.ext.3. I.6.9.
I.7.8. I.7.ext.6,8. II.7.15c.
II.8.5. III.2.ext.9. IV.1.7.
IV.3.ext.4b. IV.8.ext.1. V.1.4.
VI.2.ext.2. VII.4.ext.1.
VIII.7.ext.7. VIII.11.ext.4
Syracusani: I.7.ext.8.
VI.9.ext.6. IX.13.ext.4. -na,
Aristomache: IX.13.ext.4. -na
civitas: V.1.4. -nus Dio:
III.8.ext.5. IV.1.ext.3.
-nusnus, Dionysius: I.7.ext.6.
IV.7.ext.1

Syria: IV.1.15. VI.4.3. IX.1.ext.4
Syra mulier: I.2.4 (Nepot.)

Tamphilus see Baebius
Tamphilus

Tanaquil (wife of Tarquinius
Priscus, not Ancus): I.6.1

Tarentum (Taranto): II.2.5.
IV.6.3. VIII.7.ext.3. Cf. II.4.5
Tarentini: V.1.ext.3a. -nus

456

Archytas: IV.1.ext.1. -num bellum: II.7.15b. -na civitas: II.2.5. -na petulantia: IV.3.14a

Tarentum (near Campus Martius): II.4.5

Tarpeium, saxum: VI.5.7

Tarpeius, Sp. (warden of the Capitol): IX.6.1

(Tarquinii) (in Etruria). Tarquiniensis, fundus: V.3.3

Tarquinius, Arruns (son of Superbus): V.6.1. (VII.3.2)

Tarquinius, Sex. (son of Superbus): 6.1.1. (VII.3.2). VII.4.2

Tarquinius Priscus, L. (fifth king of Rome): I.4.1 (Paris, Nepot.). III.4.2. Cf. 1.6.1

Tarquinius Superbus (seventh and last king of Rome): I.1.13. I.8.5. IV.4.1. V.6.1. V.8.1. VI.1.1. VII.3.2. VII.4.2. IX.11.1

Tarracina (Terracina, on coast of Latium): VIII.1.absol.13

Tarsos (in Cilicia): III.8.ext.6

Tatius, (T.) (king of the Sabines): IX.6.1 (bribes Tarpeia)

Taurea see Vibellius Taurea

(Tauromenium) (Taormina, in Sicily). Tauromenitana arx: II.7.3

Taurus mons (in southeast Asia Minor): II.8.praef. IV.1.ext.9. VI.4.ext.3. VIII.1.damn.1

Taxillus (Taxippus? Gymnasiarch): 9.10.ext.2

Taygeta montes (mountains near Sparta): IV.6.ext.3

Teanum (Sidicinum) (Teano, in Campania): III.8.1
    Teana custodia: III.8.1

(Tegea) (in Arcadia). Tegeates, Stasippus: IV.1.ext.5

Telesinus see Pontius Telesinus

Tellus (earth goddess): VI.3.1b. VII.3.2. See also Terra

Terentia (wife of Cicero): VIII.13.6

Terentius: VII.7.5

Terentius, Ser.: IV.7.6

Terentius Culleo, Q. (pr. 187): V.2.5

Terentius Varro, (C) (cos. 216): I.1.16. III.4.4,5. IV.5.2

Terentius Varro, M. (of Reate): III.2.24. VIII.7.3

(Terentius Varro) Lucullus, M. (cos. 73): VIII.5.4. See also Licinii Luculli

Terra, Mater: I.7.3. See also Tellus

Tertia see Aemilia, Tertia

Tettius (father of the following): VII.7.3

Tettius, C.: VII.7.3

Teutoni, (German nation): III.6.6. IV.7.3. VI.1.ext.3. VI.9.14. -ca victoria: VI.1.ext.3

Thales (of Miletus, one of the Seven Wise Men): IV.1.ext.7. VII.2.ext.8

Thalna see Iuventius Thalna

INDEX

Thebae: III.2.ext.5. III.7.ext.5.
V.3.ext.3a

Thebe (wife of Alexander of
Pherae): IX.13.ext.3

Themistocles: V.3.ext.3e,g.
V.6.ext.3. VI.5.ext.2.
VI.9.ext.2. VII.2.ext.9.
VIII.7.ext.15. VIII.14.ext.1

Theodectes (student of Aristotle): VIII.14.ext.3

Theodorus (of Cyrene):
VI.2.ext.3

Theodorus (leading man in
Megara): IV.1.ext.3

Theodotus: III.3.ext.5

Theophanes (of Mitylene, biog-
rapher of Pompey): VIII.14.3

Theopompus (Spartan king):
IV.1.ext.8

Theopompus (4th-century
historian): VIII.13.ext.5.
VIII.14.ext.5

Theramenes (one of the Thirty
Tyrants of Athens):
III.2.ext.6,7

Thermopylae: II.5.1. III.2.ext.3

Theseus (mythical hero): IV.7.4.
V.3.ext.3a,g

Thessalia: I.8.ext.7. IV.6.1
    Thessalus, Cineas: IV.3.6b.
    -lus Iason: IX.10.ext.2

Thracia: II.6.12,14. III.7.ext.7.
IX.2.ext.4
    Thraces: III.2.12. Thraciae,
    notae: IX.13.ext.3

Thrasippus: V.1.ext.2b

Thrasybulus (Athenian general
and statesman): IV.1.ext.4.
V.6.ext.2

(Thurii) (in south Italy).
Thurina urbs: I.8.6. -nus,
Charondas: VI.5.ext.4

(Thyreatis) (tract on the border
of Laconia and Argos).
Thyreates: III.2.ext.4

Tiberis (river Tiber): I.4.2
(Nepot.). I.8.2. II.4.5.
III.2.1,2. IV.7.2. VII.3.1.
VIII.1.absol.5. VIII.15.10.
IX.2.1

(Tiberius) Caesar: I.praef.
II.praef. II.9.6a. IV.3.3. V.5.3.
VIII.13.praef. IX.11.ext.4. See
also Augustus

Tibur (Tivoli): II.5.4. V.1.1b
Tiburtes: II.5.4

Ticinum (Pavia): V.5.3

Ticinus (river in north Italy):
V.4.2

Tigranes (king of Armenia):
V.1.9,10. VIII.15.8.
IX.11.ext.3

Timaeus (Pythagorean, at
Locri): VIII.7.ext.3

Timagoras (Athenian envoy):
VI.3.ext.2

(Timanthes) (painter, 5th-4th
century): VIII.11.ext.6

Timasitheus (of Lipara):
I.1.ext.4

Timochares: VI.5.1d

Titinius (centurion): IX.9.2

Titinius, C. (of Minturnae, husband of Fannia): VIII.2.3

Titius (Caesarian centurion):
III.8.7

Titius, C. (cavalry commander):
II.7.9

Titius, L. (city praetor): VIII.3.1

Titius, Sex. (tr. pl. 99): VIII.1.damn.3

Tolumnius, Lars (king of Veii): (III.2.4). IX.9.3

Tomyris (Scythian queen, takes vengeance on dead Cyrus): IX.10.ext.1

Toranius (actually Turranius), C. and father: IX.11.5

Torquatus see Manlius Torquatus

Trachali (of Ariminum): VII.7.4

Tralles (in Lydia): I.6.12. IV.1.13

Trasumennus, lacus (in Umbria): I.6.6. III.7.ext.6.ᵣ IV.8.ext.1.ᵣ IX.11.ext.4.ᵣ IX.12.2

Trebellius Calcha: IX.15.4.

Trigemina, porta: IV.7.2

Troia: I.8.7

Τρῶες: III.7.ext.3

Tubero see Aelius Tubero

Tubertus see Postumius Tubertus

Tuccia (daughter of Caeso): IV.4.10

Tuccia (Vestal Virgin): VIII.1.absol.5

(Tuccius), Caeso: IV.4.10

Tuditanus see (Sempronius) Tuditanus

Tullia (daughter of king Servius Tullius): IX.11.1

Tullianus: VII.7.2

Tullius, (Attius) (Volscian leader): VII.3.ext.10

Tullius, Ser.: I.6.1. I.8.11.

III.4.3. VII.3.1. IX.11.1. See also Tullia

Tullius Cicero, M. (cos. 63): I.4.6 (Paris, Nepot.). I.7.5. II.2.3. IV.2.4,5. V.3.4. VIII.5.5. VIII.10.3. VIII.13.6. VIII.13.ext.1. IX.11.3. IX.12.7

Tullus see Hostilius, Tullus

Turia: VI.7.2

(Turranius, C.) See Toranius

Turullius, D. (quaest. 44): 1.1.19

Tusci (= Etruscans): I.8.5. II.4.4

Tusculum (near Rome): III.4.6 Tusculani: I.8.1a. II.7.6. V.2.2. VII.3.ext.9. IX.10.1. -num: I.4.5 (Paris). -nus, ager: I.4.5 (Nepot.)

Tyndaridae (i.e. Castor and Pollux): IV.6.ext.3

(Tyros) (Tyre). Tyrii: I.8.ext.11

Ulixes: VIII.11.ext.6

Umbria: III.7.4. VII.4.4

(Urbinum) (Urbino, in Umbria). Urbinas, T. Marius: VII.8.6

Urbinius Panapio: VI.8.6

Utica (chief town of the province Africa): III.2.14. IX.10.2

Valentinus see Valerius Valentinus

Valerius (Potitus?), C. (cos. 331?): VIII.1.absol.7

Valerius (Falto), Q. (pr. 242): II.8.2

Valerius Flaccus, C. (pr. 183): VI.9.3

INDEX

Valerius Flaccus (military tribune, perhaps one with the following): III.2.20

(Valerius) Flaccus, L. (cos. 195): IV.5.1. *See also* Porcius Cato (the Censor)

(Valerius) Flaccus, L. (cos. 100): II.9.5. *See also* Antonius, M. (orator)

Valerius (Flaccus?) Heptachordus, L. (pr. 63?): VII.8.7

Valerius Laevinus, (M.) (cos. 210): IV.1.7

(Valerius Maximus) (author): cf. II.6.8. IV.7.ext.2b

Valerius (Maximus) Corvinus (properly Corvus), M. (VI cos. 299): III.2.6a. VIII.13.1. VIII.15.5

Valerius Maximus (Corvinus), M. (III cos. 286?): II.9.2. *See also* Iunius Bubulcus Brutus

Valerius (Maximus Messalla), M'. (cos. 263): II.9.7

Valerius Messalla, M. (cos. 161): II.4.2

Valerius Messalla (Niger), M. (cos. 61): II.9.9. IX.14.5

(Valerius) Messalla (Rufus, M.) (cos. 53): V.9.2.

Valerius Publicola, (P.) (IV cos. 504): I.8.5. II.4.5. IV.1.1,2. IV.4.1,11. VIII.9.1

Valerius Valentinus: 8.1.absol.8

Valesius (rich farmer): II.4.5

Varius Severus Hybrida, Q. (tr. pl. 90): III.7.8. VIII.6.4. IX.2.2

Varro *see* Terentius Varro, Visellius Varro

Vatienus, P.: I.8.1b

Vatinius, P. (cos. 47): IV.2.4. VII.5.6

Vecilius (or Vecillus; pimp): VII.7.7

Veii (in Etruria): I.5.1. I.6.3. I.8.3. IV.1.2. V.6.8
     Veientes? I.6.3. I.8.5. V.5.2. IX.9.3. Veiens, ager: IV.4.8. Veientana praeda: V.3.2a. -nus triumphus: IV.1.2. -na urbs: I.5.1

Velia (coast town in southwest Italy): 1.1.1b

(Velitrae) (Volscian town). Veliterni: IX.10.1

Ventidius (Bassus), P. (cos. 43): VI.9.9

Venus: II.6.15. (VIII.11.ext.4). Venus Verticordia: VIII.15.12

Vergellus (river in Apulia): IX.2.ext.2

(Verginia) *see* the following

Verginius, (L.): VI.1.2

Verrugo (in Latium): III.2.8. VI.5.2

Veseris (river in Campania): VI.4.1a

Vesta: I.1.7. I.4.5 (Paris). IV.2.5. IV.4.11. V.4.6. VI.1.praef. VIII.1.absol.5
     Vestalis, virgo: I.1.6. V.4.6.ʳ VIII.1.absol.5. -nes, -les: 1.1.0. VI.1.ext.3. Virgo, maxima: 1.1.7

Vestia Oppia (i.e. Vestia wife of Oppius): V.2.1b

460

Vesuvius mons: I.7.3

Vettienus, C.: VI.3.3c

Vettius Salassus: IX.11.7

Veturia (mother of Coriolanus): V.2.1a. V.4.1

Vetulo *see* Sentius Saturninus Vetulo

Veturius (Calvinus), T. (father, II cos. 321, and son): VI.1.9

Vetus *see* Antistius Vetus

Via Sacra (Roman street): 8.1.damn.5

Vibellius, (Decius) (leader of rogue soldiery in Rhegium): II.7.15f

Vibellius Taurea, T. (Campanian): III.2.ext.1

Vibienus: VI.1.13

Vibienus: VII.7.7

Vibius *see* Accaus, Vibius

Vibius: IX.14.1

(Vibius) Pansa (Caetronianus, C.) (cos. 43): V.2.10

Victoria(e): I.1.ext.3. I.6.12. IV.8.ext.1

Vicus Longus (Roman street): II.5.6

Vicus Sceleratus (Roman street): cf. IX.11.1

Villa, publica: IX.2.1

Villius, P. (triumvir nocturnus): VIII.1.damn.6

Villius Annalis, L. and son: IX.11.6

(Vipsanius) Agrippa, M. (friend of Augustus): IV.7.7

Viriathus (Spanish leader against Rome): VI.4.2b. IX.6.4

Viriplaca: II.1.6

Virtus (temple and statue): I.1.8

Visellius Varro, C. (aed. cur. 59? see Broughton III): VIII.2.2

Volsci (Latin people): III.2.8. IV.3.4. V.2.1a. V.4.1. V.5.2. VII.3.ext.10
    Volscus miles: 5.4.1. -cus populus: VII.3.ext.10

(Volsinii) (in Etruria). Volsinienses: IX.1.ext.2

Volumnia (wife of Coriolanus): V.2.1a. V.4.1

Volumnius (friend of Lucullus): IV.7.4

Volumnius (Amintinus Gallus), C. (error for P.) (cos. 461): I.6.5

Volusius, M. (aed. pl. 43): VII.3.8

Vulcanus: VIII.11.ext.3

Xanthippe (wife of Socrates): VII.2.ext.1d

Xanthippus (Spartan soldier): I.1.14. IX.6.ext.1

Xenocrates (student of Plato): II.10.ext.2. IV.1.ext.2b. IV.3.ext.3a,b. VI.9.ext.1. VII.2.ext.6

Xenophilus (Pythagorean): VIII.13.ext.3

Xenophon (Athenian historian, 5th-4th century): V.10.ext.2

Xenophon (of Lampsacus, 2nd-century geographical writer): VIII.13.ext.7

Xerxes (king of Persia): I.6.ext.1a. II.10.ext.1.

INDEX

III.2.ext.3. V.3.ext.3e,g.
VI.5.ext.2. VIII.7.ext.4,15.
IX.1.ext.3. IX.5.ext.2.
IX.13.ext.1

Zaleucus (Locrian lawgiver):
I.2.ext.4 (Paris). VI.5.ext.3
Zeno: III.3.ext.3

Zeno of Elea (5th-century philosopher): III.3.ext.2. Cf. 3.
Zeuxis (late 5th-century
painter): III.7.ext.3
Zisemis (3rd-century Thracian
prince): IX.2.ext.4
(Zmyrna) (in Ionia). Zmyrnaea,
mater familiae: VIII.1.amb.2

Composed in ZephGreek and ZephText by
Technologies 'N Typography, Merrimac, Massachusetts.
Printed in Great Britain by St Edmundsbury Press Ltd,
Bury St Edmunds, Suffolk, on acid-free paper.
Bound by Hunter & Foulis Ltd, Edinburgh, Scotland.